the Lo...

b...

AMY LANE

T0018159

The Mastermind

"This story is a prime example of a highly complicated long con complete with a family of the heart, a reunion of two souls destined to be together forever, and Revenge with a capital R."

—Rainbow Book Reviews

The Muscle

"... Amy Lane has a way with surrounding her self with many characters and melding them into a great family. I saw this book was no exception."

—Paranormal Romance Guild

The Driver

"I just can't get enough of this crew of heroic outlaws."

—Love Bytes

The Suit

"This story was incredible, everyone using their talents was essential! It was a mystery, an education on birds... and best of all a love story."

—Paranormal Romance Guild

By Amy Lane

Published by DREAMSPINNER PRESS
www.dreamspinnerpress.com

By Amy Lane (cont)

Published by DREAMSPINNER PRESS
www.dreamspinnerpress.com

By Amy Lane (cont)

Published by DREAMSPINNER PRESS
www.dreamspinnerpress.com

The Tech

AMY LANE

Published by
DREAMSPINNER PRESS

5032 Capital Circle SW, Suite 2, PMB# 279,
Tallahassee, FL 32305-7886 USA
www.dreamspinnerpress.com

This is a work of fiction. Names, characters, places, and incidents either
are the product of author imagination or are used fictitiously, and any
resemblance to actual persons, living or dead, business establishments,
events, or locales is entirely coincidental.

The Tech
© 2023 Amy Lane

Cover Art
© 2023 L.C. Chase
http://www.lcchase.com
Cover content is for illustrative purposes only and any person depicted
on the cover is a model.

Mass Market Paperback ISBN: 978-1-64108-478-9
Trade Paperback ISBN: 978-1-64108-477-2
Digital ISBN: 978-1-64108-476-5
Mass Market published July 2023
v. 1.0

Printed in the United States of America

Here's to better times, a happier future, a time when our children bring us joy and not worry. That time is not now—but it could be later.

The Beauty of Paper

Fourteen years ago—France

"NOW THERE, Etienne—do you see?"

"Yes, Papa."

Etienne's father was a slight man with unkempt hair that fell to his collar, a pointed chin, and wrinkles in the corners of fine brown eyes. Tienne's mother had died when Tienne was very small, before the tiny family had moved to the coast using stolen passports.

"The light from the sun bounces off the clouds and hits the water so."

"Yes, Papa."

"And what do we use that looks like light?"

"White! White in the blue and white in the gray and light in the gold!" Tienne continued to sing to himself, painting the ocean view from the window of the seaside cottage looking off the coast of St. Tropez. While he did so, his father continued to labor painstakingly over an etching machine with a laminator and various

colors of ink on beautiful rainbow paper. Tienne longed
to paint pictures on that rainbow paper, but his father
told him—repeatedly—that the paper cost very much
money and the people who hired Papa to work on the
paper would be *very* displeased if he ruined any of it
before it had a chance to be used. Many other little boys
might have tested their father on this, but Tienne's papa
was so very gentle and so very kind, and he worked
hard every day. Tienne only wanted to please his father.
He knew, even as a child of six or seven, that his father
worked to feed them and that he wanted so much more
for his son than he had for himself.

So Tienne sang softly to himself while his father
muttered to the machine and the laminator and the in-
struments he used to etch letters and pictures into that
glorious paper.

The slamming of the cottage door startled them
both. Tienne's brush went sideways, and he made a gasp
of dismay, but his father grabbed his arm and tugged
him away from the painting before he could complain.
"Hide behind the couch," he muttered. "Don't say a
word."

"Papa—"

"Not a word!"

Tienne wriggled behind the couch and held his
breath, unsure of what was happening, knowing only
that his father had never spoken to him in such a tone,
not once in all of his seven years.

"Couvier! Couvier! We know you're in there!"

Tienne's father's voice was furious as he stomped
across the floor. "You are never to bother me here in my
home. *Never*."

The next sound Tienne heard was the sound of fist on flesh—and then a returning sound. Had his father been hit? Had he hit back?

"All right! All right! All right! I hear you. Never come to your house. I get it. But Mr. Kadjic wants his stuff, you hear me?"

"The order is due tomorrow," Antoine Couvier said coldly. "It will be complete tomorrow. I have been good on every order. I will be good on this one. But not if you come to my home, do you understand?"

"Yeah, sure, we understand." There was the sound of patting down and straightening. "Remember—we don't need to come to your house to make sure you pony up… or to see your pretty little son."

Tienne held his breath in the silence that followed.

"You are threatening my son?"

"I'm sayin', Couvier. Accidents happen. To everybody."

"If they happen to my son, I will be sure every member of your organization spends every day of their lives in prison. You need me. You need my skills. I am the only forger for a thousand miles who understands the new electronic implants in official documents. You can have your papers today, if you like, but they will trip every alarm in the EU, and Interpol will be down your pants so fast you'll wish you'd packed lubricant."

Tienne had to shove his fist in his mouth in fear. His father—*his* father—could talk to people like this, all in defense of Tienne.

"That is if we don't kill you first," the man snarled, but Tienne heard heavy footfalls and then the door slam. Tienne stayed hidden, keeping his breathing under control, until his father's face appeared at the other end of the couch.

"You are okay?" he asked gently.

"Oui."

"Good, then come quickly. You need to pack three changes of clothes, you understand? And a few possessions you cannot bear to be without. It all must fit in your school pack, and it cannot be too heavy."

"My paints and pencils?" Tienne asked, feeling pitiful and trying manfully not to cry as he scooted out from behind the couch.

His father's hands in his hair comforted him, and he worked hard not to tremble. "I will carry your paints and pencils," his father said gently. "We artists cannot be expected to exist without them, no?"

"No." Tienne offered his papa a timid smile and got a kiss on top of his head in return.

"Now go. Pack your treasures and your clothes." He heard a bit of tortured parent in his father's voice then. "Leave your schoolbooks. I suppose we shall obtain others, wherever we land."

Tienne nodded, also sad. Other boys hated school, but Tienne loved it. He could read and write fluently in English and French beyond his grade level, but other things too—math, science—it was all beautiful.

"It is okay, boy," Tienne's father said to his retreating back. "We shall land on our feet, if only we will jump now!"

Nine years ago—Marrakech

"So," ANTOINE said, holding tight to Tienne's hand as they made their way through the crowded streets of the bazaar. "What did you do today in school?"

"I kissed a boy!" he said excitedly. At twelve, he was well ahead of his peers, even in the Arabic language he'd needed to learn relatively quickly in the three years since they'd left Europe altogether and come to Morocco. Given that he was so far ahead of his peers in studies, Tienne had developed other goals.

He was not prepared for his father's sudden tightness on his hand.

"That is fine if you like to kiss boys, Tienne," his father said, pulling him to a quiet place in the bazaar right before their tiny apartment. "But here there are many devout Muslims who would kill you for doing so. Wait until you're in a place where kissing a person won't lose you your head."

Oh. How disappointing. Tienne had liked the boy immensely—Kamel had such amazing dark eyes. "Where would that be?"

Antoine laughed softly. "France, my boy. It would be in France. Two more years, I think. Give us two more years here. I have our passports made and ready for us. We need to be ghosts for a little while yet." His father was always so good at planning ahead.

"Being ghosts is not as much fun when there are no boys to kiss," Tienne said glumly, and his father laughed.

"Quieter, my son, or we will be ghosts for real." The rebuke was gentle, but Tienne took the hint. They'd been on the run for five years, since his father had betrayed Andres Kadjic. Yes, his father had finished the passports, but he'd purposefully included a flaw, a red flag, and some of Kadjic's men had been jailed.

It had been, as Antoine had confessed one particularly miserable night during which they'd been camped on a street corner, hiding under the eaves to avoid the rain, a stupid thing for him to do.

But Kadjic had threatened his son, and Antoine had reacted out of panic.

"Understood, Papa," Tienne said now, silently bidding the sloe-eyed Kamel adieu. "But someday…?"

Antoine smiled. "Someday you shall kiss anyone you—" He didn't trail off so much as stop abruptly, his eyes widening at someone behind Tienne, his tanned face leeching of all color, as though he'd seen a ghost.

"My boy," he said, voice unnaturally loud, "it's time to pack for Casablanca."

For a moment, Tienne was going to argue. But they'd *moved* from Casablanca, not a year ago! But then he remembered his father's code. When they were going to run, always talk about the place they'd run *from*, not the place they'd be running *to*.

"Immediately," he said, and without another word, he turned on his heel and went running up the tiny set of steps between adobe buildings to their one-bedroom apartment above the bazaar.

They were packed in ten minutes but spent the next five hours eating, drinking, and *waiting* for the cover of darkness. This time, as Tienne was bigger, he got to carry some of his father's equipment and some of their art supplies as well as the requisite three changes of clothes. Tienne thought wistfully of the next time they could paint. After they found a place, there was always a frantic bit of activity as they forged passports and plane tickets and papers of provenance and whatever other criminals needed from them before they could finally settle down to what they both loved: art!

It would be a long time before they could paint together, he mourned, but still, he and his father turned their eyes to the horizon and the coming veil of night. When it finally came, they did not leave by way of the stairs, but out the window and up and across the roof, jumping two more roofs before they finally slid down a drainpipe.

And landed right in a group of men—slick touristy men wearing leather jackets and leather coats—and one brothel boy in loose harem pants and a velveteen vest.

"Hello," said the inebriated brothel boy, who sounded much older than those men usually got. "What have we...? Andres, put the knives down. It's a man and his son. Why would you—"

"Go, Daniel," said the shorter, more muscular of the men in the leather jackets. He was clearly their leader, judging by the way the others kept seeking his approval as they shouldered Tienne's father against the adobe wall of the building at their backs. He was squat, this one, dark-haired, with a brutally planed face, and he spoke with a thick Slavic accent. "You like pretty things. You don't need to know the ugliness here."

The brothel boy—but wait. He was older than most brothel boys. Perhaps he was simply a kept man—shook his head hard, as though trying to dispel some of the alcohol or whatever had impaired his senses. "Andres, you are not going to harm these people," he said, pulling authority into his voice. "You cannot. It's a father and his son—"

"A father who has put two of my men in jail by betraying me, thinking he was protecting his son. They will not live another day!"

"Then you and I won't see another night," Daniel said, pulling himself up to his full height and moving, almost imperceptibly, in front of Tienne. "I won't sleep with a man who could do this—particularly not to a child, but not to anyone. So they saw jail time. It's the logical end for our sort. You know it, I know it. If you threatened his son, he had every right!"

"*Nobody* does that to me and mine!" roared Andres Kadjic—for this was clearly the man who had sent Tienne and his father running for the last five years. "And no lover of mine stands against me. Not in public, not in private."

"I'm not your lover, then," Daniel said. "I don't want a thing to do with you. If I hadn't been drunk off my ass, I would have seen you for the brute you are—"

Kadjic's hand came out, brutally fast, a backhanded fist that drove the slender Daniel to his knees. "You think I am a brute now?" Kadjic said with a sneer. "Before this night is over, you will know me for what I am. But first—"

He turned to his men and nodded at Antoine Couvier, and his man yanked a knife across Tienne's father's throat.

"*No!*" Tienne screamed, and he saw the whole world as in slow motion.

The man who'd killed his father dropped Antoine's body as it still spurted blood and turned toward him. At the same time, Daniel, Kadjic's lover, who would probably share Antoine's fate before the night was out, leaped at the man with the knife and looked Tienne dead in the eye, screaming, "*Run!*"

Tienne took off, running faster then he'd ever imagined he could, thinking he felt the hot breath of the man with the knife on his neck. He ran until he could run no more, finally taking shelter in an alleyway, where he sat with his back against the wall and sobbed.

The next morning, he awoke hungry, thirsty, and terrified. He knew this city, but he did not know where to go for help. He knew his father's friends, but he did not know if any had betrayed him. He knew who the authorities were, but so many were not to be trusted.

He had his pack, though. He and his father split their cash now, so with his cash and his passport and ID, he could at least get out of Marrakech and go to....

Where? Back to France, perhaps? He and Antoine had been happy in France. But Kadjic had been there too. Prague? Kyiv? Amsterdam? There were cities they hadn't been to—perhaps Kadjic wouldn't be in Amsterdam?

It was then, as he was rummaging through his pack, that he made a terrible discovery.

As he'd fled, the man with the knife had probably taken a swipe at him. There was a slice down the pocket of his backpack, and the bulk of his cash was gone, as was a tube of green paint that had apparently been slashed as well.

He was broke.

He was *found*.

And Kadjic's people were probably waiting at the mouth of the alley, intending to gut him like a fish.

He stood, frozen for a moment, until a young man appeared, right where Tienne had thought to see a mobster with a knife and an Uzi.

Instead, the man held a sizable wad of cash in many denominations, every paper covered with galway green paint.

"Looking for this?"

The man spoke English with a clear lower-class accent, and Tienne searched his face for any trace of a sneer or mockery. What he saw was a handsome young man, maybe ten years older than himself, with short brown/red hair and brilliant blue eyes, looking at him levelly as though assessing Tienne for damage. He held his robe back so Tienne could see his badge. It said something about Interpol, but Tienne didn't care.

He spat. "I know nothing about that," he said, not meeting the young man's eyes. Crooked authorities—he'd seen his father pay off his share of people with badges.

"Do you know something about the man who almost died to save your hide last night?" the young man asked softly. "Danny Lightfingers?"

Daniel. Tienne bit his lip, and his voice caught. "He is alive?"

"Aye," said the young officer. "Barely. I wanted to stay by his side to make sure Kadjic's boys didn't go after him again, but he told me to come find you. Turns out he has his own damned money to travel with, and he gave me permission to use it to get you to safety. You going to let me do that?"

Tienne met his eyes, knowing his own were overflowing. "Where is safe?" he asked gruffly. "They killed my father. Where is safe?"

"Would you believe Chicago's safe?"

Tienne squinted at him. "America?"

"Aye."

Two days later, with a neat haircut and dressed nicely, his luggage chosen to match, Tienne still didn't believe it. After flying for what felt like days, he was greeted at the gate by a woman—ah, such a beautiful woman. She wore her hair in a chignon and dressed like the women of France, in a summer dress with an elegant clutch bag.

"Etienne Couvier?" she asked softly, and he looked around, over both shoulders.

"Oui. But my papers, they say—"

"Bertrand Lautrec," she murmured. "I am aware. But I know that sometimes it's nice when somebody says your name. Come with me. I'm Julia Dormer-Salinger, and you may call me Julia."

"Am I to live with you?" he asked, confused. All he'd been told was that he would be safe. After five years on the run with his father, his twelve-year-old self couldn't imagine this woman could keep him safe.

She smiled at him gently. "I have a son, and his friend practically lives in our house. I wouldn't mind a third. Would you like that?"

He frowned, understanding from her tone that this was a surprise idea for her.

"What did Daniel plan?" he asked, remembering the brave man who had still been recovering from the injuries Andres Kadjic had given him even as Tienne had flown away.

"Art school," she said with a little shrug. "I've secured a place for you at a rather prestigious boarding school, if you like."

And part of Tienne wanted badly to go with this lovely, kind woman to her home, where there were other boys his age. But everything was so strange— down to his hair and his clothes and the clipped sounds of English in seven different accents gunning by his ears.

Art he knew. Art was his last link to his parents.

"Art school, sil vous plaît," he said politely.

She smiled sadly. "You can visit us during breaks if you like," she said and then frowned. "But let's not tell Felix where you're from, yes?"

"Who is Felix?" he asked.

She grimaced. "My soon to be ex-husband. But don't worry. We adore each other."

Tienne frowned at her, turning as she did to walk through the airport. "Then why are you...?"

"Getting a divorce?" she asked, laughing. "Because women are really not his type. Is this the only luggage you have?" She indicated his roller board and matching satchel.

"Oui," he said, remembering sadly that after his backpack had been slashed, he'd only had the clothes on his back. The young police officer had needed to buy *many* clothes in Marrakech's modern department stores to fill the small case. "Who is his type?" Tienne asked, thinking about his one kiss, and how he badly needed to know if he could die here if he mentioned who he wanted to kiss.

"Men," she said simply. "In particular, one man, whom he's pretending he's not in love with anymore."

Tienne frowned. This sounded terribly tragic. "Who is this man?"

She tilted her head. "You should know, my boy. He's the one who sent you to America and told us to make sure you had a home." She bit her lip, uncharacteristically diffident. "Did you... did he happen to say anything to you? About us, I mean?"

Tienne laughed humorlessly, remembering that one moment in the alley when a man he'd never seen, never met, had jumped on top of a man armed with a knife and defied his very dangerous lover to save Tienne's life.

"We had no time to talk," he whispered. "He… he saved me. From dangerous men. But then his friend helped me get far, far away." He saw her obvious disappointment, though, and thought of something to say. "He must have trusted you very much," he added. "Because if you were dangerous to him too, you could easily hurt him."

Her expression grew, if anything, even sadder. "And Felix and I have," she said softly. "But again, that is not your story. Come. The only interview I could get you for the school I have in mind is this afternoon. I know it's quite the whirlwind, and you won't have a chance to come home and meet the family, but if it's art school you want, it's art school you shall have."

And that was that.

Years later, after he'd met Josh and Grace and their friends, and had spent summer and winter holidays with Julia and Felix, enjoying their company very much, he would wonder at his choice.

They'd offered him family as often as they could. They found out his birthday and sent gifts or took him out to celebrate. He spent part of his holidays with them and received presents. He even painted them pictures. A part of him yearned more than anything to make himself comfortable in their home, to lie about on the couches with Josh and Grace and their friends Stirling and Molly and play games and chatter and live in their pockets as they lived in each other's.

But he'd seen his father die, and that wound, that terrible wound in his chest, it was still open, and he was still desperately afraid.

He made it through boarding school instead, and then into the School of the Art Institute of Chicago, with an emphasis on oil-on-canvas paintings. It was there that his original calling, the one his father taught him, came into play.

It helped that one machine, one stamp, one printer, one jar of ink at a time, he'd begun to build up his collection of forging equipment again. Everything from estate sales to government clearing houses and Army/Navy stores gave him items he needed, and without thinking of the reason, he spent much of his allowance on the tools of the trade he'd employed with pride as his father's journeyman.

And then he hit college at seventeen, and that foresight and patient collecting paid off.

It seemed that many teenagers were desperate to have beer.

"Tienne?"

Tienne looked up from the desk in his dorm room, where he sat with his forging equipment, and wondered if he could will the ground to simply swallow him up.

"Josh?" There, large as life—and *sixteen*—stood the son of his benefactors, along with Josh's best friend, Dylan "Grace" Li.

Tienne had seen Danny since that night in Marrakech—many times in fact. He'd shown up the day *before* Tienne's birthday dinner with the rest of the family, or the week *before* Christmas. Once a year he showed up a few days after Josh's birthday, and Tienne had understood that this was part of Danny and Felix's doomed love affair. Felix and Julia lived in a mansion, raising Josh and Josh's friend, Grace, while Danny snuck into their home like a thief and spent time with the boy he loved like his own son.

And also with Tienne, whom he treated with kindness and affection and unfailing thoughtfulness.

Tienne would look at him and see his father—not perfect, but kind. Fierce when he was needed to protect his child. Pining for a lover he could never have, although Tienne's father had lost his mother in death.

He would have gone with Danny, no matter how imperfect his life may have been, but Danny was hoping Tienne could have the family Danny left behind.

Tienne was not good enough for that family. He thought Julia and Felix and Josh lived a fairy tale life—right up until Josh Salinger made his way into Tienne's dorm room/workshop when Tienne had all his forging equipment laid out on his floor.

"Hey, Tienne," Grace said, peeking from behind Josh's shoulder and blinking at him in delight. "Good to see you. You're a criminal too?"

Josh elbowed him, and as compact and graceful as Julia and Felix's dark-eyed, dark-haired son may have been, the elbow was no joke. "The only criminal thing I'm going to do today is drop you off a building if you don't shut up," he said.

Grace—ethereally beautiful and a constant pain in the ass—smiled with all his teeth. "You promise that and promise that, and not once have I been dropped off a building." He blinked his tawny eyes at Tienne, and his smile relaxed. "And dropping me off a building doesn't change the fact that Tienne is here, making fake IDs, when your mother swears he's an angel who can do no wrong."

Josh laughed, but the look he turned toward Tienne was kind.

"You couldn't be that bad if Danny sent you," he said, and Tienne felt his face turn red.

"How do you know—"

"Danny and I write," Josh said, surprising Tienne very much. Josh put his finger to his lips. "Shh. It's supposed to be a secret, but everybody knows. One of those weird family things. Anyway, he asks me how you're doing and worries because you're alone. He really *does* wish you'd take my mother's invitation to heart, you know. She wouldn't offer if she didn't mean it."

Tienne flushed more and looked away. "I…." He didn't know how to say that he didn't know what to do with that much kindness. Instead, he scowled and peered back at Josh through the hair that had grown long again. "But what are you doing here? I…. You… why do you need my services?" he asked finally, resorting to the language of thieves because he had nothing else to explain this.

Josh looked exasperated—but not with Tienne. "Thank God, I got a tip from a guy at our school that 'some guy at the AI is the best.' Genius here"—he nodded at Grace—"left our last set of IDs in the club. I had to cancel all the cards I used with them too!"

Tienne blinked, stunned at this level of thievery from someone his age. "Who made you fake cards!" he cried.

"Oh, they were real cards," Josh said, affronted. "They were made out to fake names. Are you kidding? Felix showed me how to hide my money when I was ten." He sighed. "I was going to go after Danny, and he was trying to show me how hard it would be to trace him. I learned a *lot* the summer Danny left."

Tienne frowned, putting the timeline together. If Josh was sixteen now, and Danny had left when he'd been ten, then he must have been gone the better part of a year before the encounter in the alleyway.

Uneasily, he wondered if Felix and Josh knew how close Danny had come to death that night, on Tienne's account, and decided he wouldn't ever tell them.

And then what Josh said *really* caught up with him.

"Your father knows how to… to *lie*. To scam? To steal?"

Josh laughed kindly. "Well, *yeah*. Uncle Danny taught him and my mother all they know. But what you're doing here…." He trailed off delicately and made motions with his hands.

And Tienne couldn't help it—this was the first honest thing he'd been allowed to say about his father since he'd arrived in America by plane. "My father did this," he said. "It kept us fed and gave us money to paint." Some of his joy faded. "In the end, I think it got him killed." He shook that off. "But I never knew your family… they would understand."

Josh crouched down and regarded Tienne closely. "Was that why you never moved in like my mother wanted?"

Tienne shook his head, unable to explain, and Josh let out a sigh. "Never mind," he said, giving Tienne the uncomfortable feeling that Josh knew much more that he wasn't telling. "Forgive me for prying. Now, if you could get Grace and me our IDs, and some for Stirling and Molly too—hey, do you do fake credit cards as well?"

Tienne glanced up happily. It was a newly acquired skill. "Indeed!"

"Excellent." He gave a rather quiet smile then. "And I hope you don't mind, but I'm going to tell my father about your little enterprise. No, no, don't worry.

He won't ask you to do anything you don't want to do. But that way he'll be ready with lawyers should you get busted, you know, that sort of thing."

Tienne sniffed. "Of all the things my father and I worried about, police were not among them."

"Professional pride," Josh said, and he and Grace nodded with such understanding, Tienne wondered what sort of "profession" they'd been active in. "We get it. But there can be dangerous people in these gigs, and if Dad knows now, he can help get you out of a mess. And if you keep wanting to do it, he can get you business. All sorts of things. He has friends who need green cards, passports for people who would like to see their families. He really doesn't like the guy he uses now—says he's way too seedy, and my dad doesn't trust him. So if your work is any good…."

"We were the best," Tienne said without conceit. "It has taken me some time here. Your papers, your electronics, they're different. But my father was the best, and I worked with him until…." He swallowed. "Until I came here."

Josh laughed. "Well, excellent. You know, it would figure. I didn't think Uncle Danny would take someone boring under his wing."

Tienne had laughed then, taking it as the compliment it was. But as the years progressed, and Felix brought him more and more business, all of it protected under a layer of anonymity, none of it as edgy and dangerous as his father's business with Kadjic, he came to realize that it had been yet another sally of the Salinger family, trying to let him know he was not alone.

It was not until Danny's return—and his and Felix's rather spectacular reunion—that Tienne truly began to take that idea to heart.

Seasons Griftings

"HEY, STIRLING, whatcha doing?"

Stirling Christopher looked up from his massive computer setup in the Salingers' mansion and wrinkled his nose at his sister.

"Baking cookies," he said with a completely straight face.

Molly laughed outright, because she was the only person in his life who had ever consistently gotten his sense of humor.

"I want snickerdoodles," she said seriously, bending over his shoulder and peering at the screen in front of him.

In a panic, he changed screens with one hand while holding his other hand childishly in front of the window. "Three weeks before Christmas and you're looking at my computer? What's *wrong* with you? I'm shopping!"

She clapped her hand over her eyes and turned her back, taking this seriously, which was one of the things he really loved about her. "Sorry!" she said. "So sorry! I didn't think."

"Well, not all of us get our shopping done by October," he muttered, making sure that none of the windows with pertinent items were on display. It wasn't that Molly was picky—it was that she was *awesome*. She'd basically walked up to him in the foster home when she was eight and he was six and announced to everybody that if anyone was going to pick on him, they'd have to walk through her to do it.

And she'd been that person in his life for the past fifteen years.

So much so, that when the Christophers had been planning to adopt her, she'd grabbed his hand and dragged him to their second meeting—the "Hey, these people are interested, be your best self" meeting, and told them in no uncertain terms that she and Stirling were a package deal.

He'd been mortified. He'd tried to explain to her that hey, everyone wanted the precocious redheaded girl with the no-bullshit walk and the imperious manner. She was *desirable*. The little brown boy with the tightly kinked brown hair and gray-green eyes who rarely made eye contact was not nearly wonderful enough to add to their instafamily.

But the Christophers were, well, different. They had money, lots of it, and their one child was grown and off doing rich and powerful things. They'd found they wanted a family—children to do things with, to take shopping and fishing and to sports games. Children to spoil, in short. And Molly's hand on his, her insistence that they *were too* siblings—that had touched them.

He'd expected to be an add-on to the family, an afterthought. An "Okay, if we have to have that other kid, we will, but we really want the beautiful girl" kind of thing. But he hadn't been. He'd been as celebrated as Molly. His adoptive father had realized he wasn't a hunting and fishing kind of kid, but instead liked games and numbers, and they'd spent long weekends watching sports games and keeping book. Stirling had made predictions. Mr. Christopher had made bets and then given Stirling the money—or added it to his trust fund—and they'd spent quiet, happy time together, loving the same thing for different reasons.

Then Mrs. Christopher and Molly would get back from shopping or gallery openings or seeing a show, and they'd have dinner together and….

He pulled his mind back from the happy part of what had started out as a rough childhood and focused on Molly. Their adoptive parents had died, together, under mysterious circumstances on what was supposed to have been a second honeymoon in the Caribbean, the summer after Stirling and Molly had graduated from high school. Molly had stuck with him through that, and together they'd landed at Josh Salinger's place, his parents—old friends of the Christophers—more than happy to take them in. They both had money, lots of it, and an apartment in the city that they shared if they wanted, but the sense of being with a family? Neither one of them was turning that down.

Molly had been in the foster system two years longer than Stirling, and neither of them, not once, took for granted family dinners or a place to go on Thanksgiving that truly welcomed them or traveling with people who spoke their language. The Salingers weren't a conventional family—not by any stretch of the imagination—but they loved Stirling and Molly for exactly who they were.

Stirling was a talented hacker and an absolute whiz with money, and Molly was one of the best con artists in a generation.

And Danny, Felix, and Julia would know, because as far as Stirling could figure, they'd pulled off one of the biggest cons ever. They'd conjured a life together out of hope and sheer need.

So money they all had, but family they never took for granted. And it was Christmas, and a special one at that.

Josh Salinger was getting better.

For the past six months, he'd been battling leukemia, and for a while, it had looked as though the light of the Salingers' lives, the boy who'd drawn together the disparate group of rogues and thieves who made up their crew and family—was going to break all of their hearts.

But a bone marrow transplant from a newly contacted relative had turned the tables. Josh was still sick—and he had one more round of chemo to go, one that would end the week before Christmas—but the prognosis was good. He'd been told that he had another six months of sleeping a lot and getting his appetite and strength back, but if his blood counts came back normal after that, he should be free and clear.

The family's relief was acute—and not just Julia's, Felix's, and Danny's. The crew he'd pulled together to help bail Felix out of a jam in March had been absolutely dependent on his wellness, and now that it felt as though he'd recover for real, Christmas had become a thing they absolutely must celebrate.

Stirling was excited, and he didn't often *get* excited about holidays. He wanted to get every member of his larger newfound family something perfect.

Something that would make their lives better. Something that would tell them all that he *appreciated* them, because like the Christophers, who had first taken him and Molly in, not one of them treated him as an add-on, an inconvenience, or "that computer guy."

But imagination was not his strong suit, and shopping was driving him batshit.

He looked up from his computer screen miserably and said, "You can turn around now. It's all hidden. What's up?"

Molly's expression was sympathetic. "Still looking for something wonderful for Felix and Danny?" she asked.

Stirling scowled. "They have everything," he muttered. "And what they don't have, they can steal. And what they won't steal, they've probably *already* stolen and replaced because it wasn't fun to own anymore."

Molly laughed appreciatively and sprawled on the couch he kept adjacent to his computer setup. The basement apartment had been *designed* for Josh and his friend Grace to use as a gaming center. It had kick-ass Wi-Fi and access to several different servers with different IP addresses. Sometimes he planned and executed cybercrime from the place, because he could. Siphon some money from the oil companies to give to environmental causes? Why the fuck not?

He liked to think of himself as a very sneaky Robin Hood. "Well, yes," she agreed. "They're not into possessions so much as experiences, but...." She raised her strawberry-blond eyebrows in a way that suggested she had an idea.

Her ideas were always the best.

"What do you have in mind?" he asked, grasping for hope.

"Well, three things." She smiled and pulled on what he liked to think of as her "corporate maven" posture. She was an extraordinary actress, and although she loved the stage, her real love was human theater. "The first being that Danny and Felix love art. The second"—she ticked them off on her fingers—"being that Danny and Felix *particularly* love art created by someone they know and care about."

"Uh-oh." Stirling knew where this was going.

"The third thing being that Julia has a personal errand she wants me to run this morning that might coincide with both those things."

"Papers?" he asked, trying not to let his interest in the boy he'd been thinking about show. "Papers" was the nickname they'd given the young man they turned to for forgeries, whether painted, printed, or government-regulated. He was a shy young man with a narrow face, dreamy blue eyes, and a quiet, observant manner, who had absolutely fascinated Stirling since he'd first met Tienne Couvier/Bertrand Lautrec in high school.

"Yes," Molly said archly. "Papers."

"Molly, no." Stirling hid his face in mortification. "He doesn't even know I'm alive."

"How do you know?" she demanded. "For all you know, he's giving you the same looks you give him. You're both just… I don't know. What was that quote from Dickens? 'As solitary as a pearl.'"

Stirling rolled his eyes. Their legitimate jobs were in a local theater—he did light and sound engineering and Molly acted her heart out. Together they'd been in at least three productions of *A Christmas Carol*.

"As solitary as an oyster," he corrected blandly. "And yes, I know. Neither of us are talkers." He let out a pained breath. "It's so awkward. I… I…." *I break out in a sweat and want to kiss him all over and touch him and smell him and oh my God he's so pretty!*

"Want to have his babies," Molly stated flatly.

"Want to know him better," Stirling said with as much dignity as he could muster.

"So you're coming with me to make sure everybody's passports and IDs are ready?" Molly asked, as though he'd said anything remotely like that.

"Let me shower," he told her, not sure if it would help.

She grinned. "You're wearing the cashmere sweater, right? The navy one with the matching hat and scarf? Because there's some rocking texture, and you know, he's such a specialist with paper and such, I bet he'll notice."

Stirling tried not to preen. Molly sewed her own clothes—her wardrobe was absolutely luscious—but she also helped Stirling pick out his. Long ago, back when they were still in foster care, she'd realized that bright colors bothered him. He liked them in art or on stage or screen, but he *hated* them on his person. But *she* hated seeing him in something plain. As soon as they'd been adopted, she'd gone on a quest to make sure his wardrobe had simple, strong colors, but complex, soothing *textures.* A cashmere sweater with a simple knit/purl pattern would ground him and give him something to touch, something to soothe, in case the world got too bright and loud.

"I'll wear that, then," he said, his heart aching a little. What could he get her for Christmas? *Dammit!*

"Okay! You go shower. I'll go upstairs and get a list from Julia—I'm supposed to go over the list with Papers, and then I'm supposed to convince him to come over for Christmas Eve and Christmas. And we're going to have a full house, so he may be down here on the couch in the den, so you know."

Stirling nodded. He'd been semiprepared for that. His apartment had its own bathroom and even a mini fridge that the kitchen staff kept fully stocked with bagels and Red Bull, per his request, but Julia had warned him that the one caveat to the invitation to stay in the Salinger home was that if things got tight, he'd have to share his bathroom. He'd had no problem with that. The den itself was frequently used by the crew to plan jobs, and his bathroom was fair game then as well. He let Molly decorate it, and the staff kept it clean, and he could deal with someone else in there without hyperventilating.

But he tended to like things how he liked them and hated them to be moved.

Oh God—he was such a freak. But if he was spending that time with Papers….

"Are you sure he'll want to see us?" Stirling asked, hating himself for his insecurity.

"He's *expecting* us," Molly said patiently. "Felix commissioned him to make us all new IDs, as sort of a pre-Christmas present. And you're like bait to get him to come stay for Christmas." Her expression turned thoughtful. "I have the feeling that Danny and Julia have been trying to pull Papers into the house for a long time. They worry about him being alone too much. Which is sort of how they feel about you, little brother. Let's get a move on."

Stirling grunted, not really in argument but in dissatisfaction as to how his end of the argument had gone. It really sucked to not ever win a fight with his sister.

"He doesn't even like me," Stirling muttered.

Molly guffawed. "No! You were there last time!"

His cheeks heated in mortification. He'd shown up at Tienne's West Loop apartment with Molly, trying so hard to squash the little butterflies of hope in his stomach.

To his intense dismay, a young man had walked out, much older than Stirling and Molly, handsome, with black stubble and black hair coating the backs of his forearms. He was wiping his face lewdly with the back of his hand.

He'd given them both the once-over and snorted.

"Neither one of you are going to get *that* one hard again."

Bemused on Molly's part, and dismayed on Stirling's, they had walked into the apartment to find Tienne shamefacedly zipping up his trousers and washing his face in his kitchen sink.

"I'm sorry," he'd muttered. "That was… unanticipated. If you could, please, the packages are on the table. Simply take them and go."

And with that, he had fled to his bedroom in a huff.

Molly grimaced. "Little brother, I don't think we walked in on what you thought we walked in on."

Stirling gave her a flat glare.

"No," she amended. "I mean there was sex, but I don't think…. At least it didn't seem to me as though it was necessarily *welcome* sex."

Stirling's eyes widened. "You mean he was…." He couldn't make himself say the word.

She shook her head. "Maybe? There's a line. It's hard to explain. It's just… you don't understand." She sighed and plopped down on his bed. "When you are lonely and emotionally vulnerable, sometimes someone will want sex, and it may not be what you want, but it'll be… something. That guy, the way he left Tienne,

the look on Tienne's face—Tienne didn't want whatever happened. But maybe he was lonely and wanted
something, and that's what was there." She snorted.
"The guy was a bastard to take advantage of it, that
was all."

Something awful stirred in Stirling's chest. He'd
stayed celibate for a lot of reasons—the biggest being that he was so very guarded. He didn't want to do
something so intimate with his body unless he was intimate with the man's *person* as well. But Molly had em-
braced sex with all of the bravery and precociousness
she'd shown the world since birth, probably, and she'd
had experiences that Stirling hadn't.

Apparently, this was one of them.

"You…?" he asked, rubbing under his neck. "This
happened to *you*?"

She gave a sad little shrug. "A couple of times, before Josh rounded us up this spring. It's one of the reasons I was so excited to move in with Felix and Julia, I
think. I… yes, everybody's gay here *except* Julia, but I
also have a house full of brothers who adore me. I don't
need to have sex because I'm lonely and there's nothing
else to do. I mean, I wouldn't mind having it so I could
have a good time, or even meet someone worth having
it with. But not because I'm lonely and sad. But think
about it. There's having a lover, and there's doing what
I think Tienne was doing before we walked in. Tienne
wasn't happy with that—it's why he blew us off and ran
into his bedroom. Maybe…." She held her hands open
in an "anything goes" sort of gesture. "Now scoot! It's
an hour into the city, and I want to stop for lunch after
we have our meetup." She smiled dreamily. "Deep dish
at Lou Malnati's, you think?"

Stirling nodded. "I think," he said, and although he was aware she'd changed the subject to make him more comfortable, he was grateful. He couldn't fix Molly's loneliness; he couldn't fix that she'd been in a place where she'd *been* that lonely. She was always, always his big sister, and while it seemed like she held nothing back when talking about her personal life, he was very, very aware that she kept back anything that would worry *him*. Her long-standing habit of protecting Stirling from pain or upset would have kicked in, and he would never have known she'd felt that way if she hadn't felt the need to give him some insight on why his hopeless, stupid crush might not be so hopeless and stupid.

He was helpless to do so many things—get Tienne to notice him, help with his sister's love life, find out what had happened to their parents two years ago. The absolute very least he could do was take Molly out for pizza and make her smile.

OR MAYBE let her kick the shit out of someone.

Chicago's West Loop was known for its trendy restaurants and links to the tech world. The apartments there were upscale and high tech, and Tienne's building was no exception.

It was also, Stirling had always thought privately, very anonymous, but then, unless you got to see the inside of Tienne's apartment, he would fit that bill too.

Once you crossed the threshold of the tastefully appointed hallway with pristinely white walls, you ended up in a vast open-area living room/kitchen with framed art on the walls that ranged from brightly colored forgeries of Monet, Matisse, and Gauguin and other impressionist greats to delicate illustration plates that only a very few would be able to tell weren't the work of William Blake or Arthur Rackham.

Normally such a cacophony of color would have appalled Stirling, but something about Tienne's presentation of the works was so balanced, so tasteful. The frames were plain, good quality, and sturdy, and there was enough negative space between each work to put the focus exclusively on the work itself. It didn't bother him.

The furniture was Stirling's favorite type—solid, simple design with leather upholstery, the soft Italian kind. Everybody at the Salinger mansion had come to visit Papers at one time or another, and all of them had reported sitting on the comfortable couches and simply contemplating their favorite painting, Stirling included.

His favorite paintings were, he suspected, not forgeries at all, but original works. He hadn't yet worked up the courage to ask Papers about them.

But that was Tienne's living area. His kitchen area was a tiny office of forgery equipment, from laminators to embossers, and Stirling suspected he kept minimal food in the refrigerator and mainly paper in the cupboards.

He'd certainly been thin enough for Stirling to count his ribs the last time they'd been there.

And nobody had seen Tienne's bedroom—not even, Stirling suspected, the rather coarse gentleman who'd been exiting as they'd arrived last time.

They didn't catch the SOB leaving this time—but somebody was in there, somebody dangerous.

"No!" Tienne's softly accented voice was flat and angry. "No, I will not. Not again. I did work for you, but that is not work. I will *not* be pawed by you to convince me. No. Do you think you are the first man of your sort I've encountered? I said *no!*"

This was followed by a crash loud enough to make Stirling and Molly stare at each other in alarm.

"Stay here," Molly muttered, putting both hands on Stirling's shoulders and shoving him back against the wall of the hallway.

She pulled a Taser out of her purse with absolute confidence before lifting a booted foot—it *was* snowing outside after all—and kicking the door down like a pro in an action flick.

Stirling gave her a thumbs-up, and she stalked in.

"I thought so," she growled. "You. Get out."

"Who in the fu—"

But Molly took zero shit and gave fewer fucks. "You can leave voluntarily or my family can carry you out pissing down your own pants, asshole. Your choice."

"I *will* be back!" the man snarled before rushing out the door.

It was the same man as before, and as he turned down the hallway, Stirling stuck his foot out and caught the man in the ankle, sending him sprawling, landing on his chin hard enough to bite his tongue.

Molly and Tienne stuck their heads out of the apartment in time to see him scramble to his feet and turn a hunted look over his shoulder, blood seeping from between his lips.

"I'll be back!" he cried. "I'll be back to fuck you all!" he finished before turning to run down the hall.

Stirling met Molly's eyes and then Tienne's, but Tienne shook his head miserably.

"You should go," he murmured, retreating into the apartment. Molly followed him, and so did Stirling, because leaving him alone after that was so very much not going to happen.

"Who is he?" Molly demanded as they marched in. Tienne paused to take in the lock she'd broken and gave her a look full of recrimination. She pulled out her phone as she spoke and waved her hand. "Leave it. I'm texting Danny to come fix it. If I can bust in like an action hero, the lock wasn't good enough."

Tienne's eyes widened. "No!" he cried, almost like a child. "No, do *not* call Danny, I beg of you!"

"Danny will fix it," Stirling said, trying to soothe him. "Danny's good at that. He *wants* to do it."

But Tienne wasn't hearing him. "No, no. Do not bother him. He doesn't need to come help me from my stupidity. He has paid enough for my life already—"

Stirling and Molly exchanged a flickered look. Oh? Gossip they *didn't* know? "You will explain that," Molly said, and Stirling nodded.

"No." Tienne looked to him for support, but oh no. He did not like this situation any more than Molly did. Yes, he had a crush—it wasn't going away—but more importantly, Tienne was one of *them*. Part of their crew. And if he'd been shadowy and on the fringe by choice, that did not negate the fact that Julia had asked him to be in the house over the holidays.

"Yes," Stirling replied in answer to that speaking look. "I am *not* okay with picking up our passports and going. You aren't some random criminal, Tienne. You're one of Julia's and Danny's criminals, and that's a whole different thing."

Tienne scrubbed at his narrow face with shaking hands. His long sandy hair, usually held back by a band at his nape, had come loose, and it covered his fingers as he tried to hide from the world.

"It was stupid," he said, his voice broken like rocks. "His name is Levka Dubov. I met him at a gallery, and he said he was looking for someone to help him with visa applications." His narrow shoulders shook as he stood. "I thought he wanted *actual help* with the applications." He wiped his eyes with his palms. "I don't know how he knew me," he muttered. "But he said once he'd been told to look out for me. He knew about my father, knew what I did. I… I work with such a select clientele, you understand? Your crew, yes, and maybe three or four others. But he came over the first time—" He gave them both a look of such terrible bleakness. "—and you interrupted him then too."

"Oh Lord," Molly said unhappily. "Tienne, why didn't you say something?"

Tienne shook his head. "Danny, he already saved my life once, and at such a terrible price. He sent me here, gave me people to look after me. How could I let him know I was in with mobsters again? I…." He let out a breath and straightened his spine. "Just… go. Take your papers and go. Don't say anything, just—"

But Molly already had her phone out. "Stirling, help him get his things. Danny can move his paintings—there's storage places all over the Art Institute, temperature and humidity controlled. It'll be fine. Let me get Hunter and Chuck. We need to relocate you stat, and he sounded European to me." She looked at Tienne. "Eastern European. Russian? Czech?"

"Serbian," Tienne told her dazedly. "He claims to know Kadjic, and he's Russian. But no. Why are you calling all these people to my apartment? What are you—"

Molly scowled. "Julia said it. She said it a thousand times. She said, 'That boy needs mothering. I

don't know how to get him to stay.' I thought she was
exaggerating, you know, because she thinks we *all*
need mothering, and Good God, we're in our twenties.
But you know what? Her instincts were right on. Go
pack up, Tienne. You're coming home with us, you're
staying through the holidays like Julia had planned, and
we're going to find this guy and put him out of action
if I have to take out a contract on him with my own
money."

Stirling grimaced. "Hunter wouldn't take your
money," he said logically. Hunter was, technically, a
mercenary soldier, but he had more in common with
good guys than bad guys. From what Stirling could see,
Hunter was the one person he knew who was patient
enough to date Josh Salinger's best friend, Grace, without strangling him.

Molly's scowl intensified. "Then he'd do it pro
bono. Now *scoot*, Tienne. I'm about to talk about you,
and you don't want to be here for this."

Stirling didn't touch people without some serious
buildup beforehand, but he stood back and gestured imperiously for Tienne to pass in front of him while Molly
got on the phone and worked miracles.

"Oh God," Tienne muttered as they crossed his living room area. "I... all these paintings. They're forgeries, but they're *mine*, and—"

"They'll still be yours," Stirling soothed. "We'll
put them in storage until you're ready to move into another apartment, or back into this one. Or Danny will
rent you gallery space. Or... well, something." He was
really interested in what Tienne had said about Danny
saving his life and paying "such a terrible price," but he
knew they had other priorities right now. "Come on. In

an hour this place is going to be crawling with people trying to get you to safety. You want to be ready."

They had reached Tienne's bedroom door when he whirled and looked Stirling directly in the eyes. Stirling wasn't great at this, but he'd practiced with Molly, Danny, and Josh—and, more recently, Carl, the crew's legitimate businessman, who was a deft criminal and a stand-up guy.

Tienne's eyes were this stunning Caribbean blue, and even though technically Stirling knew that eye color was a simple genetic fact over which the recipient had no control, he was still breathless because they were *so pretty*.

"I worked very hard," Tienne rasped. "I worked to pay Mr. Danny back, but he didn't want my money. I worked to carry on my father's business, but I don't like most of the people in it. All I want to do is paint, but all I can sell are forgeries, and that man, that terrible man, knows the man who killed my father, and he thinks he has license to my art and my papers and my body—"

"The hell he does!" Stirling's chest hurt—it *ached* with the idea that Tienne had been touched by the man they'd seen coming out of his apartment the month before. "Dear God, Etienne, why didn't you tell us?"

Tienne cast him a tortured look and then stomped into his room with Stirling on his heels.

His bedroom was… simple. A plain wooden queen-sized frame sat in the corner, the bed neatly made with an off-white comforter and off-white sheets. A matching dresser stood kitty-corner to it, and a wardrobe—also matching—sat across. The bathroom was attached, and Stirling knew that the towels and linens would be absolutely as simple.

The bedroom window extended across almost the entire wall, and most of the room space was devoted to an easel and an artist's table, complete with every color in every medium from palest taupe to most exhausting scarlet.

Painting.

Stirling had been hoping to commission a painting from him—it had occurred to him what he could give Danny and Felix for Christmas—but until this moment he'd never realized how much Tienne's prowess with color, space, and brushwork dominated his every thought.

This was not a place where a man entertained lovers; it was a place where he got lost in his obsessions.

Stirling looked around and narrowed his eyes. "Okay, so I'm sure there's a bed for you somewhere at the mansion, and I think Julia has a solarium up in her wing where you can set up your painting. She frequently complains that she doesn't use it enough. She prefers the main house because she likes to be around all of us—"

"Stop!" Tienne protested. "You are talking like it's a foregone conclusion—"

Stirling scowled. "Look," he said frankly, "I have no idea what you owe Danny, but I can tell you right now that Danny doesn't care. He doesn't keep score. However you ended up on the Salinger radar, they want you to be part of them. They literally sent us to ask you to come stay for Christmas. *In their house.* I mean, you've been making their forgeries since you got Josh and the rest of us fake IDs in high school. You've helped us pull jobs before. We *like* you! Why are you freaking out if we don't want you to be pressured by the mob?"

Tienne stared at him, his eyes shiny. "You like me?" he asked, sounding like he'd been whacked out of orbit. "Why? I…." He swallowed. "I can never think of anything to say. I… I've been dying to think of something to say. You all come in, and you're so kind, and all I can talk about is price and product and—"

"Color," Stirling said, smiling a little at the paint cabinet.

"You hate color," Tienne said throatily. They were standing across the room from each other, and Stirling wanted so badly to get closer, to feel the heat off his body, to see what he smelled like. He'd noticed that Tienne didn't wear perfumed aftershave or heavy deodorants, which was fine. He smelled *clean* a lot, but not like whatever it was they put in soap to make men not smell like men.

"I love color," Stirling said honestly. "Have you seen how my sister dresses? I could look in her fabric cabinet for years." He peered down at his plain navy sweater and touched the softness at his sleeve for grounding. "I don't like it on me," he added. "It makes me dizzy. And *you* like color like Molly does. But you put it on canvas or inside paper." He felt his face relax at the memory. "You spent half an hour once explaining to me how there are tiny bits of color in the linen that makes up really good paper. That was nice."

Tienne bit his lip. "You listen so well. I… I assumed you were being polite." He swallowed convulsively. "There are so very few subjects I can talk about."

Oh, this was good. Stirling could work with this.

"Well, for starters, let's talk about wardrobe." He looked around the room. "I don't see any boots. Do you not go outside?"

"I wear sneakers," Tienne said, and Stirling shuddered.

"In Chicago? How long have you lived here?"

"Nine years," Tienne said, looking at him with worried eyes. "Julia keeps giving me boots. They are far too fine for me. I beat up the shoes I have running around the city. I sell the boots for money to give to the homeless shelter nearby."

Stirling slow-blinked. "That's lovely," he said, meaning it. "But do you happen to have a pair for yourself? Tienne, it's twenty degrees outside, and that's because it's not January yet when the real fun starts."

"I have the last pair…." Tienne gestured rather helplessly toward the plain wooden standing wardrobe, and Stirling went to it to look.

"Oh Lord," he muttered. Jeans, T-shirts, hooded sweatshirts—not many of each. He suspected the dresser would be white cotton socks and underwear, with very little accommodation to the weather extremes in Chicago. He whirled toward Tienne, feeling a helpless surge of anger that he couldn't seem to couple with words.

"Why?" he demanded. "Why would you live like this? It's freezing outside. I know Julia and Danny keep trying to give you things—an allowance, winter coats—" He flailed, so upset he could feel his ability to communicate slipping away. "Why would you reject even the shoes they keep giving you?"

Tienne's mouth worked, and he couldn't seem to look anywhere but the window that shed so much natural light onto the painting he was working on at the moment. It appeared to be a silhouette of a person, in which the form of the head in profile was filled with darkness and stars.

"It's all we ever had," he said weakly. "All we ever wanted was a place to paint. I arrive in this country and Julia gives me a choice. She said come with me to my house and be part of my family or go to art school. I chose art school. It's not fair I should have both."

Stirling gaped at him, his chest raw with pain, his brain without words—and at that point, Molly strode in.

"Okay," she said firmly. "Cavalry's on its way. Chuck's bringing a moving van, and Danny's got a place at the Institute to store the paintings. Josh is at chemo with Grace, but when they get to the house afterward, Grace is going to clear out Carl's old room— it's got best window to paint, Julia said, and Carl and Michael are all moved into their new house around the corner, so it's a matter of putting Tienne's bed and furniture and…."

She trailed off, glancing around the room in dawning horror.

"Good God," she said, looking at Stirling for an explanation. "It's like a monastery in here."

Stirling, to his horror, felt tears in his eyes for the first time since they'd found out Josh Salinger had leukemia, and the helplessness was almost exactly that painful.

"Molly," he said, his voice strangling in his throat, "he doesn't think he deserves boots."

And with that he stepped into her open arms, because his big sister was the one who made everything better, and he cried into her shoulder. Above his head he was aware of Molly gesturing imperiously to Tienne.

"You. Come here. Now."

And in a moment, they were both engulfed in her big-sister hug, Tienne shaking next to him, and he had a hope that somehow they could make it okay.

Caught

TIENNE WAS desperate to maintain some sort of dignity.

"Boots! Boots! You keep talking about boots. Why is it so important what I have on my feet?" He gesticulated wildly at Danny Lightfingers—aka Benjamin Morgan—but since Tienne had forged that entire identity, including backstopping it with travel papers and records of the fictional Benjamin being in places Danny had been for over ten years, Tienne was pretty sure he knew who he was dealing with.

Danny "Lightfingers" Mitchell was not a tall man. Slender, five feet seven or so, with curly brown hair that sported hardly any gray, golden hazel eyes, and a vulpine face, he was not, at first glance, as imposing as all that.

But anybody in the international art world had heard of Lightfingers—he was a bogeyman to tell new art dealers about when they thought of skimping on the care and feeding of their paintings or eschewed the environmental controls that kept great art in pristine condition.

"You take care of that Manet, mind you, or ol' Lightfingers'll come get it."

Tienne had overheard more than one private "collector" looking for forged provenance say something like that to somebody purchasing a priceless piece of art for pennies on the dollar.

Tienne hadn't known any of that until he'd taken up his father's employment of forging government papers. After that one chance encounter with Josh, the "cousin" he visited on occasion during holidays when he needed a home to visit, Josh's father and his distant "Uncle Danny" had continued to use his services. They'd paid well and told him repeatedly that if he ever felt somebody was asking him to do something dangerous or threatening him to make him do something he wasn't comfortable with, then he should *tell* them, and they would help him out of any jam.

He'd wondered then what exactly they could do to get him out of a jam. Who *were* these people who had taken him under their wing and were trying very hard to make sure he grew up comfortable and—to the extent that he'd allow them—cared for?

What he'd discovered had made him sad.

Danny Mitchell and Felix Salinger had been lovers for over ten years. About a year before Danny had saved Tienne's life in an alleyway in Marrakech, they had split up, but not before perpetrating the most outrageous deception. Felix had been married during much of their affair—to Julia Dormer-Salinger, who knew exactly who they were and did not mind. Together they had cared for her child, Josh, conceived before her marriage to Felix and, Tienne suspected, not *with* Felix at all. Josh had grown up happy and content with this odd family until the split, and even then, Danny had kept in contact with him. Had even snuck into the audience of Josh's plays and performances, his graduations and recitals—always with Josh in the know and Felix and Julia *not*.

Tienne knew this because Danny had done the same thing for him.

His first time had been about a year after Tienne had arrived, when Tienne had progressed from the American equivalent of junior high school to high school. Tienne's private academy had an art show with a prominent display at a local gallery, complete with parents arriving to sample canapes and nonalcoholic drinks.

Tienne had stood there awkwardly, awaiting Felix, Julia, Josh, and probably Grace, Josh's friend, whom he'd met during holidays already, when a voice behind him had called for his attention.

"Young Etienne?"

It was a cultured voice, with a European accent, and Tienne had turned to find a slight man with curly brown hair standing behind a rather large, gaudy stainless-steel sculpture.

"Yes?"

"Oh, you're looking good," the man said. "Do you…? I don't suppose you remember…?"

"Daniel?" Tienne's mouth dropped open. Not once in the past year had anybody explained how the mobster's boyfriend had managed to spirit Tienne out of Morocco and into Chicago, and why he'd ended up with the guardians who kept trying to do more than guard him.

"Yes!" Danny had given covert glances in either direction. "But I'd appreciate it if you kept my presence here quiet, dear boy. No, I'm not wanted by the police, but…." He grimaced. "Felix and I didn't part on the best of terms. I don't want to make things awkward for you when your family arrives. I wanted to check in. I understand from Julia—well, from Josh, but Julia keeps telling him to include things in his letters—that you're staying… self-contained?"

Tienne regarded him suspiciously. "Oui?"

Danny's nod had a hint of sadness in it. "I understand why," he said softly. "I do. You would be surprised. But look. Your talent—" He'd gestured to the five-painting landscape series Tienne had chosen to display. "—it's prodigious, Etienne. But your heart"—he held his hands to his own chest—"is damaged. Being in that alleyway would damage anybody's heart. I know"—his voice dropped—"that it damaged mine. Remember that being on the fringes here, that is your choice. Julia would bring you into her home in a second. Josh is always ready to accept another brother. Felix is the best of men. Don't let *my* oddness keep you from being taken in, do you understand?"

Tienne had opened his mouth then to say no, he didn't understand. *Danny* had saved him from Andres Kadjic. *Danny* had gotten him out of danger in Morocco. Why couldn't *Danny* adopt him and come stay with him and take over where Antoine had…. Oh God, Antoine—

And then he heard Felix's voice—booming, kind, calling his name—and in that split second of distraction, Danny had disappeared.

And that had been *all* of Danny's contacts after that—quiet, brief, supportive, and kind—until the March before, when Danny and Felix had reconciled, and suddenly their entire crew had come visiting Etienne's loft to try to entice him to be part of their circle.

Tienne had resisted. The shyness that had begun when he and his father had been on the run and reinforced when he'd been shipped, still grief-stricken, to a new city in a new country and a new *family* that knew nothing about him, had been ground in under his skin by eight years of prep school and private college, during which he was encouraged to use his talent and his mind but not his words, unless it was for an academic pursuit.

And he'd acknowledged privately to himself that he was well on the way to becoming the world's loneliest human and had been okay with that, until Stirling Christopher had followed his sister, Molly, into his home back in March, asking him for forged provenances to facilitate a complicated scheme beyond Tienne's wildest imaginings.

Since then, although he'd enjoyed the banter and excitement of *all* the Salingers' new friends, he'd been most excited about Stirling. Something about the young man's stillness, his terse, almost abrupt way of speaking, and his matter-of-fact movements caught Tienne's attention. He was… fascinating. Every time he stood still, he was like a mystery of planes and angles, and Tienne was helpless against the wish to explore him.

In art of course.

Until Stirling and Molly had arrived right after Levka Dubov had threatened him and put his hands—and then his mouth—on Tienne, gotten what he wanted, and left, vowing to return whenever he'd needed papers or, in his words, "a shot of virgin's come."

Tienne had lived in fear of his return since then. But Danny had asked him—personally, on Thanksgiving morning after dropping off a dinner because Tienne had politely declined the invite—for a rather large order and an interesting one, including an analysis of an ancient document he wanted to be forged by hand, not machine, because Danny thought Tienne could get more of the nuances that way.

The order had been so interesting it had helped take Tienne's worry away—right up until Levka had knocked on his door that afternoon.

Now, as he tried to disentangle himself from Stirling and his ferocious, terrifying sister in order to face Lightfingers himself, he was wondering why he'd thought Levka would leave him alone, and also wondering what would happen now that Danny had been called into this situation.

"They are worried about boots," Danny said patiently, "because they are worried about *you*." He looked around Tienne's room with a sort of grim understanding on his face, an expression that didn't lighten one bit as Felix walked up behind him, tall, imposing, and leonine.

"Remind you of anyone?" he asked, glancing around the room as well, and Danny shot him a disgruntled look.

"Yes, are you happy now?"

Felix shook his head and sighed. "Tienne, we've tried very hard to respect your boundaries, but this is a matter of your own safety. This Levka Dubov needs to be removed as a threat, and it's easier to do that if you are safe with us." He gave Danny a troubled glance. "It's also an easy, rather Machiavellian way to get you into our home so we can perhaps give you an alternative vision as to what your life can be. You don't have to live like a monk to have art in your life, Tienne. You don't have to be alone."

Tienne swallowed and nodded. "Oui. Yes. That is fine." It wasn't, really. His life was being put in a bag again and hauled away without his permission, but in the face of both the men who had given him so much, there wasn't anything he felt he could do to gainsay them.

Danny didn't say anything, just cocked his head and lifted an eyebrow, and Felix nodded. "Molly, my dear," Felix said, "if you could come with me? Chuck and Hunter are loading the paintings, and I think they need your help to—how did they put it? Tetris everything into place."

She laughed soggily. "And you need me out of the room so Danny can talk to Tienne."

Felix nodded. "And we need you out of the room so Danny can talk to Tienne."

They left, and Stirling was about to go with them, but Danny forestalled him with a cleared throat and a little shake of the head. "No," he said. "Don't go. Pack for him if you like. Make note of anything you think he needs."

"Boots," Stirling said darkly. "And a winter coat."

"I go running in the morning," Tienne protested weakly. It was his favorite time of day in Chicago— early morning. The challenge of staying upright on the icy streets—even in the lethal scalpel-wind—and jumping off and over obstacles and walls made him happy in ways he loved.

"There are running shoes made for snow," Stirling told him implacably. "And sweatshirts that will keep you warm."

He was holding his body rigidly, like he hadn't fallen apart in his sister's arms, and Tienne felt badly. Stirling was so much like him—as Danny said, "self-contained." The thought that he would come undone for Tienne…. Tienne felt as though he'd trespassed on Stirling's soul.

"I don't want to be a bother," Tienne told him, and he could not repair the crack in his own voice. "I never wanted to be a bother. Do you not both understand? I am here by luck. There is no place for me in this world, and I am here by luck, and if I'm to have this thing I love best on the planet—"

"You have to give up every part of yourself," Danny retorted. "Every molecule. Because there's no room for what Tienne wants. Only the thing that drives his soul. You think I don't know what that feels like, Etienne? I do. I did. And I took that one small piece of what I loved, and I clung to it, and I drank away the pain of not having any other part of me. And you know where that got me? That got me to an alleyway in Morocco where the man I was sleeping with ordered the death of an innocent man, and the only thing I could do for him was—"

"Save his son," Tienne supplied, suddenly understanding, maybe a little, what had driven Danny that night in Marrakech.

"Indeed," Danny said, with a terrible mixture of compassion and regret on his face. "Except his son won't let me."

Tienne swallowed and looked at Stirling, hoping his trim, soberly clad figure could ground him, and in a way it did. He was a study in contrast, his darker skin in the pale room, his gray eyes contrasting with the pale brown—even a sweetly pouty mouth in a square-jawed face. For a moment Tienne wanted to paint him, the cheekbones, the strong chin, the level gaze. Stirling would make a very, very pretty painting, and the way he was looking at Tienne....

Tienne had to look away. He switched to French because he knew Danny spoke it and most Americans didn't.

"I don't want his pity," he said, tilting his head to indicate Stirling. "Is that too much to understand?"

Danny's lips quirked up, and his gaze softened. "*Mon bebe*, do you really think it was pity that brought him here? He's been as fascinated with you as you have been with him. I'm not so old I can't recognize two birds who would be comfortable in the same nest."

"I don't know how to nest," Tienne said shortly, looking around the bare room. The living room, yes—he'd kept the art in there. It was his soul. He'd figured it was acceptable for his heart to be barren.

"Don't sulk," Danny said, before switching to English. "Stirling, my lad, is there enough to fill a suitcase?"

"Oui," Stirling replied dryly, eyes flickering between them both before he added in French, "and I'm going to take this old ripped-up backpack as well, because I assume there's some sentimental value."

Tienne's shock and embarrassment was interrupted by Danny's cackle of laughter. "Oh, I should never, ever underestimate you, my boy." He winked. "But you might have learned more if you'd simply listened longer."

Stirling looked mildly embarrassed. "This is why I'm never the shill, isn't it?"

Danny's grin made his cheeks apple. "You'll get there." He looked to the both of them. "Stirling, if you help Tienne case up his paints and his project, we can put that in the back of the SUV. Hunter and Chuck are directing some friends around to help box the paintings in the living room, but I think we need to get Tienne out of here fast."

"Why?" Tienne asked.

Danny cocked his head as though the answer should have been self-explanatory. "Because you're going to need to release all the emotion you're keeping inside, kiddo. Let's get you to the mansion before that happens."

Tienne cast Stirling a look that Stirling returned inscrutably, and it occurred to Tienne that while Stirling might not have *wanted* to cry on his sister's shoulder, he was looking very sturdy now.

Tienne's stomach felt like a thousand cascading butterflies, and so did his knees.

He turned abruptly away from Danny and Stirling and started to put his paints away into their movable cabinet, ignoring the shaking of his hands.

In his heart, he knew it for what it was: defeat.

A COUPLE of hours later, as he sat at the dinner table in the Salingers' luxe mansion in the wealthy suburb of Glencoe, he had the rather random thought that defeat tasted better than he'd first assumed—but it was a little bit louder.

He was made to know that the table was missing some of its key members. Michael, the Salingers' mechanic, and Carl, the insurance investigator who worked with them sometimes, were both at their own house, settling in. Molly told him that they'd only moved in together in the week after Thanksgiving, and they were honeymooning a little. Carl had only that week been allowed to talk to Michael's children from his former marriage over Zoom, and it was something of a delicate time.

Torrance Grayson, the YouTube reporter who made his money and reputation on hard-hitting stories revolving around social issues, was missing, although he was often missing, according to Stirling. He'd apparently promised to be there on Christmas Eve, and had, along with everyone else, committed his time to some sort of mystery gift for the three weeks after Christmas as well.

"Does this include me?" Tienne had asked, a little overwhelmed.

"Yes," Stirling said, eyes studiously on his food. They were eating london broil with mushroom Bordeaux sauce, and Stirling ate like he appreciated good food—or maybe steak.

Tienne had to admit he did too. He often relied on either fried eggs or takeout. Having somebody who seemed to know what they were doing cook for him was a luxury.

"You were supposed to ask me that tonight?"

"Well, it goes with Danny's order, which I'm *not* supposed to ask you about, and…." Stirling looked a little to his right, where Felix, Danny, and Julia sat with Josh. Josh was…well, on the one hand, he looked like hell. When Tienne had first met him, his piquant face had held an elfin charm, and health had flushed his cheeks. His dark hair had been glossy and neatly cut, and his figure, while trim and lithe, had also been bounding with energy. Tonight he was pale but composed, and his hair, which had thinned, was starting to grow back. His clothes hung on him like they were on

hangers, but he had the strength to smile at Grace and
return his sallies as the two continued the banter that
had apparently sustained them through Grace's new
relationship with the hard-eyed mercenary at his side
and several bouts of chemo that had all but killed Josh.
Tienne had seen him look worse but hated that he didn't
look better.

Cancer was an asshole—even Tienne could get on
board with that. Josh Salinger had never been anything
but kind to him and welcoming. He could have been
cold and standoffish to Tienne, who knew perfectly
well he was a weird family obligation who showed up
at the occasional Christmas or summer holiday. But
Josh and even Grace had done their best to make him
feel welcome.

It hadn't been their fault he'd found more and more
reasons not to attend, because their dynamic company
made him wistful for somebody in his life who could so
easily speak his language. They weren't even romantic
partners, but they were such… such….

Family.

The truth smacked him in the face for the millionth
time, but today, after being practically folded in a suitcase and *dragged* to the Salinger mansion, he finally
registered the pain.

They were family, as they'd been inviting him to
be since he was thirteen years old.

Tienne pulled in a harsh breath and tried to concentrate on his conversation with Stirling and on the other
people at the table: Molly of course, and Chuck and
Lucius, whom he didn't know very well.

"What…," he murmured. "What was the other
thing you were supposed to ask me about?"

Molly must have heard the thread in his voice because her head swiveled around like a toy. "Stirling?"

Stirling nodded and stood. "I'm supposed to ask you if you'd like the rest of your dinner in your room," he said, taking Tienne's full plate from the table and looking at Molly. "Glass of soda, I think," he murmured, almost as though she'd asked what Tienne had been drinking.

She wrinkled her nose but nodded before standing, helping Tienne to his feet and giving him a little nudge to follow Stirling as Stirling led the way to his room.

Tienne stumbled once, twice, and then someone— it must have been the brawny, auburn-haired Chuck— scooped him up in his arms and carried him, like a child, to his room.

He looked around helplessly when he got there, realizing they'd moved his plain bed into one of the rooms in the mansion, as well as his dresser and wardrobe. All of it was already arranged with his clothes.

"My paints…," he murmured.

"Pretty sure there's a room in Julia's wing for them," Chuck said. "Isn't that right, Stirling?"

"Yup." Stirling was setting his dinner down on the dresser. "Here, Chuck, set him down and get his shoes. Tienne, take off the sweatshirt, and we'll help with the jeans."

Tienne's brain had apparently fuzzed out completely. He did exactly what they said and found himself tucked solidly into his plain queen-sized bed under the plain white sheets and plain white comforter.

Except on top of the comforter was an ultrasoft, fuzzy blanket in a quiet mauve that didn't offend his senses but did give him a feeling of… care. Stirling made sure it was firmly around his legs as he set Tienne's dinner on a pillow on his lap.

The meat had been cut into small bites, and Tienne hadn't even been aware that had happened.

"Thanks, Chuck," Stirling said to the auburn-haired giant.

"No worries, little buddy." Chuck smiled gently at Tienne. "We share a bathroom, and I'll be in the next room for a few days, so give me a holler if you need anything." He paused. "That includes the middle of the night, if you hear a noise or if you get lost trying to find the kitchen for a snack, okay?"

Tienne nodded dumbly, and Chuck shook his head.

"I'll keep an ear out," he said, as though he knew Tienne had no intention ever of coming to him for help. Then he nodded to Stirling. "I'll have your sister get your plate up here, but I promise, no more people."

"Thank you," Stirling said, glancing Tienne's way. "He's had it."

"Understood."

And with that, Chuck was gone, leaving Tienne to eat his dinner doggedly, every bite delicious and sustaining but also an act of will.

Stirling snagged a tapestried chair—something that had *not* been in Tienne's apartment—and sat himself down next to the bed. Then, to Tienne's immense relief, he pulled out his phone and sat quietly, making small noises in the back of his throat as he played a game.

Tienne's muscles began to relax in the quiet. Bite, chew, swallow, bite, chew, swallow…. He hadn't realized how ravenous—or how tense—he'd been until his plate was empty and he was melting into the pillow at his back, staring into space. Stirling took the plate off his lap and the spoon from his nerveless fingers and set them on his dresser again and then came back and helped him get comfortable.

Finally, when his head was on the pillow and he was well on his way to falling asleep, the silence had seeped into his soul, giving him enough peace in his heart to speak.

"How did you know," he asked, "exactly what I needed?"

"I get the feeling you and I are a lot alike," Stirling said softly.

Tienne glanced up to see Stirling studying his face. Not trying to meet his eyes, no, but taking in every nuance of expression.

"Do people exhaust you too?"

"They do, but I'm getting better at processing all the chatter. It helps that I know everybody, and they're very good at accepting me for who I am."

Tienne made a soft sound in his throat. "I never wanted to be a bother," he tried to explain, and Stirling's gentle touch on his hair stopped him.

"I'm sorry." Stirling withdrew his hand slowly. "That was rude."

"I liked it." And he had, although he rarely remembered being touched since his father died.

Stirling put his hand back where it had been and stroked his head some more. "My mother left me when I was five—abandoned me in a church. She was desperate. We were living on the streets, and she couldn't feed me. I went into a foster home, and by the time the Christophers came in to adopt Molly and me, I think she'd passed away. Pneumonia, my adoptive mother said. I remember she was crying when she said it. I honestly think they would have helped my mother and helped me and done anything they could to make sure Molly and I weren't separated, even if they didn't get to adopt me. But my mother was dead, and they could adopt me, and even though I know they only took me in because Molly insisted, they... they made a place for me in their lives. They loved me. And I was really lucky."

Tienne made a little noise he wasn't proud of, and Stirling kept stroking his hair.

"They died two years ago. They were sailing off the coast of St. Bart's, and their ship went down in a storm. Molly and I were old enough to inherit our trust funds, but when Josh's parents asked us if we wanted to move in here, we did. Do you know why?"

"No," Tienne said, his throat aching with the need to understand.

"Because they understood us, and they cared about us, and we both knew, from hard experience, not to crap on that. So we live here now, even though we have an apartment in the city."

"That's... amazing," Tienne said softly.

"Your art is amazing," Stirling retorted. "Molly and I are only common sense."

Tienne smiled a little, ignoring the tear tracking down his nose. He didn't feel sobs coming, but this softness, this release of tension, it was inevitable. "What did you want to ask me to do? When you came by this afternoon. Before the world went upside down."

"Mm." Stirling kept up that hypnotizing stroke of his hair. "I wanted to commission you to paint a portrait of Danny and Felix, any style you want. I have some pictures you could use for reference. I wanted to give them a Christmas present."

Tienne closed his eyes and felt more tears. "That's a lovely idea," he said. "Since I'm here anyway, I'd be happy to."

"Good."

That's all they said, and Stirling sat there, running his fingers through Tienne's overlong hair, until Tienne fell asleep.

Slow Delicate Dance

MOLLY BROUGHT Stirling's food up—warmed and refreshed—a little after Tienne fell asleep, with a tray to go with it.

"How is he?" she asked as she gathered up the plate and utensils from Tienne's meal.

"Overwhelmed," Stirling said and then let out a happy hum as he tucked into his food. London broil was one of his favorites—he'd been sorry to leave the table, but Tienne had chosen that moment to do his falling apart, and, well, you respected that moment, even if you were really hungry.

She gave a sigh as she set everything she'd gathered down on the dresser and sank to the floor, crosslegged, resting her elbows on the inside of her knees and her chin on her palms.

Stirling glanced at her and recognized the pose for what it was—thought. His sister was often loud and rambunctious, but when she got like this, he knew to respect her mood like he knew how to respect the falling-apart moment.

He ate fastidiously, grateful for her all over again and mindful that Tienne's sleep might not be as deep as it looked. He was finishing up, mopping up the delicious Bordeaux sauce with the last bit of his bread and wondering what to get Phyllis, Julia's housekeeper and unsung provisioner of the crew, for Christmas, when Molly spoke again.

"Did you catch what he and Danny were talking about? Something about an alley in Marrakech?"

"Morocco," Stirling replied thoughtfully—not because she wouldn't know Marrakech was *in* Morocco, but because Danny had spoken of his low point as being in Morocco often enough for that to trigger their memories. "I think Danny saved Tienne's life, but he couldn't save Tienne's father. I didn't catch details, but you know…."

"That was when Danny stopped drinking," Molly said thoughtfully. "Whatever it was, it was important to him."

"So is Tienne," Stirling murmured. In rest, Tienne's narrow, appealing face could be studied. His teeth were a little crooked in the front—it spoke to what Stirling suspected, which was that he'd spent his childhood on the run, with no access to braces. But Danny and Felix had both cared about him enough to pay for his education, to try to make him a part of the family. Stirling remembered Josh missing play rehearsals to go to dinners with, as he called him, "My strange and distant cousin." The family had tried, but something in Tienne's makeup had resisted.

Stirling wanted a crack at him now.

"What are you seeing, little brother?" Molly turned her head to study him, and he could hear in her breathing when she caught the flush against his tawny skin. "Really?" she asked softly.

He shrugged. "He's very—"

"Pretty," she supplied dryly.

"And sort of—"

"Skittish," she continued.

"And I like the way he—"

"Blushes when he looks at you," she finished.

He glared at her, and she wrinkled her nose impudently. "I could have said those things on my own," he said with dignity.

"But it's so much more fun to know you!" She laughed, keeping her voice soft. Then she added, in utmost seriousness, "He's been hurt, Stirling, and I know you know what that feels like. And you and me—we both have... well, broken places. And I'm not sure if mine can ever be fixed completely, and I suspect it's the same for you. Am I wrong?"

"No," Stirling answered. "But that's all of us here, isn't it?"

"Yeah," she said with a sigh. "But be careful is all I'm saying." She gave him a grimace. "I just... you know...."

"Don't want me to get hurt." He gave her a smug smile. "You're not the only one who can do that."

Her laughter, low and throaty, was the grown version of the cackle she'd mastered when they were children. He felt moved to a sudden confession.

"Molly?"

"Yes?"

"I have no idea what to get you for Christmas. Every year I want it to be something wonderful, and every year I end up doing something stupid like updating your computer or buying you a game you could buy yourself or….." He breathed deeply, trying to find words. "Last year, you bought me fur-lined winter boots, and they're perfect. I want to get you something amazing, and I always end up dorking out." He stopped when he realized she was staring at him with wet cheeks. "What?"

"You grew up and stayed my brother," she said, her voice clogged. "It's the only present I ever wanted."

He swallowed, his throat so tight his ears ached, and risked a glance at the lonely figure on the bed. Was this what Tienne was so afraid of? This overflow of emotion so vast it had no outlet, so inexplicable it overrode all physical cues and made your eyes sting and your chest ache and….

He sucked in a gasp of air and reached down next to his chair, knowing what Molly would do next.

He wasn't disappointed when she grabbed his hand and squeezed.

"Someday," he said grandly, thinking of the best thing in the world, "I'll buy you fashion week in Milan. The whole week. You can wander in and meddle and participate in every show and—"

She scooted closer, still holding his hand, and rested her head against his thigh, like when they were children, finding any way to clutch at each other when they knew they were flotsam in an uncertain sea. He moved his hand to stroke her amazing curly red hair, paying special attention to the streaks of rainbow that she dyed into it. Ever since they'd been kids, he'd been obsessed with separating each curl. He thought she probably dyed it because she remembered him saying, "Here's a yellow curl, and here's an orange curl, and here's a

brown curl, and this one's almost white. If we had blue
or green or purple, we'd have a rainbow." He'd always
been tactile, especially as a child, his fingers able to say
the things his mouth could never manage. It was why
he gravitated toward computers so easily. His fingers
were always twitching, and computers—whether the
keyboard or the motherboard—gave him something to
twitch with.

And that familiar texture gave him words, so he
kept spinning his gift: all the things his amazing sister
could do, all the things he wanted for her. Lovers by the
score, lining up to feed her anything from strawberries
to steak. Juicy parts in plays she adored. A chance to
have her name on a line of kickass clothes for kickass
women.

They weren't things he could put in a box for her
and weren't things he could wrap, but he remembered
the way she'd been there that day, wrapping her arms
around both him and the fragile, talented man asleep
in front of them, and he thought he would put them on
the moon and give her that if he could, so she'd know
how grateful he was that she wouldn't let him be alone
in the world.

THEY SAT for about an hour before leaving Tienne
alone. Molly had made sure he had a night-light in
his room in case, which left them free to make their
way downstairs to see if anybody was up late, watching television or reading. Something about Tienne's
solitariness had made them both want to search out
family.

They came upon Josh, Grace, Hunter, and Chuck, playing poker in the small sitting room by the foyer, using candy canes as chips.

"Where's the grown-ups?" Molly asked, making herself comfortable on the floor. The room consisted of a couch and a loveseat, kitty-corner, and a stuffed chair on point to that, with a small coffee table in the middle. From what Stirling could see as he took his place in the stuffed chair, everybody was cheating wildly.

"Plotting," Josh said with a yawn. "Grace, I saw that. You can't pull cards off the bottom of the deck while we're sitting here."

"I can too."

"You're a thief, not a magician—now put them back."

"You should be nicer to me," Grace announced grandly, before putting two cards back on the bottom of the deck that were probably not the ones he'd pulled.

"Why?" Josh asked. "Show. Four aces."

Grace stared at him in outrage and threw down a pair of kings and a pair of threes. "Because we don't call you out when *you* cheat!"

"That's because we don't catch him cheating," Hunter replied, his lean mouth compressed grimly as he laid down a low flush.

"And he never cheats small," Chuck grumbled, laying down a straight. "No, if Josh cheats, it's for all the marbles."

Josh cackled and then looked sadly at his pot of candy canes. "Not this time," he admitted. "I really prefer chocolate."

Grace gave him a gentle pat on the shoulder. "Sorry, Cancer Boy. After Christmas, maybe."

Josh's stomach wasn't ready for anything as complex as chocolate. Simple carbs, gentle proteins, friendly starches.

Sugar was for people who didn't throw up at the drop of a card.

"One more hand?" he asked, yawning, and Chuck, Hunter, and Grace all folded their arms and gave definite shakes of the head.

"Save your strength," Grace said, grabbing one of the candy canes—a fruit-flavored one, judging by the stripes—and unwrapping it delicately. "You have one more week of treatment, and then it's going to be all Christmas, all of the time. Phyllis is baking cookies, Julia is doing some sort of grand present, Felix and Danny are plotting, and I know for a fact you bought all your presents in September in case you died, but you haven't wrapped a thing."

Even Stirling winced.

"Oh God, Grace," Hunter said, appalled. "That's so morbid!"

"Don't yell at me!" Grace told them between delicate flicks of his tongue. "He's the one who did it!"

Josh let out a breath and looked embarrassed. "Well, you were all off chasing down murder birds, and I was left alone to face my own mortality. I got bored."

"I am not going to be able to open that now," Molly said matter-of-factly. "I'm going to look at the wrapped present, remember this conversation, and cry. Thanks for ruining Christmas for me, asshole. I'm getting *you* ugly green gloves."

Josh grinned at her. "Are they Grinch gloves? 'Cause I'd wear those."

She stuck her tongue out at him. "God, I'm glad you're getting better. You're so irritating. Another six months and I can sock you in the arm without breaking you."

Josh groaned and covered his eyes with his hands. "So long!" He yawned and then recalled himself. "Speaking of breaking," he segued delicately. "How is my shy and strange cousin?"

"Broken," Stirling said bluntly.

"He had a long day," Chuck tried, but Stirling shook his head.

"Josh, do you know how Tienne came to be... here?" He gestured around, indicating Chicago, Glencoe, Indiana, the United States, and the Salinger family at large.

Josh cocked his head, suddenly interested. "It was about a year after Danny left," he said quietly. "Someone called Julia for Danny. I mean, I gather he was in the hospital at the time. That mobster, Kadjic, had messed him up pretty good, but we didn't know that. Julia got a call, and someone she didn't know said Danny was sending a boy to her and basically invoked Danny's name. Like Danny said to take care of him. Mom offered—I remember her talking to Dad about it. She'd *wanted* to once she'd met him, but the only bit of information she'd gotten during that phone call was that he might like art school. And—" He shrugged. "—you know Tienne. He went to art school and came home occasionally and was basically awkward and quiet in the corners for a couple of holidays. Grace and I found out he was forging IDs when we were in high school. We told Danny and Felix, separately, of course, and they gave him business. But he's never said a word about it, really. Just... you know. Always wanted Danny to be there and was really disappointed when he wasn't. Why?"

Stirling wasn't sure if he wanted to tell Josh this or not. In a way, it felt almost like a betrayal, but in another way, gossiping about each other was sort of the family hobby. *Not* sharing the information would have been wrong too.

"Because I *think* Danny got messed up by Kadjic because he saved Tienne's life. But he wasn't able to save Tienne's father. I think Tienne saw his father die. There's… there's a lot of guilt there, I think. A lot of sadness he hasn't processed. I'm not sure what to do next."

There was a moment of stillness, and he watched Hunter, Chuck, and Grace all exchange glances over Josh's head while Josh himself stayed focused on Stirling.

"Be his friend," Josh said after a moment. "Greet him in the morning, show him how breakfast works, take him to the workout shed, show him around. You're good at sitting and listening, Stirling. The rest of us— well, besides Hunter—can talk the ears off a jackrabbit. I think 'cousin' Tienne needs quiet acceptance here. You're the perfect candidate."

"Plus he's been crushing on Tienne since they met at high school graduation," Grace said bluntly.

They all slow-panned to Grace, who unrepentantly sucked in most of the candy cane and pulled it slowly out.

"Yes," he said happily. "I'm an asshole. But it's Christmas, and you *have* to love me."

"No," Stirling said, giving the irritating thief his darkest look. "No, we don't."

For the first time, Grace lost some of his swagger. "But you do, right?"

And Stirling had to relent, because he'd watched Grace wear himself thin caring for Josh in the past year. "Of course, Grace. And not only at Christmas either. It was impolite."

Grace gave it up and began crunching boldly on the remains of the candy cane. "You don't get random crushes, Stirling. I thought I'd mention your thing with Tienne because it's *important*."

Stirling blinked at him, surprised. Yes, they'd all seen Grace caring for *Josh* this last year, but this implied that Grace cared for *Stirling* too.

"Shit," Stirling muttered.

"What?" Molly asked.

"What am I going to get Grace for Christmas?"

Grace grinned pertly. "Don't worry. I'll steal my present for you."

Stirling's eyes widened in worry. Grace had a habit of stealing from the people he cared about most, but Stirling didn't possess a lot of jewelry or knickknacks for the irrepressible thief to choose from. "If you could, you know, make sure the computer isn't *running* when you pull out something vital, that would make it an especially good present."

Grace shrugged. "Suit yourself." Then he turned to Josh and said, "Are you tired *now*? Do you want my amazingly strong boyfriend to carry you to your room? Can I watch?"

Josh narrowed his eyes. "I can walk," he said with dignity, although around September, that hadn't always been true. A bone marrow transplant from an uncle he'd never met until September had made it possible and, to Stirling's knowledge, had resulted in the first deep breath the entire crew had taken since his diagnosis in late July.

"I could carry you. I've got a special pass from Lucius," Chuck said blandly, sprawling back against the couch and flexing. While Grace's boyfriend, Hunter, was the trained fighter, he was—when fully clothed— very average looking, with sandy hair and a medium build. All of Hunter's muscles were steel cloaked in velvet. Chuck, on the other hand, was a showboat, a redheaded good-ol'-boy charmer who was proud of his physique because he worked hard on it. He was also devoted to his billionaire boyfriend, and he rather enjoyed being Lucius's arm candy. Stirling suspected he played up being Lucius's himbo because it made it easier to spot marks in the crowd of movers and shakers Lucius was forced to rub elbows with.

"I'm fine," Josh said, scowling playfully. He let a smile sneak out. "I was thinking, in fact, of dancing."

The group took a collective breath. Although more adept as an actor, he was still a beautiful dancer. Not as fluid or talented as Grace, but Stirling knew it had never mattered. They had loved dancing together, even if it was sneaking into clubs while they were still in high school. For Josh, dancing was a way of keeping fit, of enjoying his body—of remembering his health. And if he was ready to dance, even for a little while, well, that was better than Christmas.

"Says you," Grace scoffed. "I'll believe it when I see it, Cancer Boy."

Josh narrowed his eyes. "Tomorrow. Nine o'clock. Before we leave for chemo."

"You're on," Chuck said. "I think we'd all like to see that."

Stirling thought of the sleeping young man upstairs and how it was going to be his job to acclimate Tienne to living in the Salinger mansion for a while, until he was squared away.

"I agree," he said simply. Then he gave a quiet smile. "But first, are you all *sure* Josh doesn't have time for one more hand? Danny has been giving me pointers for how to bluff."

This pronouncement was met with a chorus of "Oh, look out now! Stirling's going to take us for all we've got!" and he settled in happily, very prepared to win. He wasn't great at bluffing, it was true, but card counting and calculating odds was something he did very well.

STIRLING RETIRED to bed about an hour later, still miffed because Grace was not only an outstanding thief, liar, and card cheat but also because there were nuances in the game he didn't always catch. Molly had taken to giving him invisible signals under the table in a finger code they'd both worked out when they'd taken ASL in high school. The letter *J* drawn against his knee along with three taps meant Josh had three good cards. How she knew that, when neither of them could actually *see* Josh's cards, he had no idea, but his sister was every bit as smart as he was, although he'd been the one to graduate early. He always took her word for it.

They still hadn't been able to take Grace and Josh 50 percent of the time, and that didn't count when Hunter and Chuck would sneak in and maneuver around them. Poker wasn't supposed to be a team sport, but somehow, whenever they all sat down, things got competitive, and the battle lines were drawn.

Stirling snuggled under his thick comforter on rich cotton sheets done in pleasant blue stripes and thought happily that he wouldn't have it any other way.

Then he thought about Tienne, asleep in furniture and linen that was sparse and bare because he didn't think life worked in such a manner as to give him friends or lovers and company as well as the things he loved the most.

Stirling thought maybe that would be the Salinger Christmas present to Tienne. For a little while, he would know what it was like to have people who cared about him.

New Life, New Worries

"BUT WHY?" Tienne mumbled as Stirling shook him awake. "It's so early…."

It was, in fact, 8:00 a.m. He couldn't remember the last time he'd slept so long. Something about knowing that giant auburn-haired man was next door to answer his questions—and that Danny, Felix, Josh, and Julia were all guarding him in some way—had allowed him to have a better sleep than he'd gotten since the first time Levka Dubov had come to his door.

"Light breakfast first," Stirling told him. "Workout next. Then shower and a nice brunch. Then I'll show you where you paint."

Tienne regarded Stirling with surly amusement. Dressed in pristine black sweats with a black hooded sweatshirt and black tennis shoes, his short-cut ringlets all laid flat in the same direction, he'd shaved himself smooth. It was as though he'd groomed to go work out, and Tienne was resentful.

"Do I have time to use the facilities?" he asked dourly, and Stirling nodded, as though he hadn't registered Tienne's mean spirit at all.

"Do," he said. "I'll find you some suitable workout clothes. Do you prefer paint-stained or non-paint-stained?"

Tienne closed his eyes. "Non," he said, feeling small. "Paint-stained are for painting. Everything else can wash." Holes did not matter. Clean laundry was for all occasions, but paint didn't wash out.

Stirling breathed out carefully, and Tienne knew he'd said something wrong. Again.

"Fine," Stirling said. "To the bathroom, then, to change. Hurry! We want to be in the workout shed at nine!"

"Why?" Tienne asked, still grumpy. "What's at nine?"

Stirling's face lit up with anticipation. "Oh, it's going to be good. But there's no guarantees it will last. Let's get there and see."

LESS THAN an hour later, Stirling led Tienne through the mansion—which was big enough—and through a door in the back. The backyard was tremendous. It sported a covered pool big enough to swim laps in, extensive gardens lying dormant under the snow, and out beyond the gardens, a sizable outbuilding, about the size of a ranch-style home but with one wall made of tempered glass that looked into a room full of mirrors.

Tienne was busy keeping his footing on the paving stones that led to the building—they'd been recently sprayed with beet juice to cut the ice, but it was

Chicago in the winter—so he didn't get a good look into the room until they drew closer, and he sucked in a breath.

"It's a gym," he said, surprised.

"Well, yeah," Stirling said, as though this only made sense. "Treadmills, ellipticals, weights, weight machines—even a heated current pool that doubles as a Jacuzzi. The whole family uses it. See? This way you can go running without risking your neck on the ice."

"I liked exploring Chicago," Tienne defended weakly, remembering all of the times he'd slipped and fallen and had wondered as he was going down exactly who would help him up if he was seriously injured.

"Good," Stirling said, his face stony. "Continue to explore Chicago wearing boots, but if you must run, run here."

Tienne rolled his eyes because he knew there were other options, but inside he was warmed. This was a sort of care, wasn't it?

When they got to the workout room, he was surprised to see they weren't the only two people there. Chuck and Hunter were both working the weights, a tall blond man Stirling had never seen was running on one of the ellipticals, and Molly, Josh, and Grace were on the smooth stage area in front of the mirror, stretching. While he watched, Grace stood and bowed, lifting his torso and his left leg at the same time until he was holding onto his heel behind his head.

"Ouch," Tienne murmured, and Stirling laughed softy.

"He likes showing off. They'll be stretching for another twenty minutes. Go ahead and take the treadmill."

"What will you do?"

"Elliptical. I want to talk to Carl."

Tienne felt a reluctant flutter as he looked at the muscular Viking, his shoulders sheened in sweat as he attacked the elliptical course like a soldier marching to glory. "Carl?"

"He and his boyfriend just moved in together. Michael's very—" His eyes slid to Tienne in a sort of assessment. "—shy. And sweet. He's got kids, and Carl's worried about communicating with them. I wanted to see how they were doing."

Tienne nodded curtly, trying not to show his relief. He must have failed, because Stirling wrinkled his nose.

"Please. He's nearly forty. We're friends. Hurry up and get running because Josh and Grace won't wait forever."

Tienne made his way to the treadmill, watching as Stirling stashed their coats and a bag containing a change of clothes for both of them in a corner by what looked like a shower room. He thought ruefully that a shower was probably a good idea, but then he was on the treadmill, setting a midlength, high-difficulty run for himself.

He liked hills. He liked obstacles. He liked being taken out of his head and into the surrounding city. He'd brought his iPhone and earbuds to compensate, but when he started to run, he was very much prepared to *run*.

He was *not* prepared for the show.

The treadmills and ellipticals were against the back wall that separated the shower room and what Tienne assumed was the pool and Jacuzzi. They *faced* the stage where Grace, Josh, and Molly were stretching, with the bank of windows to the side and around a little, so someone working out could have their pick of views.

Right when Tienne's run was finishing up, leaving him panting and sweating and grateful for the aluminum bottle of water Stirling had packed for him, Grace ran to the sound system in the far corner and turned it on loudly enough to dominate all the other noise in the gym, including the clink of the weight machines and the rhythmic *thud-thud-thud* from the treadmills and elliptical.

Then Molly stood and briskly clapped her hands, gathering everybody's attention, and all the extraneous noise in the gym stopped.

"Dance-off," she said shortly. "Me, Grace, and Josh. No losers—not this time. Everyone wins."

There were assorted hoots and hollers from everyone in the gym. Hunter and Chuck put down the weights, and each sat on the bench closest to them. Carl and Stirling came to a slow stop on their machines, from which they'd talked in apparent grunts and monotones during the past half hour. Even Tienne felt compelled to slow down, leaving the last two minutes of cooldown hanging on his machine as he looked around to see why this would capture everyone's attention.

Following a quiet burst of cold air, Tienne looked around to see Danny and Julia step in, with Phyllis, their housekeeper and friend, on their heels. Danny caught Tienne's eye and held his finger to his lips, indicating the stage with a nod of his head.

This was a big deal.

Tienne swallowed, and it occurred to him for the first time how very close to death Josh had been. While he'd always been a distant observer in the household, he hadn't been immune to Josh's attempts to charm him to the center of the family unit, and he realized now what it was he might have lost. His heart clutched as the opening strains of the "Waltz of the Flowers" from *The Nutcracker Suite* began.

Molly, dressed in basic leotards that revealed every bit of her tall curvy figure, stood in one corner of the stage and executed a series of turns that Tienne couldn't name across the diagonal of the stage itself. Her movements were graceful and muscular, and Tienne could easily see her as a performer, although she did not have the classic figure of a principal dancer. She had a smile on her face, though, one of pure joy, and Tienne suddenly understood that this performance was not for bows or applause—it was for fun, for family, and warmth flooded him for the second time that day.

"Taking it easy on me," Josh said as she finished her last turn. He stood at the opposite corner from the one she'd arrived in, and she bowed him in. He repeated her move, and Tienne's heart clutched as he saw the strength and the surety of his movements. Josh and Molly could have easily made their living performing. Meat-and-potato dancers, yes, but still beautiful, still professional, still joyful.

He wanted to paint them to capture that joy.

Josh finished up, giving his final turn a flourish, and he bowed Grace in.

Grace inclined his head, took two steps, and blew Tienne's mind.

Grace took the same move—was it a *bourrée* turn?—and turned it into silk and flame. He added something to it, something show-offy, but as the music intensified toward the happy conclusion, Grace's flowing hands, his extra toe-flips, the flourishes he used to take basic moves and bring them to art, seemed to fit.

He finished and the audience applauded, and Tienne got to see Grace's face shining with the praise. He knew Grace *did* make his living as a dancer, when he wasn't making it as a thief, but Tienne recognized something in that expression, something that sang close to his own heart.

Grace didn't dance for the money any more than Josh or Molly did. They were all here, putting on this little bit of playful showboating, because this was a thing they all loved.

It was why Tienne kept his paintings in the living room, on display. Yes, Felix and Danny had pushed him to have gallery showings, to sell his art, but he'd always demurred. He made his money with his side hustle, and if sometimes that meant he copied the masters, well, that was a pleasure. But the paintings he loved, the ones he did because he yearned to paint—those he did for joy.

He could look at them and enjoy them if they weren't in his cloister of a bedroom. In his bedroom, it was too close to happiness.

He found himself leaning against the front bar of the treadmill, transfixed.

Grace bowed Molly in, and she stuck her tongue out at him to indicate she knew he was showing off insufferably, and then it was her turn. She executed three flawless grand jetés and finished with a pirouette and a bow to indicate Josh should go next. Josh made a face, which indicated this was a little harder on his healing body. His grand jetés weren't as grand, probably because his muscle mass had declined since his illness, but his final pirouette was lovely. Grace, of course, ate up the stage, covering it in two leaps instead of three and tumbling into a bourrée turn that practically threw him off the edge of the rise with his speed.

But God, did he look happy.

And it was Molly's turn again.

The three of them continued the game, one move, then two, then three, going as far and as high and as fast as each dared, all in time to the lovely old Tchaikovsky piece, until Josh, in a moment of overreach, failed to complete his leap and fell heavily to the floor. Molly turned off the music while Grace practically teleported to his side, and Josh smiled at him tiredly, obviously embarrassed.

"Sorry," he said, breathing hard. "Too far, too fast." His nose had started bleeding, and Julia rushed up with a box of tissues and a bottle of hand sanitizer, which Josh accepted gratefully. It was Grace who broke up the apprehensiveness of the moment by being exactly who Josh needed him to be.

"It's as well," he said with a sniff of disgust. "The way Molly was going, she was going to make me swing from the light fixtures next, and then Danny would have to replace them."

Danny, who was at his other side, gave Grace a gentle smile. "A thing I would do again and again to see such a performance," he said. Then he turned to Josh, biting his lip with worry. "Too far, too fast indeed." He put his hand to Josh's forehead and frowned. Tienne remembered that part of the danger of chemotherapy was infection and fever. "Okay, my boy. Let's get you up and bundled into the house." He looked over his shoulder. "Carl, Chuck, Hunter—draw straws."

Tienne puzzled that over for a moment, but then Chuck grinned, only a little strain on his face. "Carl's turn this time," he said.

The big blond Viking grunted. "One goddamned fight and you guys think I'm Superman," but he was moving forward as he spoke. "Grace, I know you guys had sweatshirts and shit. Go get me something to keep him from catching a chill."

Grace disappeared, and Stirling leaned into Tienne's space, breaking his fascination with the tableau of Josh bleeding and looking increasingly faint. Quietly, Stirling said, "You had to see the fight. He was sort of amazing."

Tienne gave him a distracted smile. "What sort of fight did he get into?"

Stirling shrugged. "The kind with bad guys."

"I didn't know he was muscle."

Stirling's face lit up. "He's *not.* He's our suit. He's perfectly legitimate—legit name, legit job, legit connections. He's like a secret weapon. Nobody has even put him together with us, but he does all our background checks and knows who's legitimately in need and who's pitching a rich guy's fit because something didn't pan out his way."

Tienne blinked slowly. "That's *happened* to you?" he asked.

Stirling shrugged. "Yeah, but the guy was shitty to Carl's boyfriend, so Danny and I did some digging and had Carl run his background. Turned out the guy was looking for a way to claim insurance fraud. He'd planted his stolen art in his ex-girlfriend's house. So we told her where to find it and had her tell the authorities how it got there. It was great—she got a finder's fee, and he went to jail."

Tienne digested this for a moment before saying, "But… aren't *we* criminals? Why are we sending people to jail?"

Stirling opened his mouth to answer that, but he was saved by Carl scooping a bundled Josh into his arms as though the young man weighed nothing.

"Coming through," he said. Then, more personally, "Michael's going to be really disappointed. He wants you to be better for Christmas."

Josh sighed. "Sorry. Pushing too hard."

"Yes, well, wait until Felix hears." Julia sniffed, following them. Tienne realized that when Julia had arrived, she'd been wearing a rather luscious fur-lined felt coat, but that she'd put the garment around her son and was instead sporting a hooded sweatshirt that one of the bigger men had provided—probably Carl, since he was striding out into the snowy backyard with bare shoulders and calves.

"Shit," Hunter muttered. "Grace, do you know where Carl's stuff—never mind."

Grace had slid out of the glass door before it shut, wearing a hooded sweatshirt and with what looked like Carl's gym bag over his shoulders.

There was a collective sigh from those left in the room, and Danny turned to them. "Don't worry, poppets," he said gently. "Josh will weather this fever and finish his chemo before Christmas. I know it's hard on all of you, but as foolhardy as this little display was, I also think you all needed it. We're all so very desperate to play." He gave them a conspiratorial wink. "Believe me when I tell you we have a plan. We're going to have *such* an amazing game for you this Christmas, and Josh will be damned if he's let out of the fun this time."

Molly gave a happy little grin and bounced on her toes. "Hint?" she begged. "Please, Uncle Danny? Please, please, please?"

Danny grinned back. "Not on your life." Then he turned toward the door with a little wave. "Ta-ta! Don't sweat too much! Save some muscle aches for me!"

And then he was gone, leaving them all a little happier for his having been there.

"Do you think…?" Tienne bit his lip. It was stupid.

"What?" Stirling asked.

"He did not mean me, did he? To play the 'amazing game'?" He hadn't been absent for other Christmases, but he hadn't been present, either. He'd stopped by, collected his gift, left his own gift for the family, and disappeared, frequently without saying goodbye. He'd never wanted to be a bother. But Danny and Felix had moved him in, and the thought of being left out of the Christmas celebration while he lived under the same roof caused him pain he had no right to feel.

"Oh, I think he did," Stirling said, not sounding hesitant in the least. "Tienne, Molly and I were under specific orders to ask you to join the family for Christmas—not the day before and the day of, but for weeks after. Julia made a point of telling us we couldn't come home until we had your word."

Tienne nodded, thinking about the little audience for Josh, Grace, and Molly, and how, for a moment, he'd been part of a wonderful group of people who were only there to see beauty and joy.

"Is that a problem?" Stirling prompted, and Tienne was almost surprised when he shook his head.

"No," he said. "No."

"Well, good. Did you want to run some more?" An odd jerky expression crossed Stirling's face, and he let out a frustrated sigh. "I need to move," he said. "I'm twitchy. You can leave if you want or—"

Tienne shook his head. "I will be happy on another run," he said simply. "Shower in an hour?"

"Perfect." With that, Stirling assumed his usual purposeful, sturdy walk back to the elliptical machine. Tienne watched him for a moment as he put in his earbuds and his entire body seemed to relax, his movements on the machine more methodical than graceful. He wondered about that strange rictus that had passed over Stirling's face. "Twitchy," Stirling had said.

Stirling had always been different from his sister and her friends—not quieter but truly less social. On the occasions their paths had crossed, Stirling had always been hard to shake from Molly's side, but when she'd been gone, Josh had been there, and after Danny had returned, so had Danny. Now, watching him chat with Carl, he'd realized that Stirling's face only opened up with certain people. Tienne had felt a pang of jealousy when he'd realized that Carl was a new person who fell under that category, but after Stirling's obvious assurance that Carl wasn't a contender for his romantic affections, it had hit Tienne.

Stirling's face opened up, became animated, when he was talking to *Tienne*. Whatever limitations Stirling had socially, Tienne had the potential to be one of the people to exceed those limits.

He found he very much wanted to exceed them. In fact, he felt he wanted to trespass over them, go places he suspected nobody else had gone.

Suddenly he found himself looking forward to living under the Salinger roof very much.

Solarium

STIRLING PAUSED as he tapped on his laptop and gave Tienne a covert glance, enjoying the way his narrow, pretty face was illuminated by the sun streaming through multiple windows.

When all was said and done, they'd settled Tienne's painting in Julia's sunroom. When Tienne had tried to protest, had been going to be in the room across from his bedroom, which had east and north facing windows, Julia wouldn't hear of it. Apparently Carl's boyfriend had promised to bring his children to the Salinger mansion for the next holiday, and Julia was already having that room decorated for children. Besides, she said airily, as much as she adored her solarium, she only sat in it perhaps once a week or so. Tienne could have an entire bank of windows by which to paint, and as long as they made sure to turn on the fans, she could continue to enjoy the place on the odd Sunday morning.

Stirling and Molly had enjoyed watching Tienne's face light up when he saw that his paints and canvases were set up in a hastily refurbished corner of the room, one from which all the furniture had been moved and the tile had been covered, and even the plants had been rearranged to give Tienne more space.

But Stirling had seen a hint of trepidation as well. "I'll be in here alone?"

Well, for a man who painted in a tiny corner of his bedroom, perhaps that was frightening.

"Oh, I'm sure you'll find some company some-where," Molly had declared with a wave of her hand, and Stirling had known without a doubt that everybody would spend a little time in the solarium.

It hadn't been a hardship, really. Josh and Grace went there to play video games when Josh wasn't at the hospital, and when Lucius wasn't in town, Chuck read copiously, muttering to himself while sprawled in a corner of the couch. Danny and Felix came in to play chess quietly on the weekends, and Stirling always made sure he spent an hour or two there when nobody else could.

Today, nearly two weeks after they'd moved Ti-enne in and ten days after they'd all watched Josh al-most set his health back a month with his foolish act of beauty, Stirling was happy to have quiet, uncomplicat-ed company so he could, dammit, work on his Christ-mas list.

And, well, track down Levka Dubov. Danny had gotten all his background information: name—*real* name (*not* Dubov), age (thirty-six—ew), and gener-al business (procurer for two branches of the Russian mob). Stirling was working more on the people he hung around with, as well as his current interest in Tienne. Tienne, for all he'd been blackmailed and… *exploited* by such a creature, had known almost nothing about him. After his first encounter with Levka, he'd simply done the work Levka had brought to him and tried hard not to think of the price.

The fact that he hadn't reached out for help hurt, well, everybody, but nobody had the heart to say so. Watching Tienne open up, slowly, over the last two weeks or so had been a heartbreaking act of patience.

"What are you doing?" Tienne asked, his voice intruding into Stirling's musings. With a deft tap of his keyboard, he switched to the screen that *didn't* have information on Levka Dubov or the Russian mob.

"Shopping for Molly," Stirling said with a sigh. He'd decided to go for bolts of cloth that were simply stunning, beautiful, and original.

Like her.

"And working," he added, bringing up a mock-up of a light-and-sound schematic he'd been designing for the playhouse he and Molly worked at.

"*The Tempest*," Tienne said, sounding surprised. "You do classical?"

"We do whatever catches Signor's eye," he said. The owner of the playhouse—and the producer of the shows—was originally from Mexico City. Signor Mateo Hidalgo was every bit as gay as most of the men in the Salinger house, with added points for flair and cross-dressing, often for no reason whatsoever. Stirling, who did enjoy a plain, grounded wardrobe, had come to depend on going in to meetings with Signor while he was wearing a neon-blue tiger-striped forties-style ball gown with a Carmen Miranda headdress of blue and black fruit.

Or, he might simply wear a wool suit.

Stirling—who didn't much care for surprises—found that being pleasantly surprised by Signor's whimsy, as well as his excitement over Stirling and

Molly's fresh ideas for lighting and wardrobe—made his work life extra pleasant. While not part of the inner circle, Signor did make the cut for the "pre–New Year's Eve" party being thrown by the Salingers shortly after Christmas.

"That," Tienne said, pointing to a bit of staging on the screen. "That is interesting. Have you thought of having a flat behind that, something three-dimensional that could create depth?"

"Yes," Stirling said, giving him a sideways look. "But we don't have an artist who could do that."

Tienne gave him a long look. "I find that hard to believe."

Stirling shrugged. "We have Connie," he said, talking about the designer who worked for the company. "She's very dependable, but what you're describing takes more depth than she's got."

Tienne grunted. "I could design the flat for you. It would be…." He gave a trial smile, as though he were practicing for the real thing someday. "It could be a gift to you," he said. "But not a Christmas one. Just a… er… gift."

Stirling paused, glancing at his expression once, twice, three times, and trying to put together what he knew of faces with what he knew of Tienne.

And at last it clicked.

"You're doing something kind," he said, relaxing a little. "Of course. Thank you. Using your talent to help me would be a real gift."

This time the smile took, and Tienne's entire face lit up. "Yes? You would like that?"

"Oh yes!" Stirling smiled, grateful the expression felt natural. "That would be wonderful."

For a moment, they simply smiled at each other in the sunshine, and Stirling thought it was one of the most transcendent moments he'd ever known.

Then Tienne bobbed his head shyly. "Your… your request? For Danny and Felix's picture. You would like to see?"

Oh wow! This *was* a good day for Tienne. Stirling followed him to where his easel sat, his cabinet of paints on one side, his little artist's stool in front. Attached to a smaller easel a little to the side of the canvas was a printed picture Josh had taken of his two dads at the breakfast table. Danny was wearing one of his habitual outfits of black yoga pants and a black turtleneck, and he was leaning his head on a hand propped up by his elbow, watching as Felix ate. Felix, dressed in a business suit, was sitting up straight and using his fork and knife to neatly cut up an omelet. The moment—intimate and candid—captured Felix's precision and power and Danny's whimsy and lack of convention perfectly.

But it also captured the touch of their eyes on each other's faces, as though they were drinking the other in like a thirsty plant drank water.

It had been one of a handful of pictures Stirling had offered Tienne, letting the final choice be his, and it hadn't been Stirling's favorite.

Until he saw it rendered in oil, with delicate brush-strokes and a sort of gentle reverence.

"Oh," he said, joy suffusing him. "Oh yes. That's *perfect*. Wait until Molly sees. She wanted in on the gift. We're giving it together. Oh wow. It's—"

He turned to smile at Tienne and found him standing close.

Surprisingly close, but not unpleasantly so. Just… close.

"What?" he asked.

Tienne shook his head but didn't look away. "I am *delighted*," he said. "When your face opens and you talk to me like that, I…." He bit his lip. "I always thought you were pretty."

He gave another "trial smile," but this one seemed *hopeful*.

And Stirling's heart started beating in his ears. Two weeks' worth of quiet support, quiet attention to this man, and it hadn't made him any less appealing.

In fact….

Stirling was drifting closer to him, close enough to feel Tienne's breath on his face, to realize that Tienne was maybe an inch or two taller, to think that maybe their lips might….

"Oh my God!" Molly's voice echoed through the solarium, and Stirling and Tienne both jerked back. "You guys. Both of you. Come here. I've got it! It took me a week—a *week*—of thinking, but I think I've got it!"

"Got what?" Stirling asked, adrift and a little confused. He caught sight of Tienne's rueful irritation and felt a little better.

"Damn," Tienne murmured. "I thought I'd planned that so well."

"You planned that?" Stirling asked, feeling gratified.

"I… I really wanted to kiss you," Tienne said, eyes wide and cheeks pink.

"We can try again!" Stirling told him, almost desperately. That could not *possibly* be the last time he got a chance to see what kissing was like.

"Yes?" Tienne asked, and at that moment, Molly—who had apparently yelled from across the mansion and across the street and across the mansion *across* the street—came rushing over to where they stood.

"Oh my God. Tienne, that's perfect. That's a million times perfect. Stirling, isn't that the most romantic goddamned thing you've ever seen?"

"Close," Stirling said, and Tienne's little burst of exasperation made his stomach warm. "But I love it."

"Me too!" Molly turned shining eyes to them. "And wait until you hear what we're getting for Grace. It's… it's the *best* thing!"

And finally Stirling let go of the moment that hadn't quite been. "You've got an idea?" he asked desperately. Grace's devotion to Josh this year had been, well, heartbreaking and glorious both at the same time. Stirling and Molly had been losing their minds the past week, trying to figure out something Grace would love.

"I've got the *best* idea," Molly said, eyes glittering. She held out a little bag. "I went to the Lego outlet store."

Stirling almost—*almost*—lost his temper with his sister. "You came yelling in here because of Legos?" he asked, and for the first time, Molly seemed to take in their proximity, which hadn't yet changed because Tienne was the one who needed to step back, and he hadn't.

Until now, when his face went up in a wash of crimson flame, and he gave Stirling more room he didn't want.

A slow, devilish smile curled at Molly's lips, but as Stirling gazed at her in horror, she held a finger to her lips, shook her head, and then….

Let the matter drop.

"Because the Legos aren't the gift!" she said. She opened the bag and bustled to the coffee table that still held Stirling's laptop. "Here." She dumped the Legos onto the table, and Tienne stepped back so Stirling could go look—and automatically sort through them, of course.

And then he got a good look at them and realized that they were Lego *guys*. And not just guys—*specific* guys.

A tiny one in black, with a black stocking cap like Josh wore.

Another one in black, without the stocking cap but with a pale brown face and painted on brown curly hair.

One in a gray three-piece suit with gray at the temples, like Felix, and another in a brown three-piece suit, like Carl.

A blond female Lego, wearing a Grace Kelly style ball gown.

A tiny artist, with a little painted blond ponytail, like Tienne.

And so on.

"These are *us*," Stirling said in wonder. "You found little toy people to look like us?"

"I've got a couple on order," she confessed. "And see, the thing I was thinking wasn't that the little guys would be the present, but where we *put* the little guys…."

Stirling caught his breath in excitement. "A *scavenger* hunt!" he said. "You want us to hide them all over the house—"

"And the gym!"

"And maybe Hunter's flat!" Stirling added in wonder. "And Grace's Christmas present will be—"

"*Finding them*!" Molly held her hands to her chest and danced a dizzy circle. "It's *perfect*!"

Tienne spoke softly. "There is one for me?" he asked uncertainly. "The little artist?"

"Yup," Molly said, swinging to a halt. "Make sure you hide it somewhere good, Tienne. Grace will be mad if we make it easy on him."

Tienne's smile was as excited as Molly's, and Stirling was only a little sorry that Molly had interrupted them.

But he was still sorry.

IT TOOK them an hour to text everybody and get them in on the present, and then Molly and Stirling composed the letter that would be in Grace's card on Christmas Day. When it was time to get ready for dinner, Stirling returned—reluctantly—to his room, and Molly followed him.

"So?" she said, bumping his shoulder.

They'd never played the "So what?" game. "I wouldn't know," he said crustily. "Somebody came screaming into the room about how Legos were going to save Christmas."

"Doh!" She clapped her hand to her face. "Sorry about that!"

He smiled, forgiving her. "It's a really good idea."

They took a couple of steps in silence before she said, "I can't pretend I'm not worried about you, because love can hurt sometimes. But did I tell you what he said after the dance-off?"

He shook his head. Tienne had been characteristically quiet afterward. They'd begun their routine of working out, getting lunch, and then working on their own projects until dinner, while Stirling made sure someone would be in the solarium with him while he was working. Tienne sat through the rather riotous Salinger dinners with big eyes, listening but not participating, and sometimes in the morning, he'd ask Stirling to clarify relationship points or histories of adventures that he hadn't known about.

He'd started with "Why did you send your client to jail for stealing a painting?"

Stirling had needed to think about that one for a moment, until he remembered the story he'd been telling about the douchey rich guy who'd asked them to locate a painting he was using to set up his ex-girlfriend.

"Because he was getting revenge on his ex-girlfriend and using insurance fraud to do it," Stirling had replied. He and Carl had been the ones to track down the timeline of where the painting had been and figured out that the only one who *could* have taken the painting was the person who'd reported it missing. "She'd caught him cheating and didn't want anything to do with him. This was his idea of showing people that nobody messed with him and his money."

Tienne had wrinkled his nose. "That's horrible—and illegal. I didn't realize, you know…."

"That we're good guys?" Stirling had asked, thinking about how Danny's eyes would twinkle as he said something like that.

"We are?"

Stirling smiled deliberately. "We are… levelers. We are agents of chaos, but we give the world a little push toward good." He and Danny had that conversation a million years ago, but it had stuck.

Tienne paused for a long moment. "So Levka Dubov—he had no right to me because I was as bad as he was."

A statement more than a question, it still froze Stirling's lungs. "None," he'd managed to rasp. "You're not bad, Tienne. You've never harmed anyone. Nobody has the right to your body but you."

"He said… he said we were both criminals. Nobody would care."

Stirling's breath shook, and for the only time in his memory, he wished he were big and strong. Carl could have caught that guy and beat him up. Hunter or Chuck never would have let him get away. What had Stirling done? Tripped him. Tracked him down, sure, but nothing permanent. Nothing that *hurt.* Suddenly Stirling wanted Levka Dubov hurt.

"We care," he said, trying to keep himself steady. "Just because you don't live here doesn't mean we don't care. Doesn't mean you're not one of us."

Tienne hadn't said anything that day, but Stirling had seen him, more than once, wipe his face with the back of his hand.

So of course he was curious now when Molly had new information. "What did he say?"

Molly *hmm*ed, as though aware Stirling had gone somewhere else for a moment, but then she answered his question. "He said—and give me a moment to get this right—he said, 'I am so pleased I now live in a home that gives beauty its due.'"

Stirling let out a little half laugh. "Wow."

"Right? He takes things very seriously. Does that scare you?"

Absolutely. "Uhm, a little." Stirling looked at her with some worry in his eyes. "I'm very much out of my depth," he announced. He could never be anything but honest, particularly with Molly.

She shoulder-bumped him again, which might have driven him crazy once, but he'd learned to relax over the last year, to accept basic human touch as necessary—and even pleasant. And Molly had always been the exception in that area. Her hard, bony hand in his had gotten him through three foster-care homes, one of which was abusive. She'd never let anything hurt him, and he trusted that.

"You have help," she said simply. "However you want to play this. The only thing is—" She bit her lip as she paused. "—love hurts. Crushes *hurt*. I can protect you from almost anything, but this? No. So ask for help. Know I'm not the only one."

They kept walking—they were almost to the part of the house where she would peel off to dress for dinner, and he would have to go down two flights of stairs to his little basement apartment to do the same.

When he spoke, he was probably as surprised as Molly. "Did you see him light up?" he asked. "When he got to be part of the gift?"

"Yes," she said. "It was like magic."

"Magic is pretty rare. Let's keep seeing his face light up like magic."

And now her face lit up, and much like when they were little, when he shared cookies or told her secrets, he thought it would be worth any risk to make this girl who proclaimed herself his family and then made it so, smile.

"Deal," she said, kissing him on the cheek before turning for her room.

He continued on his way, wistfully thinking that if only she'd waited *two whole minutes* before crashing into the solarium, she would have been the perfect sister.

HE WAS in the middle of changing for dinner when he heard a light knock on the door to his room. He opened the door to find Tienne, wearing clean jeans and a clean sweatshirt and looking very nervous.

"Come in," he said, beckoning Tienne in from the downstairs den. The den was the meeting place of the crew when they were talking about a job—or catching a game on the big screen. It was a comfortable, happy place with leather couches and lots of pillows for the floor and a soft squishy rug, but it wasn't designed for close conversation, and that seemed to be the only kind Tienne had.

"Thank you." Tienne bobbed his head nervously and looked around. Stirling's bedroom was neat and clean, but the covers on his bed were rich cotton and dark green, and the bed itself had a foam mattress and was designed to keep his hard, muscular body wrapped and comfortable. He had framed pictures on his walls of shows he and Molly had worked on, as well as one candid shot he'd taken of each member of the team—even Michael, who was new—and had blown up and framed. Grace had pointed out that they almost looked like surveillance photos, like he was building a crime board of the crew, and Josh had said that was a neat idea. *Someone* should have a crime board of them, even though none of the authorities even knew who they were.

He'd added the picture of Tienne the day before. It had been taken as Tienne was painting, and the sunshine through the windows had turned his blond hair and eye-lashes almost translucent.

"What can I do to help you?" he asked, looking at himself in the mirror over his dresser to make sure his shirt was buttoned at the throat. Sure, Molly and Grace always told him he could leave the top button undone, but why even *have* a button if he was going to do that?

"Tonight is a special dinner, yes?" Tienne asked, and Stirling glanced at him, surprised that he'd caught that. The last week had been spent in such an agony of introversion—Stirling recognized that sort of thing, and he knew that when *he* was completely occupied with his own inner self, he missed a lot of the things going on with other people.

"Yes," he said. "Josh's last chemotherapy treatment was three days ago." He'd had to put it off a couple of days after the dance-off. "Today he got his test results back, and while they're not sure he's in full remission yet, he's got a month of no chemo before he goes back to see. It's very big news." Stirling swallowed. "We really did almost lose him."

Tienne nodded. "I realized—when they were dancing, I realized—how much of a tragedy that would have been. I want to celebrate with the family, but I have nothing to wear."

Stirling grinned at him. "You know that after Christmas, you won't have to worry about it, right? I'm pretty sure Molly and Julia have bought out three department stores for you."

Tienne's cheeks washed pink. "I rather suspect-ed," he said. "But I don't have anything to wear *now*, and for the first time, I really want to look nice, and all I have are the suits Felix bought me when I graduated from high school and college. I know our *builds* are different, but I think our sizes are the same. Could I, perhaps—"

"Absolutely." Stirling walked to his closet, where his winter clothes hung neatly, two inches apart. "You should probably stick to the jeans that fit," he said, thinking that Tienne's legs might be longer and his waist narrower than Stirling's. "But here," he said, pulling out a dark gray cabled sweater and a white collared shirt. "They're very simple, but—"

"They're perfect," Tienne said. He bit his lip and looked around as he took the clothes from Stirling's hands. "Do you… do you mind if I try them on?"

"Not at all." Stirling gave him a smile that hurt his own cheeks. "I can leave." He indicated the door to the den.

Tienne shook his head. "No, that's fine." He turned to the mirror then, probably because that was the least awkward place to look.

This suited Stirling fine because it meant *he* could look his fill.

Tienne started to undress, pulling his hooded sweatshirt up and briefly exposing his pale body while staring studiously into the mirror. Stirling got a glimpse of long torso and sand-colored nipples, with that surprising leanness and definition that runners tended to have, before Tienne pulled his T-shirt back down and tucked it into his pants.

"Your computer setup," Tienne mumbled, probably to fill the quiet. "It's quite impressive."

Stirling nodded happily. "Computers are my thing—the insides, the code, the assembly—my adoptive father and I spent hours on them. He used to say

my genius was the best kind of genius because it let me
do practical things."

"Such as?" Tienne asked curiously.

"Well, you saw the lighting schematic," Stirling
said. "That's a fun one. But then there's things like surveillance and research. Next level B and E shit—"

"Like what?" Tienne frowned as he buttoned the
white shirt on over his T-shirt.

Stirling was so busy thinking about how he liked a
man who liked to do all his buttons that he blurted out
the first thing he could think of. "Well, we know where
Levka Dubov is," he said and then could have kicked
himself.

Tienne turned to him after pulling down the sweater and gaped.

"You're a mess," Stirling said practically, moving
closer. "Here. Let me." With movements that his sister
and then his adoptive parents had taught him, he began straightening Tienne's collar under the sweater and
then pulling down the tails of the button-down before
straightening the hem of the sweater over it. "There."

Tienne made him stop by taking Stirling's hands
in his own.

"What are you going to do about Levka Dubov?"
he asked quietly, and Stirling didn't think he was mad
because he was delicately stroking the back of Stirling's knuckles with his thumbs.

"Well," Stirling told him, trying not to be nervous,
"first we're going to see how deep in to which mobs he
is. Then we're going to see what kind of douchebaggery he's up to. Then we're going to figure out if we
need to take out *only* Dubov, or if he's got an organization we need to deal with."

"And *you* do this, all alone?"

Stirling blinked. "Well, *no*, actually. First, Danny went out to pick his pocket."

"Danny?" Tienne's incredulity was making Stirling wonder if he should actually be telling him all this. He had to remind himself repeatedly that Tienne's day job was as a *forger*.

"Well, yes. Grace is really our best thief, but Josh is our best pickpocket. Grace is too much of an asshole—he rubs people the wrong way and wants to show them how much smarter he is than they are. Josh gets in and gets out—and that's because Danny taught him from the cradle."

Tienne's sandy eyebrows were lifted in surprise. He blinked and said, "Does your sister know about this?"

Stirling rolled his eyes. "She's almost as good as they are, but, you know, she's so striking. Even if her hair is covered and she's got contacts in, her cheekbones alone make her easy to spot. I mean, yes, in a pinch, we can use her, but what we really want is anonymous white male, and since Josh is sick, Danny fits the bill."

Tienne shook his head. "Okay, so Danny lifted Levka's wallet and…?"

"And identified his false ID. *Not* one of your fakes, by the way, because if it had been, it would have been harder to spot. So I spent two days tracking where that ID has been—"

"Where has it been?" Tienne asked, wide-eyed.

Stirling shuddered. "You really don't want to know where it's been." Massage parlors, rent boys, designer drugs—Danny hadn't even wanted to burn the thing, so they'd put it in the garbage disposal with coffee grounds and sage. "Levka has some really disgusting habits. Don't ask." Chuck had come home from one fact-finding mission with his shirt covered in tearstains. The rent boy had apparently sobbed on him—*sobbed*— until Chuck had put him up in a cheap motel, bought him a bus ticket out of town, and made sure he had a halfway house waiting for him in Springfield so he could get another job and get back on his feet. And when Stirling had asked what could make a rent boy cry like that, Chuck had shaken his head and looked angry.

"How do you know that?" Tienne asked, his eyes still wide.

"Well, Chuck and Hunter tracked down the places he'd been and did the personal investigative work, found out about his habits, his contacts, and where he gets his money. I mean, *I* found a lot of cash deposits, which means he's probably getting paid off by a boss of some sort, or he's got his own drug or money operations going. They think they've got a line on the people who employ him. They're going out tomorrow to do some Christmas shopping, and then they're going to walk into dangerous places and smile and talk bullshit and come back with information."

"But… isn't that dangerous for *them*?" Tienne asked, and Stirling liked that he looked concerned now.

"Yes. They're both good fighters, which is why they go, and they work well as partners, so they usually go together. Anyway, they'll come back with some names, and I'll run them on the computer and probably send them over to Carl, because depending on what their area of expertise is, one of us should find them on the right websites to see how much it would piss these people off if we got Levka arrested for something totally unrelated to abusing their forger."

"Why? Why can't he be arrested for hurting me?" Tienne was obviously fascinated by the whole process, because he didn't blush once when talking about being coerced.

Stirling felt like he had to remind the young man that he was personally involved. "Because," he said, giving Tienne a measured look, "if he discovers that you were behind his arrest and imprisonment, either he or somebody he works with will want revenge, and then we'll have a new set of problems. I mean, in one sense, I think we're lucky—the guy is a pig. I mean, I understand pigs can be really nice creatures, but their excrement smells *vile*, so we're going to say he's a pig because the shit he leaves behind is the worst."

"Why's that lucky?" Tienne asked, and Stirling was grateful for the tiny smile he'd elicited.

"Because I don't think his bosses will miss him. It's not that we wouldn't go to war for you, Tienne, because we totally would, but that would be a shitty way for the crew to stay under the radar. We, you know, can't do anything good if everybody knows we're out to get the bad guys."

Tienne swallowed. "You'd go to war for me?" he asked, his voice thin. "I… I am an afterthought. You realize this, don't you?"

Stirling frowned. "Yes, but so was I. Molly grabbed my hand in foster care and literally said, 'You can't adopt me without him.' That didn't mean our parents didn't *love* me. It meant they hadn't imagined I'd be in their lives until Molly made them pay attention."

Tienne blinked rapidly and looked away. "This thing you are doing—it's kind. I would like to help, if you can think of a way that would work."

Stirling chuckled. "Oh, I'm sure we'll be able to make use of your unique set of skills," he said grandly, pleased when he made Tienne smile again.

In the pause afterward, Stirling became acutely aware that they were alone in his bedroom. He did a lot of his work in here, because he *liked* working alone, but he'd also become better at working in a room with other people working on the same thing. Some of his best memories were of him and Danny sitting side by side, taking turns running down leads and shouting new leads to each other as they found out something juicy.

But that didn't change the fact that he *slept* here. He undressed here. He lay in that bed and touched himself and fantasized about what having a lover might be like.

He'd imagined Tienne's eyes on him like they were right now, intent and blue and heavy-lidded with want.

He leaned forward and closed his eyes and brushed his own lips against Tienne's.

To his immense surprise, Tienne caught his breath and parted his mouth, and Stirling licked his lower lip gently. Tienne opened his mouth a little more, and this time, *his* tongue thrust forward, with enough boldness to make Stirling hope they might not be fated to stare at each other starry-eyed forever.

Tienne took his turn teasing the seam of Stirling's lips, and in a moment, their mouths were open together, fused as they explored, slowly, tentatively, but with increasing excitement.

Tienne licked along Stirling's palate, and as Stirling gasped—half in laughter—he withdrew, sucking on Stirling's lower lip.

For a moment they were silent, leaning foreheads together, their breath mingling.

Tienne spoke first. "That was so lovely, I'm almost afraid to open my eyes."

"Yes," Stirling said. He had no delicacy, no pretty words. "That's why kissing is important."

Tienne gave him a firm closed-mouth kiss, almost chaste—but with promise. "May I kiss you again? A good-night kiss at your door, perhaps?"

Stirling swallowed and nodded. "I would like that." His heart was still hammering against his ribs, and he thought maybe it would be a good thing, taking it slow. One touch, one kiss, one moment at a time to treasure.

Then Tienne lowered his mouth to Stirling's ear and spoke. "Someday, I would like to make love to you. I've never been with a man I cared about. I think I could care about you very much."

Stirling pulled back and grinned, nodding. "It's like you can read my mind," he said, eyes wide. The only person who'd ever been good at that was Molly. Then something occurred to him. "Did you *plan* to kiss me when you came down here?"

Tienne chuckled, and then, as if there'd been a signal, they both stepped back. "I had to," Tienne said. "I've had such a hard time keeping my attention on my painting because you've been in the solarium. Today I thought, 'I'm going to get him to come to me so I can kiss him,' and we almost did!"

"And then Molly," Stirling said grimly.

"She is lovely," Tienne told him, nodding with much seriousness. "But I still needed to kiss you."

Stirling's grin returned. "So you planned to come."

"I also needed a shirt," Tienne said, and for the first time, his lips quirked playfully.

"Good thinking." And oh, it was—it was the kind of planning Stirling wasn't good at, but Tienne, apparently, had learned it in his bones.

"To dinner?" Tienne asked, looking abashed.

"To dinner." Stirling gestured grandly for Tienne to proceed out the door before him, but inside he wasn't sure if he was giggling, spinning dizzy circles, or planning for the entire *Kama Sutra* in one sexual encounter.

Didn't matter. It was all good.

As he followed Tienne through the den and up the stairs to the main floor of the mansion, he was thinking giddily about what would come next.

Early Gifts

TIENNE HAD been working at understanding the conversation at the dinner table, and it was making more sense every day.

It started when he came to regard everybody at the table as a minion of a mischievous god.

Much of their conversation was wordplay, mixed with a healthy dose of one-upmanship and mutual admiration, a liberal sprinkling of irony, and the understanding that low-key insults such as "you assholes" and "needy bitch" were actually terms of affection.

Once those things were understood, conversations such as, "You assholes didn't see me make the lift—you gotta know the guy's not gonna be looking for his wallet until next month!" followed by, "Chuck, you needy bitch, we know you can make a decent lift, now stop bragging about it!" made total sense.

In this particular instance, Chuck had laughed outright at Grace, the ethereal thief, and winked. "I may be a needy bitch, but apparently I'm a needy bitch who can drive two hundred miles an hour in a stolen car on the wrong side of the road as *well* as steal a wallet with our mark none the wiser, and I'm good with that."

Lucius, Chuck's refined businessman boyfriend, arched a sculpted eyebrow. "In which case I'm not sure if that makes you more of a needy bitch or an arrogant bastard."

Chuck preened. "*Some* of us," he said smugly, "can be both."

"Y'all talk like Carl here can't crime," said Michael. He'd only been at the table a couple of times since Tienne had arrived. Small and sturdy, whippet thin and pit-bull sweet, with fathomless dark eyes and shoulder-length country-boy hair, he seemed the least likely mate for the stoic Viking at his side. Tienne had been surprised to discover that they fit together rather neatly—but part of that was mutual devotion.

"I can't," Carl said mildly, wiping at the corners of his mouth with a napkin. He had a distressingly small portion of coq au vin on his plate, and Tienne wondered if he was trying not to get fat.

Michael rolled his eyes. "Did he tell you what he did to find out about this Levka guy?"

"I know," Stirling said, surprising Tienne, partly because Stirling's eyes were looking wicked and knowing. Stirling was not the loudest or most loquacious at the table, but he did seem to know how the conversation worked.

"I don't," Josh said, his voice still rusty from chemo but sounding excited. "Tell us, Michael?"

Michael's grin at him was pure sugar. "Okay, so Danny got the first wallet—you all know that—and Chuck got the second one. Stirling ran down where the IDs and credit cards had been. Carl took that info, put it in a spreadsheet, and then broke into some sort of Interpol database to figure out which crime was being done in which places!"

"I had help," Carl said mildly, and Tienne gave him a sharp glance to see if the man was being deliberately dense.

But everybody at the table cocked their head at him and then flicked their eyes to Josh, who was obliviously chasing food around on his plate as he tried to keep his strength up after his (hopefully) last round of chemo.

He didn't notice, so Grace mouthed softly, "Liam?" and Carl nodded in return.

"He hooked me up to the database for crimes in Turkistan, Kazakhstan, Crimea, Belarus—most of them involving either art smuggling or massive amounts of fake IDs—"

"Wait," Stirling said. "What crimes need lots of fake papers?"

Carl gave Tienne a grave acknowledgment. "Either humanitarian ones to help get asylum seekers through borders, or…." He grimaced.

"Or smuggling—often human trafficking crimes so people who are being forced into slavery look legal," Hunter finished grimly.

Tienne sucked in a tortured breath, and Carl gave him a shrewd look—but not one void of kindness. "Did Levka put in large orders with you?"

Tienne shook his head. "No. I got the feeling he wanted me to do masterpiece quality work. The kind that uses the expensive paper with the dyes and etching and the raised seals. He spent time quizzing me, yes? About the things I did to make papers pass inspection. One doesn't expect my level of quality in large batches." He said it without conceit, but still he wondered how his words would be received.

Everyone at the table nodded sagely, as though criminality was a science they were all familiar with.

"Did he give you names yet, Tienne?" Felix asked. He looked so grand and imposing in his impeccable suit, and Tienne swallowed. Felix had been nothing but kind to him, but still Tienne wondered what he'd done wrong to get Felix's attention.

"No," Tienne said, carefully not looking at Stirling or Molly. "He… I think he was there to discuss numbers the night… the night he last visited."

Felix and Danny both nodded. "I'll have to put out feelers," Danny mused. "We know where he's been and who he's paying now. We need to find out where he's buying his forgeries since Tienne has gone underground and if we can't put some pressure on those sources to find out who he's working for and what they need."

Tienne swallowed, wondering if he could be brave. "You could," he said through a scratchy throat, "let me go back to my flat and start working again. Perhaps they'll send someone besides Levka because he scared me off—"

"No," Danny said flatly.

Felix looked at him in mild surprise. "No?" he asked, pausing with a forkful of salmon midway to his mouth. "I thought it was a good idea."

Danny gave him an inscrutable look and shook his head. "We don't ask anybody to play outside their comfort zone, Felix. We wouldn't ask Grace to talk to a corporate CEO or Carl to climb through a ventilation shaft because that's not where their strengths lie and they might get hurt that way. Tienne creates beautiful art, whether he's forging papers and paintings or creating original works. But subterfuge and gregariousness are a weakness for him in a place where his weakness might get him killed. We could set Hunter and Chuck with him to watch him, but that would take them away from other chores they're also suited for. So, no. No putting Tienne in harm's way."

Felix set his fork down and nodded at Danny, very carefully. "Good reasons all," he said, a smile that even Tienne could tell wasn't real tilting at the corners of his mouth. "What's the real reason?"

Danny's eyes sought out Tienne's across the table, and Tienne merely shrugged. He'd never been sure how much Danny had revealed about his past anyway.

"Because I won't risk him," Danny said simply. "I couldn't be here the way I wanted to when he and Josh were growing up, but that doesn't mean I throw them to the wolves either. Anybody here—*everybody* here— gets the same treatment. We don't put people at risk by disregarding their strengths and weaknesses. It's not right."

"So seconded," Julia said, breaking the tension between Danny and Felix. "Goddess knows I'd make a hash out of racing a car or setting an explosive—"

"And I'd trample a boardroom like a bull in a china shop," Chuck finished with a wink.

"Excellent." Danny smiled genially. "So we don't send Tienne back into the pond. We're going to have to keep doing legwork on our own."

Felix let out a breath and gave Danny a meaningful look. "But, uhm, what about that *other* project...." He trailed off with a dance of eyebrows that Tienne assumed was some sort of semaphore.

Danny let out a chuckle. "Don't worry, Felix. I'm pretty sure we can multitask." He gave Tienne a quick wink. "Besides, I think our other project will keep Tienne out of harm's way for a bit, so we'll have more time for the Levka matter to get resolved."

And now he had the entire table's attention.

"Other project?" Carl asked carefully.

"That's what he said. Josh, did you hear him say other project?" Grace demanded, not nearly so careful.

"I admit," Lucius said, crossing his silverware on his plate, "my attention is piqued."

"You mean"—and Molly was practically vibrating with excitement—"we have a *job*."

Julia, Felix, and Danny had a meeting that consisted solely of eye contact, and Julia was the one who spoke first.

"Well," she said, patting her mouth delicately, "we *were* going to ask everyone if they cared to join us downstairs after dinner for dessert and some... planned discussion."

The cheer that went up around the table was not only deafening, it was *heartening*. Tienne glanced around at the crowd—and with the addition of Lucius, Michael, and a young man Tienne recognized as a reporter, there was quite a crowd tonight—and realized what he'd been missing by simply producing forgeries in his apartment and listening to the others give him glimpses of where his papers would go.

"Is there, perchance, a gig for a reporter who needs a bit of a break?" asked the sublimely handsome young YouTube reporter at the far end of the table. Danny's gentle smile at him made Tienne pay sharper attention to the young man's paleness and the bruises under his eyes.

"If we cannot guarantee you a good story, young Torrance," Danny said grandly, "we can at least guarantee you a good time."

Torrance Grayson gave a game smile and nodded. "I couldn't ask for more," he said.

"We *are* waiting for one more person," Julia said, glancing at the clock, chagrined. "Josh's Uncle Leon should have arrived at the airport nearly two hours ago. He texted me to say the flight was delayed, but I was hoping he could get here and have some dinner before we forced him to confab."

"Uncle Leon?" Josh asked, hesitantly pleased. "I didn't know he was coming."

Julia gave him a warm smile. "He promised to stay in your life, darling. I don't know why you'd doubt that."

Josh gave her a level, not-buying-it stare, but it was Grace who said what they were all thinking.

"Isn't he the guy who keeps trying to date you, Mrs. Josh's Mom?"

To Tienne's surprise, Julia Dormer-Salinger, whose poise had never so much as fluttered in the years since she'd greeted Tienne at the airport, blushed.

"I'm not exactly sure if that's how I'd put it," she said with dignity. "But he *is* coming to visit in the hopes of helping us with our next adventure."

"It's how I'd put it," Felix said, eyes twinkling. "And it's something none of us are going to say anything about."

"But we're all going to put money on," Chuck murmured, loud enough for the other end of the table to hear him.

"I'll keep book," Lucius said softly, and Julia gave him a dire look.

"One does *long* for intelligent companionship," she murmured, and nobody bothered to hide their smirks.

Molly did give a sigh then. "Whatever we're doing, can we invite Talia?" she asked plaintively. "Since

I have no potential mate in the offing, I'd really love to have a girlfriend to play with."

"Yes," Danny said without hesitation, and Felix and Julia both looked at him in surprise.

"Yes?" Felix asked dryly.

Danny cast an inscrutable look to the end of the table, catching first Tienne's eye and then Stirling's. "Yes," he said, nodding. Then he spoke to Molly, his face assuming a tender, avuncular look. "Molly, my darling, you deserve a playmate too. Since we have no men who can appropriately appreciate your beauty, feel free to invite Talia. In fact, if you wish to go call her now, it will give Julia, Felix, and me a chance to prepare our schtick while we wait for our stragglers to arrive."

"Talia?" Tienne asked Stirling quietly, a little unnerved by the way Danny had looked at them a moment ago.

"Talia Clarke, the tennis pro," Stirling replied. "She's retiring, I think—lots of injuries this year—and she has announcing contracts lined up. She's helped us out before."

"What's *her* talent?" Tienne asked, trying not to be bitter. Danny had only meant the best when he'd set up a sort of protection fence around him, but it had left him feeling… inadequate. Not enough. Not equal to the others on the team.

"She's a delight to be around," Molly said from Tienne's other side, and Tienne was comfortable enough to send her an arch look.

She grinned and excused herself to go make the call, leaving Torrance to fill in the spot she'd vacated. "She's not a con man," he said bluntly, "and has no criminal skills whatsoever. But she's willing to help, she doesn't tell tales, and she's absolutely dedicated to Felix and Danny."

"And my sister likes her," Stirling said, and Tienne recognized Stirling's absolute adoration of his sister in that statement and would not dare to argue.

"This is a big deal?" he asked instead. "The 'confab' downstairs?"

"It is," Torrance said, some of the lines of stress and worry on his handsome face easing up. "I usually miss this part. I'm the guy they call in when they need a spin doctor at the end."

Tienne nodded. "I usually draw up the papers," he said and then added honestly, "or forge the paintings."

Grayson grinned at him. "Papers? I was wondering who you were. They talk about you all the time. Good things of course. But I was wondering if I'd ever get to meet you."

Tienne blinked and looked at Stirling. "I am... elusive?"

"Yes," Stirling said, grinning at him. "I don't know how you could doubt it."

That was disheartening. "I don't *try* to be elusive," he murmured. "I'm just—"

"Private," Stirling said with a certain grim humor. "We get it."

"What about my life do you people not know?" Tienne asked defensively, and Stirling flickered his eyes over to the head of the table where Danny, Felix, and Julia were having a conversation very much as close as theirs.

"For starters," Josh said behind them, "none of us here knows how you and Danny met."

Tienne's eyes went back to Danny, who was looking sad. Sad and ashamed. Ashamed for what? Ashamed that he didn't realize his lover was a killer? Well, Tienne hadn't realized Levka was a smuggler—or worse! And unlike Danny, Tienne had done nothing but huddle, become the victim yet again, while Danny, he had done something to stop what had happened.

"Fine," he said, standing up. "I will tell you, but it is not… a comfortable story. May I tell it only once?" He gave Torrance Grayson a narrow look. "And only for the people in this home?"

Torrance raised both his hands. "Of course," he said. "This place is very much a lockbox for me. What happens here, or is revealed here, is only for the people here, unless they need my help."

Tienne frowned. "Then why are you here?"

Torrance shrugged. He was wearing a suit—but one cut very differently from Felix's or the refined Lucius's. This suit would not be out of place on a red carpet or at a premiere, with tight fitted slacks and a mandarin collar instead of a tie. Tienne got the feeling he had dressed up for the same reason Tienne himself had—and Stirling too, who was looking very handsome in a sport coat over one of his divinely textured black sweaters.

"Because my friend's son is going to be okay," he said, giving Josh an oblique look. "And I wanted to celebrate."

Josh's return look was pure compassion. "Well, I hope you're my friend too."

Torrance gave him a truly grateful smile, and Josh made a herding gesture.

"Come on, let's get downstairs and hear Tienne's story before Danny tells Felix and Julia some other version of it. I want to compare notes with my mother at the end of the night."

Tienne snorted softly, but he rose just the same. "How do you know Danny's version will not be truthful?"

Josh made a considering sound as he guided them toward the staircase that led downstairs to the den—and to Stirling's apartment, although Tienne was going to try very hard not to think about that, or about the tender, tentative kiss they'd shared.

It had been wonderful, by the way, and so promising. Tienne had very little experience, what Levka Dubov had taken from him notwithstanding. Some scattered kisses, a few fumbles in dark corners, that made up the be-all and end-all of his consensual experience. But Stirling had been tentative as well, shy as Tienne was, but also eager to kiss some more.

And Tienne did so love the intelligence in his gray eyes and the vulnerability he saw in Stirling's expression when he was trying very hard to work out things that puzzled him. But whereas Stirling seemed more content to let things be revealed to him, Tienne felt that sometimes events required planning. He and his father had been very adept at being ready for the next time they had to run. It had taken him a long time to assemble the tools of his trade before he'd started making fake IDs in boarding school, but he'd wanted the independence, so he'd planned for it. It was time to make another plan, this one to take advantage of this offering of family given to him.

Stirling had been so open about his own past, so forthcoming about introducing Tienne to his new place in the mansion. It felt as though, perhaps, this offering of the truth would be a way to start their relationship anew, but this time as each other's focus, their own center, without the complications of Tienne's uncertain presence in the Salingers' lives. He was here, wasn't he? He lived under their roof. They protected him. Perhaps he could share the moment when Danny changed his destiny forever.

Josh drew them to the couches when they reached the bottom of the stairs, and to Tienne's surprise, the others were already there. Everybody save for Julia, Danny, and Felix—and of course Josh's Uncle Leon and Molly's friend, who were presumably on their way.

"Okay," Josh said, his voice still gruff. "The grown-ups are coming down in about soon, and they've got something cooking. Something big. It's a combined Christmas present/job whatever, and we've all cleared our calendars, and now that I might not die—"

"But your bones can still be ground to powder," Grace inserted irritably.

"But I'm still in need of recovery," Josh muttered, shooting his best friend a dire look. "I think they feel safe enough to let us in on the scam. But in the meantime…." He smiled encouragingly at Tienne, who waved a little.

"Oooh," Molly said, resting her chin on her hands. "Is it Tienne's story time already? I've been *so* good about not asking!"

Tienne's cheeks warmed, but he'd gained enough comfort to smile at her. "Indeed, you have been most restrained." He looked around at the expectant faces and tried not to quail. "You have all been very kind. Very… *accepting*," he said, finding the right word. "You all upended your lives for me, and I understand you've been searching for a way to get Levka Dubov out of my life without making me a target. I… I have no way to repay you." Heavens, wasn't *that* the truth. "I mean, besides the obvious." He tried a joke. "Free IDs for everyone?"

Grace gave a haughty sniff. "Well, since Josh is nearly twenty-one anyway, and he's the last one of us who couldn't drink, perhaps that ship has sailed."

Chuck rolled his eyes. "Please. I could *always* do with a new identity. I'll take passports if they're being offered gratis." He winked at Tienne. "Besides, I think it's enough that Tienne knows he's one of us, right?"

And the big bluff cowboy peered at Tienne soberly, letting Tienne see how very much he himself had been *seen*.

"I do now," he said shyly. "I think, maybe, that's another reason you should know this story. I… all this time, I've been so indebted to Lightfingers. More than any of you could ever guess. I did not think there was any way to pay him back. To be invited to his house, to live as a family member, it seemed like too much. Too big a gift. I did not want the strings attached. I am still—" He paused, hating to admit this. "—unsure," he said at last. "Still unsure as to what it is that I can give this crew, other than my abilities as a forger. But all you've asked from me has been that I accept your kindness—and paint." He made eye contact with Stirling then, and also with Josh and Grace, who had commissioned him as well. "Everyone has very much demanded my art, and that is almost more than I can thank you for. So since everyone is so curious to know how I came to be here, I shall tell you.

"My father and I," he said, his words summoning up Antoine Couvier's kind features, "were artists. But—as you know—art cannot always pay the bills.

My father was a very skilled forger, but not so wise with his choice of clients." He grimaced. "I have apparently learned his ways, yes?"

Stirling's quiet hand on his shoulder offered comfort.

"When I was very young—perhaps six? Seven? My father was given a job by a man named Kadjic—"

Everybody in the room gasped.

"You know this man?"

"He's the guy who carved his initials in Danny's skin and left him for dead in an alleyway in Morocco," Josh said, eyes sharp. "But that was some years after your father worked for him."

Tienne tried very hard to speak and ended up nodding instead. "Yes," he said. "My father couldn't— couldn't do what Kadjic asked. He was recruiting Chechnyan war criminals into his organization. He asked my father to make them passports, and he threatened *me* to get him to do it. My father made a plan. He left the passports on the table of our house and then took me and ran. We carried his equipment from place to place—eleven countries in five years. It took me a while to figure out why this Kadjic would pursue us so relentlessly. My father did not tell me until almost before he died. You see, he'd left the passports, knowing that Kadjic would assume Antoine would do his bidding and then try to run. If that's all my father had done, Kadjic might have let him go. But Antoine had left… time bombs, I think, in the passports. Tiny similarities in the paper, in the numbers, hints to people looking that the passports were forged, and even more, who the person really was. Some of Kadjic's recruits were seized at airports and imprisoned, and Kadjic—Kadjic was furious."

"Oh my God," Hunter said, surprising him. "I *heard* about this when I entered special ops. We were told what to look for in a fake ID so we wouldn't end up like Kadjic's goons."

Tienne gave an unhappy little shrug. "It was... it was brave, what my father did. Taking a stand. But it was also foolish. There was only us, and Kadjic, he didn't forgive."

"Eleven countries in five years," Michael said, and Tienne took him in again, an unassuming man with a rural accent. "That's some serious grudging going on. And tough on a kid."

Tienne smiled at him, liking his kindness. "I loved it," he admitted with a laugh. "I learned four languages. I attended many schools. My father brought books with us, and I learned things I found my American counterparts had never dreamed of." And so very many beautiful scenes to capture his eye, beautiful colors to fascinate him. "But always," he continued, "there was the threat. Kadjic would hear about a new forger and investigate, and we would be on the run. One night in Marrakech, when I was twelve, he caught us."

Again, another one of those sudden intakes of breath, spread out among all of his audience. These people knew the significance of the city, of the date. He was giving them puzzle pieces that, to his mind, they should have seen long ago.

"What happened?" Stirling urged softly, and looking into Stirling's eyes, he was reassured. Stirling already knew. Tienne had blurted out part of the truth that awful day, nearly two weeks ago, when he'd managed to throw Levka out of his flat because he couldn't... couldn't....

With an effort, he focused on one trauma at a time.

"It was so fast," he said, wondering if he had ever given voice to this. "We crawled down the side of a building, and there they were: three goons and Kadjic himself, and Kadjic's boyfriend." His lips twisted. "He was dressed like Aladdin, from the Disney movie. I thought for a costume party, but now that I know him, I think he did it because it pleased him."

"Danny?" Josh asked, not exactly surprised, but more in confirmation.

"Yes." Tienne nodded. "He was... he was not sober, I don't think. But I was even more surprised because Russians, Chechens, they are terrible about queer people. I thought it took a lot of balls—or power, I guess—to be traipsing around Marrakech with arm candy and goons. But in minutes, they had my father pinned against the wall, with a knife to his throat, and I thought of other things."

There was a warm, comforting hand on his thigh. He covered it with his own, not daring to glance at Stirling's face. This had not been part of the plan, but he would not reject comfort he craved. Not again.

"Danny wouldn't have it. He yelled at Kadjic, threatening to leave him on the spot, and Kadjic yelled back, ordering my father's death. The...." He remembered his father's panicked gurgle as the knife slit his throat. "It was very quick," he whispered. "But when the goon went to grab me, Danny leaped on his back and headlocked him, and screamed for me to run." He shrugged. "I did. A young Interpol officer found me the next morning in an alley. The man with the knife had slashed my backpack, and a tube of green paint had bled as I'd run. I thought young Aladdin would be the one to find me. I did not realize until Mr. Craig prepared me to leave the country that young Aladdin had almost not survived."

The entire room was silent until someone took a shuddering breath. Tienne glanced around and saw, to his surprise, that more than one person was wiping away tears.

"I'm so sorry," Molly said, coming to his other side. "That's terrible."

"Danny," Josh whispered. "We knew he'd almost died. We didn't know…."

"Fuckin' hero," Hunter said with a grunt. "All his talk about being a worthless drunk—"

Tienne gasped. "No! If he'd known how brutal Kadjic really was, I think he would have saved my father too."

"Of course he would have," Michael said, his rural twang comforting. "That's the guy we love. But that doesn't change that it must've been rough to end up here a week or so—"

"Two days," Tienne murmured, remembering the brutal culture shock.

"Holy hell!" Michael waved his arms around. "Did you hear that, Carl?"

"I did," Carl said softly. His Viking-blue eyes were inscrutable on Tienne's face. "It must have been overwhelming. Is that why you chose boarding school?"

Tienne's eyes burned. "School, I understood," he whispered. How very astute. More and more Tienne understood why these men were Stirling's friends.

"Why tell us this now?" Grace asked, and he sounded pouty and put out. "You've been haunting the corners of the mansion for *years*. Don't you think someone here could have kissed your boo-boos better?"

"Grace," Hunter began, but Grace shook him off.

"Don't 'Grace' me! Josh and I worked our *asses* off to be your friend! Invitations, hanging around during holidays—I was a six-time fuckup, and you thought you'd be the odd man out?"

Tienne bit his lip. "You all seemed so tight," he said, swallowing. Yes, he probably deserved that. "But this last week, you've been hunting down Levka and making me feel welcome. I… I wanted you to know, you see. That me, being here, it was an accident. Danny did enough for me saving my life. He did not need to give me a family too. When I thought it was him alone, I hoped perhaps…." But he didn't want to talk about that. "But a family? Mother, father, brothers? No. I did not get those things. I thought perhaps I was better off alone."

Some of them made a sort of hissing noise, but Chuck's boyfriend, Lucius, was the one who spoke. "Sometimes you are better off with none when the alternative can be worse." There was a hardness to his jaw that suggested he knew from whence he spoke.

"And sometimes," Molly said kindly, "having a good parent, even for a short time, can make all the difference in your heart. Was your father good?"

Tienne had to hold on hard to his emotions. In all his years in America, he'd never been able to talk about his father to anybody. Here, he realized, looking at all of the compassionate eyes upon him, he could.

"Oui."

Molly's smile was brilliant. Tienne would protect her, like Stirling would, because she could give her entire heart to them in a smile.

"Then good," she said. "Maybe, if you can celebrate your father here, you might also open your heart to everyone else." She glanced over her shoulder and made a flirty little moue. "I mean, I've got all the daddies and uncles a girl could ask for, right?"

Tienne had to admit that yes, she did, and suddenly he understood her need to call a friend—a female friend—that she could confide in.

"Wait a minute," Josh said, as though suddenly pulled back to something. "You said Liam Craig came to fetch you."

Tienne nodded and Josh frowned. "He must have been young—very young."

Tienne thought about it. "Our ages now, I guess. Why?"

Josh shook his head, smiling slightly. "No reason," he said. "Curiosity. He and Danny seem to be friends, and he's worked with us sometimes."

Grace made a smirking sound, and then he turned to Tienne. "Is it me? You don't like *me*, right? That's why you stayed away?"

And Tienne saw it then—what had been bothering Grace.

Hurt.

"It wasn't you," he said kindly. "It was… shyness. You are all so very easy with each other. I just sat there, for nearly two weeks, at your dinner table—it took me that long to think I could speak your language."

But Grace was still pouting. "Well, that's great. You keep 'speaking our language' and we'll try to be interesting enough to not make you run away to your painting cave again."

And with that he flounced off to the corner of the den, slid down the wall, and folded his arms to sulk.

Hunter gave him a sorrowful look before turning to Tienne. "I'm glad you decided to open up with us, brother, but you have some bridges to mend with that one."

Tienne looked at Stirling anxiously. "I don't understand," he said.

"He's hurt," Stirling said with a shrug. "I would have been too, except…." He smiled apologetically. "I get it. Too many people. Too much commotion. It's loud and confusing. Even back when we were kids, it would have been loud and confusing. So I understand. But Grace takes things personally."

Tienne nodded and swallowed, understanding a little.

"I shall have to make it up to him," he said.

Stirling grinned. "Wait until the Christmas gift. He'll be so excited."

Tienne brightened, and at that moment, there was a bustle down the stairs. Chuck and Hunter both moved, Hunter to the end of the stairwell to lean against the back wall, and Chuck to the bar. Tienne realized that they were posting themselves as sentries, perhaps to guard the proceedings in the room. Molly sat herself at Stirling's feet, and Stirling rested his hand atop her brilliantly colored, curly hair.

The first person down the stairs was a stunningly beautiful Black woman with her hair braided tightly back from her face and a pretty string of diamonds posted along the back of one ear. She was dressed warmly and fashionably in thick riding pants and a scarlet sweater, and she rushed to Molly, hugging her and dropping down to the floor in front of the couch in almost the same motion.

Following behind at a statelier pace came Julia and a brutally handsome man with olive skin, a thick dark goatee, and black hair parted on the side. He bore more than a passing resemblance to Josh, and Tienne assumed him to be the mysterious "Uncle Leon" who seemed to be enchanted with Josh's mother.

Well, lucky her. And definitely lucky him, because she seemed nearly girlishly pleased to be on his arm.

And dragging up the rear were Danny and Felix, looking at odds, which was something Tienne had never seen.

"What's wrong, do you think?" he murmured to Stirling, but to his surprise it was Michael—who was sitting on the edge of the couch next to him—who answered.

"If I had to hazard a guess? I'd guess Felix got the same story we got, and he never realized how much you meant to Danny, or how close Danny came to dying."

Next to him, sprawled in a stuffed chair, Carl grunted. "Yahtzee."

Tienne looked from one man to the other.

"How would he know that?" he asked Stirling softly so their voices wouldn't carry across the room.

"Because that's how Carl looked when Michael hung out of an SUV to shoot down a giant predatory bird," Stirling replied after an assessing look.

Carl gave Stirling a grim smile and touched his nose with the tip of his index finger. "Indeed," he said softly.

Tienne nodded, understanding, and at that moment, Danny and Felix hit the carpet and all chatter stopped.

Danny gave Felix a rather hopeful, puckish look, and Felix shook his head and responded with a pained smile. He squeezed Danny's shoulder and nodded, then looked at Julia, who nodded as well. Danny cleared his throat.

"Okay, children," he said, looking at them all meaningfully. "We have grown in both number and skill over the past months, and it's become apparent that the better we get, the more we can accomplish. Felix, Julia, and I have been talking, and now that Josh is getting better—but still needs to rest, mind you," he added with a severe look at Josh, who grinned back and gave the thumbs-up, "we think we have the perfect Christmas gift for all of you, one that will present a challenge, perhaps fix a great wrong, and definitely get us all the hell out of Chicago and into the sun and the sand for a few weeks while we work—*and Josh recovers*. Now, before I ask if everybody is on board, I do believe we need to ask permission of two of our number first."

There was a puzzled quiet, and then Danny looked toward the man at Tienne's side, and then down to his sister.

"Molly, love, I've got my little slideshow all ready, but we'll need some of your commentary. Stirling, I know crowds aren't your thing. You're welcome to stay there and add what's needed, but you can come up to stand by your sister if you're feeling bold."

Together, they both sucked in a breath, and Molly brought her hand to her mouth.

"Do you mean it, Uncle Danny?" she asked, her voice barely a whisper.

Danny nodded. "Oh yes, my lovely. Felix promised back in September. We haven't sat idle. We're going to look into Fred and Stella Christopher's death. The two of you deserve nothing less."

Adventure Ho

STIRLING'S HEART pounded hard enough to roar in his ears like the ocean.

A Caribbean blue ocean, to be exact.

Molly, her face a wreath of sunshine smiles, walked toward the console in the center of the room where Danny was, threw her arms around his shoulders, and clung.

Danny hugged her back, and Stirling found he'd stood too. He didn't go in for the power hug, but as much as he hated the limelight, he wanted to be part of this.

When the shock had worn off after their deaths, nearly two years ago, and Stirling and Molly could actually talk about it, talk about the circumstances, they'd been reluctant to reveal their suspicions.

"Lost at sea in the Caribbean. What are the fucking odds?" Molly had said one bleak day before Thanksgiving. That first year, they'd been invited to the Salingers' and had even planned to go, but it had only been Josh, Felix, and Julia then—and Grace—and the hole left by Danny was always a hidden grief, singing in the corners. Tienne would probably not show, and

Grace was almost as lost as they had been, for different reasons. It had been warmth and shelter, but not the sanctuary the Salinger mansion had become.

So, feeling angry and literal, Stirling had calculated the odds, and they'd looked at each other in disbelief.

"Those are really long odds," Molly had said.

"Even in the Bermuda Triangle," Stirling added. "Which they weren't in."

And that's when the grumbles had started. They hadn't worked with Danny Mitchell yet—hadn't seen how sometimes fixing a wrong took a vast teamwork of sneakiness, mildly unscrupulous information gathering, and sleight of hand. All they'd had was Fred and Stella's biological son, Harve, and his irritating social-climbing wife, Carolyn. Harve had told them not to contact him, while he tried to take their trusts away. It turned out that Fred and Stella had built better wills than that—ironclad, in fact—that made sure Stirling and Molly were well taken care of, but that hadn't changed the fact that they'd felt very, very much alone.

Then Danny had returned to town—and to Felix's life—last March, and he'd taken the time to teach them everything he knew. All of the savvy he'd once put into cons and grifts he'd put toward fighting for victims without other recourse, and the crew Josh had assembled had loved it. And they'd gotten very good at it as well, when they hadn't been slouches in the first place.

But once they *had* seen what it took to tackle a project like this, they'd been busy tackling other projects *like this*. Hell, they'd spent an entire week tracking down Levka Dubov because he'd touched—coerced? assaulted?—Tienne, and they still had a week or two to go before they were in a position to make sure he got his desserts and never had the opportunity to touch Tienne again. So to hear that Felix, Danny, and Julia had been thinking about him and Molly, honoring Fred and Stella Christopher, the people who had opened their hearts and their homes and their *world* to the two of them, the gift of it was overwhelming.

It deserved acknowledgment, even if it wasn't in Stirling's comfort zone.

He followed his sister to the center of the room, conscious that Tienne had left a lingering touch down his arm as he'd done so.

The touch had warmed him, and given him courage as well.

"Can we really do this?" he asked, excitement making his voice thready. "Can we go see what happened?"

"We can," Julia said. She and Leon had made themselves comfortable by the wet bar, and the look she gave Stirling was warm. "With Leon's help, we've leased a boat—"

"Yacht," Leon corrected, looking affronted.

"Does it not float?" Julia asked. "I thought that was the definition of a thing that floated."

Felix and Danny unsuccessfully tried to hide their smirks.

"What?" she demanded.

"As I recall, dearest," Felix said, manfully making eye contact, "Mr. di Rossi's 'boat' has three decks, a fully functioning kitchen, twelve cabins, and a lounge for meals and confabs. It's not quite a cruise ship but…." He made vague gestures with his hands.

"Yacht is really much more appropriate," Danny inserted smoothly.

Julia's gaze swung to Leon. "You put them up to that," she said, completely serious.

"Indeed, I did not," Leon told her, his lips pursing to hide his own smile. "Perhaps they appreciate the importance of a yacht versus a boat in a matter such as this."

Julia sniffed, all offended dignity. "*Fine*," she conceded. "We've leased—"

"Bought," said Felix and Danny in tandem.

Julia's expression was horrified. "Bought?" she squeaked.

"Leon did it," Danny said, some of the European worldliness slipping from his speech as a purely brotherly smile of deviltry crossed his face.

Julia turned to Leon, and Stirling could not ever remember seeing "Mrs. Josh's Mom" quite so unnerved. "You *bought* a yacht?"

"I do spend time in Tuscany," Leon said smoothly. "It's not such a stretch."

"Isn't that an entirely different side of the ocean?" Julia blurted. "Why would you even *do* that?"

And to the amusement of the entire room, Leon captured Julia's hand and brought it to his lips. "Because a beautiful woman asked me for a favor, and to help her in an adventure with the added benefit of getting to know a nephew I've learned to love. Merry Christmas, my lovely Julia. I hope you and I get to spend time alone on my *yacht* while we participate in this enterprise."

Julia's flush might possibly have been invisible from space, but it was certainly obvious to everybody in the room.

"Thank you so much," she rasped. "For allowing the lot of us to stay on your yacht."

"*Inviting*," Leon purred, his dark eyes avid on the hectic color in her cheeks.

"Inviting," she squeaked, casting Felix a rather helpless look.

"Indeed," Felix said, taking over the conversation. "So, as you all now know, Josh's rich uncle has purchased a yacht and invited us to vacation there with him, off the coast of Barbados. Now, we'll be traveling up and down the chain of the Caribbean isles, but we need Danny—with some help from Stirling and Molly—to help us plot our exact destination."

He sounded a bit frustrated, and Molly, who could put together a person's story from a few words and a dropped vocal tone, said, "Wait a minute." She looked from Felix to Danny to Julia. "You've been hush-hush about this for *weeks*. We've known *something* was brewing. You had us block out time and everything, but nothing until now. Why?"

Danny was the one who answered. "Well, our first thought, pet, was to surprise you and Stirling with the answer over Christmas. As Josh improved, he got more and more curious, and Julia, Felix, Grace, and I came on board. You'd both been so patient—we were hoping, I think, to present you with the information *fait accompli*. But the more we investigated, the more we realized that there were questions raised by what we discovered that we couldn't answer without you, that perhaps none of us could answer unless we actually went down to bloody Barbados to look around."

"And we couldn't do that until I was better," Josh said before grimacing. "Mostly because I'm a selfish bastard who didn't want to be left alone again." Most of the crew had left for California back in September while Danny and Felix stayed with Josh. Their reasoning had been sound—everybody was worn thin with worry, and Leon had become available for the bone marrow transplant that saved Josh's life. Josh was so tired that even talking to people exhausted him, and he often stated that he'd slept through their entire adventure. This statement, now, months later, was the closest Josh had ever come to regretting he'd been left behind.

"We made preparations anyway," he added with a little tremble, "in case, you know, I wasn't going to *get* better, and then, at least, I could go somewhere warm before I died."

Stirling's chest went cold. God. It didn't matter how often they'd all thought about the possibility in the past months, hearing Josh say it out loud always gave them all a terrible chill.

"Which is not a thing he said to us," Grace said with deep disgust, "because he didn't want us to pound his fragile bones to dust for making us all feel like crap. Asshole."

"You've been calling me Cancer Boy since *July*," Josh retaliated, and Grace glared at him.

"And not once did you sound as scared as you sounded now!"

It was true. Usually the grown-up of their tight little knot of friends, Josh couldn't seem to stop his lower lip's uncharacteristic trembling. "Sorry," he said, looking away. "I think… I think now that I might be okay, I'm finally… uhm… I can't be mad at being sick anymore, and, well, I've got to figure out how to deal." He shook his head and held up his hand. "Which is not what this meeting is about." His glare dared them to contradict him. "The point here is, we wanted to see how much I could help, and we wanted to give everybody a Christmas present they'd remember and enjoy, and we wanted to have a job we would all enjoy doing. So yes, Molly, to answer your question, we were going to try to present this to you all in a big box with a ribbon, because we love you guys and we know how this has been weighing you down. We couldn't, though. We needed yours and Stirling's input. Partly, it's because Fred and Stella's bio-kid is an incredible douchepickle, but partly because there are mysteries about their trip that don't make any sense to us but that you might understand."

Molly made a suspicious noise. "How fragile *are* your bones?" she asked thickly.

Josh grinned. "I'm never too fragile to hug," he said, and then she rocketed away from Danny and across the room to Josh.

"You're gonna be all right?" she asked, loud enough for everybody to hear.

"Unless Grace kills me first," he told her.

She pulled back and nodded. "Don't scare us like that again."

And then she wept on his neck for—Stirling checked the clock on the wall—at least three minutes while the rest of the assembly made awkward eye contact and wished she'd stop.

Danny made a *tch-tch* sound at him and then nodded his chin toward Molly, and Stirling realized this was his job.

"Molly," he said matter-of-factly. "Everyone's waiting on us to start. Come on! Don't you want to see the mystery?"

Molly sniffed—loudly—and hugged Josh one more time. He kissed her on the cheek and pushed her from where he sat on the couch that ate people to the center of the room with Danny and Stirling again, and she went, wiping her face on the inside of her violet cashmere sweater without shame. By the time she'd made it across the room, Chuck and Hunter had moved chairs to the console so they could sit, and somebody—probably Julia—had produced a box of tissues so Molly could mop her face.

"So," she said thickly, fumbling for Stirling's hand. "What do you need us to tell you?"

Stirling squeezed her hand back, and they looked to Danny, who smiled. "Grace went to fetch your keyboard, my boy. I may need you to do some actual work for this. You're one of the best partners I've ever—"

"Hey!" Grace said, coming out of Stirling's room. Stirling hadn't even noticed he'd gone, but apparently that's what made Grace such an outstanding thief. "Look at this! It's a little teeny Lego guy that looks like Stirling! I want one. Do you have one for me?"

The gentle pressure of Molly's hand was enough to keep Stirling quiet.

"Dylan Li," she said, standing with hands on her hips. "It is a week before Christmas and you're asking somebody about a toy you could only have seen if you'd been snooping?"

"I wasn't snooping," Grace said defensively. "It was on his computer desk. Looking at him. How could I not see it?"

It had been on Stirling's computer desk because he'd been planning to put it inside an unused console computer he had and marking it "Delicate—don't look here." He hadn't gotten to it yet for *this reason*.

"Well, maybe," Molly said sweetly, "if you're really good, Santa will give you an entire Lego set of little guys in black clothes."

Grace grinned and pumped the arm not carrying Stirling's much-beloved laptop. "Yes! Here, Stirling. I'm keeping the Lego guy. Merry Christmas."

"Thanks, Grace." He grimaced at his sister, but she had her eyes narrowed and was scowling at Grace as he danced his way back to the people-eating couch and Josh so they could sit practically in the same spot. Stirling had the feeling that Molly was about to perpetrate some epic criming on behalf of the Christmas spirit when Danny cleared his throat loud enough for them to hear him.

"Let it be," he murmured softly.

Molly nodded, and Stirling too. As fantastic as plotting revenge might be—and coming from Danny it could be *spectacular*—that's not what they were doing right now.

Then Danny hit the button for the big screen at the far end of the room and Stirling's attention was elsewhere.

"These are our victims," Danny said, his voice gentle. "Fox?"

Felix took this part, giving a sorrowful look to the late fiftyish couple on the screen. The man was balding gracefully, with a little fuzz of hair cut short above his ears and a gray goatee to match it, and the woman was soft and squishy, with hair dyed a gentle blond to mask her own grays. Stirling looked at them and remembered how Fred had always had a kind word, even if it was about something stupid. "Nice haircut, Stirling—makes you look handsome. Bet the boys are gonna go nuts!" He'd known Stirling was gay almost from the get-go. Stirling would forever treasure a particular basketball game between Sacramento and Chicago.

"Yeah, Sacramento sucks—they haven't been the same since they wouldn't let Karcek play because he came out." Fred had given Stirling a gentle look from across the couch. "The world's not always kind to certain people, kid. People of color, people of size, LGBTQ folks, people with special brains. It's not fair, ever, but you need to remember that even when it sucks, you're loved. Hell, your sister would fight her way through seven layers of *hell* to make sure you knew that, right?"

Stirling had swallowed rapidly and nodded before staring at the screen. "I'm not overweight," he said. "But I know I'm the other three."

"Yeah, I figured. But as long as you know you're loved *here*, that's what I wanted you to know." His father wasn't perfect, no. He liked to bet on sports, snuck cigars outside when he thought his wife couldn't smell the smoke a mile away, and was as squishy and comfortable as Stella was. Frederick Christopher had been a really good man and the father Stirling hadn't known how to ask for but had gotten anyway.

Felix's voice interrupted Sterling's thoughts, his timbre low and respectful, with a wistfulness that served as a balm to Stirling's own ache.

"This is Frederick and Estella Christopher—Fred and Stella to their friends. Fred started out as an accountant, and then he opened his first accounting *business*. Then he opened three more. At twenty-five, he and Stella had their first son—Harve, shown here with his wife, Carolyn—and at forty-five, he sold his businesses with enough money to retire a millionaire several times over." Harve Christopher resembled his father—round and with a tendency to portliness, he worked out and fasted to be muscular instead. He'd gotten hair plugs at thirty, and his blue eyes never twinkled and were never kind. His wife was two inches taller than he was, with brittle coifed hair and the same capped teeth. Stirling had never looked in her eyes—or Harve's for that matter—because he'd known that they'd never seen him. He'd once heard Harve call him "the autistic one" and Molly "the fat redheaded girl," and that was all Stirling had ever needed to know about Harve.

"But instead of retiring," Felix continued, "Fred and Stella surprised us all." A new picture popped up, this one from around ten years before, when Stirling and Molly had been with Fred and Stella for only a couple of months. "They adopted two of the most inspiring young people *I've* ever known and proceeded to enjoy their retirement by being the world's best parents."

The setting was casual—they'd all been at a picnic in the backyard, and Felix and Julia and Josh were in the shot too. Stella had her arm slung around Molly's shoulders. Molly had hit her growth spurt then and was an inch or so taller than her smallish adoptive mother, but the look of adoration in Stella's eyes was absolutely transparent. Josh was teaching Stirling some kind of adolescent-boy handshake that was cool back then, and Stirling was paying absolute attention to him while Felix and Fred laughed uproariously at a joke Stirling had never heard.

It didn't matter. He could still remember Stella's sweet voice—with a southside Chicago accent, telling Molly that her hair was absolutely gorgeous, and if she could paint, she'd paint sunsets that color—and hear Fred's laughter and know that it was only about funny jokes and never mean about other people.

He didn't realize he'd made a sound until Molly passed him the Kleenex and he found he had to wipe his own eyes as well.

"They really were the best," Molly said, her voice thick. "They… they were so kind."

"They were even nice to me," Grace said, surprising Stirling. "Remember that? I stole some of Fred's cuff links and Stella's necklace because…." He paused then, and Stirling realized that Grace had never put words to his habit of stealing from the people he loved the most.

"Because you're Grace," Josh said. Josh was leaning against the back of the couch now, and Grace was lying with his head on Josh's lap. Josh was stroking his friend's hair, and Stirling felt a sudden shaft of fondness for the two young men who had befriended Stirling and Molly in middle school and who had been their staunch defenders and peer group ever since. Grace was irritating and often irrational from Stirling's perspective, but Stirling had never doubted, even once, that Grace's heart was sound.

"Whatever," Grace muttered, pretending to be bothered. "But I did it, and I expected to hear it from my parents, I really did. But Fred dropped you guys off at school one day and pulled me aside." Grace's voice grew even thicker, and Stirling suddenly wanted to hide Lego men for the prickly thief every day of his life. "He said Stella had given him those cuff links for his birthday, and then he gave me another pair—like them, I swear, but with a slightly different diamond—and asked if I could bring the first pair back in my own time." Grace made a sound like a sob, and to Stirling's surprise, he kept talking. "And I asked about the necklace, and he laughed and said that his mother had given that to Stella, and Stella really didn't like it, but she wore it to make *him* happy, and that I was to feel free to keep it, and he'd get her something she liked."

Next to him, he saw Molly's shoulders shake, but that was mild for what was happening inside his own body. His throat had swollen, his eyes burned, and making each breath come in and out evenly was a titanic struggle for self-possession.

It wasn't until Danny leaned over and put a hand on his shoulder, murmuring, "It's okay, Stirling. Let them come. You have to grieve before you can celebrate, okay?" that something in Stirling relaxed—his back, his neck—and he leaned his head against his sister's and found he could breathe much better now that he let the tears slide down his cheeks.

"Grace," Felix said, his own voice a little thick, "you perfect little thief. I was going to give a nice speech about why Fred and Stella deserved better than what happened to them, but you stole all my good words for yourself."

There was a sniffly, snotty laugh around the room, and then a deep breath. Stirling straightened, and Felix resumed his presentation.

"Fred and Stella Christopher were, quite simply, the best," Felix said. "And while they loved taking Molly and Stirling places, the week after the two of them graduated from high school, they got to go on a senior trip to Europe. Their trip was supposed to last three weeks, and Fred and Stella, as sort of a congratulations gift to themselves for seeing Stirling and Molly through high school at the least, *leased* a *small* yacht and the services of a captain, a small crew, a housekeeper, a cook, and a guide for a leisurely tour of the islands."

The next shot was of Fred and Stella, standing on board an eighty-foot yacht, looking a little embarrassed in their tourist clothes and very excited to be starting a new adventure. They both had zinc oxide on their noses and cheeks, straw hats to protect their Chicago-spring skin from the bold Caribbean sun, and bodies that were probably not bikini and Speedo ready.

God, they looked happy.

Stirling remembered getting that picture as he and Molly had boarded the plane to Greece, the first stop on their own tour, and telling Molly he wished they were going together.

"Tell them to keep the yacht!" Molly had urged him. "I want to go too!"

Stirling had, and he'd been assured that they could go in the winter, over Christmas, and that Fred would look into buying a yacht of his own and Stirling needed to help him.

The memory pierced something fragile in Stirling's chest. He'd saved Stella's last text to him. *Fred and I will find all the good spots for you two—our vacations are always better when you're with us.*

He felt a burn of anger that they hadn't been able to make that come true.

"So," Danny said, imposing order on Stirling's chaotic emotions, "we know what they'd *planned* to do. They took a plane to Puerto Rico and boarded the yacht there. Then their plan, as outlined by our chart here, was to spend the next three weeks sailing from island to island, stopping every other day or so to come into port, get supplies, swim on the beach or travel the tourist areas. Many of the islands have designated beaches, charming tourist towns, and truly stunning scenery. Their plan was loosely drawn—Fred made that clear—and the captain was well-known in Felix's circles for taking the more moneyed set around and showing them a good time. He knew the safe places, the clubs for the younger bunch, the shops and entertainment for the less young, and after a little bit of follow-up, I gathered he was generally competent, genial, and he enjoyed his job very much. Their guide, in fact, was his wife—both of them had been born in Puerto Rico, educated in the US, and were happy to blend their love of their homeland and a life at sea with a thriving business enterprise. They appeared to be on the up-and-up—and if so, their loss, and the loss of the entire crew, in fact, was a tragedy as well."

"So what happened?" Chuck asked after a digestive silence.

"There are two stories about that," Danny said, and he pulled up the map of the Caribbean again, this time with a clearly marked path. "The first story is the route they *intended* to take. They left from San Juan, with the plan of sailing along the archipelago, hitting the islands at will, and ending up at Port of Spain, where they planned to spend three days in a hotel room, getting their land legs back, I assume, before flying back to Chicago. But two things happened that got in the way."

"The first was a hurricane, right?" Stirling asked, shuddering.

"That gave us some bad moments on our trip," Molly said. "I mean, you know. Before our lives ended."

"It was indeed," Danny said. "It was a small one—more of a tropical storm, really, but as you know, it resulted in them getting blown off course. They were quite close to Santa Lucia when the storm hit and planning to put into port there, but the storm hit early, and they were pushed down toward Barbados, which they'd been planning to visit, but, well, they arrived early."

"That shouldn't have been a problem," Molly said. "We've got property in Barbados, right? Some sort of sugar plantation that Fred bought on a whim?"

"Yes, actually," Danny said. "And while the plantation is technically on Barbados, it is more accurately on a teeny tiny plantation-sized island a rabbit's spit away from Barbados proper. Seriously. I could swim to it. It's that close."

"You once swam the English Channel with a waterproof tube strapped to your back," Felix said, sounding bored. "I'm not impressed with your rabbit. Or your lizard. Or any other creature that's trying to spit its way to an island off the coast of Barbados."

"You exaggerate," Danny muttered. "And you ruined a good metaphor, so hush."

Stirling remembered Tienne's story earlier, the one everybody in the room was still processing, about how Danny had left a dangerous, powerful man on the spot in order to throw in his lot with the people the gangster was planning to kill. He met Josh's eyes, and Josh nodded.

"Oh yeah, he totally swam the English Channel," he said softly.

"I have no doubts," Tienne added, practically underneath his breath. But he *did* say it, and it was so much a part of their banter that Stirling wasn't the only one who caught his eye and smiled.

Stirling was the only one to get a shy smile back, though, so that was something.

"So what was the metaphor *about*," Molly prompted impatiently. "They ended up on—well, I guess Fred bought an island, so that's pretty cool—"

"Not an island," Felix said. "A *plantation*, which he said was an investment, bought with his and Stirling's ill-gotten sports-betting gains."

Stirling found his heart squeezing all over again. "I had no idea," he said, wanting to rub his chest.

Then Felix hit him with the power shot. "They named it Stirling Molly," he said softly. "I know Harve made the will-reading sort of a disaster, and you and Molly left and let your lawyer handle it all, but apparently it's still feeding money into your trust. It's one of the many interests Fred and Stella left exclusively to you."

Stirling felt more than heard Molly's sharp intake of breath. "I…. Mr. Mallard never told us that," she whispered.

"Well, I wouldn't have known myself," Felix told them. "But when I contacted the charter service to see *exactly* where they'd gone before the captain called Mayday and the wreckage and bodies were found, I was told they'd gone to the Stirling Molly plantation, and, well, a little more poking and you can see for yourself."

The next photo was of a long, sun-bleached driveway through dauntingly tall fields of cane. The picture was taken from the air, and the archway in front of the drive was clearly visible. Made of wrought iron lacework, it spelled out Stirling Molly. Beyond the drive, in the distance, was a white plantation-style home, two stories, with graceful columns rising up to support a beautiful balcony.

"Oh, my word," Molly murmured. "That *looks* amazing. People *live* there?"

"Mm…," Felix said. "That's one of the things we're having difficulty sussing out. And remember, this picture was taken two years ago, before Fred and Stella made the trip. Now I called your lawyer, Chester Mallard, and he told me a few things you should know."

"Why didn't he tell *us*?" Molly demanded. "Stirling, did *you* know we've been making money from a sugar plantation for the last two years?"

"No," Stirling replied shortly. "Because I did what you did and left Harve in the room to bicker with the lawyers so we could…." God, it had been the best moment of the whole awful affair.

"Go to the Art Institute and then go for pizza," Molly remembered, squeezing his hand. "But you would think Chester would have said something to us in the last two years."

They had monthly meetings with Chester, during which the older man kept them abreast of their finances—how much their jobs brought in, how much their trust fund paid to supplement that money, and how much Fred's prudent investments had added to their trust funds. Chester was a very sweet man with a passel of grandkids, who liked to keep track of how Stirling and Molly were actually *doing*, not only how they were spending their money. (Not enough, according to Chester, who was often very amused by the fact that their trust grew bigger instead of smaller. He said it was unnatural that two young people should be so prudent with money.) He had also, Stirling and Molly had deduced, kept them shielded from much of Harve and Carolyn's venom. Harve had been furious that they'd gotten their own trusts. He'd contested the will hotly, but the document itself stated that Fred and Stella had loved their two adopted children very much, and if they couldn't be there to see them continue their journey into adulthood, they wanted to provide every opportunity they could.

Stirling wasn't great with irony, but Molly had frequently said that the *true* irony of that statement was they would have given up any claim to the will if only they could have Fred and Stella back in their lives, while Harve, who had known Fred and Stella's love into his forties, would have cheerfully killed them ten years earlier if he'd known he could get his hands on more of their money.

Neither of them said it wasn't fair, though. They'd both known too much awfulness in foster care to piss on the good fortune that had brought them into Fred and Stella's lives, however briefly.

"Well," Felix said now, "the reason Mr. Mallard didn't bring this to your attention is twofold." He sighed. "The first reason is because the proceeds from the island are, frankly, rather suspect. Danny and I did production numbers several times, and the money coming off of the Stirling Molly plantation in no way resembles how much money an actual sugar plantation should make."

"Too high or too low?" Stirling asked.

"Too *regular*," Felix enunciated. "Sugar, like any other product that is farmed, has great fluctuation in production, depending on the weather, the harvest, or the going rate for the thing being sold. Labor, processing; all of it adds up to a crapshoot. While this was a fun investment for Fred and Stella to make—and I get the feeling it was to be sort of a graduation gift, something for Fred and Stirling to play with regarding the cost of sugarcane futures while Stella and Molly went shopping in St. Barts—it was not supposed to be substantive in any way. I think he wanted a home in the Caribbean and a place to play king of the castle, but mostly he left it to his manager, Lincoln Cawthorne, who is, as far as I know, still in charge of the place. So imagine my surprise—and, I would wager, Fred's—when he got steady, beefy, but not spectacular checks from the Stirling Molly sugar plantation. Which leads us to the second variation of their schedule."

"They decided to check it out," Molly said, because she wasn't stupid.

"We think that was on their itinerary, anyway," Josh told her, and when everybody looked to him, he gave a tired smile. "Yes, I'm still alive, and yes, I *did* help with this." He managed a haughty look. "It's my present too. Anyway, the stop at Barbados was planned, and the plantation island is only about an hour away by boat. There was an extra day planned before Fred and Stella moved from Barbados to Venezuela, and while they didn't have to reserve a berth, it's only fair to assume they'd called in to the plantation to say they'd be there. The rub here is that the storm blew them off course, and we *think* they arrived at Barbados *early*."

Stirling caught the emphasis on *think*. "Did you check it out?"

Josh made a *tsk*ing sound. "Now see, that's one of the many places where we need your help."

"We contacted port authorities," Danny said, "but there was a big turnover in personnel two years ago, and…." He sucked air in through his teeth. "I don't like to make assumptions about people over the phone. However…."

"The harbormaster is as crooked as a lightning-struck snake," Leon supplied. When everybody looked at him in surprise, he grinned and waved. "I'm sure Danny would have said something far more diplomatic, but remember, I'm in imports and exports." He gave a toothy grin. "Mostly legal now, but you can bet I can spot a crooked harbormaster when I bribe one."

"Did you bribe this one?" Chuck asked in fascination.

Leon scowled. "Sadly, this particular harbormaster is either getting paid more than I offered, or threatened more than I wanted to do over the phone." He shrugged. "I find that threats are far more effective when one is in person." His gaze traveled amiably from Chuck to Hunter, with a little wink to Carl. "Accompanied by the *right* person, of course."

"Why are you the right person?" Michael asked. Stirling noticed that the smaller man was sitting practically in Carl's lap. Carl *appeared* unaffected, as massive and docile as the family Rottweiler, but Stirling had seen the two men worried out of their minds for each other, and he was relatively certain that Carl was soaking in that proximity like the Rottweiler would soak up sunshine through a window.

"I have no idea," Carl replied blandly, at the same time Grace said, "Because his shoulders are as wide as a barn!"

"Well, yeah," Michael said seriously, "but he's our least likely bruiser!"

There was a polite silence.

"Michael?" Hunter said gently.

"Yessir?"

"I once watched Carl beat the holy shit out of an abusive redneck who tried to ambush him. Please believe me when I tell you Carl is plenty intimidating."

Stirling caught Carl's narrow-eyed glare over Michael's head, aimed at Hunter.

"I knew about that," Michael said defensively. "I'm saying—he doesn't *look* like an enforcer."

Carl smiled beatifically at his boyfriend, and Stirling had to agree. He looked *besotted* but not dangerous.

"I'm an art-theft investigator," Carl said earnestly. "It's not that exciting."

Michael cackled and grinned back, and Leon cleared his throat.

"Now that we know Carl is intimidating in many ways, we should move on." After a general sound of assent from the rest of the room, Leon did. "So yes, Danny and Felix called me in to deal with the harbormaster and to flex my knowledge of crooked importing and exporting a bit. Sadly, my muscles were not impressive enough to do things over the phone, so I asked if I could be part of doing them in person."

Josh, Felix, and Danny all made suspicious sounds, and when Stirling looked at Josh, he waggled his eyebrows. Oh yes. Leon had fallen hard for the inimitable Julia Dormer-Salinger during their last adventure, and he'd obviously use the opportunity to get a bit closer this time around.

"So we don't know, *really*, if and when my parents were in Barbados," Stirling said to get the narrative back on track.

"We're pretty sure on the if," Felix said sagely, "but not full up on the when. And that's a problem. Also—next slide, Danny—so is this."

"What's that?" Molly asked, squinting at the aerial shot of… nothing. It was, apparently, pixilated beyond belief.

"That," Danny said grimly, "is every satellite shot we can get from British satellites on that tiny particle of land. Barbados? Shots aplenty. US Virgin Islands? We can see who's fucking whom and for how long— and let me tell you, there are a *lot* of scarlet derrieres on some of those sandy beaches. Martinique? Puerto Rico? A squirrel can't break wind without a tiny photonegative puff of wind appearing on film somewhere. But that tiny ten-square-mile bit of sand? Not a clue. Nothing. It is absent of light. We've got Liam Craig of Interpol following the money and electronic trail on that end, trying to figure out why six billion satellites skip that flyspeck on the map, but in the meantime, the only way we're going to know is to look for ourselves."

"So," Molly said slowly, "I know their ship washed ashore in Barbados—at least that's what the port authorities and Coast Guard told us. They told us that the storm had taken the boat out, but Stirling and I had both gotten texts that said the storm had passed, they were fine, and they were making a course correction and continuing on. We tried to show the authorities that, but…." She made a frustrated sound, and Stirling well remembered the way the French and American Coast Guard authorities had blown the two of them off. Spoiled rich kids, off on a European tour, what would they know about sailing?

They hadn't—not a thing, really—but Stirling knew lots about Fred and Stella, and they wouldn't have texted that they were okay if they'd thought they'd been in any danger.

"The authorities were useless," Stirling grunted. "But now we know they were making a stop here, at this cute little island, but they were three or four days earlier than they'd planned to be. We don't know if they checked in at Barbados, but their wreckage...." He scowled. "Danny, do we have a map of where their wreckage showed up in relationship to the—oh."

Of course Danny had a map. The beach where the wreckage had been spotted was on the point of the island absolutely closest to where the tiny island sat.

"Oh indeed," Danny told him. "And you're right. The authorities who reported the wreck to you and Molly were *not* open to reopening the case. In fact, Fox and I are paying them a visit in the next week—"

"And Grace," Josh said adamantly.

Grace sat up from his position on Josh's lap. "Really?" he asked, practically transported.

"You've been my emotional support animal for six months," Josh said fondly, leaning his head on Grace's shoulder and settling in. "*I* may not be up to ops yet, but I think you've earned yourself a little B and E, don't you?"

"Please?" Grace begged, holding his hands together in supplication toward Danny and Felix. "Please please please please please?"

"Oh," Danny said, sounding a little disappointed. "I… uhm, you know—"

Felix cleared his throat and arched an eyebrow. "Danny, *Benjamin Morgan* has the in-person appointment with them. I'm afraid you have to show." Benjamin Morgan was Danny's "legitimate" identity, the one he'd cemented by taking a job as an art curator at the Art Institute. While the rest of the world knew Lightfingers the art thief, Chicago knew Benjamin Morgan,

Felix Salinger's significant other and occasional guest on a Chicago-based television show that covered local cultural and entertainment events.

In short, Danny "Lightfingers" Mitchell couldn't be caught breaking into the records room at the local port and travel authority office while Benjamin Morgan was supposed to be in a meeting with the office that had been responsible for contacting Molly and Stirling about the loss of their parents in international waters. It was Grace's job to be the thief.

"Josh and I will be backup, though," Stirling said, almost without thinking. Then he swore softly to himself. "And dammit, I have Christmas shopping to do!"

"If you give me your list, Stirling, I can make sure it gets done," Julia said kindly.

Stirling shot her a hunted look. "No," he squeaked, remembering that he'd been going to take Molly to help him pick out a scarf for Julia. "That's fine."

She laughed softly. "I like blue," she said, "but I adore lilac. And you know I like art."

He caught his breath, having an enormous and perfect flash of inspiration. "Of course!" he said. "Whew. Thanks, Julia!"

She laughed and nodded. "Now that we have *that* settled, there is more."

They all turned toward her. "As I said, we've"— she gave Leon an arch look—"*procured* a yacht. Now, I know that Michael will be disappearing shortly to go visit his family. He'll return a few days after Christmas, and we'll be leaving on January second. Molly, Stirling, I've had Josh check with your theater company, and they've assured me that you have a full month before they start auditioning and preparing for their next production. After Danny and Felix—and Grace!—check in with the port authority liaison office, we should have enough information to travel down to the islands to do a little poking around ourselves. Keep in mind, we don't want to appear too nosy, so we'll be forced to do a little bit of touring and shopping and beach hopping ourselves." She flashed a charming smile. "I do hope that's not too awful for you all."

"Three weeks in the sun?" Chuck said, sounding horrified. "Oh dear Lord, the zinc oxide might kill me!"

Stirling gave him a complacent look, because Chuck's auburn-haired, green-eyed good looks did have their drawbacks.

Molly chuckled. "You and me both. I'll bring the sun hats and the super-gentle SPF 75, you bring the air conditioning."

Talia, who had sat with big eyes through much of the discussion, smacked Molly lightly on the arm. "I'll bring the *bikinis*." She sobered. "Also the hair products, because our hair? In the Caribbean? Without the right product, it's—"

Molly shuddered. "You're a good friend," she said sincerely. "I never would have thought of that, but absolutely."

"Will that be okay, Stirling?" Danny asked, lowering his voice to keep Stirling from being the center of attention.

"Yes," Stirling said softly. "But Danny, why do we need Tienne?" He sent Tienne an apologetic look, but Michael had Tienne's attention, talking a mile a minute about how he'd never known where being an auto mechanic would take him. "I can see how we'd need Carl and Hunter and Grace—everybody, really, but—"

Danny nodded, and gave a very gentle smile. "Besides forging papers for those of us who can't get them legitimately? Look around you, Stirling. With this bunch, that's a full-time job!"

Stirling nodded but also smiled a bit, because he suspected Danny meant it as a joke. So many of them—Chuck, Hunter, Josh, even Leon and Danny himself had need of forged documents from time to time, but he had the feeling Danny was hiding something. Stirling wasn't great at reading facial cues or social lies, but he knew Danny's little wink was meant to reassure him of something. Perhaps that his motives were benign, which was something Stirling could believe.

Danny sobered and then pitched his voice for the entire room. "But that does remind me," he said, "I realize Christmas is fast approaching, and as Stirling pointed out, some of us are still in the throes of gift-giving and shopping. As exciting as this new adventure will be, we have to keep a couple of things in mind."

He waited until all eyes were on him. "The first is that Stirling and Molly are our best source of information, but they're also having Christmas. Try to wait until the twenty-seventh to mine their brains, yes?"

Everybody nodded, and Stirling felt a moment of relief. Some people, he thought wretchedly, could both Christmas and crime at the same time, but he knew *he* couldn't.

"The second," Danny continued, "is that we are *still* on the lookout for Levka Dubov. In fact, I think we need another strategy meeting—tomorrow morning, perhaps?—to cover Levka and to plan our quiet assault on the port authority liaison. Felix and I are meeting them the day after tomorrow, and I think we can get

a lot done. In the meantime, I want to ask Stirling and
Molly a couple of questions, and we can all ponder the
answers when we break."

Again, there was that sound of assent, and Danny
turned to the two of them.

"Okay, children—and Stirling, this is why I asked
you to get your laptop. I want you to think about the
answers here. We've told you that the income from the
sugar plantation was regular, and not in a natural way.
Stirling, Molly, would Fred and Stella have approved
of anything below board? Something off the books that
might account for that?"

"Absolutely not," said Molly staunchly.

Stirling grimaced. "Gambling, Molly," he said
softly. "Remember? That's how Fred made enough
money to buy the island."

She grunted. "Oh. Okay. Well, then, maybe?"

Danny nodded. "Stirling, I've sent you the receipts
for the money that gets sent to your trust fund, along
with the other places it gets sorted into. Take a look at
that as the room dissolves into who's getting what for
Christmas and see if anything there looks familiar."

"Okay, Danny," Stirling said, glad for something
familiar to do.

"The other thing I want you to think about is this,"
Danny said. "Who would stand to benefit from—"

"Harve and Carolyn," Molly said without a moment's thought.

"Well, yes," Danny admitted. "We're looking into
them. Harve has substantial gambling debts that are
highly suspicious. Is there anybody else?"

Stirling and Molly met eyes, and while Molly appeared a little blank, Stirling had some ideas.

"I'll send you some leads," he said softly, and when Molly looked at him, surprised, he let out a breath.

"People were always asking Fred to invest his money," Stirling told her. "Sometimes, when it was just Fred and me, he'd have me look into their financials, and he showed me how to analyze the data to see if it was a good bet. He, uhm, turned down a couple of people. Some of them from this neighborhood, in fact. Harve's friends." He glanced at Danny, who was nodding perceptively. "It would be good to take a look."

"It would indeed, young Stirling. Felix and I will poke and prod that way as well. I mean, as whimsical as it was that Fred bought himself an island, it's also not something in the mainstream. So yes, let's take a look at what your father's money was doing and who was doing it, as well as what your brother's money is doing and how it's doing that as well." His speculative look abruptly shifted. "You and Molly—it won't be too rough to investigate Harve and Carolyn, will it?"

Stirling shook his head and gave a smile that felt very predatory.

"The day after the will reading, Molly had me hack into all their utility billing systems and get all their power cut off and their cars repossessed and their water cut off and their staff let go with big severance checks and—"

Danny's robust, hearty laughter was a balm to his soul.

"Oh, you two—I do wish I'd been here to see you grow up."

Stirling regarded him with troubled eyes. "That would have been kind," he said. "But I think Tienne needed you more."

Danny sucked in air through the small gap in his teeth. "Tienne needed a full-time family," he said sadly. "Which is why I sent him to the States with Fox. I know Julia and Felix tried hard to make him feel included, but…." Danny bit his lip again and studied the young man, who was now fielding questions—probably about Dubov—from Chuck and Hunter. "You must understand," he said after a moment, his voice dropping, "I wasn't even sober at the time I met Tienne. I had to spend a good two months drying out, and then another year or so making sure it stuck. Tienne didn't need to be carted through Europe by another man who didn't know where his next meal was coming from." He grimaced and looked away, and Stirling realized that Danny still carried a weight from this. A sadness. "I was a mess, Stirling. It's hard to care for someone when you're a mess. Fox and Julia—they had the home, the connections. They could make sure he was safe."

Stirling nodded, chewing his lip in thought. "My mother," he said after a moment. "My real mother. She… she left me in a church one night, because she couldn't feed me anymore and we didn't have a place to sleep. It must have been hard for her, but I always thought she'd taken the easy way out. I was wrong, wasn't I?"

Danny nodded, his eyes overbright. "She made a terrible sacrifice based on hope, my boy. But you are more than worthy. I can only say I'm particularly glad that you and your sister ended up with people like Fred and Stella, and then here. I wish…." He glanced at Tienne again. "I wish there was such a place for everybody."

Stirling nodded and then yawned. Danny laughed and cleared his throat meaningfully at Felix. Felix, using that booming voice and presence of his, called a halt to all work, insisting that they eat the dessert Phyllis was ready to bring down to them and then call it a night.

Grown-ups at the Party

FELIX WAS usually pretty canny about when to break up a group meeting, and Danny respected that about him. It must have come from the many years of running a boardroom, a thing he had learned by doing, and as painful as that period of their life had been, Danny still remembered feeding Felix information through an earpiece when Felix was making presentations to the board of the cable network that he ran for Hiram Dormer, Julia's father. Nobody had ever suspected that Felix's diplomas had been forged and he and Danny had given themselves a crash course in business law in order to run the companies in such a way that the three of them—Danny, Felix, and Julia—could be financially independent and free of Julia's monstrous father as much as possible.

It had been hard, hiding in those years—hiding had been the thing that had driven Danny to drink and had eventually driven them apart—but nobody could argue that the results had been fairly spectacular. Felix had built up the three struggling stations into a formidable network, and he had learned the stock market in the same way, building their fortunes to the point that they were all independently wealthy, including Josh.

But money had never been the object of their endeavors.

Even when Danny was dying by degrees, he hadn't begged Felix to quit being a master of the universe; he knew why Felix was doing it.

Safety. God, Julia's father had been frightening. Making sure Hiram Dormer *never* had cause to suspect that he'd been taken by two con men whose biggest con had been spiriting his daughter and grandson out of his reach had been the thing that had driven them both.

Eventually it had driven them both apart, but more recently, it had brought them both back together.

But Danny had committed a fair number of deeds and misdeeds while he and Fox had been apart, and he was afraid one of them was coming back now to roost. He'd so hoped to spare Felix and Julia the extent of the horror of his run-in with Kadjic.

Felix and Julia found him in his office/bedroom suite, where he kept a desk and a bed for nights when he had to work late and didn't want to disturb Fox.

"What are you doing here?" he asked, surprised enough to ask a stupid question.

"We have a full house, Danny," Julia said grimly. "You can take your laptop, but I'm afraid we need to put Leon up in here."

Danny and Felix met eyes, in this matter perfectly simpatico.

"And why wouldn't you put Leon up in *your* suite of rooms?" Danny asked bluntly.

Julia's high color made it perfectly obvious it wasn't a frivolous question.

"Leon and I haven't, uhm, achieved that level of intimacy quite yet," she said with delicate inflection, and Danny knew his eyes weren't the only ones that almost bugged out of his head.

"The two of you had two weeks in one of the most romantic bed-and-breakfasts in the country," Felix said, and for a moment, a hint of the young surfer boy who'd gotten lost in Rome could be heard in his tone. "What the hell, Julia! You've always had better game than me. What are you waiting for?"

She scowled and closed the door behind her. "He's Josh's uncle," she said, sounding uncharacteristically uncertain. "I mean… I slept with his brother a thousand years ago. Doesn't that make us related?"

And again, Felix and Danny exchanged glances, but this time their emotions were more on the helpless side.

"I have no idea," Felix said. Then he shook his head. "No. That's ridiculous. And you're right. You and Josh's father had a lovely moment a thousand years ago, but that doesn't mean you can't have a relationship with Leon *now*. I'm pretty sure there are situation comedies and romance books based on this exact dilemma."

Danny grinned at him, feeling some relief. Perhaps… perhaps that uncomfortable topic they'd been broaching before they'd needed to go downstairs might be tabled.

"And I don't know what *you're* smiling about," Julia snapped at him. "Do you think we've forgotten?"

Danny's grin turned off like a spigot.

"Look, you two," he said with a sigh, "there's nothing we can do about that other thing, speaking of a thousand years ago. A thousand years ago in an alleyway, I did something stupid, and it was still too late—"

He remembered. He'd thought he'd been drunk enough to erase everything—that had been what he'd been aiming for anyway. Missing Felix, missing Josh and Julia, falling into Kadjic's bed had been the act of a man who'd been desperate to prove he didn't care anymore. About anything. And never would again.

And then he realized who and what Kadjic really was in that one instant when he'd seen the man was going to kill a father and his son in a back alley, and not spare a moment's thought about it either.

He'd looked at Tienne—thin, lanky, blond, and pretty in a very European way—and for a moment he'd seen another boy, his, Felix's, and Julia's boy, and he'd been willing to die to save him.

"You almost *died*!" Julia burst out, tears in her voice. "My God, Danny, you sent that boy to us scared and broken, and we had no idea, *none*, what he'd been through. Not once in nearly ten years has Tienne told us how he came to know you, or why he was so very loyal, and…. God. I know you were mad at Felix, but couldn't you have told *me*?"

"Thanks, darling," Felix muttered, dripping irony.

She glared at him. "It's only the truth. You and I were killing him, but instead of taking it out on *me*, he took it out on *you*, and as grateful as I am that he's not mad at me, I could *kill* him for not confiding in me back then."

Danny gazed at her fondly. "How could I be mad at you?" he asked, holding out his arms. "You were doing the best you could, lovey. What happened with Fox and me wasn't your fault."

She hit him with the force of a gale wind, burying herself in his arms and sobbing, and while he had no doubt most of this was for him, in retroactive panic and a little anger, it was true, he also knew that some of this had everything to do with why she was putting Leon up in the office instead of the spare bedroom in her suite, which occupied the top floor of the east wing of the house.

Julia's father had been an abusive, terrifying, monstrous cancer of the known world—and he'd had nineteen years to bully, browbeat, and batter his daughter as she grew into a woman. That her compassion and vulnerability had survived was a testament to her strength, but that sort of thing left scars. The safety the three of them had forged when Josh had been young had been a precious thing, but it had also been fragile. All three of them had known that one wrong move, one wrong breath, one wrong name in the wrong ear, could bring Hiram Dormer banging down their door, ready to take Josh away and inflict his monstrousness on their most beloved child.

Julia had entertained lovers in the past twenty years, discreetly of course, but Danny was relatively certain not one of them had come anywhere near their inner sanctum of three, not even after Hiram Dormer was dead and scattered to the four winds. (He'd left painstaking instructions to have his ashes entombed at a local celebrity graveyard, which Julia had done. One of the few times Danny had contacted her after his split with Felix had been to tell her he'd stolen the ashes from the case and dumped them on a landfill. She'd been so grateful, she'd cried.)

Her heart had been given to her son, and Danny and Felix were her family. Those three people would never betray her, and she would *never* betray them.

The fact that Leon had entered their sphere knowing exactly who all of them were had unforeseen benefits in a relationship—but not necessarily benefits Julia was ready to deal with.

She couldn't keep him at a distance in the name of protecting Josh, Danny, and Felix. She had to determine, for better or worse, if she was ready to be close to somebody who knew that the rich and gracious socialite was actually a skilled con woman and, at times, an unrepentant thief.

Someone who knew who her father had been and who had dealt with a similar animal on his own.

Somebody who could, if it came to that, know exactly who he was falling in love with.

For a heart as protected as Julia's, it was a frightening proposition, to say the least.

It was so much easier to focus on Danny's near miss, on Tienne's surprising origins and their concerns for his well-being, than it was to think about the terrifying vulnerability of her tender heart.

"Julia, love," he said after a moment, "I'm here. I'm safe. It was a long time in the past. And I have to say that the only reason I told you is because of what I suspect about this Levka Dubov."

Felix sucked in a breath. "And that is why *I'm* mad. Don't you think we should have known that Kadjic might be looking for this boy? That Dubov might be one of Kadjic's contacts?"

Danny rolled his eyes but refused to look at him. "Fox, would it have made any difference in how you treated the boy?"

Felix made a sound of exasperation. "Of course it would have. You'd saved this boy's life. I would have *made* him stay with us. I would have tracked Kadjic down and—"

"And done what?" Danny asked, finally looking his Fox in the face. "Started a gang war that would have put you and Julia in his sights? Given away Tienne's location?" He let out a delicate snort. "Come to find me when I was still in detox? Because yes, that's how I wanted you to see me." He shook his head. "No, I sent that boy to the best place I could think of—the kindest, most protective arms in the world. And I think if Levka Dubov has any connections to Kadjic, his meeting up with Tienne is probably purely accidental. But we need to be aware. If we're sending Hunter, Chuck, and Carl into the streets to track down Dubov, we need to tell everybody about Kadjic and why he's so damned dangerous. We don't want him to know our names."

"What about Benjamin Morgan's name?" Felix asked brutally. "Because your face hasn't changed overmuch—"

Danny winked at him. "He thinks I'm dead, Fox. Both a doctor and an Interpol agent told him I'd died in that alleyway. My murder is one of the crimes they want him for. I am, for the most part, safe. But if they put Tienne's alias, Bertrand Lautrec, art student, together with Antoine Couvier, art forger, we're going to find ourselves in the middle of a gang war, and that's no place I ever wanted to lead us. So that's why I told you." He let out a breath against Julia's temple, and she resumed her death grip around his waist. "Not to hurt you both all over again."

She shook her head against him, and he didn't let go. Seeing Tienne this last week, the large blue eyes and the terrible shyness, had torn open the wound of not being there and made it fresh. He'd had very small windows in which to build a relationship with the boy and had hoped, instead, that Felix would fill the void. But as good a man as Felix was, his propensity for being larger than life had obviously intimidated the boy, although that wasn't hard to do. Tienne had been damaged long before the two of them had come into his life, and it would take more than a pleasant week or two to help him see that family had been there for the taking all along.

"We should invite him tomorrow," Felix said unexpectedly into the healing quiet. Danny looked over Julia's head and had a sudden shaft of longing to throw himself into Felix's arms the same way Julia was throwing herself into Danny's. Ten years. They'd been apart for ten years, and Danny's longing hadn't lessened one iota from the day he'd left, drunk and broken, to the day he'd reluctantly returned, knowing that all Felix had needed to do was crook his little finger and Danny would be ripe for the taking.

Felix had done more than crook his little finger. He'd presented a full-court press of contrition, regret, and longing, and Danny had consigned pride to the devil and taken love for himself.

"Of course," Danny murmured. "I'll knock on his door myself."

With a sigh, he pulled back from Julia. "Julia, my darling?"

Julia sniffled and hid her face. Danny cupped it and gave Felix the evil eye until he ventured over to loom solidly beside them.

"Julia," Danny said softly once more. "Love, look at me."

She did, and he read the truth in her eyes that he'd suspected. "Don't push me into this," she said, lower lip thrust out mutinously.

"Of course not," Danny agreed, kissing her forehead. "We'd never dream of it. Your love life has always been your business." He let out a breath. "Or it would have been, if you'd ever had one."

She smacked him on the arm, and he chuckled.

"Maybe I'm not ready," she said with a regal look down her pert Grace Kelly nose.

"And maybe you are," Felix murmured, pulling them both a little closer. "This one knows all your secrets, doesn't he?"

She sighed and said the inevitable. "Yes."

"Has it occurred to you," Felix inquired, "that this is a good thing?"

She gave him a miserable look that spoke volumes. "But it will change *everything*!"

Danny laughed, earning himself an unhappy look from both of them. "I was gone for ten years, darling. I came back and we were the same. But better, because now we all knew how much we meant to each other. You and I had forged a friendship tighter than most siblings, and we never knew we'd miss it until it was gone. You and Fox did the same over the years, and once I returned, we were tighter than ever. Do you think we won't still gather together and 'do crime,' as the kids say? Do you think Felix and I will no longer be available to you? Your wing in the mansion is most definitely your wing. I don't know about Felix, but I have no plans to move. I've finally found my roots."

"We only finished the gym last year," Felix said, sounding stuffy and dear.

"Yes, Leon has ties to other places—you may accompany him or you may stay here. But this will always be your home."

She sniffled. "He may be awful in bed. You know that. All this angst and we may be totally incompatible."

"If that man's awful in bed, Felix has a two-inch dick."

They both stared at him in horror, and he realized that, in addition to the crudeness of the statement, he'd let his real accent slip, the flat Midwestern snap he'd worked so hard to overcome when he arrived in Europe.

"As he does not," Danny added composedly, his usual vaguely European tones suffusing his voice again.

But he didn't escape Fox's thoughtful regard. Or Julia's.

"It's still there," she said softly. "You can't escape it."

Well, she was right. He'd been the kid who'd escaped the shitty foster home, spent two years working sugar daddies on the New Jersey coast, and finally hopped a ride to Rome with the first one he'd figured wouldn't kill him and dump his body on the cruise over. He'd been the one to teach himself how to pick pockets, how to scam, how to live in a foreign country until he and Felix hooked up and he'd had the idea for the one big score—the score that would get revenge on Hiram Dormer.

Right up until they realized Julia needed rescuing from him first.

But twenty-odd years of wandering the world and working the system had not erased the street kid who'd run away from abuse and into adventure any more than it had erased that oddly unstable feeling underneath his feet whenever he thought he'd come home. It hadn't been until this fall, really, when he and Felix had stayed with Josh and given everyone else a small hiatus from the worry that had wracked them all that he'd realized how firmly his feet were planted now.

And now that Josh might be okay, he would need to flex his toes a few times to make sure they really were in fertile soil and that he could really grow.

"Perhaps," he said, flexing a little, "I should talk to Tienne tomorrow about a couple of things." He pulled back from the seriousness of the moment. "Providing we can pull him away from Stirling."

"You saw that?" Felix said, being his inimitable Fox self.

"Who could miss it?" Julia asked, pulling back as well and adjusting her sweater and hair.

"You need to fix your makeup, darling," Danny told her kindly. "There's a mirror right—"

She kissed his cheek. "I know where the mirrors are, Danny." She pulled away, wiping lipstick from his skin. "And I shouldn't keep Leon waiting."

"Should we vacate…." Felix made a delicate circle around the office with the bed, and she shook her head.

"Danny was, of course, correct. I have a guest room in my suite. He should be comfortable there."

"Give him hell, darling," Felix said softly, and she straightened her posture and made her way to the bathroom.

"I'm quite good at that," she said with a triumphant smile over her shoulder.

And she went to fix her makeup, producing a lipstick from—where? Danny was legitimately curious. She didn't carry a purse with her in the house, and who kept lipstick in their slacks pocket? Did she have a lipstick in every bathroom? How would she make sure all the shades matched?

He was well and truly down the rabbit hole when Felix moved in front of him.

"What are you thinking?" he asked.

"Where does Julia keep her makeup?"

Felix's eyes widened, and then he grinned. "She's got a couple of emergency bags in strategic bathrooms, this being one of them. Seriously, you were wondering about that?"

And Danny let out a breath and relaxed, allowing his head to rest on Felix's shoulder while Felix gathered him in.

"Long week," Felix understated.

Worry about Josh, worry about Tienne, preparations for the op, all of it had taken an emotional toll that Danny hadn't been ready to analyze until Julia had come in here and forced him to.

And Felix, of course, who had probably seen their little group hug coming a mile away.

"Our boy's in the clear now," he said, hating how his voice shook. He and Felix had put on a good show of it—and so had Josh—but the two weeks after Josh's bone marrow transplant had been… rough. Josh had been hospitalized for much of it, which was something they hadn't told anybody, even Julia. The moment everyone had left for the airport, Josh had slumped at the breakfast table and started to cry. Felix had carried him to the car, and they had gotten him admitted to the hospital for the next few days' worth of chemo, as well as IV fluids and electrolytes to keep him healthy while his body remembered how to function. When the lot of them had returned from Napa, Josh had been safely ensconced in his own bed, awaiting his next round and healing, but Danny and Felix had sworn promises to Josh that they'd never, ever tell his mother how close he'd been to falling asleep in the hospital and never waking up.

It was a terrible secret to keep, but a worthy one, and until this week, Danny had felt the same way about Tienne's advent in their lives. What had really mattered was that he'd asked Julia to give the boy a place, and she and Felix had done their best. At the time, he'd believed he'd been immaterial to Tienne's emotional well-being—a conveniently placed obstacle to the boy's death and a means to facilitate his safety, that was all. But now that he was finally coming up for air after worrying about Josh, he could see how the boy had been adrift, floating in his isolation, ready to be tossed by the tides.

If Molly and Stirling hadn't come along, Levka Dubov might have drowned the boy in a trail of slime.

And bless Josh, he was so ready to worry about somebody else. He'd been the one to take over some of the tracking duties for Levka's credit cards and forged identities and such. They all knew Stirling could have done it easily, but Stirling and Tienne seemed to have a bond. Romantic, possibly, and well and good if it was, but it wasn't necessary. If Tienne felt as though he had a person he belonged to here at the mansion, it would be easier to keep him safe from mobsters and other predators, convince him to stay, to linger, to participate.

To envelop him into their fold when he'd been a wall of passive resistance until now.

But Stirling couldn't be the only one.

"One of them," Felix corrected, practically reading his mind. "Danny, how could you *not* tell us where he came from?"

Danny went from a wise man mulling the vagaries of fate to a wretched child in less than a heartbeat. "How could I?" he asked again. "Felix, you didn't know me back then. I'd spent a month in Kadjic's bed, drinking myself to death. Before that, it was like I spent a year underwater, trying to forget about you, and when I came up for air, Tienne's father was dying in his own blood, and a bloodless thug was going after a child with a knife. I wasn't *lucky* to be alive, I was *disappointed* to be alive. Apparently, Liam Craig had been tracking Kadjic's movements for weeks as well. He got there before Kadjic would have slit my throat and is probably the only reason I'm alive. He's the one who had to go after Tienne and send him to you and Julia. I... I was a *mess*. How could I bring myself into your life again after that? How could I be anything but a ghost in his?"

"How'd he know?" Felix asked, completely derailing him.

"How'd who know what?" God, this man. Sometimes Danny wondered if he made everybody stupid or only Danny.

"How did young Mr. Craig know that Tienne needed help? You say he found you in an alleyway, prompting Kadjic to run away from him and leave you to possibly live." Felix swallowed, the lines around his mouth and eyes testifying that this was not as easy to say as he made it sound. "How did he know about the boy who'd gotten away?"

Danny squinted at him. "I told him. That's how he knew to follow the green paint. What does that mat—"

Felix's mouth on his was hot and almost desperate. Felix did what he always did—overpowered Danny's self-protection, his bluster, the defenses he'd worked his entire life to erect, and forced him to be honest.

Only Felix had known the all of him. Only Felix had cared.

"It matters," Felix muttered, tearing their mouths apart and resting his forehead against Danny's. "It matters because you were half dead and you were still taking care of that boy. Don't let time and the lack of blood stop you, Danny. He's like Josh—he still needs caring for."

Danny gulped air and nodded, feeling twenty-something instead of fortysomething. "I wanted to be there for Josh so badly," he admitted, and he tried hard not to let the ten years they'd lost ride him. "I'm so mad. I finally came home to my family, and our son was almost taken from us, and…." He couldn't say it.

"You're afraid," Felix said, voice thick. "Not the least because Tienne is so remote, so prickly. I've tried, Danny. I swear I've tried. Julia has tried, but I gather the boy's mother died when he was very young. He's in awe of her, almost tongue-tied. It's going to have to be a father, and given what I seem to do to him, it's going to have to be you."

"Of course," he said, giving up and leaning his head on Felix's shoulder. "I'll talk to him tomorrow."

"Not tonight?"

Danny smiled to himself, remembering the way Tienne and Stirling had exchanged speaking looks at nearly every critical juncture of the night's briefing.

"I can't fix what's broken overnight, Fox," Danny said, dreaming in the circle of Felix's arms. "I think we can wait until tomorrow."

Over Felix's shoulder, Danny saw Julia's little wave as she emerged from the bathroom, lipstick perfect once more, before she left the room, locking it from the inside as she went. Danny raised his face to Felix's as he lowered his mouth for a kiss, and together they tried once again to bridge the ten-year gap in their lives. Some days, it felt as though the time had never been when they hadn't been together, but some nights, such as this one, it loomed unfathomable and unbreachable between them.

Danny opened his mouth and his heart and his body for the only man he'd ever loved and allowed Felix to sweep him to a time outside time, when their separation had never been and Danny had never left the haven of the family he'd longed for so badly when he'd been away.

Good Night Kisses, Good Morning Tea

STIRLING STAYED downstairs, sitting cross-legged on the couch and staring moodily at the computer in his lap while he absentmindedly ate a chocolate mousse that made Tienne's eyes roll back in his head.

He'd always had a fondness for chocolate.

Tienne wasn't willing to go back up the stairs yet, because he knew the rest of the household would be lingering. Chuck and Lucius were always starting a game of chance, and if Grace and Hunter or Molly were about, the stakes could get increasingly high. Carl and Michael would be moving slowly as well, because Michael was leaving for a week to go visit his children and ex-wife in another state, and while Carl had felt it would be better if he remained behind this trip, apparently everyone had gifts they wanted to give Michael, and Tienne did not.

He took his place on the other end of the couch, crossing his legs as Stirling did and taking an extra mousse from the tray Phyllis had brought down when all of the postbriefing conversations had been raging. He suddenly wanted to talk about nothing in particular and decided he had a good conversational gambit to start with.

"You did not have a gift?" he asked hesitantly.

"For Michael?" Stirling said, his fingers still flying along the keyboard. "Yes. Molly and I gave him lots of things to bring his children, and we went in with Carl and everybody else to get him his own car."

Tienne blinked. "That is quite a gift!"

Stirling glanced up and sucked some more mousse off his spoon. "Yes, but see, Michael moved to the suburbs, and he's Julia and Felix's mechanic. He's been so occupied driving everybody else's cars out to the airfield to work on, he never really thought of having one of his own. Carl moved to the suburbs with him—but he was in DC before that. I guess he's rarely been in town long enough to have a vehicle. So it was a big deal. But it's not happening until tomorrow morning, when they leave for the airport, so now it's all hugs." He gave a self-conscious little smile. "I told Michael goodbye this morning. Carl knows I get overwhelmed with crowds sometimes. He squeezed my shoulder before they left. We're good."

"Oh." Well, Tienne had asked. "Do you want me to leave, then?" He hated the thought of being a burden on Stirling, although he totally got how the entire crew could be overwhelming.

"No," Stirling said softly. With a sigh he closed his laptop and took another bite—almost the last—of mousse. "You can stay. I'm sorry. Tonight was a lot. Your story, then thinking about Fred and Stella again. And the idea that we're going to see what happened to them?" He shrugged. "A lot."

"You haven't thought of going to look until now?" Tienne inquired, curious. He'd been asked to provide some of the "trappings" of Stirling and Molly's present—fake IDs for everybody!—and apparently he was going on the trip with them. It hadn't been until he'd sat in the room and seen Stirling and Molly react to the background information on their parents that he realized what a hole Fred and Stella Christopher had left in their lives. This was personal to them—and to the entire crew. And he'd been invited. In fact, he'd been invited to the celebration night for Josh as well. He was feeling out of his depth, and it was such a relief to know that he wasn't the only one.

"No," Stirling said simply. He wrapped his arms around his knees and pondered. "We were devastated at first. And then, when we realized that Fred and Stella had sort of taken care of us materially, we were busy figuring out how to be grown-ups. We were enrolling in college and then working for the theater. And we were, you know—" He flashed a sudden smile at Tienne. "—doing crime."

Tienne chuckled. "Why? That is what I don't understand. You, your sister, Josh, and Grace—three of you are gifted performers. Molly's costumes are stunning, and your stage designs are very innovative. You could all be famous in difficult professions. Why the doing crime?"

Stirling thought about it and then gave him a quirky smile. "I could say the same about your art, Tienne."

Tienne caught his breath, heat taking over his face, and he realized Stirling was right. But more importantly, *Stirling* thought he was gifted. He hadn't realized until that moment how much he'd yearned to hear praise for his own work. But Stirling wasn't done talking.

"I think… I think there was something about our backgrounds, all of us, that made us believe that the powers that be weren't always in the right. In school, it was small stuff. A guy gave me a swirlie in the ninth grade. Molly distracted me, Josh messed around with chemistry, and Grace broke into his house and slipped a depilatory in his shampoo."

Tienne laughed, enjoying the image. "Fair," he conceded.

"Yes. But it was more than that. Fred and Stella were the nicest people. They opened their home and their hearts to us, and Fred had this idea that if they were going to adopt a boy, he'd do boy things: sports, girls, that sort of thing. But they met me and realized I wasn't that sort of boy, so Fred took what he was good at—sports—and took what I was good at—computers and math—and we started gambling on the weekends. Legally, not such a great idea. But Fred didn't really need the money. The whole reason he was doing it was because *I* got so excited about doing research and making odds and placing bets." He grinned. "Math excites me. Strange but true. But the point was, we hurt nobody. I think Fred gave a lot of the winnings to charity until he decided to buy an island—" He rolled his eyes. "—and there were so many worse things we could be doing. And you… you should know this better than anybody. Your father taught you how to forge papers, but he also taught you not to hurt people. Danny, in that alleyway, he's embarrassed, I think, about being an alcoholic, about being 'a mess,' as he calls it, but none of that means he didn't do something really brave by saving your life, and then he made sure you were taken care of. I think the lot of us were drawn together by the idea that good and bad, right and wrong, none of it is really covered in the law books, you know? There's lots of stuff that's legal that's wrong and lots of stuff that's illegal that shouldn't be. And Molly and I were finding our way with all of that until Josh put us all together as a crew and said, 'Let's do crime, but let's do it as a way to make things right.'"

"So it simply wasn't time yet, to fix this particular wrong," Tienne said, understanding that, if he understood nothing else.

Twin crescents of embarrassment appeared on Stirling's cheeks. "It wasn't," he said. "But now we're getting pretty good at making things right, and… well, it's happy but…." He rubbed his chest, and Tienne understood.

"Sad too," he said.

Stirling nodded. "Like you being here."

Tienne blinked. "I? How am I sad?"

And Stirling's gray eyes grew intent on a point of space in front of him. "We are all *really* happy you're here," Stirling said, as though concentrating on that distant point of light. "But we're also sad because bad things had to happen to get you here. And because we're not sure how long you'll stay. We—all of us, I think—really want you to like it here. You don't have to live here forever, but… you know. We want you to belong."

Tienne's chest ached. "That's so kind," he said gruffly.

"But you don't want to?"

And Tienne heard it: hurt. Stirling was trying to sound neutral in this matter, but there was so much hurt in Stirling's voice. Suddenly it was imperative that he answer honestly, without holding back.

"I do," he said throat thick. "I…. The story I told you, about how Danny found me, I have told that story to nobody. But all of you have tried so hard to make me feel welcome. I felt as though telling that story would help you all see who I am. Help you all know that I trust you." He fought a burning behind his eyes. "I guess I didn't tell it very well."

Stirling let out a sigh. "Tienne, I'm tired. And I'm all out of words tonight. But the first thing you need to know is that this isn't quid pro quo. If people make you feel welcome, say thank you. Everybody here understands shyness. They understand me, they'll understand you. But if you get a chance to talk one-on-one to somebody, do it. That's all." He ventured a look at Tienne's face, and Tienne sought his gaze hungrily. "The two of us are doing okay, right?"

"Yes," Tienne said softly. "But you're special."

Stirling's smile bloomed. "I, uhm, liked our kiss today."

And suddenly Tienne's smile was in full flower as well. "Me too."

"I'm taking my laptop to my room. Would you like to kiss me at the door, like a dating couple?"

Tienne's cheeks heated, and his ears grew hot. "Very much, yes." With that he rose and stood before Stirling to hold out his hand. Stirling took it, and Tienne helped him stand, then walked him across the den to the door to his suite. For a moment they stood there, and Tienne thought for the millionth time that Stirling's gray eyes were truly mesmerizing and that his face was beautiful.

"Tomorrow," he said softly in the breathless moment before their lips touched, "we can talk again?"

"Tomorrow," Stirling replied, "we can *kiss* again."

Their lips touched, and Stirling swept his tongue inside. For a moment, they both tasted chocolate.

And then they tasted each other.

And then the kiss was over and Stirling disappeared through his door.

Tienne made his way quietly up the stairs and back to his room undetected, carried on clouds by the promise of tomorrow.

THE NEXT morning he was awakened by a hand on his shoulder, shaking him gently.

"Stirling?" he mumbled, confused. He'd had dreams. Not so much erotic dreams as dreams of sweetness. Kisses. Strokes of skin on skin. Being safe and surrounded by kindness.

"Sadly no, my boy," came a voice *not* Stirling's, and he frowned and sat up abruptly.

"Danny?" He pushed the hair out of his eyes. "Danny, what…? Is something wrong?"

"No, Tienne. Not at all."

"Aren't we meeting in—" He squinted at the clock. "—two hours?"

"Indeed." Danny sighed and scrubbed his fingers through his hair. His eyes fell on the boots and the jacket that had shown up in Tienne's room—in his sizes—without a word. "Tienne, would you take a walk with me? I'll be down in the kitchen, getting us some hot coffee. Meet me there in fifteen minutes."

"Yes, okay," he mumbled, not even surprised when Danny dodged out the door. He remembered to text Stirling to tell him why he wouldn't be meeting him to go work out, and then he got busy with winter clothes, *real* winter clothes that wouldn't leave his toes cold or his ears to turn red.

TRUE TO his word, Danny was downstairs, setting the coffee maker to brew and cadging muffins from Phyllis's morning cook.

"Oh, Marco, my boy, you are going to be a magnificent pastry chef someday," he praised. "All I ask, one little thing—"

"Chocolate sour cream muffins in an hour," Marco said with a smile. Marco had straight black hair parted in the middle and a long Italian face. Tienne thought he was very handsome, but his confidence was up-front and in-your-face, not quiet and waiting.

Stirling's quiet and waiting confidence seemed to draw Tienne like a subtle, shimmering net. It was like the paint effect of layering on white to make a painting look like there were stars underneath.

"Excellent," Danny praised. "We shall be back in time. Perchance could you—"

"Cocoa will be ready in forty-five minutes," Marco said promptly. "My pleasure, Mr. Morgan."

"The pleasure is mine." Danny executed a little bow and then pulled his gloves and scarf out of the pocket of his wool greatcoat and began to don them as he headed for the door. Tienne, who had found his old scarf and gloves in the pocket of the new coat, did the same. By the time they were walking down the deiced walkway, he'd managed to pull a plain blue stocking cap over his ears as well.

For a moment, nothing was said as they situated themselves, tucking their scarves into their coats and

making sure their gloves were tight and basically secur-
ing themselves against the frigid December air.

Tienne's steps were tentative at first—the boots
were unfamiliar—but as they walked and he realized
somebody with an eye must have sized his feet, he
developed a rhythm. After a few moments of silence,
Danny turned right onto the road that marked the end
of Salinger property and ran down the block of mansions, each one with extensive grounds and its own
quarter-mile driveway to varied and lush homes.

"Wow," Tienne breathed as they walked. "This
area—it's very wealthy."

Danny chuckled. "Yes. When Felix brought me
here and told me he and Julia had picked out the house,
I was appalled at first. All I could think of was that
we were going to be fat rich marks like the rest of the
neighborhood."

Tienne laughed, surprised. "And that didn't
happen?"

"Lord no. You may not know this, but the security
system in that mansion is better than most senators possess, and possibly the president. I won't say Fort Knox,
but that's only because I haven't had the pleasure of
breaking into it yet."

Tienne chuckled again, because Danny had always
been like this, witty and effusive. He did have a way of
making whomever he spoke to feel special.

"Yet," he said, with inflection, and Danny gave
him a broad grin.

"We won't rule anything out," he said. Then he sobered. "Although for all intents and purposes, I'm trying not to commit too many misdeeds in the immediate
environs. Felix and I would like to put down roots, and

that's hard to do when the police are breathing down your neck."

Tienne *hmm*ed. "Yes. That was something my father always said. We would find a new city, and I would ask if we were staying. He would say no, we would be too busy making money off people to worry about staying. But someday we would find a place to stay, and we would only be painters from there on out."

"It's a pretty dream," Danny said softly. "Do you think you were close?"

"Mm." Tienne shrugged. "I have no idea. Perhaps by then, my father had gotten too good at running, yes?"

"Perhaps," Danny agreed. "But perhaps not. I went back and researched the two of you. Have I told you that?"

Tienne was surprised. It had never occurred to him to research Danny "Lightfingers." "No. What did you discover?"

Danny chuckled. "Your father was one of the most in-demand forgers in Europe and Africa for quite some time. If he hadn't betrayed Kadjic, the two of you might have lived quite well, but not safely."

Tienne thought about that and nodded. "I… I don't think he worked for that man willingly. It was why he risked everything trying to alert authorities to the whereabouts of his men by sabotaging their passports."

"Indeed," Danny said, his voice kind. "He did his best for you, Etienne. It was damned hard to follow your progress through Europe, particularly because he kept you with him and tried very much to keep you in school. Antoine Couvier loved his baby boy very much."

Tienne's eyes burned. "Yes," he whispered.

"I… when I sent you here, with Felix and Julia and Josh, I was trying to do right by him," Danny continued. "I had failed him so badly—"

"How?" Tienne asked, confused. "You had no idea Kadjic would do that. I remember. You were dressed like Aladdin, ready to go to a party. You… you saw what was going to happen and you spoke up, without hesitation. You jumped on that killer's back. It's the only way I got away."

"I was so drunk," Danny confessed, the self-recrimination hard to hear. "I keep thinking, if only I hadn't been so drunk—and for so long—I could have acted faster. I could have—"

"Not been with Kadjic at all," Tienne said bluntly, because he too had played the game of what-if. "Nobody sober sleeps with a monster."

Danny's shocked laugh was almost a validation. Tienne could say funny things too.

"True," he said, letting out a breath like a long plume of smoke. The big houses on their vast lawns looked so peaceful; the snow covered everything, muting the activity that was probably starting within. The emerging sun kept the lights in the windows from standing out, and the lingering gray of dawn made everything sleepy. For that moment, Tienne and Danny were awake and alive in the world, and Tienne felt a sense of peace, a quietness to the longing that had haunted him for nine years.

Danny spoke again, but he managed to pitch his voice perfectly so as not to disturb the peace in the world. "I know what you wanted from me, Tienne," he said softly. "And I wanted to give it to you. Being a father to Josh in those years before I left, that was one of the happiest things in my life. I would have done that for you. I longed to. But at that moment, in that alleyway, I was the man who would sleep with a monster. I needed to sober up, to dry out, and to learn to be myself away from Felix again. I couldn't be that father for you, so I sent you to Felix and Julia, who were the best, most happy parents I could imagine for a boy who was raised to make both art and criminal acts, both with the same talent. Do you understand?"

Tienne swallowed. "Yes," he said, suddenly ashamed. All those times Felix and Julia had offered him a home, a sanctuary, or attempted to bring him in closer. He'd only had a picture in his head of a father and a son, but suddenly…. "You wanted them to be for me what Fred and Stella were to Stirling and Molly, didn't you?"

Danny let out a relieved sigh. They were nearing a slight rise, and together they started to put their backs into pushing up to breach the hill. "Yes," he said simply. "That's exactly what I hoped for. I could only visit you every so often, help to guide you only in letters. I wanted you to have the people I thought of as safety, and… and you didn't."

Tienne sighed. "I am still afraid of so many people," he said hesitantly. The night before had been hard. Dinner when the table was full was still hard. He could eat in an impersonal cafeteria or restaurant—and he had many times—but the isolation of eating alone in those circumstances was like being wrapped in bubble wrap and Styrofoam.

"I know," Danny said. "But you're trying. You've used the gym with the others, eaten dinner. You were at the briefing last night. I know you're trying. Do you think you could keep trying? Levka Dubov is still on the loose, and he may have ties to Kadjic."

Tienne sucked in a suddenly terrified breath. "Does he… will he…?"

"No, no." Danny patted his shoulder. "No, Kadjic doesn't know yet. And why would he? I don't think he ever knew your name, and your school alias still stands. But I'm saying that going back to the city and holing up in an apartment isn't the best thing for you right now. And Julia had planned to invite you to the Caribbean all along. You had a first-class seat on that boat—"

"Yacht," Tienne corrected shyly.

Danny chortled. "By God *yes*, that *yacht*. You've had a first-class ticket there since we came up with the plan. You seem to be getting along with Stirling."

Tienne turned his face away, not sure he wanted Danny to see.

"It's fine," Danny said softly. "You two are well suited, I think. Stirling isn't shy, but he is very particular about how many people he can deal with and how. You *are* very shy, and he'll protect you. You're both uniquely suited to keep each other from being lonely, and I find it lovely. But open yourself up a little. Julia, Felix, and Josh—they've been here, trying to be family for you like they were to Grace. Let them do that for you. I'm here now. Let *me* do that for you. Nine years ago, I sent you to safety and hoped you'd take shelter there. You stayed safe, but you have never, ever found shelter. Let me give you that final push so you can find a home."

As he spoke, the two of them breached the crest of the hill, and Tienne caught his breath. The sun was on the other side, ready to pour thin winter rays over their upturned faces.

He closed his eyes and pointed his face to the sun, registering Danny's arm around his shoulder by tilting his head to rest against Danny's.

"Yes," he said, his heart full at that moment. He was wearing a coat and boots chosen especially for him. He'd been fed, nurtured, and included for the past two weeks, and he could no longer turn down the banquet that was offered. "Yes," he said again. "Okay. Yes."

"Good," Danny murmured, kissing him on the top of the head, much like Tienne's father had when he'd been small.

When they turned away from the sun and began the walk back, Tienne's face was cold and briny, but he didn't mind one bit.

THEY WERE in the kitchen, enjoying the sublime muffins and hot chocolate, when they were joined by Chuck, Hunter, Grace, Josh, Felix, and Stirling, all of whom looked freshly showered and shaved.

"Where's Molly?" Tienne asked, curious.

"Shopping with Julia," Stirling said, sounding irritated. "She's got a list from me. She promised."

"You worry too much," Josh told him gently. "You are literally with the 'thought that counts' bunch."

Stirling glared at him. "You are *literally* giving Molly and me revenge on a silver platter. No more talking, you."

Josh laughed and bowed slightly from his stool at the kitchen table.

"What about Lucius?" Danny asked Chuck, and Chuck let out a breath.

"Well, Lucius is making sure Christmas at Caraway House is a success, and it's apparently harder than it sounds. In fact, if I wasn't so worried about Levka, I'd be down in Springfield helping him."

"What do you need?" Danny asked, before adding to Tienne, "Lucius runs several under-the-radar shelters for abused women. Carraway House is for women whose abusers are prominent and powerful. It's good work."

Chuck grunted. "What he really needs is for the women to have a way to buy their own gifts for their children. They can't shop online without tipping their husbands off to where they are. The place is supposed to be under construction, so we can't very well have everything delivered there, and if Lucius has everything delivered to his place, well, that'll raise the same red flags. Apparently last year, he hired a couple of ex-residents to help with the problem—used their new digs for an address, created false bank accounts, but with the authorities coming down on those scumbags we busted last summer, well, he's afraid of getting anyone else involved." Chuck shrugged. "It's getting down to the wire, you know?"

Danny nodded. "True. I think we have a couple of solutions, though. First of all…." He eyed Tienne, who got there first.

"Fake credit cards, big balances, lots of credit."

Danny nodded. "Indeed. And as for residences—"

"My apartment," Tienne said, and when everybody looked at him, he added, "I'm not living there at the moment. If a thousand children's toys are suddenly delivered, who will know?"

Danny laughed. "Fair. But we can split it up. My old city apartment, since Carl and Michael have moved into their house, Tienne's—"

"Mine," Hunter said, and Danny nodded.

"Fair. You are very off the radar and probably not going to stay there often so close to Christmas."

Grace made an unhappy sound, and Tienne caught a frustrated look between Grace and Hunter that led Tienne to understand Grace was hoping for some more intimate time, now that he wasn't so occupied with Josh's health.

"Mine and Molly's," Stirling said, interrupting his thoughts. "We really only use it when we're working on a show."

"Excellent," Danny agreed. "Chuck, you go text Lucius while we're here and have him send Tienne a list of the women, along with their chosen pseudonyms. They should have the credit cards…." He looked at Tienne, who made a quick calculation. He had the machines and the special computer that linked almost automatically to the balances of several major credit cards, but it took a good fifteen minutes to set up each identity.

"How many women?" he asked.

"There's ten families there now," Chuck said. "With two more that are being integrated into new lives and don't have a disposable income yet."

"I can have them done by this evening," Tienne told him. He glanced shyly at Stirling. "By after lunch if I had help."

Stirling smiled back. "As long as I can go Christmas shopping tomorrow before the job, we're on."

"Good?" Danny said, and Chuck grinned.

"You guys are the *best*. Now, Tienne, I'll hook you up with Lucius's account so you can pay off the credit cards from there—"

Tienne stared at him, nonplussed. "Why? A week after Christmas, I press a few buttons and—" He kissed his fingertips. "—voila. The debt goes away. The credit card company has given a few thousand dollars to women who need it, and your very pretty boyfriend can spend more money on his very worthy causes."

Chuck grinned. "I like you," he said. "You're a good egg."

Danny laughed softly. "You sure there will be no pushback? The women need these new identities. I'd hate to burn them because something went wrong."

Tienne gave him a hurt look, wounded a bit in his professional pride. "This is what I do," he said. "I mean, yes, I paint too, and create passports and driver's licenses, but my bread and butter is the phony credit card. I'm really very good."

"I know you are, my boy," Danny said, his eyes crinkling in the corners. "I didn't expect you to be so… I don't know… advanced. But fair enough. Now, on to other matters of business. Chuck, go on. We'll brief you when you get back."

"Will do, Danny. Tienne, Stirling, thank you!"

He disappeared as the kitchen door opened and Carl blew in, looking stolid and irritated in a very practical parka and plain blue hat.

"Did Michael get off okay?" Stirling asked.

Carl gave Stirling a smile. "Yes, but he was so excited about the vehicle, he almost cried. Everybody, that was a really wonderful surprise. You know, he's never had a new car before, and the SUV was perfect."

"How's it handle?" Hunter asked, a spark of covetousness in his eyes.

"Amazing," Carl said with a little grin. "I almost want to tell Lucius to get one for Chuck."

"Why not?" Stirling asked, and Carl grimaced.

"His insurance company may actually quit on him after that whole… you know. The Bentley thing this summer. I think maybe Chuck shouldn't be on any of Lucius's vehicle paperwork for a few. I mean, yes, he's a bazillionaire, but trust me, you don't want an insurance investigation. That's a next level of bug up your ass."

"Says an insurance investigator?" Grace asked, eyes wide.

Carl winked at him. "Which is how I know."

Everyone at the table chuckled, and they made room for Carl after he'd shed his jacket and boots and gone back to the foyer for the coatrack.

"So," Carl said, "about the port authority…." And Tienne remembered that they were going to break into the records department to look for any information that had been kept from Stirling and Molly.

Felix had brought a laptop, and he shoved it at Danny, who opened it with a murmured "Thanks."

"So here's the layout," Danny said, sending the laptop toward Stirling and Grace, who were on his other side. Tienne leaned into Stirling, who gave him a sly smile under thick lashes and moved a little to make room. Together the three of them looked at the image of blueprints on the computer screen.

"Oh," Stirling said. "Oh shit. Grace…?"

"I totally know how to scuba dive," Grace said with a shrug. "I've got the gear and everything."

Tienne frowned. The job didn't look easy. The building itself was pretty no-nonsense—a rectangular structure off one of the piers of Lake Calumet with a small reception room that opened up into an office. There were a number of conference rooms that lined the sides of the building, but the back end was obviously records storage. It had windows large enough for a man—a slender man such as Grace—to slip through, which was a blessing, but the building sat on a pier, and the records room overlooked the lake itself. In order to climb to one of those windows, Grace would have to swim a lake that was on the verge of icing over, climb a piling, then climb the back wall and find a way to get in through a window.

"But there's got to be an easier way," Josh said, squinting at him. "I mean, seriously. The office is supposed to be bustling. We dress you in gray, put a hat over your hair, they'll never remember you." Grace's hair was straight, coarse, and black, but he'd had it shot through with Christmas red, green, and blue, and even the occasional sparkle.

Grace scowled at him. "But I really want to scuba dive to the back of the pier, use pitons to scale the back, and open a window with a glass cutter. What's the harm in that?"

Josh grunted. "Hunter…," he said painedly, and Hunter leaned over Grace while gripping his shoulder.

"The harm, Grace, is that nobody should know you're there," he said reasonably. "Your way would leave a cut window in the middle of December on a lake in Chicago. Josh's way has you mingling with the crowd, looking for the bathroom, and disappearing down a hallway. Really," he added placatingly, "it's far more daring."

Grace scowled at him doubtfully. "You're just saying that."

"No, not at all," Danny said. "Hiding in plain sight is the mark of a master thief. And he's completely right about the hole in the glass. The whole world would notice that in short order."

Grace huffed out a breath. "I long for a high-rise or something."

Hunter patted his shoulder. "I know you do, baby. But it'll come."

"Fine. Whatever. I have to go Christmas shopping anyway, so this way I won't need a hot bath and heating pads for the rest of the week. I'm excited." He gave a smile that was all teeth and not sincere at all.

"You can come shopping with us in the morning," Stirling said. "We're going to the Art Institute gift shop because all the art stuff is there."

Grace looked *really* excited about that, but then Danny said, "No," with a certain amount of implacability.

"Please?" He managed to give them all a hopeful glance through his eyelashes.

"I *work* there," Danny said with a long-suffering sigh. "People will notice."

"You have tons of stuff off the floor that nobody will notice," Grace argued. "And some of it would wrap up nicely."

Danny let out a sigh and looked at Felix, who shrugged. "It's Christmas, Danny. He'll bring the items back if you ask."

"Nothing from the gift shop," Danny muttered, disgruntled. "And since we're all going together—"

"We should go separately. Stirling, Tienne, Grace, and I will take the van," Josh said, his eyes practically fever bright.

"Felix and I will be coming from work," Danny said, "so we'll have the SUV for anyone else."

"Ooh…." Stirling looked at Tienne with the same kind of excitement. "We haven't taken the van out in *forever*. It's *really* comfortable and bursting with electronics. We could monitor Grace the whole time he's in the back of the records office. I could tap into their computers and tell him where to go. Yes." He looked up at Danny and nodded. "Yes, I second that."

"I third it," Carl said. "That way, I can go into the records room too while Danny and Felix are in the meeting." He grimaced. "I've been reviewing the insurance report on the boating accident, and there's some absolutely not-kosher stuff in there. For example, there was a payout on the company's behalf to the families of the captain and crew that was not actually stipulated in the contract—"

"Who was the insurer?" Felix asked sharply.

Carl gave him a grim smile. "Not Serpentus, thank God." Carl really hated the company he worked for, which was one of the reasons he used their resources to help the Salingers with such glee. He'd thought the jig was up in September, had fully expected to be fired or to quit. It hadn't happened. He'd cut his hours to the most exclusive cases and milked those contacts for all they were worth. "No, this was Atlantic United National Enterprises—"

"AUNTIE?" Grace said, his rabbit mind going to unexpected places. "There's an insurance company with the acronym AUNTIE?"

Carl gave him a flat look. "Sure, Grace. AUNTIE the insurance agency, which happens to have one Harve Christopher on its board."

"Dun-dun-dunh!" Grace sang dramatically, and Stirling shoved him sideways until Grace fell off his stool and ended up flat on his ass on the floor, staring up at everybody like a puzzled cat.

There was a bemused silence as they all contemplated Grace in return, until Hunter helped him up tenderly, dusted off his backside, and gave him a lift him back on the stool.

"You totally had that coming," he said with gentle inflection.

"Well, yes," Grace agreed, staring at Stirling, "but it so rarely happens."

"You were being an ass," Stirling said, eyes narrowed.

"I was," Grace agreed, eyeing him warily. "If I, uhm…"

"Apologize," Hunter supplied.

"Yes, that. *Apologize* for being an ass—"

"I'm sorry I shoved you off the stool," Stirling said promptly. And then, with added sincerity, "I hope you didn't get hurt."

Grace's grin was sunny and full of a sweetness Tienne had not suspected. He was starting to realize why the family might go to such lengths to make Christmas fun for the usually unrepentant thief.

"I did not. But it was good of you to remind me that I'm trying not to be an asshole. Thank you."

Stirling let out a sigh. "Thank you for doing crime with me. Now tell me you're going to wear your earbud so Josh and I can track you through the boring government building to the file storage in the back. Carl and I can hack their computers if you can hack their file cabinets. I know it's barbaric, but oftentimes government agencies like this one don't have all their information stored on network drives."

"Well, duh." Grace rolled his eyes, becoming a charming irritant again. "That's why we're doing this, right?" He gave Stirling a shoulder bump. "Besides, this is for Fred and Stella. I won't fuck it up."

"Thanks, Grace," Stirling said, and Tienne's heart clutched at the kindness on Stirling's face. It occurred to Tienne that he had assumed this entire time that he was the only character in the group who would need any sort of accommodation. He'd spent his time with the Salingers flitting in and out, trying not to be noticed in case anybody had to put themselves out for him. But it appeared that they all had their strengths and weaknesses. They did it for each other.

In another half hour, they had a workable plan for the job the next day, and Tienne was promised by a glowing Stirling that he would get to sit in the van for the gig.

"I don't know why you're so excited about asking him," Josh said with a wry grin. "Tienne, bring a book. It gets boring in there, although odds are good we may find something for you to do if you're game."

"It's very exciting," Tienne said, meaning it. "I usually make the papers and go back to my bolt-hole."

Danny made a frustrated sound. "And speaking of…. Tienne, it would appear that Levka Dubov has done very much that. We got a line on his usual haunts, his hangouts—"

"I spent three nights last week in the *slimiest* clubs you could imagine," Hunter muttered. "I must have sent three guys to the ER for trying to pick my pocket. Like… *ew.*"

"Did he show?" Stirling asked.

"The first night," Hunter said unhappily. "And we tracked his known associates there. The next night he was gone, they were gone, and I couldn't find anybody who knew them. The good news—Josh, can we tell them?"

Josh nodded. "The good news—and I got it this morning from Nick—"

"You talked to Nick?" Grace asked, his voice deceptively mild.

"He's a friend," Josh replied, as mild. "And he's a friend who has connections in the gang task force of Chicago PD. In this case, he ran the names of the known associates by the specialist for Russian gangs, and they came back to an up-and-comer. *Not* Kadjic, by any means. This guy has roots in Serbia—Dubov is Serbian by birth—and his group is known for providing weapons to the other organizations in our area. But they're smaller, less well-organized, and a little less, well, bloodthirsty than Kadjic's people. They do business with Kadjic, though, so definitely not benign."

"How high up is Dubov?" Danny asked.

Josh held out his hand and wobbled it side to side. "Higher than the knees, lower than the heart?" he said, hazarding a guess.

Chuck's belt of laughter surprised them all. "Tienne, it appears your guy is the nutbag of crime lords. I think that means we can kick him."

"When we can *find* him," Felix added over the laughter. "Because I understand that's a problem."

"It is," Hunter said. "And Chuck, Carl, and I can spend a few more evenings on stakeout."

"No," Danny said, looking at Tienne. "If he's gone underground for now, he's either caught our scent or he's on an errand for his masters. Either way, it's too close to the holiday, and Tienne is going to be in our presence until we get back from Barbados, when we can hopefully pick this up again and see if Dubov's returned. In the meantime, Josh—"

"I'll do background on Dubov's mob," Josh said promptly. "Find out what jobs they do, what their sources are, who their leaders are."

"Right," Danny said. "Chuck and Hunter—"

"We can go back one more time and look for names of scumbags," Chuck said. "Tonight'll be our last night, and then I want a steam shower to get the smell of bad liquor out of my pores."

"Very good," Danny said. "Carl—"

"Sometime not today or tomorrow, when Tienne is going to be *very* busy," Carl said with a nod in Tienne's direction, "I'm going to pick his brains for the forgeries he made for Dubov and see what sorts of things those people may be wanted for."

"What do I get to do?" Grace asked plaintively. "I want to be Tienne's friend too!"

"You're already coming with us tomorrow morning," Josh said, smiling, "and you should bring Hunter. Before we break into the port authority, we promised Stirling we'd go shopping at the Art Institute and maybe some *actual* shopping places, and he's going to need protection disguised as friends."

Grace gave Josh a wounded look, and Tienne laughed, some of his shyness crumbling beneath the onslaught, not only of information but of synergy. Everybody here worked so well together. Tienne could only be a part of it if he tried.

"Maybe not a disguise," he said, looking at Grace tentatively. "Maybe my friends could simply come with us to keep us safe."

"That's fair," Grace said, sunny mood restored. "Which means we should probably invite Molly. Besides shopping, she's pro on any sort of bonding activity. She'll be pissed if we leave her out."

"Thanks," Stirling said, gratitude evident in his voice. "I think she has other plans with Julia tomorrow—they're doing Christmas shopping and trip shopping and—" He waved his hand vaguely. "—girl shopping. But it's good of you to remember her. I didn't want to tell her she wasn't invited."

"Molly is *always* invited," Josh said with a grin. He winked at Stirling. "The fact that I didn't crush on her was the final death knell of any heterosexuality I might have possessed."

Grace cackled. "It was a very small knell. Barely a bell. His straight phase, it fell."

There was a stunned silence.

"Thank you, Dylan," Felix said with a grimace. "It's about time for Danny and me to get to work, and I was wondering how to end this meeting. Now I know."

Danny's eyes widened. "Shit! The day job!" He jumped from the table. "I will talk to you all at dinner, my darlings. I need to go find a suit!"

Felix followed him out, saying, "Really? It just occurred to you now?"

"It's a day job, Fox! I'm still learning here!"

Josh took his place and leaned into Tienne's space a little. "So, are you going to show Stirling and me how to make those credit cards? I bet Lucius sent us the list already. I, uhm…." He gave a smile that was a little tentative for the person Tienne had always seen Josh Salinger as. "I've been out of the game for a little while. I'm sort of excited about learning a new skill."

"You should see his forging equipment," Stirling said. He was looking something up on his computer, so he didn't look up. "Passport covers for nearly every country in the world, a zillion kinds of paper, stamps, seals—it's *amazing.*"

"Yeah?" Josh grinned. "I mean, we've seen some of it when we've come to your place, but, uhm, you'll share, right?"

"Ooh...." Grace's eyes lit up on Stirling's other side. "New things? New *thievish* things? Can we? We won't freak you out too much, Tienne? That would be great, you know. If we could learn things."

Josh gave him a long-suffering look. "I think somebody missed school this semester. Weren't you taking engineering classes?"

Grace tilted his head back in a dreamy smile. "Yeah, all the better to steal nuclear secrets from actual nuclear plants. I was so excited...."

"Next year," Josh said firmly. "Next year, we can all start college again. I can't wait."

Grace gave him an almost hungry look. "God, me neither." He looked over his shoulder. "Hunter, are *you* going to take classes again?"

Hunter shrugged. "I'd rather work in the family business, baby. Sorry."

"No worries." Grace smiled wistfully at him. "I'll tell you all the stuff the professor got wrong. It'll be fine."

Hunter gave a fond laugh. "You do you," he said, bending down to give Grace a surprising kiss on the cheek. "I'm going to leave too." He glanced up at Carl, who was draining his coffee cup reluctantly and trying hard not to eyeball the last muffin.

"Give it up," Hunter said. "Eat the muffin, then let Chuck drive your new car downtown so we can scout the port authority for Grace and then check a few more leads for Levka. I realize we're getting down to

Christmas here, and we've got plans for after, but…." He looked apologetically at Tienne. "Buddy, you've been putting a pretty good face on things, but I don't want that guy touching any of *our* guys again."

Tienne gaped at him like a fish, realizing that he had barely said two words to Grace's boyfriend, but Hunter apparently still regarded him as one of "our guys." "Thank you," he managed gruffly, as Carl grunted.

"Stirling, if we get back early, I wanted your help looking up an insurance thing when you're done with the forging thing."

"We'll do the forging thing," Josh said. "Send Stirling your insurance thing. You go do the undercover working-off-the-muffin thing. See? It's good to have broad skill sets."

Carl's stoic face split into a grin. "God, I'm glad you're better, kid. But don't overdo it, okay? All us old folks need a break on our tickers." He held his hand to his heart, and Josh socked him halfheartedly in the arm.

"Go," he said, looking abashed but still smiling. "I'm gonna learn how to make fake credit cards. I'm super excited about that. Stirling, the best internet is in your room—and the most encrypted too. Should we join you there?"

Stirling looked up from what he was doing on his laptop. "Yes, please. Tienne, do you need help getting your stuff?"

"We'll help him," Grace said, and when Stirling looked a little put out, he added, "Yes, we want to be his friend too. You two can be besties or whatever, but Josh and I have been waiting since we were eleven years old to be Tienne's peer group, so share until he kicks us out."

Tienne leaned against Stirling, saying softly into his ear, "It's fine. He's right. I've never had playmates before. This will be fun."

Stirling finally looked away from his laptop and gave him a searching look before smiling slightly. "Okay," he said simply. "You're right. It *will* be fun. But be prepared to send Grace on seventeen-zillion errands when his ADHD gets too bad and he needs to do zoomies around the house with the cats."

Tienne had seen the two black cats stomping about the place. Cary Grant and George Clooney were vocal and not at all covert creatures who seemed to regard their association with famous thieves with contempt. *They* wouldn't be caught dead sneaking around a mansion because *they* obviously ran things there. He'd never had pets as a child, and he wondered now what it would take to lure one of the creatures to sit on his lap.

As if in answer to his thoughts, the two of them came scampering into the kitchen, looking for the kibble that Phyllis kept on the mat against the wall by the dishwasher. Tienne had noticed a couple of boxes—the self-cleaning kind that left no mess, scrupulously maintained—in various bathrooms. The cats were well cared for, and everybody seemed to enjoy them.

Josh must have noticed the direction his eyes went because he murmured, "If you ask Grace nicely, he might make sure there's a cat in Stirling's room. Is that okay, Stirling?"

Stirling looked up, and his face—often set in stern lines of concentration—relaxed a tad. "Yes. They help me concentrate."

"Which is a total lie," Grace said, pushing back from his stool. "They help nobody concentrate, but since I like the zoomy little bastards too, I'm in."

And with that they all stood and got ready for an afternoon of—as Grace would say—learning things and doing crime.

"OH MY God," Stirling muttered. "He won't leave us alone!"

Tienne lowered his head to Stirling's ear and let loose a low laugh, both of them determined not to hurt Grace's feelings as he gamboled about them in the Art Institute gift shop. Tienne was enjoying his antics immensely, and Grace and Josh together were *highly* entertaining, but he got the feeling Stirling wanted some time alone. He understood very much—he'd been dying for a repeat of their kiss from two nights before, but at the same time, well.…

He'd never dreamed of having a friend group so much like this one.

The day before had been pleasant, actually. After a brief "class," Tienne had Josh, Grace, and Stirling creating the false identities and programming the magnetic strip for the credit/debit cards. Tienne had been told that if he could keep a record—false, of course—of the identity paying off the card, the women in the shelter who were escaping abusive men in their lives could establish their identities, and a credit line, when they moved out of the shelter. He felt like he was doing good work, and Grace, Josh, and Stirling were, well, brilliant and competent.

As he was walking them through the steps on the computer, he heard his father, teaching him the rudimentary steps in the trade. *Practice the signature, Tienne, but don't overpractice it. People dash off their names as a matter of course. Pretend for a moment you* are *the person making that mark and then go. That way, the person taking over for you will have an easier job.*

Antoine had been as gentle teaching the basics of forgery as he had been teaching the basics of art, and Tienne realized that as he passed those basics on to people who would be taking what was essentially the trade of deception and putting it to good use, he felt closer to who his father had been to *him*. Yes, Antoine Couvier had done illegal things when Tienne was a child, but his every move had been to make Tienne's life better using the only skills he had.

But that had been yesterday.

This day had started bright and early with a crash course in the basics of the heavily computerized surveillance van that Josh and Stirling had been so excited about. Tienne was decent with computers, but he was not the savant Stirling was, nor the proficient hacker that Josh was. He'd been able to comprehend the basics and to understand how he might help with the coming job by simply observing and making suggestions when needed, but beyond that, he could only whistle in appreciation for the technology the Salingers had at their fingertips. He was pretty sure his biggest contribution was going to be the small bag of provisions, water, and word games he'd packed, given Josh's warning to "bring a book" because of the boredom.

The trip to Chicago had been noisy and uncomfortable. The van had no windows, and while Chuck had been the one to drive, with Hunter in the passenger's seat, Grace, Tienne, Stirling and Josh had been in the back, holding on to their chairs for dear life while Chuck set a land-speed record from the Chicago suburbs to the downtown shopping district. Stirling—apparently familiar with Chuck's driving—was sitting on the comfortable couch lined up under a series of breakers on the other side of the vehicle. The third time Chuck hit a corner and sent Tienne tumbling across the van into Stirling's arms, Stirling kept his arms around Tienne's shoulders, holding steady, warm, and kind.

Tienne relaxed for the first time during the trip then, melting into that warm chest, the strength that was belied by the slight frame, and somehow Chuck's driving seemed to get better after that.

Eventually, Chuck pulled up in front of the Art Institute and let them out, telling them he'd pick them up in three hours near a restaurant on the Magnificent Mile, giving them time to hit shops in between.

"But won't we have to carry the packages?" Tienne asked, a little overwhelmed.

Josh, who was climbing out after Grace, sucked in a breath as the wind off the lake knocked the air out of everybody's lungs. "I've got my mother's credit cards," he said. "She's got that super-secret diamond tiara class thing where she can have them delivered. It's great."

"Diamond tiara class," Hunter said next to him, straight-faced. "Is that the thing we're going to need to get you shipped home when you can't walk the twelve blocks to our lunch reservations and the rendezvous point?"

Josh rolled his eyes. "That's a cab, Hunter. I've been whistling for those since I was a little kid."

"And talking to the cabbie in one of seven languages," Grace said in disgust.

Tienne huddled deeper into his new fleece-lined coat, suddenly very appreciative of the way the Salinger family wanted to care for him. "Seven?" he asked, stomping his booted feet before heading up the great stone steps of the Institute. "I speak English, French, German, and Afrikaans. What do you speak?"

Josh gave an insouciant shrug, indicating, oh my, he was too busy to remember right now, and Tienne suppressed a smile of amusement. Josh, Grace, and Stirling were all frighteningly brilliant—that much he'd gathered from their time the day before working on the computer, if he hadn't suspected it already. But they had also done time in American schools, in which brilliance and ability was either wielded like a weapon or highly suspicious and discounted. Josh and Grace had survived by burying their sharp minds and keen abilities under a layer of banter and playfulness that distracted observers from the things the two of them saw or knew that might have passed other people by. Stirling was not made for such subterfuge. Like Tienne, he buried himself in the things he loved and was good at, and chose the friends who accepted him for who he was.

Until this last couple of weeks, Tienne had been certain no such people existed. He hadn't seen through Josh and Grace's banter, or Stirling's self-containment. He could only be grateful they had seen past his own walls to know they wanted him in their playground too.

"He speaks English, French, Spanish, German, Russian, Korean and ASL," Grace said dryly, to fill in the silence Josh had left in the wake of that little shrug. "And Hunter, if you're here having our back, who's got Chuck's?"

Chuck had driven carefully away, which was a testament to how slick the roads were in spite of the best efforts of the Chicago road crews. As it was, the marble steps were icy, and by unspoken consensus, Stirling and Grace flanked Josh to keep him from the wind, while Hunter drew up behind him. The configuration left Tienne on Stirling's other side, feeling oddly proud of how well Stirling, who claimed not to be physical at all, would step up to keep his friend safe from the wind.

"He's meeting Carl," Hunter said. "They're doing some recon at Levka's last known. Tienne, we would *really* like to make sure you're safe, but that guy seems to have gone ghost."

"Have you checked out my apartment?" Tienne asked, and there was a long enough pause between his question and when Hunter spoke next to make him uncertain if Hunter was telling the truth.

"Yeah. That's a good idea," Hunter said, and Grace made a strangled sound, like he was trying not to say anything else.

"What?" Tienne asked as they drew up to the foyer of the Institute. "What are you not telling me?"

"I don't know," Josh said darkly, "but it's something I haven't heard yet either. I don't like being kept in the dark."

"It's not the dark," Hunter muttered irritably. "It was some new information that came in this morning, and we didn't want to put you all off your game."

They drew into the shade of the great arch, and the rubber mats made their footing a little more certain. Like a wall, the four of them turned to enclose Hunter, who rubbed his nose and grimaced.

"Someone broke into Tienne's place last night and trashed it. We've been keeping it under surveillance, and there was footage, but the three guys who broke in all had masks. Based on height and build, we don't think any of them were Levka." He blew out a breath. "Which is why the four of you get me, and Chuck and Carl are giving the last knowns one more pump before we do a little going ghost ourselves."

Tienne's shudder had nothing to do with the cold, and Stirling took off his glove to fumble for Tienne's hand.

Tienne took the reassurance gratefully. "Thank you," he mumbled, "for taking care of me. All of you."

Hunter shrugged. "Not a big deal, Tienne. Now let's go inside before Grace loses his shit and decides to rob the place."

Tienne had been in the Art Institute a million times, but he'd eschewed the gift shop because why get a facsimile of great art when the great art was right there inside the building? He had overlooked the joy of things such as silk scarves printed with Van Gogh's *Sunflowers,* or a delicate blue cashmere cardigan with cloisonne buttons done with *Irises.* Stirling, Josh, and Grace all danced around the place, enchanted by everything from books with expensive plate illustrations to stuffed animals that resembled famous paintings. And while Stirling often showed exasperation with Grace, who quite *literally* danced around, Tienne noticed that they both got very excited about a T-shirt featuring a Toulouse Lautrec painting and sporting the caption Meet the REAL Green Fairy! Every corner had a delight, including catalogs of items not on display, and Tienne found himself pulled through a vortex of people who loved the rare and the beautiful as much as he did and, like himself, yearned for the feeling of a piece of it in their hands.

They left much poorer in cash than they'd arrived, and not once had Grace felt the need to wander the catacombs of the storage rooms to steal himself a present. Or, if he had, Tienne had missed his absence in the excitement of the moment with the others.

It wasn't until they were stepping out of the gift shop that he realized Danny had been waiting for them in the foyer, sitting on a marble bench and using his phone to work until he spotted the lot of them leaving. Contrary to Josh's assertion that they could have all their stuff delivered, nobody had wanted to chance their purchases not arriving in the next few days and had chosen to carry their bags themselves.

Tienne suspected it was because there would be gift wrapping when everyone got home, and he found he was as excited to participate in that as he had been in the last hour of shopping. He'd already ordered brown paper and Sharpies for what he hoped was the best part of his Christmas surprises. He had not missed the comments about it being the thought that counted, and forethought was one of his strengths, as well as noticing small details that made people smile. The headiness of belonging enough to show that off was something to cling to, something to savor.

"Hello, children," Danny said, smiling slightly. "You're not a moment too soon. I know you'd planned to walk the shopping district, but I'm having my vehicle brought around from the parking garage. We can take that instead."

"Why?" Tienne asked, trying to keep the anxiety out of his voice.

Danny gave him a reassuring pat on the shoulder. "Nothing nefarious, my lad. I would simply like us in place for the job this afternoon a few minutes earlier, that's all."

Josh laughed and then yawned, and then looked pointedly at Grace, who gave a smile that was all teeth.

"I'm fine," Josh said, yawning again, and Tienne realized that while Grace may not have snuck off to steal something, apparently he *had* managed to text Danny about not walking the twelve blocks.

"You're tired," Danny said implacably. "And still on the mend. Six months, remember? Six months of taking it easy and long naps. Please, Josh—"

Josh held up his hand. "Understood," he said. Then he shook his head. "Seriously, I can't wait until we get to Barbados. Nobody worries about you swimming in the sun in Barbados."

Danny gave an indelicate snort and led the way outside and down the steps to the avenue that passed in front of the Institute. As they drew near the SUV that Tienne had seen him drive before, they all paused.

There was another vehicle parked behind Danny's SUV, an aging Subaru Forester with four doors and a child's seat in the back, with a tired man in a rumpled suit and basic wool coat leaning against it.

"Oh," Josh said, his voice small.

"Oh *hell* no," Grace muttered. He grabbed Josh's arm. "Don't. Just… don't."

Josh gave him a reassuring smile and disengaged. "I'll see what he wants and have him drop me off at the restaurant," he said. And with that, he took the remaining steps down to the street level and extended his hand to the tired young man with dark hair and brown eyes who had straightened when he'd seen them all.

The young man ignored his hand and hugged Josh, a great, shuddering, *private*-looking hug that made Danny groan a little before the two of them got into the battered Subaru and drove off.

The rest of them were quiet as they loaded into the SUV, with the exception of Grace muttering, "I will fucking kill him," as he slid into the middle seat next to Stirling and Tienne, leaving Hunter in the front with Danny.

"Which one?" Stirling asked curiously. "Nick or Josh?"

"Josh is trying to be nice," Grace said on a huff. "Nick is playing with his head."

"I suspect," Danny said, maneuvering the vehicle carefully onto the tricky streets of Chicago, "that Nick may have had information on Dubov. Remember, Josh was putting out a feeler yesterday."

"Hasn't he heard of email?" Grace demanded. "A fucking text? I mean, *Jesus*—"

"What is the problem?" Tienne murmured to Stirling, trying not to intrude but very curious.

"The problem," Grace said, as usual ignoring all social boundaries because he was Grace, "is that Josh has been quietly pining away for the guy for a year, and the guy is married. And no, I don't give a shit that Nick doesn't realize he's bi and is totally crushing on Josh, and no, I don't give a shit that Nick probably really cares for him. You know what I care about?"

"That seeing him does a number on Josh every time?" Stirling asked quietly.

"*Yahtzee!*" Grace cried, scrubbing his face with his hands. "And he's *married*. And he's stupid in love with his baby. And Josh is never going to fuck with that, which is fine, but it… it…."

"It hurts to see him hurt," Hunter said from the front of the car. "We know, Grace. Baby, we know."

Grace groaned and hid his face in his hands for the short journey to the restaurant.

When they got there, Nick's car was parked in front, and Nick and Josh were conversing earnestly, possibly about anything *but* what Grace had been talking about. The lot of them piled in, being led straight to the table where Felix sat, and had started to order before Josh walked in, looking both exhausted and exhilarated.

"Where's Chuck and Carl?" he asked, taking his seat between Grace and Stirling.

Grace gave him a foul look and turned away.

"They'll be meeting us at the rendezvous point," Felix said. "What did you learn?"

Josh beamed at his father. "I learned that Dubov really *has* blown town. The Serbian gang that he's connected with is planning something—something big. A big buy, a big sell. I have no idea and neither does Nick, but whatever it is, it's happening *out* of town. The good news is, Tienne, you'll definitely have a Merry Christmas, but the bad news…." He grimaced.

"This will not be resolved when *we* leave town," Tienne rightly deduced.

"Exactly," Josh said. "Which is fine. It will give us time to work on Dubov from the safety of the beach, after we give Stirling and Molly a proper Christmas present."

"Of course," Tienne said, looking at Stirling and feeling greatly rewarded when Stirling caught his eyes in return. "Anything for Stirling."

Stirling's smile went up a notch, and for a moment, there was only their warm little bubble and the vast gray wonder of Stirling's eyes.

Outside the bubble, Tienne heard Hunter ask neutrally, "How's Nick?"

"Still married," Josh replied mildly, and then Grace gave a sigh and relaxed, and the matter was dropped.

LUNCH WAS exquisite. Meals with his father had not always been regular, and the regimen of private school had not made the food any tastier. In the past weeks, Tienne had started to learn the joys of regular meals prepared with care. He thought of the time spent in his own apartment when he'd heat up a can of soup or grill a cheese sandwich and eat it distractedly while he worked, and decided that, no matter what happened, he would continue a life that celebrated sitting down with friends to eat.

The conversation had been centered around the job, including suggestions for where Grace was most likely to find actual files or computers *with* files as he explored the records room in search of the original reports from Stirling's parents' shipwreck.

Finally Grace held both hands out irritably, shutting them all up. "I'm only distracted, not stupid. Trust me. I'm a professional."

And after that, they started talking about Christmas again. This time it was songs they absolutely could not live without. Tienne remembered previous Christmases at the Salingers', and how there would always be gifts for him under the tree. It had felt very removed then. Who was he to these people? Why would they be buying him winter clothes and the paints of his dreams?

Now he was starting to recognize the suppressed excitement in his belly, the hope for art supplies—because they'd always known him enough to give him the things he loved. He recognized the yearning in himself to be an actual part of the festivities, the joy of giving to people who gave to him.

Now, as he participated in the chatter, he allowed himself the excitement, gave in to the wonder, and planned for how to contribute his unique talent. The joy was in the giving—how had he not known that was so? Among people who valued the beautiful, the unique, he felt as though he had something to offer.

After lunch, Chuck arrived for another uncomfortable trip, with Carl in the passenger seat this time, as Tienne rode in the back with Stirling and Josh. Together they navigated the short jaunt to Lake Calumet, which felt like not quite a lake after the vastness of Lake Michigan that sat adamant a few river locks away. Chuck parked the van in the back corner of the public lot and grunted unhappily at Carl, who pulled in a deep breath and met Chuck's gaze.

"Do we have to discuss this again?" he asked.

"No," Chuck muttered. "I hear you."

Carl rubbed the back of his neck. "Chuck, I can't drive like a maniac—"

"Your boyfriend tells a different story," Chuck muttered unhappily.

"I can't land a plane—"

Grace, Josh, and Stirling all made a sound like *Ha!* which told Tienne there was a story there that Carl was conveniently ignoring, and Carl went on.

"Well," he amended. "I can't land a plane *well*. I can't wield a weapon or disarm a bomb, and if someone was to wage an out-and-out attack on this bulletproof van, we all know you're our guy. The one thing—*one thing*—I can do well is read an insurance report and tell you if it's fishy. That's the only reason I'm going in with Grace and you're staying here."

"Whatever. Get out of the van before I take back your Christmas present."

Carl wrinkled his nose. "You would not take it back. Michael loves that SUV!"

"*Your* present, stupid. That's Michael's present."

For a moment the two grown, muscular men regarded each other in confusion.

"Why would you get me a present when you got the SUV for Michael?" Carl asked, cocking his head.

"Get out of the fucking van before I beat you," Chuck told him.

Carl did, muttering to himself as he did so, and in a moment, they picked up his com signature as he traveled across the icy parking lot, huddling deep inside his wool coat and stocking cap as he did so.

"Ass. Hole," Chuck muttered, cupping his hand over the com link in his ear so Carl couldn't hear.

"It's like you can't even get mad at him," Grace said over coms. He'd ridden in Danny's vehicle with Felix and Hunter, probably avoiding the last-minute instructions from the guys in the tech van, Tienne would wager. He'd never realized before how delicately balanced egos and abilities were for a job like this. Thieves really did earn their keep.

"I'll get mad at him if I feel like it," Chuck grumbled, giving it up and dropping his hand from his coms. "Did you hear that, Carl? Every time we leave you on your own, something weird happens. Mr. I'm-too-boring-for-words unleashes weirdness hell on the rest of us."

"That's unfair," Carl said, sounding worried.

Stirling was the one who spoke up next. "Murder birds, Carl. Murder. Birds. Do you remember that? Tricked-out Jeep Cherokees, emergency plane landings, and murder fucking birds. Nobody blames Michael for any of that. They all blame you."

Carl grunted. "You're all being completely unfair."

The response was a universal raspberry. Grown men—*grown men*, some of them in their forties—all stuck their tongues out and made the *plbbttt* sound into their coms so that it echoed throughout the van, and Tienne wondered if his eyes were going to pop out of his head.

Since he was the only one not wearing a com link, he leaned over to Stirling and murmured, "Poor Carl. It sounds like he's getting a bad rap for something not his fault."

Stirling snorted. "Oh no. Chuck and Grace are right. The murder-bird caper was something special. They were literally diving out of the sky trying to *eat* Carl's boyfriend, and Carl was like, 'But they were genetically engineered, so it wasn't their fault.' Carl could stand fast in a hurricane, but that doesn't mean the hurricanes don't keep trying."

"Very astute, Stirling," came Danny's voice over the computer speaker. "But we're all about to enter the building, so we need to leave the events in Napa behind us. And for the peanut gallery to quit talking in our heads."

Chuck slid out of the van then, leaning against it casually like a guy waiting for a friend, and Josh and Stirling went to minding their monitors. From what Tienne could see, Josh had the building schematics up on his, as well as feeds from all the internal cameras, while Stirling was looking at... oh dear Lord.

"Are those heat signatures?" Tienne asked.

"Mm-hum...," Stirling hummed. "There's a camera mounted on Danny and Felix's SUV, but we're getting the feed."

Stirling was looking at the heat signatures of employees and visitors on all three floors of the port authority building. As Danny and Felix entered, Hunter hot on their heels, three figures appeared with green dots on the sides of their heads, and Tienne realized those were tags for coms. Grace and Carl entered a few steps later, and they peeled off toward another section of the building.

"See the bathroom, Grace?" Stirling asked.

"Yup," Grace murmured. "There's one farther down the hall, right?"

"Yup, and it has a ventilation shaft to the records room. Remember to look for the vents when you get in so you have an escape route."

"Yes, Mom."

"And clean your room," Stirling added facetiously, making Josh snicker.

"Why do you need the heat signatures if you have the cameras?" Tienne asked into the silence that followed.

Stirling replied without looking up. "Because...." He nodded to Josh's feed, and after a few moments of searching, Tienne picked up on their guys. Danny and Felix were being escorted through a crowded tile room laid out much like a standard DMV, in which people waited in appropriate lines for everything from shipping permits to boat licenses. The man leading the way was wearing a short-sleeved shirt and a tie, and Felix and Danny were divesting themselves of their outer garments hurriedly, leading Tienne to believe the building was overheated.

In the main lobby, Hunter stood in the boat-permit line with a small file of paperwork in his hand. Tienne had missed the part where Hunter had a legit cover, but apparently somebody was getting a boat.

Tienne searched out a frame with Carl and Grace in it and saw them both striding down a long, monotonous beige corridor on cracked tile. Carl had taken off his coat but still wore a suit underneath it and had procured an ID somehow. Grace was so nondescript, moving so silkily, that Tienne had to look twice to make sure he'd spotted that pale beige-gray outfit against the beige gray of the office itself.

His eyes widened. Camouflaged indeed.

"Where'd Carl get the ID?" he asked, feeling a little hurt. He *was* a forger after all.

"Show him, Josh," Stirling commanded softly, and Josh gave him an arch look that told Tienne that Josh was usually the person in charge and not used to being bossed around.

Stirling flushed and gave Tienne a tentative glance under lowered lashes. "You know… it's, well, cool."

Josh's sudden grin flashed, and Tienne understood all over again how the world had gathered to watch this young man dance. "Sure," he muttered. "Tienne, keep an eye on the monitors that show what they're doing in real time."

Tienne murmured assent and kept his eyes glued to the screens. Felix and Danny had killed their coms, but he saw them get pulled into a small office, where the guy in the short-sleeved shirt leaned back in his chair and tried to play big shot; at least that was what his body language indicated. To Tienne's amusement, Felix and Danny listened with wide-eyed attention, both of them perched on the edge of their seats and nodding every so often as though the guy in the chair held the secrets of the universe in the palm of his fleshy hand.

That scene absorbed, he darted his eyes to the screen with Carl and Grace. Carl was still striding through the corridor as though he owned it, and as Tienne watched, he flashed his badge at a bored security guard who was leaning against a wall guarding the door to what was apparently the records room.

And Grace was nowhere to be seen.

"Where's Grace?" Tienne asked, a little panicked.

"Right here," Stirling murmured, squinting at the heat-signature screen.

Tienne turned his attention to that one, and in the same quadrant he'd seen Carl, he saw an extra heat signature about ten feet from Carl.

It was moving... oddly. And distributed oddly.

"Is he in a—"

"Ventilation shaft?" Josh asked. "Yes. He and Carl should meet in a moment. In the meantime...." Josh's quick nod dragged Tienne down to a corner of Josh's screen that depicted a scene from moments before, when Danny and Felix stood blocking the door to the lobby. As they waited, Tienne saw two things: one was their contact coming up in front of them, getting ready to extend a hand, and the other was Carl and Grace hitting the doors behind them almost at a run.

In a moment of time over so quickly it almost blurred on the screen, Grace barreled into Hunter, who knocked into Felix and Danny. Danny was driven up against their contact's chest for just a moment, and when he came back, the lanyard with the ID badge that he'd worn on his chest was gone.

And while Tienne was watching Hunter make sincere apologies to Danny and Felix while Grace disappeared like smoke, Carl came in from the cold and brushed by the lot of them, taking the ID from Danny's hand as he held it behind him and to the side. In a moment, Carl was striding down the hall behind an invisible Grace, the ID around his neck and his coat over his arm, Hunter was in the line for boat permits, and Danny and Felix were making with the big eyes and absolute attention.

Tienne whistled lowly. "Wow," he said, meaning it. His father had forbidden him from picking pockets—in some of the places they'd lived it could have gotten him maimed or killed if he wasn't good at it—but he'd seen his share of street lifts in his time.

What Danny, Felix, and Carl had just done was a thing of beauty, right down to the timing, and he was most impressed. He even wanted to do one himself, to see if he could.

Stirling and Josh, though, had moved on to other things, and Carl's voice, stolid, hushed and unruffled, echoed through their speaker.

"I hear you, Carl," Josh said, and his fingers flew as he pulled up what looked like a filing schematic on the corner of his screen where the picture loop Tienne had been watching had sat. "Yes, Grace is looking for the files in the C cabinet—Christopher or Caribbean. All of the computers are networked, and they're designed for an open office. Anyone can access them with the code of the day. Well, yes, find a computer and I'll give you the code of the day."

Carl sat down at a console just as Grace popped out of a ventilation shaft at his feet. Carl barely raised an eyebrow, and Grace rolled his eyes before heading for the filing cabinet.

For a moment, everybody was busy with their own individual tasks, and then Tienne noticed Felix raising his hands above his head in a stretch and surreptitiously tapping his ear as he did so.

"Josh," he said softly, "I think Felix wishes to be on coms again."

Josh's eyes flickered. "Good call, Tienne," he said before shoulder-bumping Stirling, who hit a button on his keyboard. And suddenly, they could hear the director of something or other droning on and on about…

Wait. What was he saying?

"Well, yes, Mr. Salinger, I do realize you're trying to recover the personal effects of your friends for their children, but while the Christophers' ship *has* been salvaged, I'm afraid their effects are part of an ongoing investigation."

"Oh my!" Danny said, his voice dripping ingenuousness. "You mean you're still investigating the cause of the wreck? I thought it was a storm!"

"Well, yes," said the man in the tie. "But it has come to our attention that the area where the boat was found is experiencing heavy traffic from unusual sources. We think it's best to keep the effects until the investigation is—"

"What unusual sources?" Felix asked, his natural authority causing the other man to thump heavily forward in his chair.

"Just boats leased to people we're not sure of—it's nothing related to the Christophers, really. It's simply an inquiry of the area. That's really all I've been told, you understand. Barbados and the Caribbean isn't my jurisdiction." He gave an ingratiating smile at odds with his grandiose gestures of a few moments before. "I'm the holiday temp for the usual harbormaster who runs the Lake Calumet office. He might have more information for you, but I don't think so. When you made your appointment yesterday, I went searching for the effects and found them all classified, so—" He shrugged. "— you know. There's nothing I can do."

"Carl, Grace," Josh murmured into his com, "there is a file cabinet in the far corner of the room, right under the window, labeled Classified. Grace, you're going to need to pick the lock, but it appears to be bursting with ultrasonics—"

Tienne gave a quick glance to Stirling's screen, which showed the file cabinet as a big mass of red and yellow underneath an icy blue front from the window, which was cracked open a tad, probably in deference to the many computer terminals running.

"Wait," Stirling said. "See?"

Josh followed Stirling's finger on the infrared screen to a place one floor below but in the same area. There were a number of glowing lines to and from that spot, which seemed surrounded by a giant blank blackness—a cooling unit, most likely.

"Grace," Josh said, his voice taking on an urgent tone, "you're going to need to go down one floor to the electrical room and cut the power there. If you do it from your floor, you'll trigger an alarm, but the box is supercooled. Cutting it at the box juncture would—"

They all heard Carl's calm voice say, "Someone is coming."

"Fuck it," Grace said, sounding almost gleeful. "Hunter, beast mode."

"You little shit," Hunter muttered into his coms. "No!"

"But I thought you loved me!" Grace whined.

"Grace, get in the fucking ventilation shaft before I shove you in there like a sausage," Carl said shortly. "You assholes always underestimate me."

Grace disappeared from the records room, and his heat signature reappeared in the ventilation shaft, moving at an almost impossible speed for someone who was, at the very least, on all fours or slithering like a snake.

Tienne watched, as mesmerized as Josh and Stirling, as an employee hustled down into the records room, produced a key, and started to rifle through one of the unclassified file cabinets. A practically dressed woman in sweater and slacks, she'd hauled her hair out of her plainly pretty face into a careless ponytail and was obviously more intent on her job than her surroundings. She didn't notice Carl until she'd spun on her heel and was on her way out of the room.

"Oh my goodness," she squawked, startled. "Who are you?"

Carl gave her a winsome smile that made Tienne suddenly aware of him as a handsome man and not the stolid colleague Stirling seemed to regard him as.

"So sorry to startle you—" He hunted the ID on her chest. "—Millie. Oh, what a lovely, old-fashioned name. I love that."

Millie, who appeared to be in her midforties, gave him a shrewd glance that told them all she was not buying his attempts at flirtation. "No, seriously, what are you doing here?" She frowned at his badge, only to see that he'd turned it backward.

"Carlson," he said, extending his hand. "Carlson Sternburg from Serpentus."

"The insurance company?" she said in surprise, and he shook her hand briskly but then lingered on the release, winking at her as he did so. Oh. This was why the adorable Michael would die for him.

"Yes. We had a ship lose cargo in the Mackinac straits last year, and while most of the shipping containers have been accounted for, there was one...."

Millie's eyes got big. "The container from *Dominant Ecstasy*?" she squeaked, turning an unattractive shade of plum. Oh wow—Carl was using a real case. Go Carl!

Carl shrugged, looking sheepish. "Yes, I'm afraid. Anyway, an unnamed source said the container hadn't been lost, it had been hijacked, and I wanted to confirm a couple of checks on the cargo manifests. I hope I'm not in the way."

For a moment, Tienne thought the coy little look under his eyelashes was too much and the woman would realize he was a total fraud, but instead...

"She blushed," Josh said, sounding surprised as they watched the woman saunter away from the file room with a secret little smile on her face.

Felix and Danny exchanged puzzled looks on the other screen in front of them, and Josh muttered, "You guys, Carl's got game."

"Get *out*!" Grace exclaimed, and as they all turned their heads to Grace's blotch on the infrared screen, he cut a wire without consulting anybody.

Josh, Stirling, and Tienne all let out a sigh of relief as no alarm filled the com waves, and Chuck stuck his head inside. "We okay?" he asked, his anxious tone indicating he'd been listening to his coms with his heart in his mouth.

They all nodded, and Tienne wasn't sure about his own expression, but he could see that Stirling and Josh had wide eyes and looks of anxiety of their own.

"Fine," Josh said, keeping his voice casual.

And *that's* when the alarm—probably delayed by the cold box—started to ring fiercely, the noise feedback in the coms forcing Josh and Stirling to grab their ears in pain.

"Shit!" Josh snarled. "Danny, Felix, get out and evacuate with everybody else. Hunter, go back and help get Grace out of there. Carl—"

"I'm going through the filing cabinet right now," he said, his voice fuzzing out over the speaker because of the blare of the alarm. Millicent had apparently dashed for the fire door already since she'd been in the hallway, the security guard at her heels. Once Hunter cleared the lobby, he had a free shot to the back of the record room.

"Got it," Carl said, solid voice still working under the alarm. "The other files were sent to Carlson Sternburg's email."

"Who in the fuck is Carlson Sternburg?" Chuck asked in exasperation.

"A cover identity I made him after his last gig," Stirling said, eyes riveted to the screen. "He's an employee of Serpentus and has an email that Carl can access but can't be traced to him. The identity even draws a paycheck."

"Which I donate to Lucius's shelter," Carl muttered. "Where's Hunter?"

"Helping me out of the ventilation shaft." Grace's voice over coms had a tinny, echoing quality. "It was a ten-foot drop to the bend."

"Fuck *me*!" Hunter snapped. "Carl, get out."

"I'll be right there," Carl said calmly. "Where's Felix and Danny?"

Chuck poked his head outside of the van and sighed. "Helping their contact guy not freeze to death. He apparently ran out of the building without his coat."

"Jesus fucking hell," Josh muttered. "Okay. Hunter, let Carl help Grace out. Chuck, grab the fireman gear from the back of the van—there's two jackets. You need to sneak those into the back employee entrance so you and Hunter can clear the building. Herd Grace and Carl out the front, and tell that poor asshole in the polyester shirt he can go back in. Everybody clear?"

"Got it, Josh."

"Understood."

"Jesus, you're fuckin' bossy."

"Really, Grace? You couldn't have waited to ask somebody if that was the wire you should cut?"

There was a pause in the com chatter.

"Sorry, Hunter."

"Move it, people," Josh urged. His yawn was unfeigned. "It's time for Recovery Boy's nap."

Pennies

AT STIRLING'S urging, Josh, Hunter, and Grace rode in the back of Danny's SUV for the trip home. Carl sat up front with Chuck, where Stirling was sure the shit would fly fast and furiously, and Stirling and Tienne had the back of the van to themselves.

"Carl?" Stirling begged as Carl handed him the file folder and a couple of thumb drives through the back door of the van. "Could you ask Chuck to be kind?"

Carl nodded. "Sure thing, Stirling. You and Tienne feeling a little sick?"

"If the trip here didn't do it," Tienne said thickly, "the adrenaline dump would."

Carl chuckled. "Well, every job has its hiccups. Between what Felix picked up from the manager's office when everybody fled the building and what I got you there, it was a trip worth making."

Stirling stared at his friend, never sure when Carl was understating things for humor or understating them because not much got to him.

"What are you going to tell Michael about today?" he asked suspiciously.

Carl gave a smile that was all teeth. "That we went to the port authority and got some information on your case, why?"

"Because I need to know what to tell him that you forgot to," Stirling said, not blinking.

Carl gave him the same look of speculation that Stirling had given him and closed the door thoughtfully. Good. Carl would have to *think* about how much of the day's activity he wanted Michael to know, and that might make him think twice about underestimating Stirling the next time they went in on a job.

With a sigh, he slouched back into the swivel seat that was mounted in front of the screens and gave Tienne, who was curled up in the corner of the couch on the other side of the van, a tired smile.

Stirling blinked and ran through facial cues in his head.

"You look very scared," he said, taking a guess.

"That was very scary," Tienne said with a flicker of a smile. "We were almost caught."

Stirling shook his head. "No, that wasn't even close. Felix and Danny have enough money to smooth things over if we had been, but you've got to understand. That's what our guys *do*. People *believed* Chuck and Hunter were firefighters. They *believed* Carl was a Good Samaritan who happened to be on scene. Did you see Grace under the foil blanket? He practically swooned in Hunter's arms. Running a con is like running a theater show, but seven-eighths of the show is improv, and sometimes your props explode."

Tienne managed a smile and a faint laugh. "Then what am I?" he asked. "I'm not an actor, I'm not crew—"

"You're a prop master," Stirling said seriously. "A very specialized one. How many IDs have you done for Hunter and Chuck?" Stirling knew the answer, down to which passport each one had and how many stamps on it, but he thought it was important that Tienne regarded the bulk of his work himself.

"A lot," Tienne murmured.

"They're our two pilots," Stirling said. Carl had been taking lessons from them, but he didn't count yet. "If you didn't fake their IDs and licenses, they couldn't fly us, and believe me, we've used that. We asked you to fake a zillion provenances with a week's lead time in March. Those were absolutely essential. The entire con would have fallen apart without them, like it would have fallen apart if Grace hadn't been able to switch them out in the safe, or Hunter hadn't been able to help Grace out of the ventilation shaft. You understand? Every prop, every player, every techie—it's all needed to pull off a show."

Tienne leaned his head on his hand as the van made a blessedly smooth right turn into traffic. "That sounds like a very good story," he agreed and then gave Stirling a rather sweet look of need. "Do you want to come over here and lean against me and tell it?"

Stirling felt his smile in his toes, and he met Tienne's eyes, thrilled at the request.

"It'll be like champagne in celebration," he said, particularly proud of the analogy when Tienne laughed.

After a moment to see if Chuck was going to do anything stomach-dropping from the driver's seat, he pushed himself over to the couch and leaned against Tienne's chest. Tienne wrapped his arm around Stirling's shoulders and held him.

"I was very afraid for everybody," Tienne confessed into his hair. "You and Josh were so calm, giving directions and using the technology to guide everybody, but my heart almost burst out of my chest like a rabbit's when that alarm went off."

"At least it wasn't gunfire," Stirling said, remembering when it had been.

"Oh dear God!" Tienne's arm tightened around his shoulder. "You all are so brave."

"Because we're doing it for other people, I think," Stirling said. "And this is nice. Being held like this. What do I have to do to be held like this every day?" Tienne's arm was warm, and his chest was hard, and he smelled nice.

And he seemed to like to tighten his grip around Stirling's shoulders every so often, and it made Stirling feel safe and cared for.

"Keep putting up with me and my anxiety," Tienne muttered brokenly. "Holding on to you seems very easy after what you did."

"It's not a crime to be nervous," Stirling said, sitting up. "Not at all."

"I certainly wasn't a help," Tienne told him sadly.

"You were!" Stirling said, remembering this. "Josh and I weren't watching Felix and Danny's screen. You were. Felix was trying to get our attention, and we almost missed it. You're definitely a help. You notice details." He looked at the backpack on the floor, with granola bars and water—both of which had been distributed after everybody had been clear of the building. "You plan ahead. That's *so* important, even if we have to improvise sometimes."

"Really?" Tienne smiled hopefully, and Stirling nodded.

"Oh, absolutely." He meant it too. "I'm not a very patient person, Tienne. I wouldn't bear with you if you were a drag on us and not a help."

"You say the kindest things," Tienne murmured, but he was smiling puckishly, and Stirling hoped his confidence would build. Tienne cupped Stirling's jaw tenderly and rubbed Stirling's bottom lip with a thumb. "You have seen me vulnerable and helpless," he said. "I would like very much to be the kind of man you could depend upon to protect you."

Stirling gave a lopsided little smile, because it was an amazingly sweet thing to wish. "I can depend on you to never hurt me," he said, thinking about Molly's talk about crushes and what she could and couldn't do to keep his heart safe. "Molly and Carl and Chuck and Hunter can protect us from any outside forces. But I've never had a lover before, because they're scarier than bullies or criminals. They can hurt you worse. So if you're going to be the guy who wraps his arm around me and holds me close, you've got to be the guy who doesn't hurt my heart. That's all I want. It's like forgcry—or painting. It's a very specific skill set, Tienne. I… I think you have it."

Tienne smiled shyly, and Stirling had to kiss him. With a happy little sigh, Tienne settled back into the cushions on the corner of the couch, Stirling on top of him, their mouths exploring without urgency. They were in a vehicle with witnesses up front—they weren't the sort of people who would get naked or down and dirty in so public a place. But for a little bit of time, they could hold each other and kiss each other and grow comfortable in the knowledge that they each fulfilled a very specific, important niche in the other's life.

Every kiss made Stirling tingle, and every kiss made Stirling want.

Every brush of Tienne's lips upon his own told him that this was the right person to touch him for the first time, and this was the person he trusted with his most precious possession.

Tienne didn't have to run a con or pretend to be a fireman or crawl through a ventilation shaft to make Stirling happy. He made Stirling happy by being Tienne.

MOLLY AND Julia listened to the recap at dinner with the sort of expressions on their faces that Stirling usually associated with shock or horror.

Leon held his hand over his mouth and hid his amusement.

"Oh dear God," Julia said after a moment. "Did they buy that you were firemen? You didn't have a truck. You didn't have equipment."

"We put a cherry light on top of the van and magnetic strips on the side," Stirling said, not sure why Josh sent him a pained look. "It was really smart of Josh. I didn't even realize he'd had those made up. There were some for Danny's SUV too."

"Yes," Julia said archly, "*Josh* showed some presence of mind." Her tone made it clear that everybody else had fallen short of her expectations.

"Felix did too," Grace vouched. "He got information when the alarm went off, and we didn't even know that was going to happen!"

He smiled winningly at Felix, who gave him a bemused smile back. Stirling knew for a fact that Felix intimidated the snot out of Grace, and he thought that maybe Grace's proximity to *Josh* for the last six months had also made him closer to Josh's parents.

"And don't forget Danny," Felix added smoothly. "If Danny hadn't charmed the socks off of Mr. Weaselburger—"

"Wiessenburger," Danny said, mouth twisting with humor. "It's German."

"The man was a toady," Felix said. "I don't care if he was this year's Miss Norway, it wouldn't have made him less of a toady. He spent half his time telling us why we couldn't get any information and the other half telling us what sort of information we could get if only we kissed his ring."

"Well, it was good information," Carl said. "No matter how we got it." He glanced at Stirling and Molly. "Guys, I think we've got some suspects for whatever happened to your parents. I mean, yes, we definitely need to go explore the island—"

"Because sunshine and beach reasons," Molly said soberly, and Carl grinned at her.

"For sunshine and beach reasons," he confirmed, his voice as sober. "But depending on what we find there, we've got enough information about who benefited from the wreck and who wanted it covered up to build a first-rate legal case."

"Do we really want to build a *legal* case, though?" Hunter asked, eyeballing Stirling and Molly speculatively.

"Yes," Stirling said at the same time Molly said, "Maybe?"

They looked at each other, and Molly sighed. "We'll see," she said darkly. "If Molly goes Hulk Smash…."

"We've got your back," Felix told her, his eyes kind. "Hulk Smash is a very understandable mode of operation for what we're doing here, as long as you can live with the breakage."

Molly nodded slowly. "I'll think about it," she murmured and then looked at Stirling. "We will."

Stirling nodded back, relieved. Molly was still including him in her plans for revenge—it made him feel better thinking about revenge as a whole. Watching Tienne fret about not being a warrior had made Stirling wonder. Tienne hadn't needed to be a warrior; he'd had protectors for most of his life. So had Stirling. But being a protector was costly. It was hard. Grace had made himself Josh's protector while Josh was ill, and he'd grown up a lot, but he was also... needy. Hurt. Hunter indulged him as often as possible, managed his mercurial moods, reined in his propensity for self-destruction. Hunter knew that Grace was acting out against how much this last year had hurt his heart.

It made Stirling wonder who had been there for Molly in that way. He knew part of the answer was Julia and part of it was Chuck, who was particularly protective of Molly. He said it was because they were both redheads, but Stirling knew something of Chuck's history and knew he had a habit of protecting little sisters. But Chuck and Julia—and even Talia—weren't the same thing that Hunter was to Grace.

Or what Tienne was becoming to Stirling.

Stirling worried that Molly wouldn't have somebody to rein her in when her heart got too dark and her first impulse was to lash out.

The fact that she took Felix seriously—and Felix took her as seriously—settled something important in Stirling's heart.

But that didn't mean he wouldn't still worry.

"So, Tienne," Julia said kindly, looking at Tienne as he fidgeted in the seat next to Stirling. "Did you enjoy yourself today?"

"Yes." Tienne flashed a shy and brilliant smile. "Josh is very smart. He leads wonderfully. And everybody else is so talented." He looked away. "I play such a small part in your adventures," he admitted softly. "I'm surprised you invited me along."

"Well, we might not always be able to let you sit in the van and wait it out," Julia said, keeping her voice warm. "Someday you may be invited to come out and play. But until then, we most assuredly appreciate the help you give us so willingly."

Tienne gave another one of those smiles. "Always," he said, bobbing his head. "Anything for you."

Stirling saw his eyes flash to Danny's face like a child's to a parent's, and Danny's answering wink.

Underneath the table, he fumbled for Tienne's hand, relieved when Tienne's elegant, strong fingers gave his a squeeze. Tienne may not have seen the progression, but Stirling did. Tienne might not give his heart to strangers, but every day Tienne was at the Salinger mansion, Stirling could see him bonding with the family.

THERE WAS no briefing that night. Since Levka Dubov was out of the country and they had a week after Christmas to prepare to set sail, Julia had declared the next three days Christmas presents, baking, and wrapping days. Stirling, who was pretty sure his last gift was going to arrive the next day, still had to wrap, and he was grateful.

He was also grateful that Grace, Josh, and Molly came downstairs to play video games with him and Tienne, making the night casual and normal and happy. It wasn't that Stirling didn't like how close the family got during jobs, but vacations were vacations for a reason.

"So," Molly said, pounding her video game controller with all her might. "Have we talked about the elephant in the room?"

"You eat *one* cookie…," Grace complained, and Stirling watched Tienne hide his laugh.

"No," she said patiently. "I meant the fact that Stirling and Tienne are holding hands while they're waiting for their ups."

Stirling's entire body flushed hot, and he glanced at their twined fingers in surprise. He looked up to meet Tienne's eyes and saw that he was staring at them too, and they met eyes in recognition that it had seemed the most natural thing in the world.

"I think we all noticed," Josh said, yawning. "But we were trying to give them space because we love them."

"I wasn't," Grace announced. "I don't notice people unless I'm trying to pick their pockets."

"Which is why you're a jewel thief and not a street thief," Josh said with a laugh. "Molly, did you have a point?"

"Yes. Find me some straight men, you assholes. I'm begging you. I need one penis that swings my way. That's all I want."

Stirling bent down with his free hand and stroked her hair. "I'll do my best," he promised. "Because you're a good sister."

"I am. Tienne?"

"Yes, Molly."

"Hurt him and they'll never find your body."

Stirling's blood ran cold, and he looked at Tienne in panic to see if he took the threat as seriously as Stirling did.

But Tienne raised their joined hands to his lips and kissed softly, and Stirling flushed again, feeling happy and rosy and full. "You saw my last relationship," he said. "I know when someone is kind."

Molly grunted, and her game avatar died a noisy, bloody death. She turned and glowered at both of them. "Stirling?"

"Yes?"

"Your job—your only job—in this relationship is to convince him that whatever was going on between him and Dubov was *not* a relationship. Do you understand me?"

Stirling nodded, his lips parting slightly in dismay.

They hadn't talked about it.

It had been two weeks since he and Molly had crashed into Tienne's apartment and Molly had beaten the crap out of Levka Dubov—and they had not yet had the conversation.

How did one say, "What happened?" without violating all personal boundaries? But how did one go beyond merely hand-holding and a few lovely kisses without blurring those lines?

But this was Molly, giving her best relationship advice, and she wasn't doing it so Stirling could ignore her.

"Understood," he said softly. And then he leaned back against Tienne and relaxed, wondering if Tienne would be up to more kisses that night after they'd talked.

EVERYBODY WENT to bed shortly after that, leaving Stirling dozing on the couch against Tienne's lithe, warm body. For a few moments, Stirling was content with that, and then he recognized the feel of Tienne's hands smoothing along his chest, down his stomach, and then returning to touch his face.

"Learning me by feel?" he asked.

"My hands do know best," Tienne replied modestly. Stirling had seen the art he was preparing for Christmas, had seen the pieces Danny had stored at the Institute. He wasn't lying about that. Something about Tienne's hands knew the shape of things, the texture, and he touched with that sort of reverence.

Stirling captured his hand and traced the strong veins along the back of it to the knuckles. "Tienne?"

"Mm?"

"How do you feel about what Levka Dubov did to you?" He hated the "how do you feel" questions—Fred and Stella had gotten him evaluated when they'd first adopted the two of them, carefully explaining that they thought Stirling's brain was very wonderful, but that they wanted to treat it as gently as possible so Stirling would always know how wonderful he was. He'd had his share of "How do you feel about that?" and hated that he was inflicting it on another person.

"It made me feel dirty," Tienne murmured. "I... I have not had another lover. Ever. I was always afraid someone who didn't really *see* me would touch my body and not know who I was."

"He wasn't a lover," Stirling said. "It doesn't count. I want to touch you very much, but I don't want to make you afraid or dirty. I just... you know—" He smiled a little, knowing it was inadequate. "—want to feel your skin."

"Good," Tienne whispered, and Stirling felt the ghost of a kiss on his crown. "I want to feel yours."

"You don't have to go back to your room tonight," Stirling said softly. "We don't have to make love, but maybe we could just... touch."

"Could we take off our shirts?" Tienne asked, and Stirling smiled because he thought this might be as close to flirting as they'd ever gotten.

"We can even take off our jeans," he said.

"But not our briefs," Tienne said, as though he understood Stirling's boundaries.

"We'll see."

The thought of them in bed together, touching bare skin under the covers, was enough to make Stirling shiver all over.

It was enough to make him ache, and to want, and to need.

Tienne must have been feeling something too, because he tugged gently at Stirling's sweater and the shirt underneath and lazily rubbed Stirling's stomach.

"Mmm...." Stirling grew hard, but suddenly he very much didn't want anybody coming down the steps into the den to find them like that. "Tienne, I'm tired. I think we should go to bed now." Had he done that right? Would Tienne know it was a joke?

Tienne's soft chuckle gave him a sigh of relief. They could do this. They could communicate about what they wanted and not be shy and awkward. They could move their personal boundaries to include their persons.

Until he realized that they could do that, he hadn't realized he'd been holding his breath in fear that they might not be able to.

They moved to Stirling's room together, and he closed and locked the door, then dimmed the lights. They undressed in a soft yellow glow bright enough to see what they were doing, and when they were down to their skivvies, Stirling killed the lights and slid into bed, shivering a little.

Tienne joined him, and they turned to each other, staring at each other soberly while their eyes adjusted to the dark.

Stirling could see first, probably because Tienne's pale skin glowed like the moon in the bare tint of the night-light coming from his bathroom and his blue eyes glinted in anticipation as they locked gazes. Stirling's stomach muscles relaxed as he realized he could do this too. Tienne's soft stroke of his chest made him shiver, but in a good way.

"I like your muscles underneath your skin," Tienne murmured. "And your sturdy body."

Stirling smiled. "I like your slender body," he said. "Everything about you is very… appealing."

The shyness of Tienne's smile made Stirling ache more. "Yes? You too."

Their hands got bolder. Stirling stroked Tienne's chest, his stomach, his lean hip. Their mouths met naturally, an extension of their hands, and soon they were clenched in an embrace, and touching skin, all of the skin, was still not enough.

Stirling's cock strained against his briefs, and while he knew what he'd do if he was alone, he didn't know what Tienne would want him to do, here in this dark cave of safety that he'd worked so hard to build.

Then Tienne clutched suddenly at Stirling's backside and ground hard against Stirling's leg, his erection pulsing fiercely even through his briefs. Stirling made an executive decision and hoped Tienne wouldn't mind.

"Underwear *off*," he panted. "And I'd like to stroke your cock, if that's okay."

"Please?" Tienne whimpered.

Their movements were frantic and a little violent as they both kicked off their underthings and then lay facing each other again. Tentatively Tienne reached down and grasped Stirling firmly, stroking up, while Stirling did the same. He'd thought they might kiss while they did this, but kissing was all-consuming and greedy, and this—the silken feel of Tienne's barest skin in his palm, the briny stickiness of his precome—it seemed to demand his immediate attention and care.

As did Tienne's grip on his own erection, firm and gentle, the thumb skating across the bell. Ooh yes— that was exquisite. "Do that more," Stirling begged and did the same thing in return. He wanted more of it. He wanted it in his mouth, wanted to taste the clear sticky brine on his fingers. He had just opened his mouth to beg, say, "Please can I suck you?" when Tienne took him in a rapturous kiss, ripe and greedy with everything their hands were doing, everything their bodies were doing, until Tienne's thumb caught him on the ledge of the bell and he cried out into Tienne's mouth and came, body thrusting without conscious thought as Tienne groaned, his come scalding Stirling's fist as he spilled over again and again.

Finally, the tsunami of need seemed to have washed through them, and Stirling collapsed against the sheets, spent emotionally and physically, ready to fall asleep covered in his come and Tienne's as well.

"Clean up," he mumbled. "So we can snuggle."

Tienne's gentle chuckle warmed him. "I'll go get a cloth."

A moment later, Tienne was cleaning him and then drying him with a towel that he tucked under Stirling's hips on the bed before stretching it out for his own hips.

"Wet spot," Tienne mumbled, sliding back in next to Stirling. They kissed again, and Stirling had the sensation of being lost in a sky ship, tossed among the clouds, happy in a dream he hadn't known he'd coveted for his own heart.

"I want to do this again," he murmured. "I want to do this a lot."

"Yes," Tienne replied, tucking Stirling's head against his chest. "There's a reason for all the songs and poems about lovemaking."

Stirling grunted. "Is that what that was? Somehow, I thought there'd be more lubricant and a bigger mess."

Tienne laughed softly. "My father used to say that everybody assumed lovemaking was sex, and sometimes it is. Sometimes lovemaking is putting a cock or a mouth somewhere specific and doing a specific thing. But sometimes it's touch that makes both people happy."

"We've done that!" Stirling said. "And now I'm happy. And sleepy. But also happy."

Tienne kissed his temple and sighed against his ear. "Then it was perfect."

And Stirling was back on the sky ship, tossing in the happiness of dreams.

THEY WERE awakened at five in the morning by a man in black pajamas sitting on the foot of the bed.

"Grace?" Stirling mumbled.

"I found this tiny Lego guy that looks like Carl and this one that looks like Chuck. See? Carl has the suit and the blond hair, and Chuck has auburn hair and a little detonator. They're awesome. Is there one of me?"

Stirling squinted at him. "Yes, but... oh God. It's like the one on my desk. You're not supposed to find all of those until Christmas Day. It's your present, dumbass. You have to find all the Lego guys."

Grace's face lit up. The thief was already quite beautiful—and knew it—but his heart-shaped features grew transcendent, like moonlight, with joy.

"You gave this to me?" he asked.

"Me and Molly and Tienne," Stirling muttered. "But it's no fair if you find them now. Put them back. You don't want people to think you ruined the surprise."

"Well, if it's supposed to be a surprise, people need to hide the little guys better." Grace sniffed, but it was more a *sniffle* than an expression of disdain. "You guys really came up with this present? For me?"

Stirling sighed. He might as well say it. "We love you, Grace. You're a really good friend. Now go hide those where you got them from and go back to bed."

Grace gave an ecstatic little shiver, like a puppy, and then ghosted out of their room. As the door closed, Tienne mumbled, "I could have sworn you locked that."

"I totally did," Stirling told him, eyes drifting closed.

"You'd think con men would be better at hiding Legos."

"I'll talk to them about it."

"HE FOUND *what*?" Carl demanded over breakfast. Josh was sleeping in, and Hunter—prodded by Stirling, who'd told him Grace was going to drive them all batshit—had taken Grace back to the Art Institute, this time to steal something to take the edge off.

"He found your Legos!" Stirling told him, and Chuck, who was sitting between Carl and Lucius, stared at him with the same sort of indignation.

"I hid mine in Lucius's garment bag," Chuck said. "In the little safe pocket underneath where the shoes are supposed to go."

"That's a good place," Lucius said. "How did you know that was even there?"

Chuck grimaced. "Drug dealers try to smuggle stuff in there a lot. If there's no dogs and the DEA agent is new, they can get away with it."

"Great," Carl said. "I hid mine in between the leather and the lining of my shaving kit. I've smuggled thumb drives from careless thieves in there. How on earth would he know to search it?"

"He didn't," Molly muttered. She was eyeballing one of the chocolate cheesecake muffins over the kitchen table, but she'd been making whining noises about appearing in a bikini, and Stirling thought she was try-ing to hold back.

"Then what was he doing rooting around in there?" Stirling asked in exasperation.

"Here," Tienne said, handing Molly the muffins and the butter. "You can ask for one, you know. I'm good at passing things."

She smiled at him with sort of a stupid affection that made Stirling glad he'd chosen Tienne. "Thank you," she murmured.

Julia, who had been running around the kitch-en with Phyllis, making ingredient piles for cookies, paused to answer Stirling's question. "Stirling, if I'm not mistaken, things got a bit sticky yesterday. Carl and Chuck came to Grace's rescue. He was probably looking for something to steal anyway, because he real-ized he could have lost you and didn't have anything of yours in the collection. That's how he stumbled across the Legos." She paused and frowned. "And my poin-settia Christmas brooch. I spent ten minutes searching for it this morning. Goddammit." She pulled in a shaky breath. "I'll have to hide the earrings someplace really good so he can gloat about finding them."

"Mm." Chuck regarded her thoughtfully. "That's a good point." He smiled at Carl. "Carl, my man, I've got a really good idea."

"What?" Carl, too, was eyeballing the chocolate muffins.

"First, give it up and have a muffin. This close to Christmas, all diets are blasphemy, particularly when Marco baked his heart out for us. Second of all, let's hide each other's Christmas presents somewhere for Grace to find. So I hide my present for Grace in your guest room, and you hide yours in mine. He'll be breaking the rules and hunting for presents, and that way, he'll know we know he's going through our stuff. And he'll know…."

Carl gave a faint smile, but one Stirling had come to recognize showed true affection—with a little bit of bemusement as well. "He'll know we love him. Of course." But he shook his head and held his hand out, palm raised. "But no muffin. Christmas Eve, yes. Christmas Day, yes. But two days before Christmas, I'm still pretending diets exist."

"Masochist," Chuck muttered.

"Realist," Lucius retorted. Stirling had noted that Chuck's super-rich boyfriend seemed to exist on dry toast and fruit.

"You're both crazy," Chuck snapped. "For God's sake, who told you hip bones were sexy? It's like banging a washing machine, no?"

Next to him, Tienne reached out and grabbed his third muffin and began to munch immediately. Stirling smiled but kept his observations to himself.

As Chuck and Carl began discussing the pros and cons of hiding places, Stirling leaned close to Tienne and whispered, "I don't mind hip bones."

Tienne's response was to turn his head and sneak a quick kiss, and Stirling preened smugly about that all morning.

CHRISTMAS EVE was formal dress at dinner, games and movies in the den, and a promise for everybody to meet in the living room at 10:00 a.m. sharp, although a rotating brunch would be available at the table throughout most of the day.

The entire lot of them, including Phyllis, ended up in the den at eleven o'clock at night, watching *A Christmas Story* in their pajamas before the big day. Per usual, Stirling sat on the couch, this time with Tienne leaning against him, and Molly sat on the floor in front of him, leaning back between his legs. He stroked his sister's hair absentmindedly, a thing he'd done since they were young because her curls were so soft and bouncy and because it reminded him again and again that if he had nobody else in the world, he had Molly.

"Mm," Molly said, leaning her head against one of his knees. "Remember our first Christmas with Fred and Stella?"

Stirling laughed a little. "Everything was magic," he said. "We were so scared, though."

"Yeah," she said. "What if we woke up and it was all a dream."

"I remember," Stirling said. "You were like, 'Magic can be stolen, you know.'"

She *hmm*ed. "All those young adult novels couldn't be wrong."

He smiled a little but then looked worriedly at Tienne, surprised to see Tienne's eyes soberly searching his face.

"I can't be stolen," he said.

Stirling nodded. "I was thinking more the other way around. This can't be stolen from you."

Tienne closed his eyes but didn't answer. Instead, he snuggled a little tighter, and Stirling stroked a hand down his arm, wondering what he would have to do to make Tienne think this family was his too.

After the movie, everybody shuffled off to sleep, including, Stirling was amused to see, Carl, who had joined them wearing Garfield pajamas that Michael had bought him. Michael had called too, in the middle of the movie, and they'd put it on hold to share the phone and listen to him talk about the exploits of his children and ask excitedly about what they were doing. Not a soul mentioned the Chicago port authority, and after Carl ended the call, he'd let out a sigh of relief.

"Thank you," he murmured.

"Merry Christmas," Hunter muttered. "But why you don't think we'll tell him on vacation is beyond me."

"This will let him concentrate on his children," Carl said with dignity. "And I didn't really do that much."

They all threw popcorn at him, and that had been that.

But now Stirling and Tienne were left on the couch, and Tienne stood and stretched. "I... I have presents for everybody tomorrow," he said.

"You put them under the tree, right?" Stirling asked. He'd actually watched Tienne doing so without comment, but Stirling was hoping Tienne hadn't gotten an attack of shyness and pulled them all back. *Under the tree* was actually getting a bit ridiculous by now. Stirling was wondering if people were going to have to open presents spilling into the hallway or sitting at the breakfast table or hanging from the ceiling.

"Yes." Tienne's cheeks colored. He'd used plain brown paper, Stirling had seen, but he'd drawn a quick caricature of the recipient instead of using names. Stirling had seen Molly's package, and if she didn't keep the paper, he would. "I... my contributions were small."

Stirling shrugged. "Most of us have money, Tienne. It really is the thought that counts. Carl can buy dignified pajamas, but Michael liked the Garfield ones, and it made Carl happy to wear them. Lucius may be able to get Chuck a Maserati for Christmas, but instead he had me hunt down the hood ornament from one of the earliest Formula 1 Ferraris. It cost about a twentieth of what a really awesome race car would cost, but I think Chuck's going to enjoy the smaller present more because it's not a show of cash, it's a show of thought. Chuck can bore you silly about the history of European cars and car makers, and the only person who can follow him is Carl, who had to study the same thing. The fact that Lucius remembered all that and tracked down a thing he'd love? It means more."

Tienne's smile was incredibly boyish. "It's like Grace's present," he said. "Not expensive but interesting. That's what I hoped. I wanted to give interesting presents."

"The wrapping paper alone is a present," Stirling told him, letting his admiration shine.

That boyish smile grew even more. "I... part of me is torn. I have your present, but I didn't put it under the tree. It's...." His face turned a very sweet shade of pink. "Tomorrow threatens to be very loud. I would like for your present to be special."

Stirling grinned. "I have yours in my room," he said. "I was, uhm, sort of hoping to give it to you tomorrow morning, before things get crazy."

"Yes! I'll go get yours." And with that, Tienne—dressed in Stirling's sweats, which he seemed to prefer for pajamas—scampered up the stairs, leaving Stirling to clean up the last of the blankets from the den, pick up the few remaining pieces of popcorn, and retire to his bedroom.

Tienne joined him there in a moment, and they sat on the bed, touching shoulders.

"It's...." Tienne sighed. "It's probably stupid. I looked at what your sister got for you and...."

"Let me see!" Stirling studied the package first, pleased with the dreaminess of the caricatured figure on the paper. The item itself was wrapped like a tube and tied off at both ends with ribbon, but Stirling could feel the soft center, like clothing. Ooh. Stirling had mentioned his sister's gifts—which were usually clothing—and wondered how Tienne had interpreted that.

Tienne reached for his own gift, which Molly had helped Stirling wrap in a brilliantly water-colored piece of silk. She said his apartment—the part with the paintings in it—had been a study in color, although he'd saved all of the plainness for his own room. Maybe, Stirling had thought, this would persuade Tienne to invite a little color into his inner sanctum.

"On three?" Tienne asked, smoothing his fingers down the silk and closing his eyes.

"Sure," Stirling murmured. "On three."

For a moment there was the rustling of paper, and then Tienne caught his breath.

"Oh...." His voice broke. "How did you—"

Tienne stared at the framed picture in his hand. Grainy, with the washed colors of a photo taken over twelve years before, it was a close-up, and looking at it, Tienne was holding his hand to his mouth like he was holding in his emotions.

The picture showed a man in his midthirties, with a thin face and a divot in his chin, walking down the streets of Marrakech with his arm slung around the shoulders of a young man, nearly a teenager, both of them oblivious to being photographed. They were dressed like natives, in linen robes, their heads covered, but the man's face could be seen enough to make out the blue eyes with the kindly crinkles in the corners, and the fond smile.

The boy looked up to his father—but only by a little. Stirling imagined Tienne would have surpassed Antoine Couvier in height within months.

"The Interpol officer," Stirling murmured in answer to Tienne's question. "The one who was tracking Kadjic. He'd figured out you and your father were being tracked by Kadjic's men, but he didn't know why, and he took surveillance photos. I asked Danny if there was a picture, anywhere, of your father, and this is what he found."

Tienne brushed his fingertips along the glass of the frame and then gave Stirling a watery smile. "That's amazing," he said. "Like you said, thoughtful. So thoughtful. I… I cannot thank you enough." He didn't have to say that he didn't have a picture of his father. There had been nothing in his room when they'd helped him move. His story of the backpack with the green paint told the rest. He'd barely gotten away with his life.

Stirling shrugged. "Well, Danny helped. I mean, his name is going to be on the big-ticket stuff from him and Julia and Felix, but… you know. He wanted you to have this too."

Tienne nodded as though his throat were too thick to speak, and then he glanced at the thing in Stirling's hands.

"You like?" he asked anxiously, and Stirling rubbed his fingers over the texture, closing his eyes.

"I like," he said, rubbing the yarn of the hat against his cheek. It was impossibly soft.

"It's qiviut," Tienne told him. "It's rare. The undercoat of a musk ox. It needs to be brushed from its coat. You only like things that are pleasing to the touch. The color—it is quiet, but it is also like your eyes."

A cool charcoal gray with a tint of green.

"It's perfect," Stirling told him. Molly would probably steal it, because she did that, but Stirling didn't mind. Molly and Grace were very much alike. Stirling loved the hat—Molly would steal it because she wanted to be part of the things Stirling loved. It was part of the reason Stirling had followed her into theater—they could steal little bits of each other's grown-up lives to prove to themselves that they had the same bond they'd forged as children.

Tienne gave that devastatingly shy smile. "I… you are so kind. And the stillness inside you, it gives me so much peace. Everything about you makes me want you more." His laugh was self-conscious. "And not in a peaceful way, either!"

Stirling clutched his hat to his chest. "I have been fascinated by you since Josh introduced us in high school. So quiet and alone. And all I knew was that I wanted to be inside your space. I… I'm mad that Dubov tried to force himself inside your walls. I was dying to be invited."

Tienne reached over to Stirling's hand and clasped it, which was the only thing that possibly might have made Stirling let go of the deliciously soft garment.

"I would say you are the only person I want in, but you're the only person I want to touch my body." He ducked his head. "I am finding, more and more, I love being part of a family that doesn't give you a chance to be completely alone. I see what Josh and Felix and Julia and Danny have tried to offer me for so many years, and I wish I'd taken them up on it sooner." Stirling could hear his throat work. "Every day with all of you seems like a lesson on how not to be lonely."

"It is," Stirling confirmed. He leaned his head against Tienne's shoulder. "But I do like that sometimes it's you and me, alone."

Tienne smiled and kissed the crown of his head. "Do you think it's snowing outside?" he asked.

"Yes, probably. It's Chicago. Or, you know, Glencoe, which is part of Chicago."

Tienne chuckled. "My apartment was cold and lonely, but I got to see the snow falling. And I'm so happy right now. Can we go upstairs and watch the snow from the small foyer? I think it would be very beautiful."

Stirling gazed at him with admiration and put his hat on over his ears. "Of course."

Together they made their way cautiously up the stairs to the living room, which was barely lit. Danny was under the tree, delivering packages, and when he saw them, he held his finger to his lips and winked. "You may have to go around through the kitchen," he murmured, "if you want to see the snow fall."

Neither of them asked how he'd known that was what they'd intended. Instead they nodded and tiptoed their way to the small sitting room off the foyer, where they curled up on the couch, Stirling leaning back into Tienne's arms as they peered out the wrap-around windows to the snow-laden darkness beyond. The room itself was lit softly, and the outside twinkle lights illuminated the fat flakes falling past the window.

Stirling fell asleep like that, his head on Tienne's chest, a throw from the couch over his shoulders, feeling as at peace as he ever had in the world.

HE AND Tienne were awakened the next morning by Molly bouncing on his bed, dressed in a billowy floral flannel nightgown straight out of a Victorian romance, with fleece-lined slipper-boots that went midcalf and a basic microfleece sweatshirt worn on top like a robe or wrapper. Her wild hair cascaded over her shoulders and around her face, and Stirling couldn't help but smile at her as she shook the mattress on the frame.

"Get *up*!" she crowed, as excited as a ten-year-old. "You guys! The whole world is waiting for you!"

Tienne sat up and yawned. "How did we get here?" he asked. "Didn't we…?"

Stirling went to run his fingers through his hair and encountered the whisper-soft qiviut hat instead.

"We did," he muttered. It *hadn't* been a dream. They *had* fallen asleep looking at the snow. "Molly, how did we get here?"

She stared at him. "Who *cares*, little brother! Merry Christmas! Come *on*. Grace woke up this morning and read the note I left him on his door last night when he and Hunter were having loud, noisy sex. He's going *apeshit*. You need to come up and see!"

That was enough to send Stirling out of bed, finding the slippers he'd worn up the stairs right next to the bedstand. He turned to Tienne with a grin. "Are you ready?"

Tienne grimaced and stood up himself before going to the dresser, pulling the two sweatshirts they'd been wearing around the house from the top, and tossing one to Stirling.

"Now," he said, nodding.

"By the way," Molly said as they left Stirling's room and went up the stairs, "nice hat. I want it."

"No," Stirling told her. "Tienne gave it to me. It's special."

She gave him a sideways glance. "Is it as special as *I* am?"

"Nothing is as special as *you* are," he told her, seizing her hand. "But it's still special."

She cast a speculative glance behind her. "Can Tienne get *me* such a hat?"

"Oui," Tienne returned playfully. "So long as your brother can keep his."

"He can," she declared and then paused as they reached the top of the stairs to kiss Stirling's cheek. "And definitely keep *him*, little brother. I adore him. Now come *on*!"

And with that she pulled them both into a bright swirling *loud* kaleidoscope of ripping paper and happy thank-yous, of excited greetings and warm exchanges. People were respectful of the two of them—there was always a "May I?" before the hug or the ruffle of hair or the playful slug on the shoulder—and by the time the rush of presents was done, Stirling felt as though he and Tienne could go back downstairs and sleep for a week.

He wasn't sure if hunting down the mystery of his parents' death would be more or less rewarding than this moment here, surrounded by the family he hadn't known he'd needed, but he did know that the one was not possible without the other, and he could only be so full of gratitude his heart felt as though it might break out of his chest.

Stepping Outside the Van

AFTER THE initial rush of gift giving and excitement, Tienne and Stirling left their gifts in a small pile in the living room and took some breakfast to the foyer, where they listened to the noise—frequently punctuated by Grace's triumphant crowing—from a bit of a distance while they drank hot chocolate and ate quiche and fruit in blessed quiet. Unsurprisingly, Stirling fell back asleep on his corner of the couch, while Tienne took his time over an illustrated book of heroes throughout the ages, flipping each page slowly and reading the captions as well as the legends behind the heroes. It had been a gift from Danny, with a note that said it was from his personal collection and an inscription in the front from the editor to one "Mitchell Benjamin" to prove it. Tienne had made that ID three years before Danny had returned to Felix and his family, and he'd clutched the book to his chest, eyes absurdly bright, when he'd seen it.

Now he was staring at a plate of Gilgamesh and Enkidu when he heard a quiet clearing of the throat and looked up to see Carl in the doorway, still in his ridiculous and dear Garfield pajamas, with a scarf that Julia had hand-knitted wrapped around his neck, Tienne's gift, packaging and all, tucked under his arm, and his hands full of hot chocolate and a small plate of pastries and quiche.

"No diet today?" Tienne teased gently, feeling brave and pleased with it.

"It's Christmas," the big man said soberly, setting his food and mug down on the table across from the stuffed chair. "Calories don't count on Christmas."

Tienne grinned at him in agreement and replaced the burgundy cashmere throw that had fallen from Stirling's shoulders when he'd curled up in a tight little ball to sleep. Sleep softened him. Awake, his jaw was square and set, his gray eyes sharp and assessing, and his posture almost frighteningly solid. Asleep, he was content.

"All the people," Tienne said in explanation. "He loves the family, but...." He shrugged.

"We're exhausting," Carl conceded. "I get it." He smiled a little and picked up his mug. "He didn't wake up even a little when Chuck and I carried you two to the bedroom."

Tienne groaned softly and buried his face in his hands. "That is so embarrassing."

"No," Carl demurred. "It was sweet. I mean, I'm going to be a stepfather eventually. I understand it's part of my duties."

"But we're supposed to be *grown*," Tienne protested.

"You are." Carl tried to look modest and failed. "I've been working out a *lot* in the past year. That was like my little Christmas present to myself."

Tienne chuckled, understanding Stirling's bond with this man. He was a favorite uncle or a big brother. "I'll tell Stirling you said so."

Carl wrinkled his nose. "Let him think it was Santa," he said, and Tienne grinned back. Carl winked before taking Tienne's gift from under his arm. He'd opened it carefully, so the caricature of him and Michael was intact, and he showed it to Tienne and looked suitably impressed. "These were *awesome*," he said. "Everybody was excited about them. You could have simply given us drawings in Sharpie and your Christmas work would have been *done*."

Tienne's cheeks warmed with the praise. "It's my favorite thing," he admitted gruffly. "The forgeries were to pay the bills." They were also such different parts of his brain. The forgeries required planning and foresight, but paintings? They required almost an instinctive recognition of the beauty of things and how to portray that beauty with color and line. It was the difference between covering Stirling's shoulders with the throw and trying to capture that softness in sleep.

Carl held up the passport, the credit cards, and the Maryland driver's license that had been in the package. "But they are also things of beauty," he praised. "All under Carlson Sternburg. It's fabulous. The identity is backstopped in the computer, and I've got the paperwork—this is going to get me through a lot of fun adventures, I have the feeling. Thank you, Tienne—it was a very thoughtful gift." Carl nodded at Stirling again and indicated the hat. "But not quite as romantic as that."

"He likes the textures," Tienne murmured. Lots of little cables on that hat, and some lace as well, not to mention the exquisite feel of the yarn itself.

"He's a young man who pays attention to details," Carl said admiringly. "Much like yourself." Carl's gift to Tienne had been a way out of the lease on his apartment and the option of subletting it and making a small income from it should he decide to stay at the Salinger mansion. A pesky detail, and a thing that Tienne would have muddled about in, lost and flailing, unless someone stepped up to help. It was odd how the most practical and un-Christmassy of presents was one of the things Tienne was most grateful for that morning.

"Only artistic ones," Tienne said, feeling inadequate.

"Tienne, I am not a leading man. I'm not Josh or Danny or Felix. I've always been a bit player, even in my own life. Until suddenly Michael Carmody saw me as the star of the show. It doesn't matter that you're not the mastermind or the grifter. And Stirling is more hacker than any one crew deserves. When he and Josh work together, they can reprogram the world. We've got Torrance, who's our spin doctor or our face man, not to mention Molly. And God knows, Chuck and Hunter could probably take over small countries together. All you need to be is Stirling's leading man."

Tienne looked fondly at Stirling clutching that cashmere throw. It had been a gift from Josh, and when Stirling had asked him about the burgundy color—a little bit out of Stirling's usual array of grays, blacks, and browns—Josh had told him that he deserved a small taste of the rainbow.

Stirling had chuckled and clutched the throw to him for the rest of the morning. Tienne understood then that Stirling was being invited to do more, *be* more to the organization than the man behind the computer, and he realized how much this meant to his stalwart hacker that Josh and his family saw more to him than a computer genius.

"I'd say it's all I want to be," Tienne murmured, "but I think I'd like to be something to all of you as well."

Carl's low rumble warmed him as much as hot chocolate would have. "I think that can be arranged."

Tienne leaned his head against the side of the couch, abruptly as tired as Stirling, but he still managed a smile. "I've never had a Christmas like this one," he confessed gruffly. "I don't think there's a card big enough to thank you all."

Carl stood. "I'm going to go get you some chocolate to drink when you wake up from your nap. Don't thank us, Tienne. *Play* with us. It's all anyone here wants from you. It's our favorite gift."

Tienne was humming bars of music from the Offspring, "Come Out and Play," as Carl walked softly from the room.

A FEW days later, the house had been cleaned up, the presents sorted, and only the cheery decorations and extra pounds remained as obvious reminders that the season was still in session. Grace had found all of his little Lego guys, including the one that represented himself, and he'd spent two days indulging his hyperfixation and building a little Lego castle showcasing all of his people doing their people things. Most of the crew was still indulging in naps—and fudge—but some of the faithful had resumed working out, and apparently the zealous had indulged in everybody's favorite pastimes: snooping, conning, grifting, and theft.

Which was made very apparent when Felix and Danny began making requests to Tienne for IDs and passports and to Stirling for, "Just a little background here," and, "Maybe you want to dig there."

And after a little more of this and a little more of that and before people had finished their packing, a briefing was in order.

Stirling was more than ready.

Tienne had learned more and more of his moods over the past couple of weeks and had come to recognize that when he sat at his computer for hours, needing to be reminded to eat and drink—and sometimes, even to use the bathroom—that meant something was consuming him. Yes, Stirling and Molly had been very reasonable, putting the search for their parents' mystery on hold, but now it was time to work, and they were more than ready.

Tienne respected Stirling's needs. He knew who had killed his own father, and why he'd need nothing short of an army to get revenge, but Stirling and Molly had a chance to get some badly needed justice. But that didn't mean he didn't want more time to make love.

They spared some time every night to touch, to pleasure, to gasp and come, but Tienne, who had never thought of himself as a sexual being—who had, in fact, been shocked when Levka Dubov had made his first aggressions, because he hadn't imagined anyone would see him in that light—was suddenly yearning for those moments when he had Stirling's complete attention on him, on his body, on his needs.

He'd started to wonder if maybe he should, perhaps, assert his wants. Molly would come down and drag both of them to dinner, in spite of Stirling's objections that he only needed one more moment to finish what he was doing. Tienne, who knew what it was to be consumed with his work, and who spent mornings deep inside his art in the solarium, was always amused at how happy Stirling seemed to be when he was pulled away for something as simple as food.

Could Tienne, perhaps, *seduce* Stirling away from his computer?

He wondered.

But not tonight.

Tonight, they had important things to think about.

"Okay, children, are we all here?" Danny, who was usually their self-proclaimed MC for briefings, glanced around the room. All the people Tienne had come to expect were there—Danny and Felix, Julia and Leon, Josh, Grace and Hunter, Chuck and Lucius, Stirling, Molly, and Tienne—all of them in their most comfortable of casual clothes, with plates full of Christmas goodies, because nobody felt like giving those up yet. Even Torrance Grayson was there that night, looking altogether different from his usual nattily dressed self in a slim sweat suit with a zippered collar and ankles. Something about the tousled hair and unusual amount of stubble told Tienne that Torrance had allowed himself to truly relax during the holidays, and the people in the household were getting to see a side of the young YouTube news star that nobody else did.

The only person *not* there was Michael, who had three more days with his children before he returned home to leave again the next day. Carl was there, though, in jeans and a sweater, sitting next to the audio/visual island with Josh, looking very much like a second in command. Stirling was sitting cross-legged on the couch next to Tienne, his computer in his lap, his concentration wholly on the screen in front of them.

"All accounted for, Danny," Molly chirped gamely from her spot in front of Stirling on the floor. "What do you got for us?"

Danny winked at her. "Well, for one thing, some advice not to shove me in any ventilation shafts—I've eaten like a horse over the last couple of days. Grace, I'm afraid it's all up to you."

"I found all my Lego guys," Grace said happily. "I can do anything."

"Then could you stop going through Lucius's underwear?" Chuck asked, pain in his voice. "Gotta tell you, it's a real cock-kill."

Grace gave him a raspberry, and Tienne assumed that meant Grace was going through everybody's drawers twice that night. Well, some people had cats that stole socks.

"And moving on," Danny murmured. "Step one, buy new underwear."

Everybody laughed uneasily, and Felix added, "Step two, burn what we have now."

Grace rolled his eyes. "You people act like I haven't seen all of it before. One word for all of you— when it starts getting holes, throw it out."

There was a collective sigh, and Danny soldiered on. "Okay, Carl, on screen."

Carl hit a button, and what appeared was a series of photographs of photographs—this was, Tienne surmised, the pictures of the effects from the shipwreck that had been in the classified folders they'd risked so much to get access to at the port authority.

"This," Danny said, "was in Fred Christopher's pockets when his body was recovered. You will notice two things—"

"The phone seems to be on," Josh said. "And—" He paused and looked around and, to Tienne's surprise, paled and backed down. "—you say it, Uncle Danny. I was… really mad about this."

Danny sighed. "Yes, son. I know." He gave Stirling and Molly a truly compassionate look. "Josh was right. He saw some of this earlier. The phone is still on, and there are papers that were found in Fred's pockets that have very little water damage. The same with Stella's effects, which were found in her purse. The luggage seems to be missing, and some of that is theft, which I understand happens sometimes in small ports, but the most disturbing thing here is while the cause of death on their certificates says 'drowning….'" He left it for Stirling to finish.

"None of their most personal effects were wet," Stirling said, voice hoarse.

"No, they were not," Danny agreed. "In fact, we can read the receipts in Fred's pockets and see the last few entries Stella made in her checkbook. Now, Fred and Stella were thoroughly modern with all their banking, but Felix told me they kept what they called a 'vacation balance' and then withdrew against it when they traveled."

Felix added, "It was typical Fred. He could literally buy an island, but while he was never stingy, he liked to know where he stood."

Tienne heard Stirling's indrawn breath and put a comforting hand on Stirling's knee. To his surprise, Stirling took his fingers off his keyboard long enough to give that hand a reassuring squeeze.

"So yes," Danny said. "While there was nothing else to indicate that the Coast Guard report and the actual circumstances were different, that alone is suspicious. As were some of the things marked in Stella's 'vacation balance.' It indicated that Fred and Stella made some very *large* withdrawals, far above their means. Now, we checked the withdrawal amounts against their bank account, and anybody want to guess what we found?"

"Don't have to guess," Stirling said excitedly. "I did the checking, and now I can see why. Those withdrawals were wired from their account when they were *supposed* to be lost in the storm. Except the time's wrong. The times for those withdrawals are *after* Fred and Stella texted us that they were okay and *before* the Coast Guard told us they'd discovered the wreck. So sometime between when the yacht was in the clear and Fred and Stella were found dead...." He paused, frowning.

"They were suddenly very interested in making other people richer," Felix supplied grimly. "But that's not the only suspicious thing."

"It is, indeed, not." Danny shook his head. "We didn't get a chance to photograph the effects of the captain or the tour guide, his wife, but... Carl?"

"But I saw several forms from Atlantic United National Enterprises in their paperwork—" He gave Grace a frustrated look. "We call it AUNTIE. It's a rival insurance company to Serpentus, and while yes, Serpentus is the devil, AUNTIE is the devil's excrement. Let's say I've never been told to overlook a line. I've been pressured to cut a corner *without* the line, but I know people who have left Atlantic United who did so because their board of directors is fine with doing things that are completely unethical. Given that, I took a look at the paperwork. It's what I was doing before Grace cut the alarm."

Two documents appeared side by side on the screen. "Now, Fred and Stella's life insurance papers were not in the files I looked up, and they shouldn't have been. In fact, *those* folders should be in a storage vault somewhere at Serpentus, where Fred and Stella *were* insured. I checked. But these papers from Atlantic United *are*, which is strange because...." He paused, as though to let others draw their conclusions.

"Those are life insurance payouts to the captain and his wife," Lucius said. It would figure, Tienne thought dryly. Lucius wasn't a grifter, a thief, or an insurance agent, but he did know his paperwork.

"Bingo," Carl said, putting his finger to his nose. "And they are, in fact, quite large. Anybody want to look for the other anomaly?"

"They're forged," Tienne said, suddenly aware that his skill set was valuable here. "They were filed *after* the accident, although the dates have been fixed to make it look like they were filed before so the couple's children could benefit from their death."

"How do you know that?" Stirling asked. "The numbers look identical to me."

"They're identical *between* the pages," Tienne said. "There are usually minute differences, particularly on numbers. People hesitate over the date all the time, even if they've written it a thousand times in an hour. These are almost a stamp. This was very carefully done, and the signatures as well."

"And points to the forger," Torrance Grayson said with admiration. "Now, can anybody tell me what that means?"

Josh gave a delicate snort. "You—get out of the driver's seat. It's our trip."

Torrance's grin, Tienne noticed, had the teeniest bit of infatuation in it. Interesting. Closeted policemen, out and proud YouTube reporters—who else had been quietly pining for Josh Salinger?

"Well, then," Torrance told Josh flippantly, "drive!"

"It means," Josh replied, pitching his voice for everybody, "that someone wanted an insurance payout to the family of the two dead employees—and a healthy one—retroactive of their deaths. Carl, did you find anything about their effects?"

"No, I did not," Carl said. "And I looked. The cook, the maid, the one engineer as well. In fact, they *all* had insurance payouts like this one, but that was *all* they had." He glanced at Tienne and put his finger to his nose again. "All with the same forged date, I might add. The *exact* forged date."

"So," Felix intoned, "we have what appears to be blood money paid to the families of the islanders who were killed on the yacht, which, of course, implies that they're either all dead or all part of the cover-up."

"According to the searches you had me do," Stirling said, "they really are all dead. There are burial plots and cremation receipts. I have names of family to talk to, most of whom live in the islands as well."

Tienne cocked his head. Stirling hadn't said what he'd been working on over the last few days. It occurred to him that he and Stirling enjoyed their stillness so much that they might need to work on their words some more.

"It also," Danny continued thoughtfully, "implies that whoever did this is local. Maybe not legitimate, but somebody who was settling in for a while."

"Again," Molly murmured, "Fred's island folly. Not moving anytime soon."

"No, it is not," Felix agreed. "But it *is* getting more mysterious the more we discover."

"Did the insurance forms get us anything else?" Leon asked, and Felix grinned at him. Julia's suitor had been kind and attentive—and seemed to fit seamlessly into the family fun and games. Apparently he was much like Tienne, in that he'd only recently allowed himself to be absorbed into the Salinger crew. But unlike Tienne, he didn't seem to have a shy bone in his handsome, muscular body.

"You're enjoying this very much, aren't you?" Felix said happily.

Leon shrugged. "Indeed I am. Although the getting fleeced at poker is something I could have lived without."

There was a suppressed snort from various parts of the room, and Tienne and Stirling looked at each other in confusion. Grace, who was sitting on Stirling's other side, leaned over and cleared that up.

"There was a late-night game the day after Christmas. All the old men went. Apparently, Mr. I Own a Yacht and Can Con the Best is a little rusty at poker."

He spoke in the world's worst stage whisper, and Leon di Rossi gave him an amused look.

"Consider me schooled," he said with a regal nod.

Hunter spoke up. "And you were," he said. "But you were also a damned good sport who asked a damned good question. Felix?"

"It was indeed a good question," Felix said before winking and adding, "and Danny and I can spot you money if you want a rematch."

Leon gave him a narrow-eyed glare that was obviously all play. "Game. On."

"Answer, Felix," Chuck prompted. "I think Molly's about ready to levitate on nerves alone."

Felix gave Molly and Stirling an apologetic look. "Sorry, children. I'm afraid it's been an eventful vacation. But Chuck and Hunter are right. Carl did track down who paid for the insurance policies, and he found out a couple of interesting facts."

"First of all, there were a number of shell corporations disguising the identities." Carl nodded to Stirling. "Stirling got through all of that noise, and once I had the names of the actual companies, we discovered they were Chicago based." He nodded to Felix and Danny. "They were, in fact, people that Felix and Danny work with on a regular basis."

"But since Felix and Danny need to appear legit," Torrance Grayson said, "and it's my job to be sort of rogue and in your face, I'm the one who made contact."

Stirling and Molly both turned to Torrance in surprise.

"Torrance," Molly said. "My man. I'm so impressed."

Torrance inclined his head modestly. "Well, you all have given me such delicious stories—and Felix, of course, gave me my start. It was the least I could do." Torrance, in fact, had been one of the premiere up-and-coming newscasters in Felix's cable network before an attempted coup had caused him to walk out in protest. Although Felix had since regained control of his businesses—and had reclaimed his reputation as a fair and equitable boss—Torrance had remained independent and had amassed a following on YouTube that he used to their benefit on occasion. Tienne had long understood the distinction between covert business dealings and actual criminality, and Torrance Grayson was a sterling example.

"What was?" Grace asked, obviously as stunned as Stirling and Molly. "What was the least you could do?"

"Apparently it was something Carl did first," Torrance told them. "I visited the corporations under the guise of interviewing their CEOs about humanitarian causes. Which I did, by the way. It was a nice little fluff piece for the holidays. But while I was there, I had Felix call to distract the honchos, and I got into their open computers."

"Nicely done," Danny said. "Charm, guile—you would have made a top-notch grifter."

"High praise indeed," Torrance replied. "But I sent emails to Danny and Josh so they'd have the foothold to do a little digging."

"Not me?" Stirling asked, his voice laced with hurt.

"This is supposed to be a present, darling," Julia said, her laughter soft. "There will be plenty of work for everybody. But Josh and Danny wanted to spare you some of the digging." Her voice dropped subtly. "You had other things on your plate."

Stirling cast Tienne a sideways look, and to Tienne's delight, a dark red crescent appeared over each sharp cheekbone. Absolutely, he thought to himself. Absolutely, he needed to seduce Stirling away from his keyboard that night.

"Thank you," Stirling said, his voice low but intense. "Everybody. This was a lot of digging. What did you find?"

There was a pregnant pause, and Danny let out a low whistle. "Stirling, do you remember that list of people you sent me? Fred's friends who had asked your father for money but who had been denied?"

"Yes?" Stirling and Molly exchanged looks, and Tienne could tell they were shoring themselves up for hurt.

"Three of those names cross-referenced with VPs in the three companies," Danny told him, compassion written large across his face. "And that's not all."

"Hit us," Molly prompted. "We don't talk to those assholes anyway."

But given the way Stirling was clutching her shoulder and she was covering his hand with hers, Tienne could tell the betrayal hurt.

"All three of them have funneled money into a company that as far as we can tell doesn't *make* anything but money," Josh said ruthlessly. "It's called Fosters Incorporated, and we've all read the description about six times. There's shit about leveraging synergy and a whole lot of pirated rhetoric from MLMs about a think tank needing natural space or whatever, but it's bullshit. And the guy with his name on all this bullshit…?"

Oh, Tienne could answer this one, but Molly and Stirling needed to be the ones to actually say it. "Harve and Carolyn," they said in tandem.

Felix, Danny, Josh, and Carl *all* put their fingers on their noses. It seemed their suspicions about Fred and Stella's birth son had proved more than accurate.

"Got it in one," Danny said. "In fact, you were exceptionally accurate. I predicted it would *only* be Harve, but Carolyn has family money that she's invested in this enterprise as well, whatever it may be. And are we all ready for this, people? Because it's not going to be a surprise."

"Let me guess," Grace said. "The company's located in Barbados?"

"Not just a pretty face," Danny praised. "It is indeed. But that was almost predictable. There was one wrinkly carrot in the bag that did throw us for a loop, and you all need to take a look at it before we pack our bags and apply our sunscreen." He nodded at Carl, who obliged with a slide that made Tienne gasp.

Levka Dubov appeared on the screen.

"For those of you who missed the briefing about Tienne's nasty little attacker, this is Levka Dubov, and he's an asshole. He is also—"

Chuck broke in. "He's also attached to a new, up-and-coming branch of the Serbian mob. He's midlevel. High enough not to kill, low enough not to know everything." He paused. "And I hesitate to mention this, but it's necessary. His mob has ties to everybody's favorite scumbag—"

"Kadjic?" Tienne asked, a low buzzing in his stomach.

Chuck nodded. "Yes. He's not *in* Kadjic's mob, but he deals with them. I'm not saying we're going to turn the corner and run into this guy, but don't be surprised if his name comes up."

"What exactly was Levka's dealing with Tienne?" Leon asked apologetically. He eyed Tienne with gentle eyes. "No offense, Tienne, but you're not exactly mob material."

Tienne gave Leon a faint smile. "He sought me out at a public event, but I think it was because he'd heard about my skill as a forger. I... I wouldn't have worked with him, except...."

Chuck saved him from more personal revelations. "He was trying to threaten and intimidate Tienne here into making him and his mob buddies fake IDs and passports." Chuck turned toward Tienne. "Tienne, we never asked you, but what country were those passports issued to?"

"Guyana," Tienne said in wonder. "I… I should have put it together before. It was such an obscure choice."

"But very handy," Chuck said. A small smile flitted across his good-ole-boy features. "And you were occupied with so many other things. And not to state the obvious, but you all know where Guyana is, don't you?"

"About a four-day sail from our destination vacation," Hunter said. "But it's attached to the mainland and probably easier to smuggle things to and from. So we've got the Serbian mob, a desert island, insurance payments to the families of murder victims, and prominent Chicago businessmen fronting a corporation getting money from nowhere. Wow." A smile split Hunter's lean, predatory features. "This is gonna be a kickass vacation."

"It is indeed," Felix said. "But I'm afraid we're going to have to do a bit of questioning on the islands before we know how to approach this. I propose we do a little more poking around our crooked businessmen and then make a few stops between Puerto Rico and Barbados while partying on the islands and sending out feelers."

"We're going to have to go to the island," Molly said, voicing the obvious.

"Oh, we are," Felix said. "But forewarned is forearmed. We've got Serbian mob involved here, Molly, my darling. We want to bring these people down, but we also want you and Stirling free to live a long life reveling in your revenge too. They're good goals, and they needn't be mutually exclusive, but they do require a bit of planning."

"You people," Torrance Grayson said, looking tired and pleased and excited all at once. "You *do* bring me the best presents. I am forever in awe."

THE MEETING broke up after that, and at Stirling's urging, they played poker with Carl, Chuck, Lucius, Josh, and Torrance for a few hands. Tienne noted that Stirling was not a very good poker player. It wasn't that he didn't know when to hold or when to fold, and he was good at masking his emotions. But he couldn't bluff. The few times he'd tried, everybody at the table had marked the moment he'd decided to pretend he had a hand and said, "Hold." For a moment, Tienne had felt a surge of anger. Everybody at the table was taking terrible advantage of him. But then he watched Stirling analyze the cards, analyze everybody else's reactions, and ask questions.

"But you knew I had a hand and you held anyway. Why?"

"Because I bluffed last time too," Chuck said. "You calculate odds—odds were good I actually had something this time. You were sure to bow out, and you did."

So yes, the losses and the lessons were hard, but everybody at the table was good at explaining what had happened and why. They weren't being kind to Stirling, they were *teaching* him, and God, Stirling was so smart. He was learning. On the last hand of the night, he bluffed on a pair of fives without hesitation or calculation—and won.

Tienne and Stirling took their winnings—they all played with real cash this time, which shouldn't have surprised Tienne but did—and bowed slightly before disappearing to Stirling's room. As they were walking down the stairs, it occurred to Tienne that he'd stopped sleeping in his bedroom entirely in the last few days before Christmas.

"Stirling, do you need your space from me?" he asked as they approached the landing to the den.

"No."

Tienne suppressed a spurt of exasperation. He'd known Stirling wasn't one for small talk or too much explanation; it had been one of the things that had drawn Tienne to him in the first place.

"Good," he said simply, pleased when Stirling took his hand and turned to him as they neared the door to Stirling's quarters.

"Why would you ask?" Stirling's gray eyes searched his questioningly, and Tienne felt that breathless anticipation that had tinged all of their kisses.

He really, really wanted Stirling's fine mind, his solidly beating heart, his unique soul, to focus on *him*. It made him feel seen as he hadn't felt seen since he was a child.

"I seem to have moved into your room," Tienne said apologetically. He had to tell his lungs to work. Gah! They'd slept in the same bed for a week, and he still had to tell his lungs to work.

"Do you want to move back?" Stirling's head was cocked, as it often was when he was processing emotions like computer functions, hoping to come up with the correct equation.

Tienne thought about it. "No," he said. "My room was bare. My art space in the solarium is... is more me, but it's as though I had no soul to put into my own room. I feel like I have more soul to put into yours."

Stirling's smile—sometimes an ephemeral thing in his square, plane-and-angle face, sometimes as solid as a church foundation—flitted across his lips. "I should object to that," he said, "but I won't. I like that you put your soul in my space." His eyes darted up and to the right, not as though he were lying, but as though he was looking for the perfect words. "I'm very bad at choosing artwork or color. If you like, you could put something interesting but not too—" He shrugged. "—jumpy. You could put a picture up." That wonderful dark red appeared on his cheekbones. "I love *your* work. If you like. I know you have lots to do. Commissions from everybody. You're working on passports. But I'd love it if you put some more of your soul in... uhm, our room."

Tienne smiled shyly. "Our room?" he asked.

"Yes."

And then their lips met, and, still kissing, they made their way inside Stirling's suite. The door clicked behind them, and the kiss became harder, more urgent, Stirling's mouth dominating Tienne's, his sturdy presence pinning Tienne in place against the door behind him as his body took charge of everything in front.

Stirling's hands—soft, sleek but firm—shoved under Tienne's sweater, smoothed across his rib cage, palmed his nipples. Tienne raised his hands above his head, and Stirling seized that opportunity to haul his shirt and sweatshirt off over his head and then took over the kiss again. Tienne allowed it, going liquid against the wall as Stirling ravaged Tienne's mouth before moving to his throat.

Tienne tilted his head back and gasped at the sensation of Stirling's lips trailing down the base of his throat, of his teeth grazing Tienne's collarbone, his hands still taking ownership of Tienne's stomach, his ribs, his hips.

"Oh God," he murmured. "This is wonderful. What prompted this?" He'd been going to beg for it, seduce this attention out of Stirling, draw him out of his laser focus on his computer, his cause. But that one mention of Tienne, more at home in Stirling's rooms than in his own, had brought those plans crashing down in the most wonderful way.

"Lots of things," Stirling whispered as he lowered his head to Tienne's nipple. He played with it for a moment, making Tienne gasp and clench his fingers against Stirling's scalp. His hair was too short, too tightly trimmed to stroke or to pull, but Tienne needed something, anything, to anchor himself in his pleasure.

"Like?" Tienne murmured on a breathless little moan. Stirling moved his head to the other nipple, licking and tantalizing first before answering.

"I realized you were in my room voluntarily. That you chose to be mine. That's important." He lowered his head again, sucking a little bit harder, and Tienne moaned.

"I am yours," he pledged. "And being with you is important—*so* important—ah! God! Stirling!" Tienne thrust his hips forward, grinding up against Stirling's hips and whimpering with need at the pressure on his cock.

Stirling backed up enough to shove Tienne's sweats down his hips, along with his briefs, and Tienne kicked them hurriedly off, aware that Stirling was undressing too.

In a moment they were both bare, and Tienne got to skate his palms along Stirling's skin with the same awe he'd felt since the very beginning. It was like his hands drank in the beauty, the color, all of the tiny unique textures that made up his lover, and pulled them deep into his pores—into his soul.

"Anything else?" Tienne whispered as Stirling danced him to the bed. He paused to strip the covers down before laying Tienne on clean sheets and covering Tienne's long slender body with his own shorter, sturdier one. He kept up the kissing, the sucking, the laving, the *marking* as he moved his way down, but paused with his head directly above Tienne's groin.

"I've been studying," Stirling said, before darting out a quick little tongue to tease Tienne's cock.

"Wha—ah!"

Stirling engulfed the head with his mouth this time before pulling back and smiling, all the while keeping up a firm stroke in case Tienne forgot what they were really doing in bed at that moment. As. If.

"I realized I didn't have a clear picture as to what I wanted to do during sex," he clarified, and Tienne choked on a laugh at the same time he widened his knees, exposing himself, making his body vulnerable and available to anything Stirling had in mind.

"You needed a picture?" Tienne managed.

"So I did some homework," Stirling said soberly. "And it was the *best* kind of homework, where I looked at pictures and read firsthand accounts. And now I want to do some hands-on practice!" He punctuated that with a stroke of Tienne's backside, and Tienne's breathless moan was not enough to show his appreciation. "Now that I have a picture in my head, I want to savor you. You are a gift. And we have tonight, and I don't want to look up all the things that are dangerous about Barbados tonight. Do you know why?"

"Because they have acid fruit and green monkeys and that's terrifying?" Stirling was not the only one who could use a computer, but Stirling had been sending them all briefings about what he'd termed "unfamiliar terrain."

"Well, yes, but...." Stirling licked him again, squeezing his shaft and swirling his tongue on Tienne's bell, playing with the slit and the harp string with his tongue.

"What?" Tienne rasped, his body so aroused he was surprised his brains hadn't completely scrambled.

"Being gay—doing gay sex things—is *illegal* on Barbados," Stirling said. "And here, in my rooms, surrounded by people who would fight for us, I want to do really illegal things to you. All of you. I want to lick your asshole and finger you and stretch you and fuck you and make you come. It's all I can think about, and it's a gift, and I want to *take that gift*."

"*Please!*" Tienne moaned. No more words. He'd been a fool to think they were needed. The way Stirling was touching him, *taking* him right now, should have been more than enough.

Stirling kept sucking his cock, stroking and teasing, and Tienne stroked the crisp, trimmed ringlets on his scalp, gasping for air, for invasion, for *something*.

"Stirling?" he begged.

"Mmf?" Stirling stared up his body, his mouth full and stretched with Tienne's cock, and Tienne could have swooned with the raw carnality of it. From Stirling. Who could have guessed his lover had such rawness inside?

"You said you would fuck me," he gasped, trying not to come, trying not to end first.

"Come in my mouth first," Stirling murmured, quickly sticking a finger in his mouth before swallowing Tienne down to the root again.

As Tienne struggled to assimilate the command, and the motion, he felt Stirling's slick finger at his entrance, doing what he'd promised—stretching him. He lost all cohesion and cried out, his hands flailing at his sides as he did what Stirling had told him to and came.

He pumped solidly into Stirling's mouth, and Tienne felt him swallow once and then hold the come inside his cheeks, the heat and slick of it heady and erotic.

As soon as Tienne fell back against the sheets, sweating, dreamy from orgasm, Stirling shoved his thighs up to his chest and spat come on his asshole.

Tienne's whole body trembled from the *idea* of what he'd done.

And then Stirling lowered his head and began to lick.

Tienne's words fled; any thoughts of dignity fled. He was simply a vessel for Stirling's wants, a thing to be pleasured and give pleasure in return. His eyes rolled back in his head, and he shuddered, coming to again only when Stirling reached for the end table for the little bottle of slick with which to oil his cock.

As Stirling lined himself up at Tienne's slippery and stretched entrance, he paused. "You're ready, right?"

Tienne managed a garbled, "Pllss…." as Stirling fitted himself in and thrust, firmly and gently, inside.

Tienne's consciousness exploded, and he was aware only of the feel of Stirling inside him and all of the lovely, exciting things his body was doing in reaction. His cock had filled again and was burgeoning, *aching* to be stroked, but Tienne *couldn't*…. He could only clasp Stirling's biceps, muscled and defined, and wrap his thighs around Stirling's hips.

He found he was panting words after all. Nonsense. "I want, I want, I want… ahhhh…." as Stirling picked up the pace and thrust harder and deeper, hitting his sweet spot, hitting his soul.

His orgasm wasn't so much a climax of body as it was a destruction of worlds. Planets turned to dust behind Tienne's eyes, and his body was rendered limp and useless as pleasure electrified him into plasma.

Stirling gave a satisfied little groan and came, spurting come inside him, so hot and real that Tienne could feel it fill him, feel it slide outside as Stirling collapsed and softened, still rutting furiously as though he never wanted to stop.

For several moments, the roaring in Tienne's ears eclipsed all sound.

When his heart had slowed enough for him to breathe again, he whispered, "I love breaking the law."

Stirling gave a ripe chuckle but didn't move from his sprawl across Tienne's chest. "There's consequences," he mumbled.

"Damn the sheets and wash the torpedoes," Tienne said nonsensically, and they both giggled, breaking the almost deadly serious spell that their lovemaking had cast.

Many more minutes after that, they managed to move, to stumble to the bathroom and wash up, to get out clean sheets and shove the well-used ones into the hamper.

When they wiggled under the blankets and comforter again, though, they were still naked.

"Tienne?" Stirling murmured, fitting his head on Tienne's shoulder.

"Yes?"

"I forget people a lot. Molly has to drag me to dinner sometimes. When we roomed together in Chicago, she'd bring me coffee in the morning if we hadn't seen each other the day before. Promise me something?"

"Anything," Tienne murmured fervently.

"If you ever feel neglected, like you need my attention, please ask for it. Please don't think I don't care anymore. I don't really forget you all. Time goes faster than I expect it to. Do you understand?"

Oh. The words were so close to what Tienne had been thinking that he felt the burn of tears.

"I understand," he murmured, kissing the top of Stirling's head. "I was planning to seduce you tonight for precisely that reason."

Stirling's grin was a thing of beauty. "That would be good too."

All of it—*all of it*—all of them together was good. "Is being gay really illegal in Barbados?"

"Yeah." Stirling snorted. "I mean, I don't think anybody's going to come arrest our entire yacht, but, you know, it's not nice to invade an island and start having sex in the shadows like bunnies to prove a point."

Tienne paused, thinking about the most unusual— and very gay—crew. "I'm not sure if we should tell your friend Grace or not."

"I know, right?" Stirling asked, laughing softly. "On the one hand, it would be good if Hunter knew so he could put a rein on Grace if it's needed, but on the other—"

"Grace might end up having sex in the town square, to be—"

"Grace," they finished together.

"Grace does pride himself on getting away with things," Stirling murmured. "I say we tell him and see if Hunter survives."

Tienne chuckled sleepily. "Not a bad way to go, really."

"Mm…." Stirling's voice had gone dreamy. "I could go that way."

A thought occurred to Tienne. "Do you… do you want me to penetrate?"

"Do you want to?" Stirling sounded almost asleep.

"Selfishly, no, but someday…."

"We can have lots of sex," Stirling slurred, "and see."

That was a good note to fall asleep on, Tienne thought. That promised good things in their future.

He couldn't ever remember having a moment so replete.

Travel

STIRLING DID not necessarily love traveling. He liked routine, he liked space, and he liked physical comfort. He disliked heat, humidity, sand, being jostled, and not knowing where his next meal was coming from. While he'd looked forward to the adventure, and being with his friends, he had not particularly looked forward to getting to the yacht or exploring off of it.

When he realized that Leon had volunteered his private jet to get the bulk of the crew to San Juan, where the outfitted yacht awaited, he'd felt the burn of tears in the back of his eyes and the obligation to actually search Josh's uncle out as they traveled and say thank you personally, rather than as part of the group.

The plane was spacious to an extent, but given how many of them there were—fourteen—it was still pretty crowded. Thankfully, Lucius had volunteered to have Chuck fly his private plane, with Talia, Molly, and their luggage. This lessened the jostling, and while Stirling usually didn't like traveling without his sister, having Tienne in the seat next to him, smelling vaguely of linseed oil and listening to an audiobook in French, seemed to calm him right down.

Stirling waited until Julia had left her seat next to Leon to go chat with Danny and Felix for a moment before moving to take her place.

"Hello, Stirling. Are you enjoying the flight?" Leon di Rossi was devastating as an urbane business-man, but Stirling always thought he couldn't escape the tiniest bit of being a pirate, either. Julia couldn't be blamed for being fascinated.

Stirling grimaced. "I don't like traveling," he understated. "But it's much better than commercial, and I wanted to thank you. It was nice of you to fly us all out." He cast a look over his shoulder to where Josh and Grace were sitting cross-legged, sleeping on each other's shoulders while Hunter read a paperback and rubbed Grace's thigh in absentminded affection. "It wasn't necessary. Josh seems to like you okay."

Leon let out a low laugh. "It wasn't easy," he confided, "but it seems that the key to Josh's heart—and his lovely mother's—is to simply embrace this mad crew of criminals." He gave a self-conscious smile. "Myself included."

Leon ran what was now a successful import/export business, and most of it was legit, as far as Stirling had been able to dig up. But the business he'd inherited from his gangster father had needed a lot of cleaning up and a few ruthless decisions on Leon's part, and on the part of his brother, Matteo di Rossi. Neither of them had known about Josh. Julia had done that on purpose, knowing that Matteo, like herself, had been trapped by a monstrous parent in a life full of fear. She'd found her own way out, with the help of Danny and Felix, but Matteo had gotten a scant year of freedom before he'd been killed trying to do the right thing. Leon's desire to be a part of Josh's life, and to donate his own bone marrow to see that his nephew would recover from leukemia completely, was absolute and devoted.

The fact that he seemed to embrace all of Josh's family—his two gay fathers, their quixotic enterprise to "do good crime," his odd assortment of friends and all—made him even easier to like.

And the fact that he'd been immediately smitten with Julia and seemed intent on courting her like a chevalier didn't hurt.

"Josh has a talent for being kind to people," Stirling said. He frowned, trying to find words. "I was worried at first when you came into his life. He holds us all together. We didn't want anything to tear him apart."

Leon nodded and smiled sadly. "It took me very little time to figure that out. But you've all been wonderful at embracing me." His smile quirked up at the corners. "And of course Carl's boyfriend and your sister helped by showing my children a wonderful time when I came out this fall."

Stirling remembered that. "Molly's like that," he said fondly. "She could make giant sea creatures who only want to inflict mayhem fall in love with her."

Leon arched his brow, and Stirling remembered Molly's other facets.

"And if they didn't, she'd rip them limb from limb," he added in the name of truth.

Leon's rich laughter warmed him. "That's the fiery redhead we love," he said.

And that reminded Stirling of the other thing. "And thank you, too, not for the plane," he added, "but for the yacht and doing all this for… well, us. I know you were trying to please Josh and Julia, but you're helping me and Molly too, and I thought I should say something."

"You're very welcome," Leon said, and for a moment Stirling thought that was his cue to get up and leave, but then Leon cleared his throat. "I feel compelled to thank you as well."

Stirling blinked at him. "Me?"

"Well, not you—everybody. I know that you all put yourselves in a great deal of danger this fall to find the people responsible for Matteo's death, and I'm grateful. But for more than that."

Stirling frowned. "I'm not sure I did any work for you on anything else," he said.

Leon looked like he was trying not to smile. "Well, yes and no. Matteo and I, we grew up in privileged circumstances, yes. But we also grew up not knowing who to trust. The friend who was nice to you at boarding school could have been the son of your father's fiercest competitor, so it didn't pay to get too close to people. Even our wives were chosen for us because of their use to our father's business. And of course, once you become the head of such a company...."

Stirling scrambled to pick up on the cue. "Friends are hard to find?" he hazarded.

Leon nodded. "Indeed they are. Imagine my delight when I found my brother had a son, and he wanted for nothing *but* my bone marrow. There was even an offer to pay me for it." He snorted, and Stirling blinked. He hadn't been part of that offer, but Carl had.

"You said no," Stirling said, figuring that out for himself.

"I did." Leon crossed his legs, ankle on his knee. "I said no, and Josh's family welcomed me, and then all of you did the impossible. You not only found the boy responsible for my brother's death, but you...." He shrugged. "You allowed me to forgive him. And I'd grown up seeing myself as constantly the king of the mountain—but not in the glorious way. In the way that I had to do constant battle to keep someone underneath me from lobbing a knife at my back. But here was another mountain, a peaceful mountain, with people who enjoyed it when I visited and had no interest in my mountain at all." His smile returned. "Yes, in a way the yacht and the jet are quid pro quo. You all jumped into my quest, so why shouldn't I jump into yours? But the truth is, I wanted a chance to play on your mountain. So thank you, Stirling, for a chance to go tilt at your windmill and to be your good guy." He glanced around the plane, his eyes landing on Josh and Grace and then on Julia. "Somehow your little group has convinced me that it's better to play on the mountaintop with friends than to be an angry, battling king. I know you won't believe this, but it's made me a better father—and a better prospect as a partner. It's almost the best con of all."

Stirling smiled back at him, at a loss for words. Then his eyes fell on Josh again, and he sobered. "Will he really be okay?" He hadn't wanted to ask Felix or Danny this, and would have died before he put a doubt in Julia's mind. But Leon loved Josh too, and Stirling didn't feel quite so afraid of hurting him in this matter. He had children.

"God, I hope so," Leon said. He bit his lip. "Nobody will talk to me about this," he murmured, lowering his voice, "but what is the status of his love life? I know young Mr. Grayson is interested, but Josh appears to have only a friendly interest. Any other prospects?"

Stirling thought of the friendly hug Josh had given Nick, his policeman friend. "Not that I know of. His last crush was married with a baby. I think the guy returned the feeling, but Josh is no homewrecker."

Leon *hmm*ed. "Good boy," he said happily. "Raised right. But that's a shame."

"What is?" Julia asked, scooting in on the other side of Leon so Stirling didn't have to get up.

"Josh's love life," Leon said promptly and without embarrassment.

An enigmatic smile graced Julia's perfect features. "Mm. Yes. Well, we do have our young Interpol friend who is meeting us in San Juan. We can always hope."

"Interpol?" Leon asked, and Stirling wasn't the only one who heard the undercurrent of alarm in his voice. Well, Stirling had seen his financials; Leon had done his best since inheriting his father's empire, but nobody got out from his mob ties completely.

Julia waved her hand reassuringly. "Don't worry about Liam, darling. He's a friend of Danny's. In fact, we've enlisted his help once or twice, and he's been rewarded with a few stunning case clearances. He has no interest in your formerly criminal behind."

Leon gazed at her with complete besottedness. "That is so very good to know," he murmured, taking her hand and kissing it.

Stirling took that as his cue to leave, but as he stood, Leon belayed him with a nod. "Stirling, I was serious. Thank your sister for me as well. I'm so glad to play a part in your adventure."

"We're glad you're here too, Mr. di Rossi," Stirling replied.

"Leon," he said, and Stirling ducked his head and made his way back to sit next to Tienne.

Tienne was still awake, regarding him with wide blue eyes. "What were you doing?" he asked.

"Pretending to be a grown-up," Stirling told him. He'd need to tell Molly that too.

"Well done. Can I lean my head on your shoulder?"

Stirling smiled and retrieved his own earbuds so he could listen to his favorite sci-fi podcast. "Yeah."

Tienne's warmth in the air conditioning, his firm contact, and the husky voice of the audiobook reader all helped to settle his bones.

Traveling. Still not his favorite, but there were moments.

BECAUSE THEY'D been traveling aboard the jet, they had the option of changing from their Chicago cold-weather gear to their vacation gear before the plane landed, and as they stepped down the ramp into the warm, humid salt air, Stirling had never been so happy for his privilege. The ocean breeze kept the heat from being too oppressive, but if Stirling had walked onto the tarmac wearing jeans and a wool sweater, he might have gone catatonic with overstimulation. He'd never done well in the heat.

Leon had thought of everything, including transportation to the port, and as they were chauffeured through the colorful streets, Stirling felt a curious sense of loss. A part of him yearned to be out on the streets, looking in the shops, turning his ankles on the cobblestones. The people out there looked as if they were having so much fun!

But even as a child, he'd known his limitations. Stella and Fred had been kind enough not to push him.

"Stirling, don't you want to go to your friend's birthday party?"

"I like Josh, but people are really loud there. Do you think he'd mind if I sat in the corner and read?"

Josh had not, and neither had Grace, for that matter, although Grace's birthday parties were usually big dinners at Josh's house. As he'd grown older and been able to control his environment more, he'd gotten better at adapting to noise and confusion—and even at enjoying it sometimes. Christmas in Chicago with this widening loop of people he considered his family had been wonderful, but part of that was because he'd had his room or the den to hide in when things got too loud.

There didn't seem to be many places to hide in the streets of San Juan.

Tienne, with that uncanny ability he had to be on the same wavelength, leaned over to him and said, "I grew up on streets like these. We always lived on a second floor above a shop or a business, and I could hide in the quiet and watch all the noise on the streets. It was my favorite way to know a city."

"I could know a city like that," he said, thinking of his and Molly's big loft in Chicago. They'd gotten it because they could look out on the streets through a big plate glass widow in the living room.

"All the people, otherwise," Tienne said, and Stirling found his hand as they sat in the air-conditioned car and squeezed.

"Yeah."

But the trepidation of the celebrating knots of tourists died down when they got to the port and saw the yacht. Big—not quite Salinger mansion big, but big—it obviously had enough lounges and cabins and nooks and crannies for all of them, with the added bonus of places to sit on the upper deck of the prow and deck chairs on the top deck, along with a hot tub.

Three levels, over 200 feet long, it was spacious and elegant and looked like it could hide the timid and showcase the bold in turn.

"Whew," Josh said as he got out of the car after him. "I've got to tell you guys, I had some reservations. Being in the sun as much as I have is making me a little bit queasy and tired. I know I'm supposed to be done with chemo, but recovery is kicking my ass. This looks great, though!"

While they were all pale from the Chicago winter, Josh's face was extra pasty, with two crescents of unhealthy color at his cheeks.

Tienne and Stirling met eyes, and Stirling ran to find Leon or Felix or Danny.

He ran into Liam Craig instead.

Liam Craig was in his early thirties, younger than the oldest in the group but older than the college students. He had curly dark brown hair, teeth with a mild overlap in the front, wide cheekbones, and merry indigo eyes. He looked like a mischievous uncle or friend of the family—or even a con man or grifter. The one thing he absolutely didn't resemble was a police officer of any kind, particularly when dressed in a madras shirt over a ribbed tank, cargo shorts, and deck shoes. It was practically the uniform of the Chicagoans as well, with variations in pattern. Sometimes it wasn't a madras shirt, it was a Hawaiian shirt—hooray!—but on Liam, coupled with the straw hat and a smear of zinc oxide on his nose, it looked like he'd been born to be a tourist.

"Heya, Stirling," Liam said, his British accent as charming as the rest of him. "Did you get lost?"

"I was looking for Julia or Danny or Felix," he said unhappily, peering back to where Grace, Josh, Hunter, and Tienne were grouped. "I know this is supposed to be Leon's yacht, but Josh can't really wait—"

At the mention of Josh's name, Liam's head came up like a prized pointer's.

"Is he not feeling well?"

"Recovery lasts a long time," Stirling said, remembering Josh's collapse on the dance floor weeks earlier. He'd seen—they'd all seen—that Josh had needed to nap a lot to recover from their holiday festivities, and the entire family had an unspoken code to put Josh's needs first.

"I know it," Liam muttered. "Here. I introduced myself to the captain while I was waiting and—oop! Shit!"

They both watched in dismay as Josh, who had been standing on the dock looking around like the rest of his friends, suddenly turned the pastiest shade of white and went down.

Hunter caught him, damsel in distress style, and Liam trotted across the quay, disregarding the uneven footing, catching Hunter by surprise.

"Over here," he directed, walking up to a tall dark-skinned man with the white uniform and cap of a captain. "Captain Griffith!" he hailed. "Captain Griffith, this is one of Mr. di Rossi's guests, and he's taken ill."

When the man spoke, it was with mildly Dutch/French flavored English, but something about his careful politeness made Stirling think the man could erupt into a full Bajan dialect at any time.

"Yes, please, bring him in. This is our young man who's been sick? We have a ship's physician on call for him."

"Fuck," Josh murmured. "Hunter, put me down. Please. If the dads see me like this, I'm toast. I'll be on the mid-deck in the shade for the rest of the trip."

Grace let out a high-pitched, almost frantic whine as he practically danced at Hunter's side. "You said you'd be healthy—you promised! I'm telling. We'll be grounded. We can sleep in the shade. I can do that!"

"That's all fine. Nothing wrong with a bit of shade at sea," Liam said. He turned to Hunter and held his arms out. "Here, I can take him."

Hunter paused for a moment. He and Josh had been good friends before Josh had pulled them all together to work jobs, and Stirling could see the reluctance on Hunter's face.

"Trust me," Liam said with a wink. "I work out too." He gave a playful flex, and Stirling's eyes almost bulged. How had he hidden those shoulders and arms under a madras shirt?

"Don't drop him," Hunter growled, shifting Josh over.

"Not on purpose, right, mate?"

Josh let out a low groan of mortification. "You know I can never speak to you again after this," he mumbled against Liam's chest. "You've carried me *twice*."

"Right, then," Liam murmured, and it wasn't Stirling's imagination. The young man's eyes, his voice, both dropped and became tender as he spoke. "We'll email sitreps. Nothing awkward about that."

"You never email back," Josh said, his voice taking on a sort of dreamy quality. It occurred to Stirling that someone as independent and self-contained as Josh Salinger must be quite over being carried as an adult, but he never seemed to get angry or frustrated.

"Well, it's always a group send," Liam chided him. "What's there to say but 'roger that'?"

"Don't be a dick," Josh replied, sounding grumpy, and Liam shifted Josh's weight—he was still slight after such a long illness—and seemed to hold him closer. If Stirling hadn't been behind him, he wouldn't have heard what Liam said into Josh's ear.

"You've got to invite me in, boyo. I don't trespass where I'm not wanted." And then, before Josh could reply, he said in a slightly louder voice, "I was supposed to inundate you with spam, then? Did you *want* all my kitten videos?"

"Dick."

"Ooh," Grace said, a little bit of delight penetrating some of his worry. "You pissed him off, Mr. Interpol Man. Don't piss off Recovery Boy."

"Recovery Boy, is it?" As they spoke, Liam shouldered his way across the gangplank and into the ship, following the lead of Captain Griffith. Stirling had grabbed his two duffel bags—one with his computer equipment—as they'd started for the yacht, and he realized everybody else had claimed their own luggage as well.

Apparently thieves weren't big on trust, even when there *was* honor among them.

"Better than Cancer Boy," Josh mumbled. "Oh, the breeze feels good."

They were walking down a hallway with cabins on either side, and Liam got to the end of the corridor and hip-checked his way through a semi-open door. "If you like the breeze, wait until you feel the AC," he said.

"Captain Griffith? I'm putting him in my quarters for the moment. You said his quarters were on the second deck, and I think he needs the bed right now."

Because Stirling had been closest, he watched as Liam tenderly placed Josh's body on the covers and pulled a cotton throw from the bottom of the bed up over his shoulders.

"There ya go, mate," he said, his British accent dropping a level or two down on the income scale as he spoke to Josh and Josh only. "I'll go fetch the ship's doctor—"

"Done," Grace said, darting out of the room.

Stirling glanced at Hunter, a pained expression on his face, and Hunter sighed. "I'll go fetch Grace before he wheels the doc back here on a dolly," he said and disappeared.

"Tienne and I will—" Stirling said, but Liam shook his head.

"You hang here with Josh a minute," he said. "I'll take your bags and show Tienne your quarters." He paused and looked back and forth between them. "I got that right, didn't I? Julia said you two would want to bunk together?"

That July, Liam had been there to help him and Josh out of the van after Chuck had disarmed an explosive device installed under the engine. The crew had bonded with Liam then, and some of them had met him on various adventures since, but most of their communication had been via email. It had only now occurred to Stirling that this young man had once saved Tienne's life as well.

"You remember Tienne?" Stirling asked, hoping he could remember manners. Tienne was looking shyly at Liam from under his lashes.

Of course he'd crush on Liam. Liam saved him from an alleyway and helped him to his new life.

"Good to see you, lad," Liam said kindly, moving to squeeze Tienne's shoulder. Tienne was a few inches taller than Liam Craig, but Liam had that vital presence. And Tienne had a lot of practice making himself invisible.

"Nice to see you too, Officer Craig," Tienne replied, his accent a little thicker than usual. "I'd hoped to—"

Liam nodded, cutting him off. "I'd hoped to catch up too. But let's get Josh settled and then meet the rest of the troops. I understand there's dinner in the lounge tonight, and then we cast off tomorrow morning." He sent a look back at Josh that dared the young man to contradict him. "As long as some of us are feeling better," he added archly.

"Go away and let me vomit," Josh moaned. Stirling looked around in alarm, and Liam produced a basin from the tiny attached bathroom.

"Here," Liam instructed. "Help him use this if he needs it. I'll get the luggage settled."

And then he was gone, Tienne trotting helplessly in his wake, trying to keep up. Stirling was alone with Josh, something that rarely happened because *everybody* wanted time with Josh, so Stirling had to settle for spending time with him on jobs.

"Hey, Stirling," Josh murmured.

Stirling sank to a crouch next to the bed and smoothed back Josh's sweaty hair from his temples. Maybe because of all those hours they'd worked side by side on computers, or all those times in middle school when Josh had comforted Stirling after driving away bullies, but Josh was one of the few people whose space Stirling felt comfortable enough in to do this.

"You weren't supposed to be sick when we had this adventure," he accused.

"Not sick," Josh protested. "I really am cancer free. Just… you know. The airplane, the humidity—can't cross continents like I used to."

"I know." Stirling sighed and continued to stroke his friend's hair. "I just wouldn't have agreed to this if I'd known you were still not feeling well."

"That would have been a shame," Josh murmured. "I really love working with you. When we're running a job together, I feel like there's no one else I'd rather have by my side."

"Me neither," Stirling admitted. "It's hard to explain. I'm glad Tienne isn't jealous of it, whatever it is."

"It's like having a work partner," Josh said softly. "That simple. It's like Grace isn't my lover, he's my friend. You're not my boyfriend, you're my partner." His voice was wandering. "So many different good people in my life. I'm so blessed, Stirling. So lucky." He swallowed hard. "And you're lucky too," he added.

"I know I am." Stirling's mother had loved him enough to keep him safe. Molly had loved him enough to grab his hand and never let go. Fred and Stella had loved him enough to give him a home. And Josh and his family had loved him enough to take him into their hearts, even when all his material needs were already met.

And Tienne cared about him enough to stay with him, to lodge in his quarters, to seduce him away from himself when he became too involved. Stirling could very well be the luckiest boy in the world.

"You're especially lucky because the air conditioner is working," Josh said, laughing a little. "You might not need to hold my hair back as I puke."

"That *is* luck." Stirling recognized this joke and laughed with Josh, who closed his eyes then and fell asleep.

Half an hour later, Julia was escorted in, and she fussed over Josh as Liam took Stirling to his quarters, thinking gratefully that Tienne was probably there already.

"Where are you going to stay?" he asked Liam anxiously. He didn't like the thought of Liam displaced on board this sort of floating hotel.

"Probably there." Liam winked over his shoulder. "Josh gets one of the bigger rooms, you know, because he's Josh. I'm sure they'll move him when he feels better."

"And in the meantime?"

Liam shrugged. "I brought a book, you know, and the lounge is pretty nice. There's chairs and a settee on the middle deck. The city really is something to see from here." The famous view of all the multicolored buildings was something Stirling could watch forever. "Don't worry about me, Stirling. I don't need a whole crowd to be happy."

Stirling paused, and to his surprise Liam noticed right away. "Tienne is shy like that too," he said by way of segue. "I… I can't believe you found him in an alleyway."

Liam's face always seemed so jovial, so merry, but now some of that energy bled away.

"He was covered in his father's blood," he said, and Stirling gasped. "He probably doesn't remember. He was so terrified, so *traumatized*. And I thought, 'Oh no, that Lightfingers chap miscalculated. We lost that kid when we lost his father.' But Danny insisted. Said Felix and Julia would make him whole if anyone could. I gather it took a while."

"It did," Stirling rasped, voice tight. "I... I think he didn't realize he could be safe until this last month."

Liam smiled, some of the sadness around his mouth and eyes lightening. "And I think having someone he can hide in corners with has helped him more than you will ever know. Stirling, you probably think we don't know each other well, but Josh, Danny, Carl, Chuck—even Hunter—all email about you. Particularly for this trip. Every step in this plan was made thinking about you and your sister. Hunter was the one who suggested we wait a breath before casting off. Carl was the one who made sure you and Tienne got a room in which both of you could work, far away from the noise of the upper decks. I've got mad dyslexia and a few quirks of my own. My whole life I've had to fight to function like any other typical lad in the world, but you've got an entire family fighting to let you function in the way that suits you best. The fact that you're doing that for Etienne, giving him that space? Never doubt you made a difference in his life, the same way your adoptive parents did in yours." He paused and winked. "But I assume with slightly different rules."

Stirling managed a blush. "Very much so," he mumbled. "Thank you."

Liam shrugged. "Thank *you* all for inviting me." A small smile played at his mouth. "My life could have been very boring if Lightfingers hadn't been in it. He'll

never know it, but I was rooting so hard for him to return to Felix. It was such a fairy tale, you know?"

Stirling nodded. "Sometimes we need those to believe in."

"We do. Now come on, I'll install you and remind
you that dinner is at six, but there's a small craft table
if you need lunch before then. I know breakfast was a
while ago."

"Thank you." Then, a question. "What were you
doing here so early?"

Liam's face opened up. "Running around the island, of course! Got here last night, stayed in that really colorful hotel that overlooks the harbor. I mean,
this whole job's a vacation for me, and I've never
been to San Juan or the Caribbean. Too much fun to
be had."

"You and Josh would have fun together," Stirling
observed. "Once he's better."

And now it was Liam's turn to blush, although it
probably stood out more on his fair, freckled skin than
it did on Stirling's darker tones. "Josh probably has better people to go running off to dance with than this old
copper, you think?"

"No," Stirling said, not willing to play that game,
"I don't. But thank you. If this is my room, now I really
am ready for some quiet."

Instead of being offended, Liam simply laughed,
the sound rich and rolling, and Stirling thought that
when Josh was better, he and Liam would have an
exciting courtship rife with bickering, banter, and
conflagration.

The thought made Stirling yearn for the shy artist in his room who looked at Stirling like he hung the

moon and would spend Christmas Eve in a darkened foyer to see the beauty of snow.

He opened the door and found Tienne stretched out on the bed, facing the porthole so he could look at the ocean.

With a happy little sigh, Stirling threw himself on the bed next to him and ran his hand along Tienne's neck and between his shoulder blades, smoothing out the kinks under his skin and glorying in Tienne's sensual sigh.

"Is Josh okay?"

"Yes. His mom came in, and you know Julia. She makes things better."

"What ever happened to the doctor?" Tienne asked, and Stirling remembered that Grace had been sent to fetch the shipboard physician but they had never shown.

"I have no idea—"

At that moment there was a clatter in the hallway outside their cabin.

"Grace! The hell!" That was definitely Carl. "Hunter said you ran off the boat like your head was on fire and your ass was catching!"

"I had to get a doctor!"

"Oh my God," Carl muttered. Then, solicitously, "Ma'am, I'm so sorry. Are you okay?"

The voice that came next was female with a decidedly Puerto Rican accent. "I was told it was an emergency?" The doctor—however Grace had gotten her on board—also sounded very confused.

"I was told it *was* urgent, but this idiot didn't hear the part about a *shipboard physician*." Carl sounded like he was taking deep breaths.

Tienne looked over his shoulder at Stirling, and both of them listened with all their attention—and their hands over their mouths.

"Shipboard?" Grace said, obviously caught flat-footed. "As in, here on the ship and not out on the island?"

"Oh my God," Carl muttered again. "Ma'am, thank you so much for coming. There's a doctor with the patient now, but if you follow me, we can compensate you for your time. Grace, Hunter is in the middle of the city trying to track your phone. Go out on the dock and call him and then do whatever you have to do to make it up to him. Jesus Christ almighty, kid, could you think for once in your life?"

Grace's voice when he spoke next was desolate and a little pathetic. "Sorry, Carl. I didn't mean to be stupid."

Stirling could imagine Carl massaging the back of his neck in that way he had when he was dealing with the mass of confusion that came from herding a bunch of people who were very brilliant. And very unpredictable. "I know. You were thinking we were in the all clear and then Josh passed out on you. I get that patience isn't your thing. Take a lesson from Josh and be ready for this stage to last a while, okay?"

"Sorry, Carl." Beat. "Sorry, Dr. Nice Lady."

"It's fine," she said, obviously taking *her* cues from Carl and showing Grace kindness instead of massive amounts of exasperation. "And don't worry about compensation. I was off duty anyway."

"Oh Lord," Grace muttered. "Lady, do you have a favorite charity?"

"Hurricane relief," she said promptly.

"If you give Carl the name of an organization, *I'll* write the check," he said, and there was a level of determination in his voice that made Stirling think that he truly meant to make amends.

Gah! There was a reason they'd all killed themselves to hide tiny Lego guys for the unpredictable thief.

"The heart of an angel," Tienne said accurately. "In the body of a remote-controlled mouse."

He paused, and Grace said, "Come on, Mrs. Nice Doctor Lady. I'll take you to see Josh and make doubly sure he's not going to die."

"With a drunk god on the controls," Tienne added, and Stirling muffled his quiet laughter in the hair at Tienne's nape.

A few moments later, though, when the hallway in front of their room had apparently cleared out and Grace had managed to set right his folly, Tienne said something that nearly broke Stirling's heart.

"I wish sometimes," he said, "that I was Hunter or Carl or Liam. One of the men who could catch you or save you if you fell. It's not even that I'm so slender, you see, it's that I never respond in the moment. I'm afraid I can never be that man for you. The one who can carry you to bed."

Stirling was nearly asleep, in what promised to be a truly necessary nap, and he barely had the wherewithal to murmur, "I don't need someone to carry me, Tienne. I need someone to hold my hand."

There was more he wanted to say about that, but he didn't know how.

Perhaps it was this thought, though, the thought about being in the moment, being the kind of man who could catch his lover and keep him safe, that made him resolve to push his people-comfort boundaries during this trip. After all his people had done for him all his life, it was the least he could do in return.

THAT NIGHT at dinner, Stirling tested that resolution. Liam had really underpraised the appointments in the lounge, which were done in brightly colored fabrics that echoed the iconic rainbow brilliance of the buildings that greeted visitors at the port of San Juan. A linen and microfiber blend, the furnishings would breathe in the humidity while cradling the body in comfort, and the polished teakwood and brass gave an illusion of shade against the brightness of the sun out on the upper decks. Stirling was looking around, thinking he wouldn't mind setting up shop here for the next couple of weeks, when a grim-faced Hunter managed to corner him. Everybody else was milling about with juice drinks and talking about their drive in and the things they'd seen in the city that they were going to go check out after dinner, and Stirling was even contemplating joining them, although clubs and nightlife weren't usually his thing. Something about walking hand in hand with Tienne with *their* people laughing and bantering around them held more appeal than such an outing did with strangers.

That line of thought was held off, though, when Hunter walked by him and, with a pass worthy of Danny Lightfingers himself, shoved a familiar item into Stirling's pocket.

Stirling only caught a glimpse of fabric, but he'd recognized a black microfiber balaclava/face mask that Grace had specially made and never left home without.

Grace had a couple of them, in fact, and with Hunter's next words, Stirling realized he'd be seeing *all* of them in the next couple of hours.

"Two words," Hunter murmured, gray eyes restlessly scanning the room as they always did. "Tracking device."

"All of them?" Stirling asked before taking a bite of a canape made of bacon and fig and munching blissfully.

"This one first. I'll get you the others before we leave the ship tonight." Hunter frowned. "You're coming with us, right? To La Placita? It's like the ultimate pub crawl, and we're here on a Friday night right after New Year's. You should come."

Stirling frowned back. "I should ask Tienne. I... you know. Crowds." He grimaced and caught sight of Josh, hanging back on the cushions of one of the couches that lined the walls and looking out the windows onto the water. "Besides, someone should stay and keep Josh company *besides* Grace." Stirling gave Hunter an apologetic look. "He *really* needs to get out."

Hunter let loose with a strained laugh. "Yeah, Grace does. But San Juan is an amazing city, and, you know. This is sort of your Christmas present from all of us." He grimaced. "I know you won't be partying at every discotheque in the islands, but could you, you know, for us, this once here?"

Stirling was as surprised by the request as he was by his desire to fulfill it. "Let me speak to Tienne," he said. And then, remembering, "*After* dinner. Think I've got ten minutes to slip out and get this done?"

Hunter eyed the group. "Yeah. I saw the kitchen on the way in. They won't be ready for the salad course for a good fifteen."

"I don't even want to know—"

Hunter's shrug was eloquent. "You've got to know how to time things," he said. "Also, when a kitchen is vulnerable to an attack. Don't worry. You'll be back in plenty of time."

Stirling timed himself. It took six minutes to hurry down the hallway, pull a waterproof, *sweat*proof, fuck-up-proof tracking device the size of a pinhead from his kit and shove it in the lining of Grace's trademark thief's hat/mask, then scan it into his computer so the tracker was active. He tucked the hat into his pocket and was making sure his phone was online with the tracer as well when he entered the dining room right before the chef came out and rang the bell to sit.

Stirling pulled up his seat next to Tienne and found Hunter on his other side. He tucked the hat into Hunter's cargo shorts pocket much as Hunter had tucked it into his and got a brief shoulder bump in return.

Stirling ignored the bump and turned to Tienne, who had missed the exchange entirely. "Do you want to go ashore tonight?" he asked. "To La Placita to dance?"

Tienne turned toward him in surprise. "You want to?"

Stirling gave a look around at the smiling faces of his family; at the people who had committed to this entire adventure to right a wrong for his sake and that of his sister, and who considered it play, a treat, a chance to go out and do some good and enjoy working with a group of people who had their backs.

"I think it would be something we could do for our friends," he said. "Something we might enjoy ourselves."

That sweet, bemused smile flickered across Tienne's features. "Of course," he said. And then his eyes lightened in a truly amazing way. "I would love to see the city as the sun sets and the lights at night. I think many things would be lovely here."

Ah, Tienne—always looking for beauty. "Then we're on."

Hunter, who had apparently been listening shamelessly, said, "Good!" He dropped his voice. "And by the way, Liam said he'd keep Josh company tonight. I, uhm, wouldn't feel too bad for leaving him alone."

And Stirling didn't.

By day, La Placita was a conglomeration of businesses open to a farmer's market in an open courtyard. By night it was teeming with bars and dance floors—and one of the most LGBTQ friendly hot spots in the islands. Not everybody went. This trip seemed to be mostly for the college-aged crowd, which meant, oddly enough, that Michael and Carl came, probably so Carl could help chaperone, although he'd be mortified to admit it. It also meant that Chuck came and Lucius stayed behind, much to Chuck's dismay.

"I really wanted to see him dance too," Chuck declared wistfully on the car ride over. "Apparently he's got grown-up business stuff to take care of." Chuck sent Carl a dark glance. "And Michael told me you tried to weasel out of this for the same reasons."

Carl rolled his eyes. "No, I tried to weasel out for completely different reasons involving Michael not needing to be saddled by his old, staid boyfriend while people his own age are out enjoying themselves."

There was a digestive silence in the limousine, broken by Michael's indignant, "You are *not* old! Oh my God, I'm the one with three kids and an ex-wife! For fuck's sake!"

A predictable chaos ensued, during which time Stirling leaned into Carl's space and murmured, "He's really sensitive about that."

"I know," Carl muttered. "Go figure."

The lively debate—Was Hunter too old for Grace? Did Lucius count as older than Chuck because he was obviously way more mature? How old was Leon di Rossi? Was he too old for Julia? Was he good enough for Julia at any age? The yacht was nice and all, but zillionaires were a dime a dozen, and people like Julia Dormer-Salinger were rare and precious gems. Were Stirling and Tienne really both twenty-one? Wow. What was *that* like? And did anybody know any single gay men for Torrance or straight men for Molly and Talia?—was only halted by their arrival at La Placita. The car pulled up, and they all clambered out, Talia and Molly dressed in their most colorful clubbing dresses, the men all still wearing their tropical island uniform, and everybody cheerful and ready to have fun.

To Stirling's surprise, that was exactly what happened. He was, in fact, nearly a year younger than Tienne, and had only recently turned twenty-one. For the first time, he could drink legally, and he found he liked rum punch very much—but not enough to get drunk on it. Tienne seemed to enjoy Hurricanes, and they both had fun dancing under the stars, particularly when the tempo of the music was not too fast and not too slow.

Dancing, returning to the group's table to drink some water, talking to whoever was there, and then hopping back on the dance floor had always seemed to be a frenetic waste of time to Stirling. He'd watched Molly, Josh, and Grace indulge in this pastime often enough as they'd cleared high school. But on this night, with people he trusted, in the balmy tropical air under a clear bed of stars, he suddenly felt free enough to let go, a little, of the things that had always held him back.

He would forever hold a very clear memory of dancing in Tienne's arms, their hips swaying together to something Latin and exciting, the strung lights over their head seeming to wrap around them in a dazzling net. Tienne kept him safe—and being safe meant he felt free enough to turn his face to the sky and laugh, while Tienne's lips found his throat and together they moved joyously and without care.

When the car returned for them, he climbed in next to Tienne, loose and buzzed and a little bit horny from dancing and stupidly happy. They all quieted as a group as they walked down the pier and took the gangplank to the ship, and the hushed excitement of their whispers as they made their way to their cabins—or, for some of them, back up to the lounge to see if the others were awake—held the same sort of excitement as any job they'd ever pulled.

Finally, *finally*, Stirling and Tienne were back in their cabin, and Stirling wasn't even aware of undressing, or even consciously needing, but suddenly Tienne's mouth was on his and they were kissing the same way they had danced—seamlessly, breathlessly, without reservation, without care. There were no worries about whether they were making love right or if they knew what to do next. They'd done this before, and they wanted that moment, that same coming together, that same trust, that same release, and like magic, with each moon-saturated kiss, with each velvety dark caress, with the feeling of Tienne's hands on his body and his flesh embedded in Tienne, that stunning mixture of the familiar and the new, the safe and the free, made their hearts soar in climax like starlight riding the night.

Stirling didn't even remember coming down.

Clear View

THE WATER between Tienne and his prey was the most stunning color blue.

Tienne stalked silently, the noise of his breathing through the snorkel loud and rhythmic, his feet paddling slowly behind him as he simply stared down at the reef below him and looked his fill.

Yellow, green, purple, and pink, large and flat or tiny and shaped like little darts, the myriad fishes scattered from his shade, and he hunted their swirl of color with the same awe he'd use for magic sparkles coalescing before his eyes.

Oh! He could understand why so many artists were inspired by the ocean.

He himself had always imagined a cold gray ocean, with white gauze curtains fluttering through open windows, mimicking the surge of swell and spray. That had always been the ocean he'd painted. But this was the opposite of that. This was a warm, *gay* ocean—full of little rainbow fishes excited by their freedom, suffused in that peaceful, sense-affirming blue.

He yearned to paint it.

TIENNE HAD spent the day before on the reef too, protected by an SPF suit, and at the end of the day, as he'd fallen exhaustedly into bed next to Stirling, he'd realized his face ached from smiling.

Stirling had spent the day in the shade, side by side with Josh, both of them researching the financials and business dealings of the three men who, along with Fred and Stella, had purchased life insurance for the dead members of the crew of the wrecked boat. Apparently, Felix had sent in a request to the Barbadian authorities for the official coroner's report on Fred and Stella. They'd been cremated before being shipped home to Chicago, on Harve Christopher's request, and the sight of the undamaged documents that had made up their last effects had sparked a fierce and angry curiosity in every member of the crew.

Felix's request had been denied on their third day out of port, and Liam, Chuck, and Danny had taken a small outboard motorboat to the nearest island—St. Kitts and Nevis—to charter a small plane to Barbados so Liam could flash his Interpol identification and perhaps get some better cooperation.

"Do you think Liam's credentials can get that information?" Julia asked Felix. She, Felix, and Leon had been lounging on the top deck at the time, all of them tanning perfectly in the sun. Tienne had been up there for the short briefing, and he'd needed a big floppy straw hat and zinc oxide on his nose and cheekbones to walk the stairs to the upper deck.

"Do you really think it matters if they can't?" Leon asked, turning toward her with his eyebrow arched high enough to be seen over his sunglasses.

Julia had laughed richly and taken a sip of her mimosa. "I think one way or another, we'll get what we need," she said. "But I don't want to get young Liam in trouble."

Felix snorted softly. "Julia, you do Danny and Chuck an injustice. Please, dearest, have some faith. They won't even know their security has been breached."

"Nobody would have known if I'd gone with them," Grace pouted. "Why couldn't I go with them?"

"Because," Hunter snapped. "We were afraid you'd come back with another doctor, and this one wouldn't have a handy charity to pay off in return for kidnapping!"

"Oh. Yeah." Grace had run his hands through his straight black hair. He'd had little streaks of Christmas-colored tinsel shot through it for the holidays, and they stuck out with his fingers, making Tienne think he was a little off-kilter. "Sorry about that."

"Grace," Josh said, from his perch on the couch that surrounded the deck space, "I've *got* to get out of this sun. Could you come keep me company in the lounge? Get us some smoothies or something? God, I could really use some downtime."

Grace popped up from his own pouty sprawl on the couches. "Okay. Sure. Absolutely. Peach smoothies? Or we could do mango?"

"Why don't you go ask the cook and surprise us," Josh said with a smile. "Have them make a couple. We'll have a smoothie-tasting contest and cool down."

"Yes! Absolutely! I'll get our tablets. We can play video games and yell at the TV and—" Grace disappeared like an escaping hamster, and everybody on the top deck gave a sigh of relief.

"Thanks," Hunter murmured.

"Don't thank me yet," Josh said grimly. "Hunter, I'm going to need help down the stairs."

Hunter went to assist him, and as he ventured into the shade of the deck, he called, "Stirling, join us? Tienne, you too if you like. Stirling and I can multitask."

"What will you be doing?" Tienne asked as Stirling put his own tablet in its sleeve and stood, positioning his straw hat carefully so it didn't blow off his head.

"Josh and I are still researching financials. There's a heckuva firewall up—it's going to need both of us and maybe Danny to crack it, as well as to hack the satellite feed to figure out who's blocking the pictures from the island."

"Why didn't Josh say that?" Tienne asked, and Stirling grimaced, which meant it had a lot to do with emotions he wasn't good at explaining.

"'Cause Grace is losing his shit," Michael said, the twang in his voice comforting. "I think he's afraid Josh won't need him anymore."

Everyone left on the deck had turned to Carl's sweet dark-haired boyfriend, their mouths open a little in surprise.

"Michael," Julia said in wonder, "I do believe you've put your finger on the pulse of the problem. Of *course* he's driving us all up a wall!"

"Oh…." Talia let out a sigh. Tienne had tried not to be jealous that, like Stirling, she could survive with some SPF during the day and coconut oil at night, but otherwise she simply got darker and more beautiful. He was starting to think that between himself, Liam, Chuck, and Molly, they'd all cornered the market on aloe and ibuprofen.

"Oh what?" Molly asked. She'd managed to make wearing a tent beautiful—but only because her tent was flowing white-and-blue linen and shaped to flutter in the breeze, revealing her buxom figure while it kept her covered from the sun. Her straw hat had also kept her scarf-wrapped and bundled hair under cover and, Tienne suspected, well-oiled to keep the humidity from creating a mass that might very well take over the yacht. Talia did the same thing with her own straightened hair, and Tienne marveled both at how beautiful the women managed to keep themselves and at what a science it was. He felt like he could paint them sunning themselves on the deck of the yacht as a study in joy, but he'd told Stirling privately that the only reason his hair was long was because he usually forgot to cut it. Stirling had dragged his fingers through it and whispered that it was turning white-blond in the sun, before kissing him senseless, and by the time they were done making love, Tienne had been lucky he even remembered he *had* hair.

Talia bit her lip. "He… well, even I could see it. He's grown up a lot in the past six months. He had a purpose. I mean, *Josh* was his purpose. I bet he's wondering what his purpose is now."

"Oh!" Molly said, echoing her friend.

"Well, shit," Carl muttered. "Come on, Michael."

"Where we going?" Michael asked, standing up from his spot by the rail and following Carl without question.

"We're going to go find some vocational advice for our friend the thief. I mean, we'll have plenty of work for him, no problem, but he's pretty good at taking care of people. I bet if we find a way for him to do that that's semiregular, we might be able to keep him out of trouble."

"Ooh, that's a good idea. I'd look for myself, but, you know."

"You hate school and you love working on cars," Carl said, looking at his boyfriend besottedly.

"Yeah. Sorry."

"No worries."

Together they'd gone down the stairway, so adorable Tienne wanted to hold his hand to his chest, and he stood to go with them.

"Tienne, wait!" Molly said, looking at Talia, who nodded and stood with them. "They're going to do computer things. Want to come with us and snorkel?" She gestured toward the leeward side of the boat. "The reefs start within sight of the ship that way. If we ask the captain to anchor, we can take the skiff and some paddleboards out and look at the pretty fish!"

Tienne paused, wondering if he should leave Stirling, but Molly grabbed his arm, irrepressible as always. "Come *on.* All the grown-ups are going to be sunning themselves here, including Lucius!" She pitched her voice on purpose, Tienne suspected, so Chuck's boyfriend, who was currently napping in the sun, would know they hadn't forgotten he was there, since he'd been left behind too.

"I can hear you," Lucius replied fuzzily. "Tell me what it's like and I'll come with you tomorrow." With that, he shifted to the part of the deck under the canopy so he wouldn't burn, then resumed his nap. Well, he *had* been working on the computer until the night before, when he'd pronounced himself done with business and ready to play with them on the yacht.

Of course, that had been before Chuck had gone with the "away party" to go be muscle for whatever Liam and Danny might need.

Tienne imagined Lucius might be fully justified in catching up with some sleep today.

"We'll hold you to that," Molly chirped gaily. "Now come *on*, you two! I've got another two hours in the sun before the zinc oxide welds itself to my skin!"

What had followed had been lovely. The snorkeling itself was perfection; the feeling of being alone and one with all that surrounded him was something he'd only felt before when painting. But almost as good as visiting this alien world had been coming to the surface and exchanging stories with Molly and Talia. Everything from, "Oh my God, the size of that ray! I thought it was your average little one, and then Talia swam by and it was humongous!" to "And I turned around and there was a *turtle*, and it was *right there* looking at me!" The fun in sharing the experience with people who were as excited, as vibrant about it as he felt was extraordinary.

And then they'd returned to the yacht and regaled Stirling with their day, watching the interplay of wide-eyed fascination and laughter on his face as they spilled their adventures excitedly, like children.

Tienne hadn't done that since he'd walked through the streets of Marrakech with his father.

Realizing that he could have adventures not with Stirling, but with Molly and Talia and the other members of the crew, was almost a revelation. But that didn't mean Tienne didn't like Stirling best.

A BODY drew near his in the water, feet paddling evenly like his own. Tienne couldn't make out details, but he assumed it was Talia or Molly. The face masks didn't allow for unobstructed peripheral vision.

Whomever it was bumped his shoulder gently, and he pulled up, keeping a slow paddle with his feet to keep him upright, and was delighted to see his new companion was Stirling.

"You came!" He pulled his face mask up to the top of his head. His voice sounded unnaturally loud to his own ears, but it felt as though he was shouting over the sea and the wind, and Stirling didn't seem to flinch.

"You loved it so much yesterday, I paddled out from the yacht to join you." He indicated his board, and Tienne grinned.

"Cheating," he said, holding his hands up. The skiff was bobbing nearby, so they'd have a place to convene or rest without having to paddle all the way to the yacht.

Stirling laughed, and Tienne was so incredibly charmed. God, he was pretty, his square jaw set for whatever came his way, his sturdy, muscular body charging through the water, determined to power through the waves.

"Do you want to see the fun stuff?" he asked, excited to show off his favorite place in the reef. "There's a pincushion fish thing over there. The floor's about ten feet below us, but—"

"I know—no stepping, no touching." Stirling pulled his mask down with a free hand. "Let us observe."

Tienne did the same, and with bumps on the shoulder and quietly predatory intentions, he pulled Stirling into his glorious little world of color and motion, light and silence, flickering gentleness, and above all, beauty.

An hour later, they pulled up breathlessly alongside the yacht with nothing more in mind than to rinse the salt off their skin on the aft deck and catch lunch and maybe a nap, only to be greeted by a grimly cheerful Chuck, who helped haul them up the ladder, one hand-up at a time.

"We didn't hear you come back," Stirling said when they were all gathered on the aft deck, using a hose to rinse themselves off.

"We skirted the reef out of general politeness," Chuck said, "but we've got some fun stuff to tell you." Tienne wasn't sure if anybody else noticed, but the corners of his mouth tightened, as though "fun" was a less than satisfactory description. "Dry off and meet us in the lounge." He threw towels at them all and then grinned at Stirling's sister. "And Molly girl, you might want to start on the aloe and ibuprofen right now. Babydoll, you need a vacay from the sun."

Molly's green eyes widened in consternation, and she raised a hand up to her nose, which, Tienne could see, was already starting to blister. "Oh goddammit," she muttered. "What's a girl gotta do? Sunproof Kevlar?"

"One word," Chuck said kindly, pointing to his own peeling nose. "Shade. Now let's get busy. Lounge in ten. We need to talk."

Tienne and Stirling hurried to their quarters to swap their board shorts for cargo shorts and their SPF wear for plain tees. Tienne had slipped his cargo shorts on when he felt a soft hand on his shoulders, smoothing something cool and soothing as it went.

"Am I red?" he asked, craning his head to look.

"So red." Stirling bent his head and gave a pink shoulder a gentle kiss. "But you looked so happy. I'm glad you went and did something while I was busy, but, you know, I was jealous. Looked fun."

Tienne closed his eyes as Stirling kept applying the burn cream, realizing for the first time how very crisp he'd become on the edges. "I'm glad you joined us," he said. "Your sister...." He chuckled. "She's such a dork."

Stirling burst out laughing on a chuff of air. "A dork? I don't think I've ever heard her described like that!"

"In the best way!" Tienne protested. "We were all looking at the shallow end of the reef. We were being very careful, you understand. No feet down where we could touch. But Molly turned around and came face-to-face with a giant turtle, and she *wanted* to flail. *I* would have flailed, I have no doubts, because I was ten feet away and it scared *me*. She *wanted* to lose her mind and get scared, but she didn't. Her eyes got really big behind her mask, and she kept paddling gently in the other direction and the turtle passed by without so much as noticing she was there, and then we all took a break in the skiff to talk about what we'd seen—"

Stirling's chuckle told Tienne he knew what came next.

"And she had an epic freak-out?" Stirling guessed.

"I was quite surprised! She's normally so...."

"Self-possessed," Stirling said. He rubbed the last of the aloe on Tienne's neck, and Tienne shuddered and realized that maybe tomorrow would be a good day to stay in the shade with the redheads.

"Yes," Tienne agreed. "It was really quite amazing to watch her so discomfited." He turned to Stirling for a quick kiss—which Stirling gave him—before Stirling pulled back.

"She trusts you," he said, a small smile on his lips. "That's wonderful."

Tienne frowned. "She trusts me? What—"

"Talia has been her friend for a little while. Molly would let Talia see her freak out a bit. But she only does that when she knows someone. Otherwise, she would have held that epic freak-out until she got into her quarters." He gave a small shrug. "Maybe she would have let Chuck see it. He's, like, her favorite uncle. Like Carl is to me. But other than that, she trusts you, or you'd never know what a dork she was."

Tienne opened his mouth, wanting to take back the word "dork" because now it felt harsh compared to the gift Molly had given him. But Stirling was dressed and it was time to go.

THEY WERE the last two people to walk into the surprisingly tense room. Felix and Danny were standing in the middle of the lounging area in what looked like a possible shouting match, although Danny was wearing a sling around his arm and had a white bandage around his shoulder with a bit of blood seeping through.

Without a word—or even a glance exchanged—Tienne reached for Stirling's hand and found it. Together they entered cautiously.

Danny glanced at them as though they were a welcome distraction. "Oh, hello. Don't you all look a bit deep-fried. Good. I'm glad you used your time wisely." With a sigh, he turned toward the group and gave his shoulder a cursory nod. "As you may have guessed, I think the job has officially begun."

"What. Happened?" Julia asked, her voice icy and controlled.

"It wasn't his fault," Liam said, and Tienne was getting the impression that Liam was used to playing peacemaker or fixer, but he hadn't counted on the mass amounts of concern in the room.

"Was it yours?" Grace asked, not meanly, but he was most assuredly upset, shifting from foot to foot, practically twitching uncontrollably. As they watched, Hunter leaned over the smaller thief and wrapped his arms around Grace's shoulders.

"Easy," he murmured, and to Tienne's immense relief—and probably everybody else's too—they saw Grace relax.

"We're not blaming you," Josh said to Liam, glaring at his best friend from his "throne" of cushions in the far corner of the room. "But you, Chuck, and Danny haven't said anything." He gave a gesture to Danny's arm. "*Somebody* damaged our thief. What *happened*?"

It was not a request.

Liam nodded and gave Josh a level look. "For starters," he said with a sigh, "the police force wasn't in a position to help us. Somebody at the government level had declared the entire matter of the wreck of the Christopher yacht as classified. I was given a sheaf of paperwork and told to come back in six months. The whole thing reeked of payoff. So since we didn't have six months, and we'd left our expert in port affairs back on the yacht"—he nodded to Leon—"we went with plan B." This time he nodded to Danny.

"Which was to break into the harbormaster's building, the better to steal *their* records," Danny said with a grimace. "Now, the harbormaster's building isn't like an outbuilding, like back at Calumet Lake. It was a government building, this one built in the Victorian era and maintained nicely because, well, Barbados is a very pretty island."

"You guys," Chuck added, looking very serious. "There were cobblestone walkways, hanging baskets of flowers, the smell of fruit in the air…." He kissed his fingertips in a classic chef's kiss. "It was exquisite. It's a shame none of us will ever be invited back."

Danny cleared his throat. "But as we were saying…."

Chuck recalled himself. "Yeah. Anyway, so Danny figures out the best place to go in is a second story window. I give him a leg up and start patrolling the back alleyway to keep his exfil clear."

"I was driving getaway," Liam said. "Small vehicle, parked nearby, ready to go fetch when they needed."

"So what happened?" Hunter asked, his arms still in that comforting circle around Grace.

"Bad guys with guns," Danny said. "I made it in and out of the building—and make no mistake, I have the documents we need—but as I was climbing down the wall—"

"Like a fucking *spider*," Chuck muttered. "It was terrifying. Josh, Grace, I hope you guys are taking lessons."

"Anyway," Danny said, "suddenly I hear a shout and the alleyway is absolutely flooded with bad guys with Glocks, speaking Serbian. I freeze, because I'm above them in the shadows and they can't see me, and Chuck—"

"I dive through an open window. The doors were locked, but it's a stucco building with no air conditioning, and some of the windows were still open for air flow. Anyway, I dive—"

"Wriggle," Danny supplied dryly.

"Yeah, it wasn't very big. I wriggle through an open window, and I take a peek outside and realize Danny's trapped like a rat in a cage."

"Very apt," Danny said. "So Charles here starts running through the bottom floor of the building, turning on every light he can find. The building starts lighting up like a Christmas tree, and the gunmen prove they're *not* aligned with the Bahamian government because they're like cockroaches. They can't get away fast enough. It was a good plan—"

"Obviously not," Chuck said, sounding angry at himself.

"There were no perfect plans," Danny said soothingly. "The only problem was that it exposed me. I got winged climbing in a window, but by then, there were police all over the grounds, including our handy dark alleyway and in front of the building as well."

"Oh my God," Michael said, obviously entranced. "What did you do?"

"Well, that is where our young Mr. Craig got very inventive," Danny praised. "Remember, we were supposed to take the car to the airstrip, but that was right out. So young Liam here drove the car up *over* the courthouse steps, telling Chuck to hang back and wait until the police followed us. He was driving a tiny car—"

"A Mini," Liam said. "Chuck was practically origami in the nonexistent back on the way there."

"So I was relieved *not* to jump in the car on the way back," Chuck supplied. "Liam literally drove that thing up the steps to the front door, and Danny jumped through the roof into the front seat before they took off."

"What did you do?" Lucius asked his boyfriend, obviously trying not to get too upset.

"I hid," Chuck said, looking like that was only natural. "Once the cops saw Danny jump through the moonroof—which was not a bad feat considering—"

Danny sent him a killing look, and the whole room sucked in a breath as they realized he'd done this wounded.

"Anyway," Chuck continued on as though nothing had stopped him, "the cops followed Liam, and Liam drove the Mini into the harbor."

"We escaped out the roof," Liam said, "and hotwired a Zodiac with half a tank of gas, and drove it out of the harbor like a bat out of hell."

"Did the police follow you?" Carl asked clinically, and the three of them nodded.

"We expected them to," Liam said. "But it took them a while to scramble and find their own crafts to coordinate. In the meantime, Chuck—"

"Under Liam's direction," Chuck added, tipping his head at Liam in admiration.

Liam tipped his head in return and continued on. "Chuck had caught his own ride to the airstrip."

All eyes turned to Chuck, who filled in the rest. "I stole one of the police motorcycles. Can you believe they left the keys in it?"

"And…." Molly made a "go on" gesture, because the entire room was obviously riveted.

"And I hotwired a Mosquito Air," Chuck said, "and flew out to sea to fetch them from the Zodiac."

Felix frowned. "How did you… fetch them?"

"They climbed a ladder," Torrance supplied, half laughing, half appalled. "Because by now they had a news reporter on one of the police boats, and there's a picture—it's damned hard to see, and you both were wearing microfiber masks—of Danny and Liam climbing into the smallest, dumbest helicopter I've ever fucking seen."

"It barely got us back to St. Kitts," Chuck confirmed. "We had to ditch it in the shallows so we could… uhm, swim to our boat and come back here."

There was a horrified silence.

"Oh dear God," Julia said at last. "That's—"

"That's *amazing*!" Leon said, eyes wide.

"I'm so jealous you assholes didn't even fucking ask me," Hunter muttered.

"Or me!" Grace said, obviously not letting this go.

Into the chatter, Felix utterly lost his cool.

"*You got hurt!*"

He stood, hands inches away from Danny's shoulders as though he *wanted* to shake his smaller lover but was afraid to hurt him further.

"Well, yes," Danny admitted, "but we didn't get *caught*."

"*Augh!*" Felix, whom Tienne had always assumed was cool as a cucumber in a summer hurricane, *flailed*. His arms waved, his feet shuffled, and his mouth worked as he went fishing for words that wouldn't come.

"Felix," Danny said, using his good hand to tentatively stroke Felix's bicep to calm him down. "I'm fine. We did not expect the Serbian mob during a simple B and E. It was like the Spanish Inquisition!"

Felix's body calmed down, but his mouth worked helplessly. "The Spanish Inquisition?" he finally managed.

Tienne felt it. The entire room opened their mouths to finish the Monty Python quote. Everybody knew it, but—

"Nobody expects the Spanish Inquisition, Dad," Josh said, before looking out at everybody else. "You. Cowards."

Felix closed his eyes and breathed. And one more time. And one more time. Finally, when he appeared to have calmed down, he took a step back and grimaced.

"I walked right into that one, didn't I?"

"Both feet, no hesitation," Danny confirmed. Then his mouth quirked in concession to Felix's anxiety. "It hurts like hell, Fox. I could really use some ibuprofen and R and R to recover. But we need to tell the kids what's up so they can help us solve our little problem, okay?"

Felix nodded and massaged the back of his neck. "Understood. You know, I'm starting to think the way we spent our youth was a little dangerous."

Danny grinned at the rest of the room. "He once outran the entire police force in Dublin to hide in a bog. Smelled like peat for days."

Felix shuddered. "It was not as glamourous as it sounds."

"That's good," Grace said, "because it sounds like you almost got your ass busted while covered in rotting veggies."

"Well, I did not have the option of escaping in a helicopter so small, Charles probably had to break wind to let Danny and Liam fit inside," Felix snapped.

After a moment of shock, because Felix was *seldom* crude, Chuck said, "Who told!"

The resulting laughter was more of a tension relief than anything else, and Felix dragged a chair from the dining table in the pause, urging Danny to sit.

"Danny is right," he said, making it clear he'd reclaimed his cool—and his position as leader. "I got a look at the documents Danny obtained, and we need to make some decisions. Gather around, children, and let's have a conversation."

Into the Breach

WHEN THE briefing was over, Stirling and Josh sat in the lounge, working side by side on their computers, while Carl took over the dining room table. Danny promised to join them after his one-on-one with Felix, but as the discussion had progressed, it had become increasingly obvious that Danny, Liam, and Chuck had really had quite an adventure and maybe needed some more sleep before they could coherently plan so much as a trip to the bathroom.

Tienne had grabbed a sketchbook from the cabin and had fallen asleep, charcoal in hand, as he attempted to sketch a flat blue-and-gold fish that had figured prominently in their adventures that morning, while sitting on the couch that stretched by the window. Michael—who had apparently spent the entire morning down in the engine room, talking to the chief engineer and helping him out of sheer delight—had done the same thing; only he'd fallen asleep while composing a letter to his children, complete with pictures.

Stirling paused in what he was doing to watch as Carl stood up, stretched, retrieved the tablet from Michael's lap, and set it down beside the couch. Carefully, so as not to disturb him, he pulled a cotton throw from the back of the couch and wrapped it around Michael's shoulders, smiling a little as Michael burrowed in.

Then Carl caught Stirling's regard and blushed.

"He's so sweet," Stirling said, enjoying the normally stolid man's shy smile.

"Could say the same," Carl told him, nodding at Tienne.

Stirling gave him a smile of his own—but even he knew it wasn't complete. Carl frowned and moved closer, snagging his chair at the table and moving it so he could look sideways onto Josh and Stirling's computers.

The papers Danny had stolen from the port authority had been troubling, as had been several things about the adventure itself.

The fact that Liam, an Interpol agent, had been stonewalled when asking for what was, essentially, a professional courtesy, had rung their first alarm bell, but not the loudest. The loudest had been that their break-in at the harbormaster's building had been anticipated. Danny was a superlative thief, but even if he'd been a mediocre thief, Liam and Chuck both knew enough about security to not let him walk into a trap. He hadn't gotten caught *going into* the building. The mass of thugs—all of them dressed in black jeans and madras shirts—had shown up expecting something to go down.

And none of them had been police. The police, in fact, had sent them scattering like cockroaches.

"No," Liam had said, shaking his head and catching Chuck's eyes. "These gentlemen were somebody's muscle—not real cops. For one thing," he added, looking grim, "the Barbadian police aren't trigger happy like the American bobbies. There's no reason for them to shoot a guy clinging to a building. This was a criminal action designed to keep anybody who might want to see those papers from following up on the request. I think *they* had probably planned to storm the place and rob it, but they saw Danny and fired shots and bolloxed their own chances."

"So," Chuck reasoned, "well-funded but not bright."

"And they spoke Serbian," Liam added, and that reminder brought a whole new level to the proceedings.

So Levka Dubov's group, the up-and-coming Serbian gang, was very likely there, in Barbados, and highly functional.

And apparently they had a reason for not wanting the details of the wreck of the Christophers' yacht to see the light of day.

After looking at the hidden details of the wreck, Stirling could figure out why.

The ship had not—as had been reported to the port authority in Chicago—"wrecked." It had, in fact, run aground. The people who had died—and as reported, neither the Christophers nor any of their crew had survived—had not been drowned or injured in a shipwreck.

They'd been shot.

There had been no pictures—thank God—but there had been coroner's reports, and those had been enough.

The thing that had made those papers so important was the time stamps and locations. When the ship had reported coming through the storm, it had been around eleven in the morning, island time. The captain had radioed the port and said the ship had been blown off course, but since they were so close to Stirling Molly, they would dock there, and the Christophers could take an early inspection of their island.

The ship had run aground on a beach in Barbados nearly eight hours later, giving plenty of time for the murders and for the ship to be turned loose.

"There was another tropical storm due the next morning," Danny had said when they'd dropped that bombshell. "I think the ship pulled into Stirling Molly, and whoever was behind whatever illegal operation was going on there decided it would be better to kill all aboard. Then they probably turned it out to sea and set the engines for a putter into the void, hoping it would get capsized in the oncoming storm." He paused then, his eyes going from Stirling to Molly with undisguised compassion. "This news... it's going to hit you both hard, though probably not now, when you're surrounded by people. But whenever and however it hits you, children—remember. You don't have to be alone when it does. There's not a soul in this room who wouldn't throw themselves on that emotional grenade for you. You're loved, both of you. And we are all so terribly sorry."

Stirling had swallowed, dry-eyed, and he'd looked at his sister, whose jaw had been clenched along with her fist. Danny had given her a grim smile, and not a soul in the room doubted the channel Molly's grief would take.

Rage. Stirling would be content with justice, but his sister would need vengeance, and that was such a tricky line.

Stirling had tried to catch up with her after the meeting broke up, but she'd been charging for the gym, which was opposite the lounge. Hunter had held up a hand and said, "I'll take care of her, Stirling. This is in my wheelhouse," and then he'd disappeared, Grace at his heels.

Well, Grace had been getting twitchy too. Maybe the three of them would beat the hell out of each other and bleed off some extra energy so everybody's brain could engage.

Stirling knew his own brain felt thick as pudding as he tried to slog through his task at hand.

"How you doing?" Carl asked now, his low, rumbly "dad voice" a comfort even if Stirling couldn't fathom an answer.

"He's doing shitty," Josh answered, shooting them both a glance. "Ask me how I know."

Stirling stared at him in awe, because Josh, who seemed to have so much else going on in his life, in his *brain*, really had put his finger on the pulse of Stirling's emotions.

"How?" he asked. "How do you know?"

"Because you sent me the data on Fred's three business buddies that are part of Foster's Inc. twenty minutes ago and you haven't started their phone traces yet."

"I was trying to figure out what other business contacts they had besides Harve," Stirling told him logically.

"Nothing legit," Josh said, waving his hand. "If they're crooked, they're doing their business dealings on the dark web with burner phones. Or in cash, of which they've all got substantial withdrawals at regular intervals." He pointed to his screen, and Stirling and Carl both angled themselves to look. "See? Here, and here. By the way, everybody note this date?"

"Oh shit," Stirling said, his entire body going hot and cold. "All three made withdrawals and deposits to the same bank account on the day my parents' ship went…." He swallowed, and what Danny had foretold reared its ugly head. "The day they were murdered."

"Yes," Josh said softly. "And look at the amount."

Stirling blinked at the single amounts from each account, and then blinked again and tried to kick his brain into gear. "The entire amount," he said slowly, "put all together—that's the *entire* amount paid into the life insurance policies." Oh, he wasn't going to lose it. He knew what that meant, *knew* that meant betrayal by people Fred had thought of as friends, but he couldn't… couldn't….

Josh nodded and interrupted his spiraling thoughts. "Three guesses as to what that means."

Carl chuffed out a breath and answered, which was good because Stirling's throat and mouth weren't doing so hot in conjunction. "It means we have a clear bit of evidence connecting these four with the criminals down here who carried out the orders."

Josh nodded again. "All we need to do is find that." He tapped his screen where the mystery account number sat, all but glowing red. "Where that is. Who those people are. And I think I have a way to do that."

Carl and Stirling looked at each other, and although he was reassured that he wasn't alone, Stirling still felt breathless. Like an elephant was sitting on his chest, and he couldn't move it alone. But they were planning, and his brain was needed, his prodigious brain that could jump light-years with the press of a key. He couldn't let it wander.

"Yes?" Carl intoned, moving his hands in a classic "Give me more" gesture.

"Well," Josh continued, "we all know where they have to be, right? I mean, Liam asks for the papers, and that night, bad guys fill the square. They can't be that far away."

"The tiny island," Stirling said, his voice sounding far away to his own ears. "We all know that. Fred and Stella landed there early because they got blown off course, and they saw something they shouldn't have and…."

Josh nodded. "Exactly. So that's got to be the source of our bad guys. We drop a bug in bad guy central in two days—"

"Why two days?" Stirling asked. He couldn't seem to *think*.

"Because that's the pattern, see?" Josh pointed to a document on his own keyboard that Stirling should have seen. "The seventh and twenty-first of every month. In two days, it will be the seventh of January and our guys in Chicago will be sending money here." He tapped the mystery number on his screen. "One bug in their software and we can know who they are, how often they get paid, and where the money goes afterward."

"But isn't that risky?" Stirling asked. "I mean, I wouldn't even send Grace into an unexplored island and expect him to get that bug there."

"Well, no," Josh agreed. "But the island isn't named Dylan 'Grace' Li, now is it?"

Stirling sucked in his breath, his panic crystalizing into this one thought. "No—no, it's not."

"Do we have a contact number for Stirling Molly? The island, I mean?" Carl asked.

"Only one," Josh said. "But he's sort of a relative, right, Stirling?"

"Harve," Stirling murmured. His ears hurt. "Do you think he'll do it? Or do you think he'll set a trap?"

"Oh, he'll definitely set a trap," Carl predicted. "But I think we can pretty much foil any trap he sets—"

"The island is probably inhabited by the Serbian mob," Stirling cautioned, suddenly afraid for his friends. "Even Carl, Chuck, and Hunter aren't enough to defeat an army, and I'm not going to let anybody else get hurt on my account." He had to suck in a hard breath then.

Carl snorted. "And how will you stop us, Stirling? Isn't that why we all do this? To right wrongs? What happened to your parents—it doesn't get much more wrong than that. I mean, yes, we looked into this because we all love you and Molly, but that doesn't mean we wouldn't have wanted to get to the bottom of it anyway."

Carl—God! Why did he have to be right so much? "But Danny got *shot*," Stirling said, his voice cracking, his breaths coming shorter and shorter. "He got *shot*, and Fred and Stella, the nicest people on the planet, they got *shot*. These people are dangerous. What if I lose a whole other family? You're only supposed to get one, but I lucked into two, and what if I lose them as well and—" He couldn't breathe.

He *couldn't breathe*—

"Shh...." Tienne was there, where Josh had been, pulling Stirling against him and putting a cool hand on the back of his neck.

"You're supposed to be asleep," Stirling said, surprised out of his panic spiral enough to think.

"You needed me," Tienne said simply, and Stirling looked at him in awe.

"How would you know that?" he whispered. "How could you...?"

Tienne's hands—dusted with charcoal—smoothed along his cheek, his forehead. "I don't know. Usually, I don't understand people at all." He gave a winsome smile, and it was enough, enough for Stirling to trust him.

Enough to allow himself to break down.

"I don't want to lose anyone else," he gasped, the hole that Fred and Stella Christopher had left suddenly gaping in his chest as he hadn't allowed it to since he and Molly had been informed of their deaths. Oh God. The Salingers—Danny, Felix, Julia—and Carl, Grace, and Josh.

Molly. Oh Jesus. Molly, who was planning even now to go do battle with the people who had robbed them of the parents they'd loved so fiercely.

Tienne. Gentle Tienne, who was cupping his cheeks and breathing evenly, trying to get Stirling to breathe with him when all Stirling wanted, *all* he wanted, was to... was to....

His first sob sounded strangled and thin, like a dying cat, and his second was loud and awkward, like a coughing bear. His third came easier, but it still shook his body like a giant with a rag doll, and his next one wasn't much better. He was going to fly apart; he was going to disintegrate. Not even Tienne's arms could hold him.

Except it wasn't only Tienne's arms he felt.

Carl was enveloping them both in a bear hug from his other side, and Josh was here too, rubbing his back.

And as Stirling lost all cohesion, lost all control, he realized that this was what Danny had meant.

Nobody on this ship had to be alone.

SOMEHOW, TIENNE got him down to his room, where he lay still for a long time, eyes closed, brain in a foggy limbo. He slept briefly and awoke feeling odd and disconnected but also clearheaded. Tienne's hand, dragging from his shoulder down his arm to his waist, pulled him slowly, sensually, into the here and now.

"Crap," he muttered, lacing their fingers together across his stomach. "I'm so embarrassed."

"I don't know why," Tienne mumbled against his neck. There was a pause, and as though it only now occurred to him, Stirling felt his lips in the same place. And then the tiniest bit of tongue.

Against everything that had happened, he felt a smile starting.

"What do you mean?" he asked, but he snuggled backward, realizing the fan was on overhead and the porthole was open. Outside, it was cool enough to render the air conditioning unnecessary, and the fresh air felt sweet moving across them.

"Your emotions. They were… they were very true," Tienne murmured, bending his attention to Stirling's ear.

Stirling had a terrible thought. Turning over in Tienne's arms, he searched his lover's eyes. "Who was there for you?" Nothing about Tienne's story of the night his father died, or the morning he'd found himself being dragged through Marrakech by Liam Craig, spoke of a time to give in to grief or anger. It occurred to Stirling that one of the things he most treasured about

Tienne, the stillness inside him that gave Stirling such peace and comfort, had been born of Tienne's knowledge that nobody would hear him scream, nor comfort him should he cry.

Tienne's face, with the high cheekbones and dreamy blue eyes, assumed a suddenly adult, very *present* expression.

"Nobody," he said. "You knew that."

Stirling had always been afraid of strong emotions. Perhaps it was what had made his undoing in the lounge so very hard to come back from. But now, seeing the desolation on Tienne's face, he realized he would do much to be able to go back and be the rock in Tienne's storm.

"I want to be there for you," Stirling rasped, tracing his fingertips along Tienne's cheek. "If you need somebody to hold you, like I needed you—I want to be there. I may not be able to do it alone, but I still want to be part of the rescue party."

Tienne turned his head and kissed Stirling's fingertips. "I do not need rescuing right now," he said, almost winsomely, but then he sobered, and Stirling was reassured. "Although perhaps, like you, there will be a moment when my heart remembers again what it has lost and will want to tear itself apart."

Stirling swallowed. He wasn't sure if it was that Tienne's first language was a poetic one, or that Tienne surrounded himself with beautiful art and the stories therein, but he was always so eloquent.

"If that happens," he whispered, "I'll help you put it back together."

Tienne licked his lips and took a deep breath, which told Stirling that those emotions, for Tienne, were still very near the surface in this hushed, breathless moment.

"I shall learn to trust in that," he said. Then he kissed Stirling gently on the lips, a searching kiss, to see if Stirling had the desire in this moment, when their souls were bare and, perhaps, would need covering with the sweetness of flesh.

Stirling responded, the thrum of arousal already a steady beat in his veins.

"But now," Tienne continued, feathering a kiss down his jaw, "I would rather be there for you and take you someplace where you are happy, so you remember that you can survive the screaming of your own heart."

Stirling moaned, as much from the touch as from the sentiment and the glorious offer of pleasure and escape from pain.

"Come with me," he said, thrusting his hand under Tienne's T-shirt, enjoying the sudden intake of breath, the way Tienne's concave stomach drew tighter under Stirling's palm.

"I'm so happy you asked."

They went slow—achingly slow. Every kiss, every touch, had a comment, a murmur, a moment of "Ah...."

Their sighs mingled, and their gasps lingered, and their touches... oh, their touches sizzled nerve endings, became more than fingertips stroking, tongues laving, teeth nibbling.

When they were naked, Tienne pushed Stirling to his back and reached for the lubricant under the pillow. At first Stirling was afraid he planned to top, and Stirling wasn't ready for that, not now, not when he didn't know what to expect. But Tienne surprised him, reading emotions and the moment so readily, Stirling thought he must be clairvoyant, with a solid view into Stirling's soul. After dripping a little on his fingers, he reached around behind and, giving Stirling a coy look from underneath his blond lashes, began to stretch himself.

"Oh!" He moaned softly, and Stirling spanned his slender waist between his hands, stroking him, grounding him, until Tienne raised his face to Stirling's, eyes closed, lower lip caught between his teeth.

"Good?" Stirling asked, everything aching with the need to be inside him.

"So good," Tienne told him, moving his shoulders and arm in an unmistakable way. The thought that he was penetrating himself, *fucking* himself, made Stirling's hips buck, and he released a little precome spurt.

"Please?" he begged. Tienne had driven this moment, had placed Stirling at his mercy. Stirling wouldn't take the reins from him now.

"Yes."

Tienne's hand, slick with lube, wrapped around Stirling's cock, placing him just… right… there.

With a groan that shook them both, Tienne slid backward, stretching to accommodate Stirling's girth, and then, oh God, bit by bit his length. Down, down, down, until finally he was seated flat, his breath coming in little pants, sweat popping out on his chest, along his throat, dripping from his brow.

"Stirling!" he cried, leaning forward and putting his palms on Stirling's chest. "*Please!*"

He trusted Stirling with his heart, to hold it when he finally allowed it to break. The very least Stirling could do was take this moment and bring it home.

He grabbed Tienne's slender hips to hold him in place and began to thrust.

"*Yes!*" Tienne threw his head back, and his slick hand reached for his own cock while his other hand reached for his nipples, and Stirling pleasured his ass—and himself. Every thrust, every slap of flesh, drove them both higher, higher, *oh God higher!* Until finally Tienne began to shake all over, his skin—still pale, even after all that sunshine—blotched with passion, his face taut with arousal. With a deep cry, one that Stirling felt vibrate through his cock and to his balls, Tienne came, spattering come across Stirling's abdomen, across his chest, the sight and scent driving Stirling over the edge.

With a final thrust, he drove into Tienne and cried out, his eyes closing as fireworks tore through the darkness behind his gaze. On and on, as though the slow burn had built passion behind a dam, the orgasm ripped through him, each ripple building, each spasm ramping him up again, until they shook together, the aftershock almost bigger than the first quake of flesh and come.

Finally, Tienne gave a little whimper of completion and rolled off, dripping come onto Stirling's thighs as he went. For a moment they simply panted into the quiet, and it was only in that space that Stirling realized the slanting shadows of late afternoon had darkened into evening.

Hunger hit him with so much force, he was almost light-headed.

"That was wonderful," he muttered. "Food?"

"God yes," Tienne agreed, and Stirling turned his head in time to see a gorgeous, utterly innocent smile bloom across his face. "To both."

Stirling's chest swelled, tight enough to threaten his breathing, but it didn't feel like the tears that had rocked him hours before. What was this?

"Is this love?" he asked aloud.

Tienne blinked, but the smile stayed in place. "I hope not. It's making you frown."

"It's not bad," Stirling said, trying to breathe past the fullness in his chest. "It's… it's wonderful. But…." He swallowed. "But it's still making me cry."

Tienne rolled over and kissed him, his smile still one of the most beautiful things Stirling had ever seen. "Then save it for another day," he murmured. "Because I would cry with you, and then we may be too overcome with love to get food, and that would be a shame."

Stirling found his humor with this. "They would find two dried-out husks and think, 'Wow, it's true—you *can* die of too much sex!'"

Tienne's laughter burbled out, and the tightness in Stirling's chest eased up, and he realized he could do this. He could contain this brilliant, full emotion suffusing his body with light.

And if he couldn't, it would transcend his flesh and simply make him bigger in spirit.

"And only we would know," Tienne said huskily, kissing Stirling's jaw again, "that it was love, and it made angels of us and left our bodies behind."

"How do you do that?" he asked in wonder.

"Do what?"

"Read my mind."

Tienne caught his mouth and kissed him, a solid, sturdy, real kiss that made becoming an angel less of an option and dying from too much sex more of one. Then he let go of the kiss and planted a brief one on Stirling's forehead.

"I read your face," he said. "It is so beautiful, I cannot look away. I want to paint it—but not now. Now get up! We need to clean up and dress or we *will* waste away, and that would be a shame."

"It would," Stirling said, rolling off the bed and stretching. "There is so much more lovemaking to do!"

THEY CLEANED themselves up and made their way up to the lounge. Dinner appeared to have been served and cleared, but Leon had instructed the galley staff to keep leftovers and lunch fixings available in the snack area, where a small refrigerator, a counter, and a microwave sat, along with cases of water, cookies, and snack bars in the cupboards. And there was always fresh fruit.

Stirling rooted around the fridge and pulled out two covered plates with what he assumed were his and Tienne's dinners and put the first one in the microwave for two minutes.

"What's for dinner?" Tienne asked, getting glasses from over the counter.

"London broil with mushrooms and baked potatoes," Stirling said happily. He sniffed the air. "Although I think everybody else had fish."

Tienne chuckled. Stirling tried—he really did. But apparently his dislike of fish had not gone unnoticed. Three days into the cruise, he'd begun to get hamburgers instead of halibut, or chicken instead of tuna. On this night, when he and Tienne had been missing, the kitchen staff had gone out of their way to make sure there was a dish they both could enjoy.

"Leon's staff is the greatest," Stirling groaned as the microwave dinged.

"Perhaps it is that *Leon* is the greatest," Tienne reminded him. "I have the feeling he is invested in getting to know all of Josh's friends."

Stirling thought about it, and about the extravagant gift of the yacht, of the trip, of the adventure.

And of the way he blushed like a schoolboy every time Julia Dormer-Salinger walked into the room.

"Mm" was all he said, and Tienne let another one of those devastatingly shy smiles slip.

"And his fondness for Julia is quite apparent."

Their eyes met in a moment of shared laughter—of affection for friends—and Stirling put the other plate in before setting the table for them both.

"Placemats too?" Tienne asked, bringing over two tumblers full of orange juice and the bottle itself.

"Fred and Stella had us set the table every night," Stirling said, remembering. "And I know it was supposed to be a chore, but Molly and I were used to, well, depressing dinners. Basic food on chipped plates, sort of thrown down. 'Hey, it's edible. We did our duty. Do yours.' But even though they had, you know, money and help, Stella would make us set the table and assist in the kitchen. She arranged for Sherri, the cook, to give us basic lessons so we wouldn't exist on takeout when we were on our own. It was…." He smiled fondly. "It was a nice gift, that sort of gift of ceremony."

"Mm…." Tienne sat and regarded his food thoughtfully. "My father, well, he was like me. He would often get lost in his work. No ceremony for us. But there was always a moment—and sometimes you could *see* him jerk himself painfully into the here and now—but he'd call himself to the present and ask me if I'd eaten, and sometimes if *he'd* eaten, and ask me about my day. Sometimes, if he was between jobs, he'd greet me from school or set up my easel and give me lessons as we worked together." His eyes grew far away. "He was a good man, my father. There were hugs. He did much to protect me, you know? From the decisions he'd made when he was desperate."

Stirling thought of his own mother, the glimpses he could remember. The idea, always, that he'd been left in a church—not abandoned in a street, not ditched with strangers. She'd left him in a place where she believed that someone would feed him and keep him safe.

"It's funny," he said, knowing that funny wasn't really the word. "We both... I mean, we know so much wealth now. But I don't think, for either of us, it's the wealth that matters."

Tienne blinked, as though surprised to learn this about himself. "It is the people," he said, reaching under the table to pat Stirling's knee. "And the work. It's having an obsession that drives us, yet knowing we have a net to catch us if we fall."

Stirling caught his hand and laced their fingers together, squeezing gently. "I'm so glad you believe in our people now."

They resumed eating while still holding hands, but Stirling was pretty ambidextrous, so it wasn't awkward at all.

They were finishing up when Liam Craig wandered in, rooting through the cupboards restlessly and coming up with cookies. He turned to the two of them and gave a quiet smile.

"So you finally woke up, did you?"

Stirling wasn't great at looking people in the eyes most of the time, but tonight it had less to do with making contact and more to do with embarrassment. "Sure."

Liam's low chuckle was nothing but kind. "I can tell you, Carl needed a hug by the time you were done, poor chap. He's got a fondness for you, Stirling, make no mistake. And Josh was beside himself."

Stirling frowned. "Wait, where *is* everybody now?" He'd lost some time while he'd been overwrought. He knew he'd cried himself out before Tienne had guided him down to the cabin, and then he'd lain in a fog, napping a little, before waking up, and… *waking up*. But it had been midafternoon at the latest when they'd left the cabin, and it was after dark now.

Liam thought. "Well, I think Felix and Danny had your idea but with rather a bit more shouting at each other. That's how some folks get it done, right?"

Stirling ducked his head in embarrassment. "They're very volatile," he mumbled.

"That's a good word," Liam agreed. "I'm gonna remember that word. Anyways, so they're being *volatile*, and Leon and Julia took everybody else to the island on—"

"Which island?" Tienne asked. "I mean, I lose track of which one comes where. And you, Danny, and Chuck all jumped forward to Barbados and then came back to us and… which island?" he finished at last, a little desperately, and Liam's laughter reassured them both.

"Martinique," he said, amused. "It's about a two-hour trip from where we're at. We're still cruising toward Barbados, and your teeny tiny island at the tip. That's over a hundred and fifty miles from where we are now and maybe six, seven hours. And I don't blame you for getting confused. What's even more of a mind-blower is remembering which islands have their own governments and which ones are territories."

Stirling grunted. "Don't even get me started on Puerto Rico. I'm still mad about the hurricane."

Liam held his hands up. "As are a lot of folks. One crisis at a time, right? Anyway, they're on Martinique, for happy volcano reasons, I understand."

Stirling squinted at him. "Volcano reasons?"

"Not the museum dedicated to Gaugin?" Tienne asked. He frowned. "Although that would probably be closed by now."

Liam let out a breath. "Yes, in fact the only things not closed by now are probably the restaurants in Fort-de-France." He let out a sigh. "I think they wanted to get off the bloody boat, if you ask me, although I understand there's lots of nature things to do during the daylight hours. Scenic gorges, peaceful gardens…." He couldn't seem to stop a distasteful shudder, and Tienne laughed.

"You prefer city life?"

Liam winked. "You caught me. Yeah, I do. But I got my adventuring in last night, so tonight, I stayed back with—"

Stirling made the leap. "Josh? You stayed with *Josh*?"

And for the first time ever, the unflappable Liam seemed a little discomfited. "Not like you're thinking! He was a bit tired this afternoon, and…." He shrugged, his eyes going to the breezeway he'd come from, probably thinking about leaving Josh in his cabin.

Wait. "Did Josh ever move out of your cabin?" Stirling asked, wondering how Molly, with her love of all things gossip, did not know about *this*.

"He stayed in mine, I moved to his," Liam said, looking embarrassed. "He was out almost that entire first day and night. It was easier." And that seemed to get his feet back under him. "And not an errant thought or word from either of you, yeah? We've been keeping company is all. He"—Liam's expression went troubled—"doesn't want to hold the lot of you back, but you do realize that it's at least a six-month recovery for someone who's gone through what he has, don't you? From muscle mass to wind to strength, he was used to being the guy in the away party, going mach five."

"Which is too bad," Tienne said guilelessly, "because he's quite apt as the guy behind the computer with Stirling, giving all the orders."

"Who is?" Danny said, wandering in from the same direction Liam had come from.

"Josh," Stirling said, watching the older man carefully. He'd changed into a fresh outfit, but he was still wearing what Stirling thought of as "thieves' clothes," which consisted of black yoga pants and a black T-shirt, something he often wore when he was restless or thinking about a job. He also still wore his sling tight against his body, and while usually as fluid as Josh or Grace in his movements, he seemed a bit stiff in the shoulders. Yes, Stirling deduced, being shot and battered about for the night still hurt.

"Josh is the best grifting mastermind to come along in a generation," Danny said without conceit. "It's a good thing he was born to a family of criminals or he would have ended up in prison."

Liam's face darkened. "I don't like that word," he said stubbornly. "I wish you wouldn't use it."

"Criminals?" Danny rolled his eyes as though bored. "Tienne? Stirling? How many laws have you broken today?"

Stirling thought about it. "Well, there was the hacking I did on Foster's Inc., the tracing of the money to the mysterious account offshore in the Caymans, and the gambling tips I sent back to the theater manager in Chicago." He paused, wanting to make sure this was understood. "We channel the winnings into the theater," he said seriously. "That way they can stay independent. But Molly and I donate monthly too."

"Of course," Danny said with a completely straight face. "Tienne, you?"

Tienne thought about it too. "I updated a couple of passports." He frowned. "I don't know why so many of you have forged papers. You're almost all legitimate." He gave Liam an apologetic glance. "Except for you, Officer Craig. You needed something with your alias on it, in case you get caught with us." He paused for a moment and then brightened. "Oh yes! I sold one of my forgeries back in Chicago."

"I did *not* want to know that," Liam muttered.

"They're pigs," Tienne said, completely without apology. "They don't know Monet from Manet. They wanted to tell their pig boss that they have a priceless work of art on their walls."

Stirling looked at him, appalled. "Can they trace the forgery back to you?"

Tienne stared at him. "Of course not! Josh set up the fake identity and the bank account and even false papers for a pretend art-dealing middleman. They'll buy the painting and get it delivered and never see our faces. Good Lord, Stirling, Josh and Grace have been helping me with this business since boarding school. I'm not as bright as you, but I'm not stupid!"

Danny was regarding Liam with complete aplomb. "And that's Stirling and Tienne, Liam. They're practically virgins compared to the rest of the crew." He paused. "Except Michael. Technically, that boy hasn't done anything illegal since he got out of prison for armed robbery."

Stirling looked miserably at Tienne, realizing that both of their faces had gone hot and blotchy at the word "virgins."

At the sink, Danny and Liam both stared at them, raising their eyebrows.

"Criminally speaking," Danny added, "that is."

Stirling nodded, feeling marginally better.

"But my point," Danny continued after a delicate clearing of his throat, "is that they're not working within the law, but—" He gave Stirling a tender look that felt like rainwater when he said this. "—they're not doing any harm, either."

Liam chuffed out a breath. "It's hard to argue with the gentleman who forged my credentials," he said with a wry smile. "I don't like the thought of any of you in jail."

Danny winked at him. "Like any of *us* would be there long."

Liam shook his head and muttered to himself, and at that moment Danny's pocket buzzed. He automatically reached for his phone, wincing when he pulled his shoulder too hard before he had it.

"It's Hunter," he muttered. "I wonder…." He hit Speaker, and Hunter's voice smacked them all like a thunderclap.

"Grace is missing. Get Stirling to activate his tracker."

Stirling's brain blanked out for a moment, and then he turned to Tienne. "Do you remember where my laptop is?"

"I'll go get it," Tienne muttered, hopping up and running toward their quarters. In a daze, Stirling reached for his phone in his pocket while Danny kept Hunter on the line.

"What happened?" he asked gently.

"The lot of us were walking by a restaurant, and we heard voices," Hunter said. His voice was crisp and military, as though he was reporting to a CO. "They were Serbian. I told Grace that and that he should stay alert. We split up then. Leon took Julia and the girls shopping. Something about fabrics. Carl and Michael went out to the bay to watch the ocean at night because they're too sweet for words, and Chuck, Lucius, Grace, and I went to a club so Chuck could see Lucius dance." Hunter chuffed out a breath. "And that's when I noticed Grace was gone. The little asshole took advantage of the splitting up and—*goddammit*, I am *trained* to keep track of people, and he's the *one person* I need to keep track of, and he's *gone!*"

Hunter's voice cracked, and Stirling's heart cracked a little with it. Grace was a flutterby pain in the ass that none of them could live without. He pulled out his phone and accessed the app that tracked Grace's microchipped masks. Two were on board the yacht, but one....

"Okay, he's on the move," Stirling said, wanting the bigger screen of his laptop badly. "And moving off the island fast. Is he on a boat?"

"Boat?" Hunter's voice pitched again, and they could hear another, deeper voice—probably Chuck—calming him down.

Then Danny grunted. "Hunter, I need you to chill a minute. Carl's trying to call me too. I'm going to put you on hold."

Carl's voice was as calm and stoic as ever, but there was a suppressed urgency in it that made Stirling's hackles rise. "Danny, Grace and Michael stowed away on a big cabin cruiser on its way to… somewhere."

"It gets worse every time I click on my phone," Danny muttered to himself. "What, why, and *somewhere*!"

Tienne slid Stirling's laptop in front of him, and he gave a brief nod before booting it up and tapping frantically.

"We were walking along the pier when we spotted Grace," Carl was saying. "Barely, and only because Hunter had texted and told us to look out for him. He was following a group of assholes wearing tacky polyester shirts and black pants and talking loud enough in Russian to wake the whole island."

"Russian or Serbian?" Danny asked quickly, and Carl's exhale told them what they needed to know.

"I'm not great with either. Could have been Serbian. Anyway, Michael and I ducked behind an equipment shed, and the guys got into a cabin cruiser *right* across from us. Slick, big—at least thirty feet long—with two decks, it had a couple of smaller inflatables lashed to the sides. The guys climbed in, and we watched as Grace wriggled his way between the boat and the inflatable, and Michael said, 'Someone needs to watch out for that boy,' and before I could do a *goddamned thing*, Michael *followed* him. And now the boat's taking off!"

Stirling rubbed his chest. Hunter and Carl were unflappable—the most solid people on earth. But their lovers were in danger, and it devastated him to hear them come undone.

"Calm down," Danny said and looked at Stirling, who pointed to the screen. "We've got a line on where they're going. How do we have that again?"

"Well, I could track their phones," Stirling said, "but I put a more efficient device into all of Grace's special thief masks because Hunter had a bad feeling about him taking off."

Danny blinked. "It's like it's in the water in Glencoe," he said. "Okay, can you track both ways? In case somebody drops a phone or a mask?"

"Yes." Stirling frowned. "In fact… yeah, I think Michael dropped his phone."

Danny flailed. "For fuck's sake, hush!" he hissed. Then, "Carl, we have them—"

"I heard what he said," Carl told him, sounding very logical. "Okay, so I'm in our Zodiac." They all heard the roar of the outboard. "Which direction am I going?"

"*For fuck's sake, wait for Hunter!*" Danny roared. "God*dammit*, Carl, it's a big fucking ocean, and he's on his way to the fucking pier!"

"Yes, of course," Carl said, seemingly by rote. "But *Michael!*" His voice cracked, and Stirling thought of Carl's sweet-faced, happy, adorable, more-honest-than-sunshine boyfriend and tried not to hyperventilate with him.

"Wait," he said, looking at his screen. "Wait, I know where they're going." He pulled back the map a little so he could see more than a red dot in blue water with the green of Martinique behind it. "Look at the direction. There's only one place it could go."

"Okay," Danny said. "Carl, go toward the island off the coast of Barbados. They're heading toward the northern tip of Barbados, and the only thing out there is Stirling Molly. I'll call the others. Hunter can hotwire something."

There was a thud and a grunt from Carl's speaker, and Carl, unflappable again, said, "No worries. Hunter, Chuck, and Molly hopped in. How far is Barbados?"

"It's about five hours to where you're heading. You might want to come to the yacht first and—"

It was probably a good plan to regroup at the yacht. Like Danny had said, Barbados and the tiny plantation island were a good six hours away. But Carl was hearing none of it.

"We'll follow them in case Michael or Grace go overboard. We're heading for Barbados. Out."

And Carl's phone clicked off, leaving silence in the lounge.

A thin, strained voice in the doorway from the hall interrupted everybody's stunned inaction. "What the hell?" Josh Salinger demanded, while Stirling's brain shorted out completely.

"Molly?" he stammered. "*Molly*?"

And then Liam strode forward to catch Josh before he could fall, and Danny hit his phone again and snarled, "Felix, get your ass out to the boats. We're taking the other Zodiac."

Tienne shook Stirling's shoulder slightly. "Do you have a waterproof case for your computer?" he asked. "We should go, don't you think?"

Stirling blinked away Josh and Liam and Danny and Felix and focused on Tienne's calm eyes, his gentle expression, and felt his rational, step-by-step brain kick in.

"Yes," he said. "We'll need the waterproof case in my electronics suitcase, extra trackers, sunblock, hats, long-sleeved, breathable shirts, sunglasses, fire blankets, and a first aid kit."

"I'll go gather that," Tienne said, disappearing like somebody who remembered what it was like to gather a few possessions in order to cut and run.

Feeling reassured somehow—they were doing this together, hurray!—Stirling turned to Josh and said, "How you doing?"

"I'm pissed," Josh muttered, head between his knees. "Goddammit, I want to go."

But he couldn't. It was obvious. Recovery Boy or not, he wasn't recovered enough for this.

"Are you good enough to grab your computer and come copy me on this tracker?" Stirling asked, preparing to transfer the program over to Josh. "Because I'm about to take my computer on a very small boat that bounces."

"I can do that," Josh said stoutly, sitting up. His voice dropped to sweet politeness. "Thank you, Liam. I really am fine. If you could bring my computer from the corner, you can get ready to go with everybody else."

"Get ready to go?" And it wasn't Stirling's imagination; Liam sounded surprised.

Stirling turned his head in time to see Josh's glare. "That's my family out there, Liam, and not the gun-toting yeehaw side of it. And I can't lose *anybody*."

Liam took a breath and nodded. "Of course," he said, and to nobody's surprise dropped a kiss on Josh's forehead. Ah. They were in that stage of a relationship. "And I need you to look something up for me while you're waiting."

He stood and made ready to dash to his cabin.

"What do you need?" Josh held out his hands for his computer, and Liam obliged, also with a hand up so Josh could move to the table.

"I need you to look up a communication timeline. We know when the Christophers' ship docked and when it washed ashore. Look up communications in that area and try to see if this group of thugs is acting alone or on orders, and from whom. Figure out how long the yacht was probably out there before running aground and if any of our Foster's Inc. rich guys answered any phones before or after it departed. It would have taken about twenty minutes to do everything—kill everybody, set the yacht up to cruise, and get off it. Narrow that time frame down." Liam swallowed. "If your guys get captured, we need to know whether to go storming the castle or if we've got a communication lag to sneak them out. It could make all the difference in the world."

Josh swallowed, and so did Stirling.

"Cops," Josh said. "Go figure." Liam turned to go, and Josh grabbed his hand before casting a covert glance at Danny, who was busy on his phone again—probably texting everybody left on Martinique. "Take care of the dads if you can?" he begged. "I mean, you know. Grace, Michael, Molly—them first. But the dads?"

Liam nodded. "'Course. You take care of you." Then he grimaced. "And try to calm your mother down when she gets here. If the dads are gone and she's stuck on the boat...."

Josh shuddered. "It'll be epic and ugly. I can manage it." He gave a weak grin and let go of Liam's hand and placed the back of his own against his forehead as though swooning. "Recovery Boy to the rescue!"

Liam was chuckling as he ran out of the room, and Stirling went back to sending all his tracking data to Josh, who didn't drop a stitch.

"Okay, what kind of tracker did you use?"

Stirling told him, and Josh gave him a quick, tight smile.

"Hunter asked you to do that?"

"Yeah, when Grace went to kidnap that poor doctor for you. His Grace sense has been apparently tingling this entire trip."

"Well, remind me to never doubt his instincts," Josh muttered. "Okay, they're good to go on my computer." He let out a growl of frustration. "I need to be there!"

Stirling turned toward him and broke his physical-distance habit by squeezing Josh's shoulder. "It's okay. I mean, I've got to get out of the van at some point, right? And Molly can take care of herself. She's amazing at it."

Josh grunted. "You may need to *save* her from it," he said, and Stirling was grateful for his honesty.

"That too." His sister's heart was so pure; he would hate to see her do something she regretted forever. "I'm worried about Tienne," he admitted quickly, before Tienne could return.

Josh looked away from his computer—he already had phone records up, and Stirling thought he'd probably been worse than useless that afternoon, because Josh seemed to have done a lot of hacking while Stirling had been freaking out. "Tienne is quicker on his feet—and more street smart—than he seems." Josh tapped a few more keys and then gave Stirling a grim smile. "He also runs really fast. I think if shit gets hairy, tell him to run, and you smart it out." The smile faded, and Josh fought a tremble in his mouth, and Stirling was reminded all over again how close they'd come to losing Josh Salinger—*their* Josh Salinger—forever. "But take care of yourself, Stirling. I.... You and Molly have been my friends so long. I swear, when I started running us as a crew, all I could think of was I would get to play with my friends, like we did in school. I—"

"Can I hug you?" Stirling asked, testing his boundaries. Carl would hug him sometimes, and it felt very avuncular. Tienne's hugs were boyfriend hugs. But Josh, his friend, his workmate, his brother—they had not, in his memory, ever hugged.

"I wish you would," Josh said. "And then get going. We need to hurry, and we need everybody back alive."

Concrete parameters to an important assignment.

Josh looked away from the computer and gave Stirling a quick two-thumps-on-the-back sitting bro hug, but Stirling needed more. This was his brother, and he was worried, and so was Stirling. After a deep inhale, Josh relaxed and really held him, and while Josh's body was still thin and unsubstantial, Stirling felt for the first time since his diagnosis in July that his friend might really be okay.

"Don't let Julia get too mad," Stirling murmured and then grabbed his computer, moving to where Tienne waited with a neatly packed knapsack and Stirling's waterproof computer case.

Together they turned toward Danny, who was pacing back and forth, his voice rising.

"No, Julia, we are *not* waiting for your helicopter to get you here because we can get to the tiny island without getting shot out of the sky. Do I *know* they have anti-aircraft artillery? It's a guess, dearest. Josh needs the rest of you here. Felix and I have to go now." He paused. "Well, of course I love you back. You know that. We wouldn't desert you now—not after all we've done to be a family again. Come back to the big bloody boat and be there for our boy."

Julia said something tart, and Danny's look had none of it.

"You can call me an alliterative asshole when we return. Now good*bye*." He ended the call and put the phone in the pocket of his slim yoga pants, then turned to Josh. "Josh, son, do me a favor and make sure your mother isn't armed when we return." He bent down and kissed Josh's cheek, every bit the father Stirling had expected him to be when Josh had told them in middle school that he really had two dads and a mom.

"Stirling, my boy, let us depart," Danny said briskly. "Tienne, good packing, I expect." He paused and then grabbed one of the cases of water that sat next to the refrigerator and turned to Stirling. "Grab a couple boxes of protein bars, too, and some fruit. The journey is about five hours, and one thing grifters learn is to eat when you can."

Stirling did so, turning in surprise to see Tienne holding his knapsack open so Stirling could dump the bars into it.

They worked okay as a team, Stirling thought when they were finally trotting down toward the lower deck, where they could board the Zodiac. They would be okay.

Molly, Grace, Carl, Hunter, Chuck, Michael....
Please let them be okay.

The Watcher

TIENNE AND Stirling had lots of time to think—and not much time to talk—while hunkered down on the floor of the Zodiac, taking shelter from the wind under one of the fire blankets.

Danny, Felix, and Liam all took turns piloting the craft, one to steer, one to navigate and watch for other boats on the water, and one to duck under the shelter with the two of them and rest. Tienne and Stirling would stand and stretch—or sometimes do yoga if it didn't mean disturbing someone else in the back of the craft—but in the end, Tienne was exhausted anyway and questioning his value to this mission.

Who did he think he was?

Stirling's handy waterproof case doubled as a fully charged battery and Wi-Fi hotspot—he kept an eye on Grace's progress through his phone but kept working with Josh through the rest of the night to get the information they'd need. Occasionally he'd talk lowly into Tienne's ear to have him pass on information to the guys at the helm, but other than that—and being the disburser of protein bars, because Danny had called it on the needing-food part—Tienne felt pretty useless.

Some of that must have shown when he went to tell Felix and Danny that Julia had threatened to skin them both and wear their pelts as motorcycle leathers and their teeth as jewelry, and that she was on the yacht by now and in the process of chartering a helicopter that she claimed to be armed to the teeth so she could drop bombs on their heads and laugh while she did so.

Tienne had balked at passing that message along, but Stirling had shown him the bold-faced all-caps text that said TELL THEM WORD FOR WORD, and he'd realized that Julia wasn't fucking around.

Tienne did his duty as messenger boy, passing the news to Danny, who was piloting as Liam dozed at his feet and Felix stood by his side.

Danny laughed and spared Tienne a glance. "Don't look so miserable, Etienne. She's not including you and Stirling. And she probably thinks we forced Liam on this mission with an electric cattle prod."

Felix sighed. "She… you know, as much as I love her, I'd rather hoped…." He bit his lower lip apologetically, and Danny recoiled as though he'd been slapped.

"No," he said, the tinge of outrage in his voice. "No. Fox, I refuse to give her up to the marriage gods. That's not fair. *You've* had her for the past ten years, but I just got her back."

Tienne blinked at them, wondering what they were talking about. Then it occurred to him. Danny had left Felix, Josh, and Julia for nearly ten years—he'd been cut off from his family when he'd rescued Tienne. As he'd confessed to Tienne, he'd been "a mess" and unable to tend to himself. But that split hadn't been *voluntary* so much as it had been *necessary*. And Danny had missed his lover very much, but more than that, he'd missed his *family*. And with Julia most obviously getting closer to Leon di Rossi, it was possible that his family would change again.

And like that, it struck him like a soccer ball to the chest.

He'd miss Grace and Molly and Carl—and even Hunter and Chuck, whom he didn't know as well— should anything happen to them. When he'd started to pack, had planned what to take and how to move, he'd been doing his planning for *Stirling*. He'd been trying to anticipate what *Stirling* would need to rescue the people *Stirling* loved. But now, watching these two men—still young, in their early forties—try to hang on to a woman they did not love romantically but loved perhaps more fiercely than many married couples who did not know their own mettle, he understood the greatness of what Danny had tried to give him all those years ago.

Danny had wanted him to have *this*. Not adventure—and the lover was a bonus but not a necessity from Danny's perspective—but people to go to bat for, who would go to bat for him.

That moment, more than a month ago, when Stirling and Molly had crashed into his apartment, fought off the bane of his existence, and dragged him into their riotous, loud, chaotic den of thievery had been fate's equivalent of shaking him by the shoulders and splashing him with cold water: *This—this is what you could have. You could love and be loved by a raucous household of people, and you could help them as much as they wish to help you.*

And he could have Stirling, and they could be a quiet eye in the storm. Or, when they were needed, a mighty wind.

"Whether or not you end up as motorcycle leathers will probably depend on how whole your skin is when you return, yes?" he asked Danny, who gave him a brilliant grin.

"It will indeed. Now tell me what Stirling's doing when he's working down there. He seems more absorbed than a man relaying a message."

So Tienne updated them both on Stirling and Josh's race to trace the phone messages and establish a timeline giving them an idea of who was giving the orders and who was carrying them out. When he'd finished, Danny and Felix met gazes, and Felix called Liam from his repose on the deck of the prow, out of the wind, and nodded to Tienne.

"Good thought on the phone timeline," Danny said, leaning into Liam so he didn't have to shout. "Now I want you three to join Stirling under that tarp and come up with a plan."

"Sure," Liam said, but he cast a look to Felix. "As long as Felix mans the helm for a good hour or so. You're looking a smidge pale, my friend."

Danny grimaced, and Tienne remembered the stiff way he'd held himself when he'd come rooting through the cupboards that night.

"It's a deal," he said, yawning, and Felix helped him down to where Liam had been sitting, chin to chest as he'd nodded off.

Then Felix turned to Tienne and Liam and shooed them on while he took the helm. "We're cutting power and switching to paddles as soon as the island's in sight." He nodded toward the state-of-the-art navigational system in place by the wheel. "According to this, we've got two more hours—but dawn's coming. Get to it, gentleman. And don't hesitate to ask Julia or Leon—or even Lucius—for anything, including lawyers, guns, and money."

Liam grinned wickedly. "The shit has hit the fan. C'mon, boyo, let's go plan."

Tienne went with him and snuggled under the fire blanket, finding that Stirling had fallen asleep, chin to chest, much as Liam had been. Gently, Liam disengaged his laptop, and Tienne put an arm around his waist and pulled his head to his shoulder. Perhaps it was the chill of the wind outside the boat or the cold of the predawn, but the animal comfort of Stirling's dozing body gave Tienne hope.

TIENNE MANAGED to catch a little sleep himself, but he was still, like the others, windblown and a little discombobulated when Felix killed the motor and broke the paddles from their lashed home on the side of the pontoons.

According to Stirling's maps, the southwestern, windward side of the island was also the only place to dock. There was an obvious cove—sheltered from the wind, with enough space and depth to home a cabin cruiser at the least—that they planned to avoid as a good place to get shot.

But to the eastern side of the island was not a cove so much as a place where the jungle overgrowth met the water. Small bodies sifted through the shadows up there, and Tienne was amazed to see monkeys, as common here as birds might be in Chicago. Surprisingly enough Liam was the one to voice a bit of squeamishness about potentially crawling through the jungle in order to get to the inhabited southwestern side of the island.

"There's not, you know, snakes here, are there?" he asked as they approached, engine off, oars dipping quietly into the water. They were lucky because they *were* approaching the windward side, and they'd set a course to come in from the southwest—the wind gave them a gentle little push and they made good time.

"The fer-de-lance is rarely seen and pretty shy," Stirling responded. "But don't pet the pretty frogs, watch out for banana spiders and manchineel trees, and for fuck's sake, don't touch the giant snail shit."

Tienne was not the only one in the boat who paused rowing and turned to stare at him in horror.

"Giant snail shit?" Danny was the one who voiced it.

"It carries rabies," Stirling told him matter-of-factly. "Also, brown recluse spiders are bad, but they're bad everywhere. I sent you all a briefing! If we didn't get bitten in that hotel in Napa, we probably won't get bitten here."

"We moved you to the B and B after the case was solved," Felix said, sounding wounded.

"Where I watched the sunsets from my window in peace," Stirling retorted dryly, and Felix chuckled. "You would like California," Stirling told Tienne. "Those sunsets would make a beautiful painting."

"So would fish," Tienne replied, thinking fondly that only Stirling would be remembering sunsets he'd seen at his desk in California when they had tropical fish on a Caribbean reef that he'd seen *in person.*

"Not poison dart frogs and giant snails?" Liam asked sourly. "How are we supposed to know what giant snail scat looks like, anyway?"

There was a thoughtful silence. "I'm thinking it's slimy?" Stirling said, but he did not sound positive.

"You don't know?" And now Danny sounded a little alarmed.

"Well, *you* try googling giant snail shit!" Stirling retorted. Then, "And frankly, the poison dart frogs were what really freaked me out."

"And the acidic fruit," Tienne reminded him. "And the monkeys."

"Did I mention the screw worms?" Stirling asked, in the same tone he might have used for "Did we remember sunscreen?"

"Oh dear God," Felix muttered. "Do we even want to know?"

"Don't let any flies on an open wound," Stirling said. "Not even a mosquito bite. They lay eggs that turn into flesh-eating maggots. And not the *dead*-flesh-eating maggots—these guys burrow into your body and aim for vital organs."

Incongruously, Liam started to laugh. "You're a treasure, Stirling. Next time I'm in Chicago, can you tell me about street crime? AR-15 death stats? Ceramic knives? You could save me some skin and help me keep my blood in my body with those skills."

"I can look those up, but you have to read the briefing," Stirling replied with dignity, right before Danny shushed them because they were getting close enough to the island for their voices to carry.

A Very Bad Thing

AS THEY drifted up against the beach, they realized that the foliage—or more specifically, the canopy of a really big lignum vitae tree, handily keeping this area of the island from eroding—would make good cover.

"Hey, Stirling," Liam whispered as they ducked low and pushed up against the beach. "Is there anything we should know about *this* tree?"

"It's not a manchineel?" Stirling said, keeping his eye out for the deadly "beach apple trees" that had toxic sap, wood, and fruit. Then he remembered what he *did* know about the tree Liam indicated. "And there are potions made from its bark that are said to heal syphilis, croup, *and* arthritis." Oh yeah. "And it's supposed to be good luck to build a hut from the wood, because it's really hard."

"That's my boy," Liam murmured.

"I'm glad you approve." Stirling narrowed his eyes, trying to keep out the dark thoughts. The time spent in the bottom of the Zodiac, researching timelines and getting information from Josh on Harve's buddies and Harve's involvement with the shell corporation had made him angry. Six hours of a *really* uncomfortable, sensory overloading boat ride had transformed that anger into electrified rage. "See that tree to the right? Sort of alone on the beach? Stay away from that, and definitely don't touch the fruit." He wanted to shove a ton of it down Harve Christopher's throat with a broom handle.

They all sucked in a collective breath. "That's good to know," Felix murmured. "Do you think the others know—" At that moment they saw the other Zodiac, pulled deep into the foliage by making use of a tributary stream that had hollowed out the sand.

"Of course we know," Carl murmured, popping his head up over the edge. "*We* read Stirling's briefs, and if we hadn't, *Molly* read them and told us all what to look out for on the way in. Here, Danny, let me grab your bowline. We've got enough room to fit both boats side by side."

"How did you get settled so fast!" Danny asked, sounding vaguely outraged. "You were closer, to be sure, but you had to paddle in just like we did!"

Carl snorted. "Not only do Chuck and Hunter *drive* like bats out of hell, they also know how to *modify engines*. Call me if you see my eyebrows floating around—they blew off shortly after we left Martinique."

"Where are they?" Stirling asked, his voice taut. "You say 'we,' but I don't see—"

"Molly, Chuck, and Hunter went off toward the main house," Carl told them, his voice taut. "Stirling, I don't know when you last checked your tracker, but about half an hour ago, Grace's phone and Grace's mask took two different directions."

Stirling frowned, but he couldn't figure out what that meant. Danny and Felix, however, had an idea.

"Michael really *did* drop his phone," Danny said shrewdly. "And when the ship docked, they were probably about to be discovered."

"Yes, that's what we thought," Carl told him. "Because it looks an awful lot like Grace gave Michael one of the things he knew he was being tracked with so people could find him. The phone is heading steadily on an obvious path through the jungle straight for the house."

"So that's Michael," Felix said, and Stirling appreciated the solid way Carl nodded, as though they weren't talking about Carl's most loved person in the world. "What's the other tracker doing?"

"Heading in the same direction, but it's sort of dodging—in, under, around, and through." Carl's mouth twisted as he tried to smile. "Give you three guesses."

"Grace," they all breathed, and Stirling's eyes burned.

"Hunter was probably much relieved," Danny said, his good hand to his chest as they all processed some relief.

"Unless Grace gave his mask to a monkey and threw a banana at the house," Carl hazarded, "but yes. We're thinking it's Grace. We landed about two hours ago—but it took us a little longer to paddle in than it should have. Hunter took Grace and Molly, and Chuck went after Michael—"

"Not you?" Liam asked, and Carl grimaced. For the first time Stirling caught sight of white lines of pain around his mouth and eyes.

"I may have neglected to mention a few things," he muttered, and by now, they were close enough to look into the Zodiac and gasp.

Carl was wearing a white T-shirt, obviously worse for wear from the shoulders up, and he sat at the pilot's console of the Zodiac with his leg extended in front of him. They saw that what looked like a *torn* shirt hanging off his shoulder was his, Hunter's, and Chuck's madras and Hawaiian print overshirts, folded, ripped and tied into a gauze padding for a wound that was still bleeding. Stirling swallowed as he realized how close that blood was to something really vital.

"We were spotted leaving Martinique," Carl said gruffly. "Not Michael and Grace—they'd successfully stowed away. But I was diving for the Zodiac, and Hunter, Chuck, and Molly were racing for the end of the pier to hop in as I pulled out. One guy in the aft of the cruiser saw me and threw a knife—"

"No guns?" Danny asked, wincing.

"We figured they might have learned from Barbados," Carl said with a grim smile. "Anyway, he got me in the chest, Hunter got him in the throat, he fell off the back of the boat, and nobody seems to be missing him."

"And you kept going?" Stirling asked, appalled.

Carl tilted his head gently. "Michael's with the bad guys, Stirling. They bandaged me up, and I could help spell them with the steering and navigation, but I'd lost a lot of blood and…." He took a slow, deep, even breath. "We're not sure if he nicked my lung or not, but Hunter seems to think the tissue *around* the lung is inflamed. We figured it would be better if I stayed here and didn't slow them down." He gave a surprisingly sweet smile. "The stakes were too high to cut and run. For all of us."

Stirling rubbed his face and scrubbed at his hair. "Molly can take care of herself," he said, trying to re-assure himself.

"That she can," Danny said, squeezing his shoulder. "Good thing Chuck's with her so she doesn't have to." He looked at Felix and Liam, who both nodded. "Okay, so here's what we're going to do." He looked at Stirling. "You're not going to like it."

"Tienne and I stay here and work with Josh to blackmail Harve into calling his guards off?" Stirling guessed. "Yeah. That's what we figured on the way out. And this way, we can take care of Carl too."

Danny chuckled. "And don't forget—you're op center. Now that we're here, everybody's earbuds will work. Carl, am I to understand—"

"They've probably put them in by now," Carl said. "Stirling was pretty good about updating us on where you guys were."

"Right, then. Stirling, you're the mastermind. We're the muscle. Josh is the hacker. Tienne's the lookout."

"And Carl's the poor schmuck bleeding on the floor of the boat," Carl supplied dryly. "Danny, Felix, Liam? There is a *path* through that forest. I haven't seen another troop of guards coming through in a while. It's probably safer on the path than it is trying to crash through the underbrush. Do you all understand?"

They all nodded, and Carl let out a sigh of relief. "Stirling's not wrong. I've seen three of those god-damned frogs in the last fifteen minutes—a fucking *rainbow* of deadly colors. Gloves and hats to keep things from slithering down your neck. Please, only one of us can fit on a medevac chopper at a time."

Speaking of....

"And if you all let me work," Stirling said, opening his laptop and getting to it, "I think if we order a medevac chopper *now*, it will probably get here by the time this whole thing is over."

Danny and Felix both nodded, and all three of them put their earbuds in. "Go to it, control," Felix said, and they both pulled on knit hats that they tucked into their long-sleeved microfiber "thieves" clothes.

"Be careful," Tienne bade them before the lot of them disappeared into the brush. He turned to Stirling. "Why are you smiling?"

"Did you see how they were dressed?" he asked, thinking that microfiber was very breathable, but the clothing was very protective.

"Yes?" Tienne obviously didn't understand, but Carl chuckled softly.

"Yes, Stirling, you're right. They really *did* read your briefings."

And yes, that probably meant they had pretended not to in order to calm him down, but the good news was, it worked.

And nobody was getting giant-snail-poop rabies on his watch.

TIENNE, USING the quiet competence and foresight he'd displayed so very often, had positioned himself behind a screen of leaves to the side of th`e inlet that overlooked the beach. From this distance, they could see a modest dock, along with the cabin cruiser with inflatable boats lashed to the side.

He sat, scanning the beach and the path that could be seen from his position and sorting through the pack full of goods.

Stirling glanced up from the information Josh had sent him and cocked his head.

"What are you doing?" he asked, watching as Tienne dumped the supplies in his backpack into a bag Carl was holding.

"One of those beach apple trees is about fifteen yards from our little spot here," Tienne said. "There is fruit on the ground. I'm going to fill the bag with the poison fruit."

"Why?" Stirling asked, giving Tienne his complete attention.

Tienne looked at him. "What is the first thing they will do if they find us?"

"Shoot us?" Because *look* what they'd done to Carl!

"No." Tienne's expression grew grave. "Because your friend Michael is still alive. Carl would have told you if he'd heard gunshots. The island is not that big, and the only sound is the ocean. No. They will want to know who these people are and what they're doing. And the first thing they'll do is—"

"Search us," Stirling said, getting it. "While you're at it, get that pack of tiny waterproof transmitters you dumped in Carl's lap and shove one in the hem of each of our shirts. Earbuds they check, but not clothing. Scan it with my phone. Carl—"

"I can do it if Tienne can bring me the phone," Carl said.

"Good. And there's also a little bag of tiny lock-picks you can shove in the hems of our clothing too."

"Should we have remembered this for Danny and Felix?" Tienne asked, getting to his tasks with alacrity.

"Danny and Felix already have theirs," Stirling said. "And so does Liam. I gave them out near dawn, when you were sleeping. And I don't think Danny goes to *bed* without his lockpick."

Tienne gazed at him with so much admiration, Stirling wanted to squirm. "So very smart," he said. "Can we think of any more booby traps?"

"I've got a Beretta behind me on the seat," Carl said, reaching painfully to the space where the back and seat met and pulling out the gun. "It's got a full clip but no silencer."

"If it's close enough, you won't need a silencer," Stirling said grimly. "Anything else?"

"A hunting knife," Carl said, equally as grim. "The balance is shitty, but it's pretty sharp."

"Why would you carry a hunting knife with shitty balance?" Tienne asked, and Stirling winced.

"I wouldn't," Carl replied dryly. "Let's just say someone threw it my way."

"Oh," Tienne said, and for a moment, Stirling knew he didn't get it. Then, "Oh!" And then he got it. "Oh dear God. What a terrible joke."

Stirling smiled to himself. *Now* he got it.

"I do what I can," Carl said modestly. Then, on a more serious note, "Tienne, get a move on, okay? Usually organizations like this have guards circulating at intervals. It's been an hour since those two signals split, which means we're due for another round of guards to come by on patrol. Stirling, how're you doing?"

Stirling paused and took stock.

"Okay, so Josh traced the phone calls and times, and I traced the emails to Harve and his friends and between them. Together, we've got a solid time bomb. If we send this to the Department of Justice, the trades and security commissions, and Interpol, there is enough here to start an investigation against the lot of them for conspiracy to commit murder and smuggling—"

"Smuggling what?" Tienne asked, and Stirling grimaced.

"We have no idea." He blew out a breath. "We've got payments into and from this shell corporation—it's obviously a money laundering front, and we can prove that too. But we don't know where the money is coming from. I *assume* the Serbian mob, but…."

"You don't know what they're selling," Carl murmured. "Probably because whatever it is, it's all done *here*."

"On this tiny, uncharted, unnamed plantation island," Stirling muttered. "I mean, Josh looked up the history—it used to be a sugarcane plantation, but you don't kill a boatload of people—two of them your *parents*—over sugarcane."

"What about the timeline?" Tienne asked. "How much time do we think they had, the people on the boat?"

This made Stirling's stomach roil. It would have been so much easier—so much less cold-blooded—if they'd simply stepped out of the yacht and were gunned down.

"They had two hours," he said softly. "Two hours between their last contact—a radio to the port of Barbados saying they'd been blown off course but they had a safe place to make port between storms—and when they must have been cut loose to end up washing ashore in Barbados like they did. Josh apparently studied tidal maps and simulations since Danny gave him the news yesterday." His mouth twisted, thinking about how tired Josh had been and how his normally super-competent hacker partner had been moving at half speed over the long night. "Maybe you'll both need a medevac helicopter. Wouldn't that be special? And Leon helped too. He got hold of the port master in Barbados and apparently paid him a small fortune in bribes to turn over the records Danny *didn't* get during the break-in, which had the last radio call to port."

"That's reassuring," Carl said. "That gives us something to go on. As does the number of our people out there in pockets. Danny and Felix are practically ghosts, and Hunter, Chuck, and Molly can be their own army."

Stirling had seen his sister fight many times before. "Molly is pissed," he said frankly. "And everybody adores Michael. I, uhm, think he's going to be all right." He didn't want to lead Carl on; false hope was a terrible thing. He'd learned that as a child, hoping every day his mother would come back for him. When Molly had grabbed his hand that day in the foster home, she'd done more than saved him from bullies, she'd saved him from *himself*. He'd had no idea how to continue on, how to learn to trust in the world again, but he'd done it, clinging to his sister's hand. But trusting in Hunter, Chuck, and Molly—and in Danny, Felix, and Liam— wasn't false hope. Trusting that Grace was keeping an eye on Michael and tracking him to make sure he was okay—that wasn't false hope either. These were people he'd depended upon time and again, and while their plans didn't always go perfectly, they'd always worked hard not to let people down.

And everybody really did love Michael.

It wasn't *false* hope. It was hope, plain and simple. Miracles needed elbow grease. Their crew had lots of elbows. It was as easy as that.

"Thanks, Stirling," Carl said, tilting his head back and closing his eyes. He opened them again when Tienne reached over his shoulder and offered him a bottle of water and some ibuprofen. "And thank you, Tienne," he said gratefully. "Got any—"

And mango.

"You can use your big off-balance hunting knife for that," Tienne said.

Carl grinned. "I can indeed."

Stirling went back to his computer, suddenly cracking a smile. "And you know what?" he said to himself. "We got a little bit of luck."

He messaged Josh. *Guess what?*

What?

The island has its own Wi-Fi.

BRILLIANT!

Yup.

Now all we need is to get a worm into their system.

I've got an idea about that. Stirling smiled to himself. It was a great idea.

What?

I'm going to get captured.

NO. NO. NO. ABORT ABORT ABORT ABORT

But right then, voices from the cove where the cruiser was parked could be heard drifting along the water. Carl's guess had been right on schedule. The next batch of guards were there.

Commence Operation JUICY. Track my phone and my computer—you should be able to piggyback off the Wi-Fi shortly.

STIRLING—

Trust me! Remember—Operation JUICY.

And then Stirling closed all his windows before pulling up a screen he and Josh had built for a high school prank, and made sure it was the only thing showing when his laptop was opened. Then he shut his computer and put it in the waterproof, bulletproof case. He turned to Tienne and Carl, who had also heard the voices down on the beach.

"Do it," Carl said, nodding, and Tienne looked from one to the other.

"Do what?"

Stirling swallowed. "How many rounds do you have in the Beretta?" he asked. Oh, he was putting an awful lot of faith in this man to leave him behind and pray he'd still be breathing when Stirling got back.

"A clip in the chamber and one to spare," Carl said, nodding. "I'll lay flat and wait until somebody looks in—"

"Have Tienne cover you with the fire blanket before he goes," Stirling said. "And have him leave you lots of water."

"Wait," Tienne said in surprise. "Before I go where?"

Stirling set the case down for a moment so he could take Tienne's hands. "Baby," he said very carefully and then paused, taking the earbud out of his ear and tucking it into Tienne's. For the last twenty minutes, there had been nothing but steady breathing and quiet subvocalizations—and the occasional curse as somebody tripped or made too much noise.

"Do you hear them in there?" he asked, and Tienne nodded.

"They can hear us. Tell someone to let you know they're okay. Say, 'Stirling needs a coms check.'"

"Stirling needs a coms check," Tienne repeated automatically. His eyes widened. "It's Danny. He says to be careful, he knows what you're doing. How does he know what you're doing?"

Stirling winked, amazed at his own audacity. "Because it's what they would do. Now I'm going to go turn myself in. Don't worry, they won't shoot me."

"They won't *what*?" Tienne didn't raise his voice; he too was cognizant of enemies right over the hill. "How do you know that?"

"I've got it handled," Stirling said, his heart thundering in his ears. "Trust me. But I need you to do me and Carl a favor, okay?"

Tienne shook his head, suddenly putting everything together. "No," he said weakly.

Stirling put his cell phone, which had scanned the trackers that they'd all had put into their clothing, into the pocket of Tienne's cargo shorts. "You have to," he said soberly. "You're the only one who can tell them where I'll be. Now I swear to you, I have a way to make them not shoot me. Operation Juicy. Remember that. Grace will know what it means and explain. But you have to promise me you'll get this phone to Danny and Felix and the others. The minute I walk out of here, you have to follow that trail. You do parkour through Chicago, Etienne. You run ten miles a day. You're smart and you're fast, and you'll get there."

"But what about Carl?" Tienne asked, his eyes watering.

Stirling swallowed and gave Carl a tortured look.

"It's my only chance," Carl said. "If the bulk of them go with Stirling, I'll only have a couple here." He waved the gun.

Tienne nodded and then said, "You have to go do your hero thing, Stirling, but let me defend Carl." He gave Carl a rather proud smile. "I have an idea."

Stirling's eyes burned. "We'll trust each other," he said gruffly. "We're smarter than they are, and we've got a plan." And with that, he kissed him, their lips hard and passionate and knowing.

They'd become lovers. They'd fought past the smallness that their worlds could have been. They didn't have to be the guys in the van anymore. They could be Grace and Hunter and Chuck and Carl and Danny and Felix and Josh, by being themselves.

"Love you," he said, not caring that they were big words. They were necessary words too. "Be safe."

And with that he grabbed the backpack of poison fruit, which he put over his shoulders, and the bulletproof computer case, which he held in front of his chest, and snuck out from under the shelter of the lignum vitae tree.

Operation JUICY

TIENNE'S HEART was thundering so loud in his ears, he almost didn't hear Danny calling through his earbud.

"Tienne, what's happening? Tienne?"

Tienne watched, barely breathing as Stirling walked out onto the blinding sand of the beach, holding his computer in front of him, both hands showing to whomever was approaching. He couldn't hear what they were saying as he neared, but he could see that all four men, dressed in black slacks and white tanks, were aiming their very deadly ARs his way.

"*Tienne*!" Danny hissed, louder this time.

"Nobody's shooting," Tienne muttered. "They're talking. Wait, one of them took the backpack from Stirling. He's rooting through it." Tienne started to laugh. "They're eating the beach apples. Good."

"Tienne, whatever you were going to do, you need to do it now or get out," Danny said. "You, they'll shoot, and Carl can't play possum to take them out if you're there."

"Oh! Wait, no. I have an idea."

Without talking anymore, because some of the guards from the beach were looking in the direction from which Stirling had come, Tienne grabbed the plastic bag containing the rest of the beach apples and a couple of the gloves he'd found stashed in the Zodiac's supply chest. They were solid gloves, rubber, going up far past his wrists, and he wondered if they were for fishermen or assassins. Either way, it didn't matter. They would protect his skin from the pulp of the fruit and the acidic skin, which was important.

He put the gloves on and looped the bag around his wrist, hoping the gloves were strong enough to let him climb the lignum vitae tree to the larger tree behind it. The bigger tree had a smooth bole that would have been harder to scale, but the lignum vitae tree would mask his body until he found a perch there.

He climbed it easily, finding a spot from which he could look down on anyone approaching the two boats but not be so easily seen himself. "Carl," he murmured, trusting in Stirling's technology. "Can you hear me?"

"Yes, I can."

"I need you to play possum, as you said. Under the fire blanket, hiding the gun, eyes closed. If you feel anything dripping down, make sure it doesn't touch your skin."

"Roger that." Tienne heard him rustling and used his perch to look out to see what was on the beach. He gasped. "They hit him!"

"Shh…," Carl soothed. "Are the guns still out?"

"No, but… but they hit him in the stomach and the face." Tienne's voice pitched, and Danny's came in loud and clear. "He knew this was coming, Tienne.

Don't worry. They can't beat him too badly. They need to bring him back to the house, and it's easier if he can walk. What else?"

"Okay, there are six of them. Four are with Stirling. Two are doing what you said. They're coming this way to see what he told them." Tienne paused. "What do you think he told them?"

"Hopefully that I'm dead," Carl whispered. "Now stop talking so we can sell that."

Tienne made a soft noise of assent and gazed wistfully up the beach, where he saw that indeed, Stirling had been pulled up by his arms, still clutching the computer case. After some rough words from the leader of the guards that penetrated Tienne's leafy fortress, Stirling opened the case and the computer with it, showing the screen with a defiant cock of his head.

To Stirling's surprise, the four men stood back, looking at each other in panic. The leader shouted at Stirling; even Tienne could hear it.

"Make it stop! Make it stop! We'll kill you right here!" He was so loud, the two men who had been heading for Tienne and Carl's position under the tree stopped to watch the show.

Stirling's voice, those simple, unruffled accents that had so soothed Tienne from the very beginning, echoed across the beach.

"If you kill me, I can't make it stop."

There was an uneasy silence, and the leader said hopelessly, "Make it stop."

Stirling moved stiffly, but he still gave a nonchalant shrug. "I need the island's Wi-Fi to stop it, and unless you have the password, I can't get in. You'll have to take me to Harve Christopher himself. I'll stop it then."

"Mr. Christopher is not on the island." The man's Serbian accent was more pronounced, now that Tienne knew to listen for it, and it told Tienne the man was uncertain and a little bit afraid.

"But you've got a computer with his face on it, am I right?"

The leader's face was probably pale by ordinary standards, but stress and sunlight had made it almost purple under a crew cut of coarse black hair. He started to shift his weight in acute discomfort, and Tienne hoped he was not yet developing symptoms from the beach apples.

"We will take him," he announced, nodding three of the lackeys toward the path. He waved at the other two. "You two, check out his story! Make sure that body is dead!"

Tienne saw the last two guards moving again toward their hiding place under the lignum vitae tree and started to pulp the manchineel fruit in the plastic bag. The bag itself was getting dangerously thin, and Tienne was grateful for the gloves. He ceased his movement as the guards got nearer and used a twig to poke a hole in the bag.

Oh! There they were, about six feet below him, the tops of their heads and bare red necks clearly visible. As they ducked under the protective fronds, he very carefully dripped the acidic oils of the manchineel fruit on their crowns.

The guards spoke in Serbian, but Tienne didn't need to translate. Their noises were obvious.

"There, the boats, like he said," he imagined the first one saying.

"The body too. Do you think he's dead?" The man was pointing toward Carl in the Zodiac.

At the same time, both of them began to rub the oil from their heads, ears, and neck with bare hands, moving restively as the discomfort began to set in.

"Hey, what is this stuff? Is there a monkey pissing on my neck?" The guard was pointing at one of the monkeys nearby, and the idea of monkey piss made Tienne smile even as he stopped dripping and pulled quietly up into the branches, waiting to see what would happen next.

"Ouch—ouch—ouch—"

As Tienne watched, they began to rub their hair, their necks, their foreheads more and more vigorously, and then, glory be, their eyes.

And then they began to whimper, dropping their guns and rushing for the tributary outlet, probably hoping for some fresh water before it hit the ocean.

It must have still been salty, though, because as Tienne dropped soundlessly from the tree to the ground, they were gibbering in pain as the water touched their faces and their hands. Tienne could see the blisters and reddened, peeling skin as he approached. Quietly he grabbed one of the guns and grimaced. It was practically plastic. It wouldn't do at all. Then he spotted one of the solid wooden oars that someone had dropped on the ground as they'd hopped out of the Zodiac, and he decided that would be perfect.

It would be like swinging a cricket bat, right? The thought was both funny and sickening, but all he had to do was remind himself of Stirling, bleeding on the beach and needing him, to swing.

Once, twice, and both men slumped to the ground, their blistered and bleeding hands still in the tributary stream. Tienne went back to their weapons and gave Carl a helpless glance.

"Throw them in the ocean," Carl murmured, and even though it meant tossing the weapons over the heads of the incapacitated guards, Tienne complied.

He couldn't use such a weapon, and if he couldn't use it, he had to make sure his enemies couldn't either. When he was done with that, he peeled his gloves off and washed his hands from the water coming under the two watercrafts, just in case.

When he was done, he turned back toward Carl, who subvocalized again, his words carrying clearly through the earbud as they could not against the roaring of the ocean.

"Grab water before you go," he murmured.

Tienne nodded and pulled a bottle out from the flat Danny had made them bring and shoved it in the pocket of his cargo shorts. He was the only one who hadn't worn black microfiber to this little jaunt, but next time he'd know better. He knew Carl had plenty of water by him, so he gave him another anguished look.

"Stirling will kill me if you're not all right," he said, and Carl winked.

"So will Michael. Don't worry. You've got to run, Tienne. Now go."

Tienne turned toward the jungle and remembered his time on the Chicago streets. Just him and the whooshing in his ears and the obstacles in his way.

He'd put on his brand-new tennis shoes before he'd packed for Stirling that night. Something about them made him feel like he was ready for adventure.

Stirling was counting on him to be ready for this adventure right now.

"Stay safe," he said to Carl.

And then he ran.

THE TWO hits—one to the face and the other to the stomach—that Stirling had sustained had not hurt *nearly* as bad as some of the beatings he'd received in middle school before Josh and Grace had joined Molly as his defenders. Of course, Molly had been teaching him self-defense since then, and he'd learned how to take a punch. His core, back, and even his neck muscles were very strong, and he'd tightened those up when he'd seen the leader of the guards getting ready to do his thing.

Stirling had assumed it would happen; maybe it was the surprise that had made it suck so bad as a kid.

Either way, he was really in pretty good shape as he was pushed through the jungle, still holding his computer case in front of him.

In fact, he sort of wanted to crow.

They'd *bought* it.

The countdown screen looked *really scary* if you were a seventh grader looking at your dad's porn, which was what Josh and Stirling had programmed it for. Stirling had made some tweaks. Instead of *This Hard Drive Will E-Mail Your Last Known URL to Everybody at Your School and then Self-Delete in T-Countdown,* Stirling had replaced the copy with *This Information Will Automatically Disburse to the Following Agencies Unless the Password is Entered in....* Stirling had given them forty-five minutes, because he'd seen the island schematics, and it should take about half an hour to tramp through a basic jungle path to the plantation house in the middle. After that, everything was theater.

And Stirling was counting on Tienne and the others having something in place to save him and Michael by then.

The countdown screen—done in dramatic black, red, and toxic-green—was all theater too, of course. They'd designed the screen to get the kid who had outed Grace to his entire seventh-grade class by telling everybody "That squinty-eyed pervert keeps looking at my ass!" Besides being racist, he'd been mistaken. Grace had retorted, "Your ass looks like a squashed potato. Why would I want to look at it when your best friend is *juicy*?"

Which was how that kid had found out that Grace and his best friend had been necking behind the handball wall during PE.

He'd immediately turned on his best friend, bullying *him* out of school since Grace, Josh, and Stirling were unrepentant, but nobody in Josh's crew was willing to forgive and forget.

Josh and Stirling had hacked his home system and realized the kid snuck into his father's office to look at porn and beat off at the same time every night. Grace had done a little B and E, and Josh had designed the front page while Stirling had come up with the more complex program that actually did what the front page promised, *immediately* after it was activated.

The threat wasn't the sham; the countdown was.

Which was what gave Stirling some of his chutzpah as he walked—shoulders back, head up—through the foliage.

The other thing was the vast array of gastrointestinal noises coming from the guards, as well as the frequent moans and mutters as the skin around their mouths and hands began to heat.

The lead guard turned toward them and shouted something along the lines of "What the hell is wrong with you!" and was met by whines, moans, and whimpers.

He pulled out his gun, and one man—the man who had opened the backpack and eaten two or three of the small round green fruits—fell to the ground in the fetal position, groaning.

Stirling watched impassively, wondering if they would make the connection between the fruit and the symptoms. He'd been hoping for a bigger gap between the two—all his reading had suggested it would take a good eight hours for absolute misery to set in, but then, most of those reports had been from people who'd taken experimental bites. These guys had gone to town on the fruit, eating much of what had been in the backpack, and Stirling had a moment of guilt that he might have killed them all.

And then he remembered that these were some of the same people who had probably gunned his parents down, and his guilt disappeared.

The leader of the guards started shouting at his men, waving his gun and gesturing. In desperation, he fired a couple of shots into the air, and Stirling watched as the men who were still standing reluctantly continued on in obvious misery.

The gluttonous one, though, stayed fetal, his eyes half closed, in obvious pain, uncaring whether he lived or died. After prodding him with the gun for a moment, the leader turned his back on his comrade and said a terse word in Serbian that started everybody forward. Stirling witnessed it all without comment. He knew that his resting expression tended to be completely neutral—it was one of the reasons he worked so hard on recognizing and mirroring happiness when that was what he felt.

But now he knew that a completely neutral, unaffected expression would be an asset. No amusement—and no guilt either.

The leader of the guards gave him a half-furious, half-fearful glance, and Stirling didn't so much as raise his eyebrows. With a nervous gesture of the gun, he forced Stirling to precede him into the jungle.

Head up, shoulders back, Stirling did that.

Which was why he was the only one who caught the merest flash of dark fabric out of the corner of his eye as they neared the bole of another banyan tree.

His eyes widened, but he kept walking, not sure if he'd just seen Hunter, Chuck, Molly, or even Grace, but he was reassured all the same.

He'd never be able to do this alone.

AFTER BEING on board the yacht for nearly a week, Tienne was relieved when it only took him a couple of strides to get into his street-running groove. While there were no fallen limbs or unexpected lizards in Chicago (and the gecko in the path nearly gave him a heart attack, as small as it may have been) there were potholes, pedestrians, icy patches, and mad cabbies to contend with. Like with his art, his focus had always been details, the small moments that made up the big picture. The exact placement of the foot that made up his mad dash through the jungle.

He kept his eyes on the road, his head out of the clouds, and ran, depending on the people he was looking for to see him first.

He was so intent on his path that he didn't see Levka Dubov until he literally bounced off the man's solid, muscular body, doing a back roll into the underbrush before popping up to see what he'd hit.

Levka was sitting on his ass, looking a little befuddled but unharmed, and for a moment, Tienne froze.

He remembered those moments, both of them, when Levka had intimidated him in his own home, had bared his teeth in a lewd smile and shucked Tienne's pants down his thighs without permission or consent. Tienne's brain had shorted out both times, and in that moment, he'd been the scared child again on the streets of Marrakech, seeing the unthinkable, the bloody and heartbreaking, in front of his eyes while a complete stranger screamed, "*Run!*" at him in a desperate bid to save Etienne Couvier's life.

In those terrible moments in his kitchen, he'd wished to go back to that time and simply let death take him, because he could not fathom how to make this— the helplessness, the violation, the awful sense of being a watcher in his own life—stop.

And for this moment—a breath—he was that watcher again.

Levka scowled, pushing heavily to his hands and knees, preparing to regain his feet, and Tienne remembered the satisfying thud that body had made when Stirling had stuck his foot out and tripped him.

Stirling.

Who was counting on him not to freeze, and not to get beaten to death or shot either. Stirling was counting on him to get his phone to his friends so they could get him out of the bad guy's house and they could all make it to safety.

Stirling, who had pulled Tienne's passive, resisting body into his home, his family, his bed, his *life*. And he was counting on Tienne to make it through this damned jungle.

Levka Dubov was still on his hands and knees when Tienne burst from the underbrush again and ran over him, head, neck, back, and ass.

With a grunt, Levka was pushed back into the soft jungle floor, full of rotting vegetation and rich volcanic soil. He grunted, but Tienne turned around as Levka tried to get his hands and knees under himself once more, and Tienne ran over him again, taking care to stomp particularly hard on his thick neck between his shoulders. Tienne was aware that he weighed very little, and Levka was very big, but Tienne had to keep the big man stunned until he had a better strategy.

On his third pass over Levka's body, when the man was howling in frustration, a quaking volcano of muscle and rage, Tienne spotted it. A gun. A heavy gun, like the one Carl had been hiding, had been knocked from Levka's hand when Tienne had first run into him.

Once again, Levka tried to get his hands and feet underneath him, and this time, Tienne placed one foot on Levka's shoulders and leapt to the side, bending to scoop up the gun.

He had it too, the weight reassuring and deadly in his palm, when he felt a rough hand wrapping around his ankle, yanking his foot out from under him.

Tienne twisted, landing on his side, letting the fleshy upper part of his arm take the impact so he was on his back as Levka hurled himself on top of Tienne's struggling body.

Levka was swearing in Serbian, spitting and snarling with rage, his face caked with mud and dirt, dried leaves and twigs imprinted on his cheeks, dirt falling from his teeth. None of that mattered when his filthy hands wrapped around Tienne's throat.

Oh God—it hurt. It hurt so bad! Tienne gasped, unable to breathe, unable to think anything but no, no, no…. This man was going to win again. He was going to violate Tienne in the worst way. He was going to take his life! Tienne's arms sprawled at his sides, and the weight of the gun became unbearable, and his fingers spread to release it.

"Levka!" Tienne choked, his vision going black, and for a moment, a terrible moment, time stopped.

"You?" Levka said, surprised. "The forger?"

He was so stunned to recognize the man he'd assaulted the month before, his grip eased for a fraction of a moment, and Tienne suddenly remembered that he was *not* helpless.

His grip tightened, and he swung the gun up in a clumsy arc, using all his strength to clock Levka on the temple.

Levka's grip on Tienne's throat relaxed some more as Levka gasped in shock, obviously reeling from the blow, and Tienne hit him again.

And again.

Levka collapsed, unconscious, on top of him, and Tienne scrambled out from under the body and kicked Levka in the face, his foot connecting with the nose, because he heard a crunch and a squelch.

Oh God. Oh God oh God oh God.

Levka was *bleeding*. He was *bleeding*, and Tienne was….

Tienne gasped. He was alive. Oh God, he was alive, but the phone—

Frantically he checked the pockets of his shorts and found it, the weight solid near his thigh.

And his water was twenty feet away, where he'd first gone sprawling.

Tienne crouched on Levka's shoulders and took the man's pulse, relieved to find his heart was still beating.

But he was in a conundrum.

He had a gun—he had a *gun*—and it would be easy, so easy, to hold the Beretta to the base of this man's skull and pull the trigger. Nobody would know.

Without thinking, Tienne felt himself positioning the gun and fumbling for the safety.

Stirling would know.

Tienne stopped fumbling and made sure the safety was on. Then he clocked Levka in the head—the back this time—hopped off his back, and kicked him once in the ribs before running to get his water bottle and shove it in another pocket. He took a few more strides, and then a few more, and then he fell into a rhythm. When he'd gone far enough away from Levka and knew in his gut that the man wasn't following him, he threw the gun as far into the underbrush as he could.

"Ouch! Hey! The hell!"

Tienne was so surprised at the voice that he tripped over his own feet and went sprawling again. He came up, sputtering swear words in French and German, and squinted into the jungle, trying to find the owner of that very familiar voice.

"Grace! What are you doing here?" he hissed, not wanting to shout when there were patrols seemingly *everywhere*.

"They took Michael to a house," Grace said, gliding through the underbrush on cat feet. When he emerged completely, Tienne was amused to see he was wearing his club clothes, which, with the exception of the long-sleeved amber-colored shirt, doubled as thieves' clothes, given that he was almost invisible. On his head was one of the microfiber caps Stirling had inserted the tracker in, rolled down low over the back of his neck.

Stirling would be so proud. Even Grace had read the briefing.

"So why does that explain what you're doing in the jungle?" Tienne asked, still rattled. He looked behind him on reflex, and the fact that he didn't see Levka was not enough to reassure him. "Come on. We want to make sure Dubov doesn't wake up and come after us."

"Dubov?" Grace asked, matching Tienne's stride as they jogged. "I knew he was here, but why would he come after us?"

Tienne sucked air in through his teeth. "I... I may have whacked him on the head with the gun."

"Good move," Grace said approvingly, and Tienne appreciated that Grace had no other suggestions for what to do with the gun, because he felt stupid enough as it was.

"And I ran up and down his back a couple of times and pushed his face in the mud."

"Excellent! Did you kick him in the balls?"

"No!" Tienne retorted, putting a hand out when it looked like Grace was going to turn around and rectify that oversight. "No, and we don't have time."

"Later," Grace said, nodding judiciously. "Good call. What are you doing here?"

"Coming after you! And all the people who followed you! Jesus, Grace, you smuggled on board that ship and the whole world lost its mind."

Grace stopped abruptly.

"Wait, what?"

"Well, you got into the boat, and then Carl's boyfriend got into the boat, and then Carl, Chuck, Hunter, and Molly followed you, and Michael—"

"Michael," Grace said with a sigh. "He lost his phone. Dropped it right into the ocean as we were hanging on for dear life. Poor Carl. He must have been panicking."

"And Hunter wasn't?" Tienne wanted to shake him. "And Josh? Because we were all there when Josh got the call, and he fell into Liam's arms—"

"Again?" Grace said smugly. "It's, like, their thing."

Tienne turned around and smacked him in the arm. "*You worried us*. My God, Grace, I have spent most of my life reasonably sure that if I fell into a hole in the world, nobody would know I was gone until my body started to stink. You wandered off to follow the Serbian mob, and *everybody who loves you* shit a brick. Danny, Felix, Liam, Stirling, and I spent hours in one of those inflatable fucking boats getting here so we could rescue you and Michael. Do you know that? Stirling had to give himself to the damned mob—"

"I saw that," Grace said. "They're taking him back to the house. Why did he do that? Why didn't you two hide?"

"Because Carl is hurt and in the bottom of the other inflatable boat—"

"Hurt?" And for the first time, Grace's wandering mind with all the questions seemed to focus. "Carl got hurt? Why?"

"Because one of the bad guys threw a knife!" Tienne exploded.

"But that's the whole reason I followed the mob!" Grace returned, and he sounded legitimately distressed. "None of this was supposed to happen. Danny got *hurt*. Do you understand? Josh spent our entire lives together wanting his Uncle Danny to come back, and he did, and then Josh got sick, and then Danny got *hurt*. And I decided, enough of this bullshit. I was going to follow the bad guys back to their lair and email Josh, and he and Stirling could do all their magic stuff. *Nobody was supposed to come here.* Did you not understand? *Nobody else was supposed to get hurt*!"

Tienne took a deep breath and stared at the unusually despondent Grace. Poor baby, he thought, feeling older than the young man for the first time in their acquaintance. Tienne had his demons, but it was obvious that Grace did too. And part of what drove him was protection of the family they both loved so much.

"Don't you get it?" he asked Grace gently. "We didn't all jump on a stupidly luxurious boat and cruise down here so one guy could go in and save the day. We did it so we could be with Stirling and Molly as they confronted what happened to their first family. So we could be their second family and make sure they were okay."

Grace nodded miserably and wiped his face on the shoulder of his tarnished gold shirt. Then he gave a little smile. "Stirling probably doesn't need me anyway," he confessed. "I spent most of middle and high school trying to keep him from getting the shit beat out of him, but it turns out he just needed the right tools. I think he poisoned an entire contingent of guards."

Tienne started to grin. "That was my idea. Did the beach apples really make them sick?"

Grace brightened even more. "I swear, one guy was going to die." He shrugged, unconcerned about the plight of the hapless guard. "Which is what they get for not reading the briefing."

Tienne gave Grace a gentle smile. "Never ignore Stirling's briefings."

"I'm saying. So where to next?"

Tienne patted his pocket, the phone still there. "We find Felix and Danny and the others. I've got Stirling, Michael, and even you tracked on the phone in my pocket. I think it would be great if we could come up with a plan."

Grace nodded and turned to run forward. "Another mile and we'll be at the clearing where you can see the house. I'll bet they're close to that spot. A plan would be good."

Tienne grinned and thought of a way to engage Grace, whose heart was apparently much larger than his self-awareness. "Race you!" he gasped, and they were off.

Perhaps five minutes later, if that, an average-sized man wearing cargo shorts and a panama hat stepped into their path and caught Grace around the middle as he was about to sprint by. Tienne skidded to a halt as Hunter crushed Grace to him, and through their earbuds, they could hear him growling—*growling*—his frustration at Grace about the last panicked hours.

"What did I say, huh? *What did I say* about running off on your own? What did I tell you?"

Grace's reply was muffled. He'd been without communication all this time, and he was clinging to Hunter, burrowing his face against the larger man's chest.

"Sorry?"

"No! No sorry! *Baby*, you can't do this to me—do you understand? That place you came from? There's a dead rapist back there. I was there. You can't go running off without us, right?"

Chuck and Danny had drawn up to Tienne's shoulders, and they all watched—and listened unabashedly—to the reunion in front of them. Both of the other men, and Hunter as well, sounded out of breath, as though they'd all been sprinting and had screeched to a halt in this small space around the path.

"Dead?" Tienne asked, distressed. "I left him alive. What killed him?"

"Broken neck," Chuck said, voice uninflected.

"A tiny nick in his carotid," Danny said in almost the same voice.

"His nose was smashed up into his brain pan," Hunter said, taking a moment from scolding Grace to glance at him, and Tienne had a sudden awful suspicion.

"How do you all know this? I came from there, and I ran here trying to find *you*!"

Danny scratched the back of his neck, a deceptively innocent gesture that made Tienne's eyes widen even more. Felix came up alongside him and gave that genial, everybody-gets-along-here smile that had probably been the terror of the boardroom.

"Well," Felix said conversationally, "we could hear everything you were saying and doing, Tienne. You realize that, right? So we knew you left Carl—and good for you, taking care of his attackers like that—but we were a little bit worried, and so we, uhm…."

"Checked your progress, so to speak," Danny contributed. For the first time, Tienne noticed the green streaks across their clothes and faces, as though they'd raced pell-mell through a jungle without any thought of stealth at all. "And as it turns out, the jungle is thick, but it's not entirely impassible… I mean, we *did* read the briefings, right?"

"Oh yes," Felix nodded. "And the path you were running on—the one the guards seemed so attracted to—well, it does loop around quite a bit. It was as easy, really, to, you know—"

"Cut through the jungle?" Tienne asked, still numb, although his heart was warming with every word. Those awful moments with Levka, when he'd assumed he was alone and helpless—he hadn't been helpless at all. And he'd never, *ever* been alone. They'd been running for him, running to his rescue, through the thick of the jungle, while he'd been fighting for his life. And when they saw that he'd taken care of himself, they had, well, they had taken care of a loose end. And they'd done it for him.

"Oh yes." Felix gave a smile that was all teeth. "And we were so proud of you. You did very well against what was surely"—his voice gentled and dropped—"*surely* a difficult opponent. But, uhm, he seems to have sustained some other injuries after your little altercation, and I'm afraid he won't be joining us for, well—"

"The rest of his life," Chuck said matter-of-factly. "But I for one don't plan to miss him."

Tienne nodded and gave a weak smile. The knowledge that Levka Dubov was no longer a threat—in fact, was *no more* period—would have to seep in. Tienne realized that, on one level, he'd been expecting Levka's attack for a month. Levka had been the monster in the back of his mind that had sat waiting to jump out and get him, and he'd *tried.*

But Tienne had fought him off, and his friends had gone in and made extra sure that this one bad guy would never bother Tienne again.

"He would have been a terrible guest at parties," Tienne said, and Danny's reassuring squeeze on his shoulder told him that the attempt of humor was appreciated. Tienne looked around and realized that their group was not complete. Suddenly the fate of Levka Dubov was the least of their worries.

"Where's Molly?" he asked. "And Liam? Oh my God—*Stirling*!" And with that he pulled out the phone and thrust it into Danny's hand. "Danny, *Stirling*. He let himself be captured, and they had *guns*, and they *hit him*—"

"And do you think Molly would let her brother be alone for long?" Danny replied gently, turning Stirling's phone and entering the passcode deftly.

"He told you the passcode?" Felix asked, one hand on Danny's hip protectively as he looked over Danny's shoulder.

"Don't insult either of us," Danny told him with a sniff. "I got it from Josh, in case."

"When?" Felix challenged.

"Before we got on the boat, dearest." Danny turned his head enough to touch Felix's bicep with his forehead—it was a very subtle, very tender gesture of affection. "I try not to be *too* stupid. Now hush. These youngsters and their newfangled apps…."

Tienne heard a few soft snorts and saw some rolled eyes. It occurred to him that while Stirling and Josh were both known for their computer skills, Danny must have been in on the first floor of hacking, particularly if he'd been a successful thief over the last twenty years.

Danny, like Tienne and Stirling, did not like to make much of himself.

The thought was like a soothing whisper in his ear. His casual assumption at the beginning had been that he was different, and so alone. But no. He'd run to Stirling's people, and they had run to take care of him. His heart swelled.

And now they were going to take care of Stirling.

"So where are they?" he asked.

"Well, Molly heard your plan—remember, they all put their earbuds in when we thought you'd be arriving. She anticipated Stirling on the other path. I am assuming she's finding a way to follow him into the house."

"And Liam?" The young Interpol officer had been both kind and funny, and Tienne hoped he was okay.

"Liam is following at a distance—he wants to keep an eye on her, yes, but he also wants to see exactly what the MacGuffin is. What *are* they dealing here that makes this island so very deadly?"

Hunter's diatribe at Grace had faded, and all that was left was the two of them, clinging tightly together in the middle of the path. Chuck interrupted reluctantly.

"Hunter?"

Hunter looked up, and Chuck nodded down the path. "I'll flip you for Carl."

In their ears, they could all hear Carl say, "Fuck you both. I'm fine. Get Stirling and Molly back." His voice shook, though, constrained by lack of oxygen, and Tienne felt a pang of remorse for leaving him there alone. Stirling had ordered a helicopter, but they still had another half an hour at the least before it arrived.

Felix grunted and gave Danny a stern look. "Danny will come sit with you, Carl. And that way, should Julia find a helicopter, he can persuade her not to skin us all and use our hides as a sunshade."

Danny made a sound of protest. "*Stirling* and *Michael*—and *Molly*," he enunciated, but Felix shook his head adamantly.

"On a normal day, I'd bow out and leave you to it," he said, and Tienne took in his drawn features and recognized worry. With new eyes, he gazed at Danny and saw he was almost gray with fatigue and what was probably pain. While it was hard to spot through his black clothing, the bandage at his shoulder looked wet, with a rime of rust-colored dried blood around the stain.

"Fox," Danny complained, but he sounded peevish and plaintive. *Not* the pillar of strength they had all come to follow, but a tired man who had suffered a really brutal two or three days.

"Oh, come now," Felix murmured, brushing his knuckles along Danny's cheek. "You'll have the children thinking I can't do the job. That's not fair." He gave a playful yet tender smile. "The takedown is the best part."

Danny sighed and let some of the weariness of the past few days sag his shoulders. "I dislike being benched," he muttered.

"Join the club," Carl retorted in their ears. "Now hurry. Stirling has been *captured*—and as much as the bad guys don't know what's heading their way, the idea of that kid in danger makes me stabby!"

Felix bent and gave Danny a hard, no-bullshit kiss—the kind that would make any recipient go a little stupid and boneless, Tienne was sure—before turning Danny gently by his shoulders and murmuring into the ear without the earbud.

Danny kissed him on the cheek and passed the phone to him before he started a tired jog back along the path, and Felix turned to the rest of them.

"All right, children. We've got Stirling's whereabouts and Grace's cell phone here, and both signals are converging, so I assume they're getting moved to the same place—the big house down in the valley beyond the undergrowth. Liam? Molly? Can you hear me? You've both been awfully quiet out there."

"Molly can't talk right now," Liam whispered. "She's a little busy."

"Molly," Tienne said, remembering something. "If you can hear me, Stirling told them his name to keep from getting shot. If you're trying to get to him, it may work for you."

They all heard the quiet hum of assent from her, and that reassured Tienne very much.

"Liam," Felix murmured. "Have you discovered our MacGuffin?"

"Who had guns in the pool?" Liam asked quietly. "Was that Hunter?"

"I had drugs," Hunter replied. "Chuck had human trafficking, Danny had counterfeiting, Julia and Felix had diamonds, Leon had priceless artifacts—Carl, did you have guns?"

"I did," Carl wheezed, and Tienne watched everybody's mouth tighten. It was good that they'd sent

Danny back to take care of him. He needed medical attention soon. "You assholes owe me money, but I'll take getting my boyfriend out of danger if you're too cheap to pay up."

"I think we can manage both," Felix said, and while his voice was mild, his forehead was drawn into lines of concentration. "Liam, where's their stash of guns?"

"There's a mushroom crop of small outbuildings on the other side of the house, bunkhouses and such. Only one building's in use. It houses about sixteen, and it looks to be fully occupied, so look for between twelve and twenty-four lackeys when all are accounted for."

"Minus Levka Dubov," Hunter said dryly.

"And the guy Stirling poisoned," Grace said excitedly. "He might not be dead, but I think he wishes he was."

"Guys," Tienne supplied. "Four guards ate the fruit. It normally doesn't work that fast."

"And don't forget the two assholes who are still out cold by me," Carl panted. "I've got a bead on them, but they're moaning in their sleep right now, so I think they're out of the game."

"Wow," Danny panted, obviously in midrun. "That's eight of twenty-four for Tienne and Stirling and the poison beach apples. I don't think any of you are going to beat those numbers."

"And Molly took out three," Liam said on a whispered chortle. "God, she's violent. Okay, Felix. Orders?"

"Liam, you and Hunter secure the guns," Felix said. "Liam, can you get some of your chums to come confiscate them? Tell them we have permission from the island's rightful owners, Stirling and Molly Christopher, for the helicopters to land."

"Will do. Hunter, head east and skirt the jungle. I'm on the far side of the house from you all, near the big rock outcropping close to the ocean. See you in ten."

Hunter nodded and looked unhappily at Grace. "Do what Felix says," he rasped. "God, Grace, you and me, we're going to have to—"

Grace kissed him quickly. "Don't get hurt," he said. "You can talk about whatever you want, but that's my only rule."

Hunter let out a breath. "Mine too. Don't get hurt." His lower lip quivered for a moment, a thing Tienne had never thought to see in Hunter's absolutely calm, self-contained stoneface. "I'm begging you, baby. Please."

Grace kissed him again. "I'm like a cat. Sometimes I fall off the couch, but I usually don't get shot. I'll be fine."

"Augh!" But on that note, Hunter was gone, turning toward the path leading out of the clearing.

"Grace," Felix said, and it was obvious he was trying to capture the thief's attention before he simply wandered off. "I need you and Tienne to keep a bead on Stirling and Molly." He held up the phone. "I'm betting that Michael is being held somewhere—a side room or something—but Stirling and Molly will need an audience with the boss." Felix frowned. "Tienne, did Stirling say anything else after he took off his earbud? Anything that will help us anticipate what he had in mind?"

Tienne thought about it. "He said something about juicy…. Wait—*Operation Juicy*. I think Grace was supposed to know what it is."

Grace looked up, suddenly alert and in the moment, not wandering after Hunter in his mind. "Uh-oh," he muttered. "People, we've got to hurry. Operation Juicy means the police are about to start banging down the doors of the guys in the States—the guys leading the operation. We don't have much time to get them out of the house before shit goes tits up."

Felix's eyes went wide. "Of course not. Okay, you and Tienne, go! Get Stirling, Molly, and Michael out of the house."

"What are you and Chuck doing?" Tienne asked, wanting to know ahead of time so he didn't get in the way.

"Chuck and I are going to make sure nobody goes in the house after you and Grace. Stirling will have an easier time intimidating people if there isn't a surprise contingent of panicked guards running through." He gave Chuck a grim smile. "Are you up for that, Charles?"

"Do I get to blow shit up?" Chuck asked wolfishly.

Felix winked. "Liam, is there anything down there that can help a brother out?" he asked.

"Electric vehicles and kerosene?" Liam was breathing a bit heavily, as though running at near capacity.

"We're on." Chuck held his hand out for some action, and Tienne took him up on it, smiling widely to be included. "Let's be good guys."

The House of the Rising Son

BY THE time Stirling and the lead guard had rounded the final bend from the jungle to the plantation house clearing, two other guards had simply dropped where they stood, shit themselves, and rocked back and forth, whimpering in pain.

Well, seriously. Who eats random fruit carried in by someone they're thinking about killing?

And the last guy was not looking that great either.

The lead guard was livid. He cast Stirling fulminating looks, as though any indication of guilt on Stirling's part would cause him to simply burst into flame, but Stirling had his game face on. No guilt, no fear, no satisfaction.

Well, he was a *little* satisfied, but he didn't let it show on his face.

What he *did* let show on his face was admiration, though, as he finally got a look at the clearing with the plantation house.

It had been designed to be so pretty!

The house itself was modeled after the antebellum mansions of the American South, with tall Grecian pillars and two stories and a veranda. Done in white stucco with red trim, it had high ceilings, probably with the big fans installed that kept the place cool and breezy and shaded, even in the summer. The house itself sat in a little valley of what had once been acres and acres of cultivated farmland. The land had lain fallow for quite some time, and the jungle was obviously encroaching the borders, but there was still a double line of shady beech trees leading from the path to the docks, and rich grasses, grown waist-high, on either side of a once-white gravel path.

Stirling could imagine Fred and Stella buying this, thinking about family vacations and small local businesses. Thinking about weekend retreats and getting out of Chicago in the winter. Even spending Christmases here as a family, because they could.

Oh, this place could have been so beautiful, such a dream. Bought with money, yes, but imagined with kindness and whimsy.

But the house was about a quarter mile away, and Stirling could see the ruts through the grass where trucks had been driven and the belch of smoke from some sort of industrial machine on the edge of the vegetation on the far side of the house itself. He could see other guards or soldiers or mobsters or whatever hauling crates from a truck to outbuildings, and he noticed a trash pile started on the other side of the jungle as well. Cigarette butts and crumpled coffee cups littered the white-graveled drive, and Stirling shuddered to think of what these men had done to the inside of the gracious plantation house that Fred and Stella had bought out of love.

A knot of rage had built in his chest, strand by strand, like a tangled ball of fury and bloody yarn, from the moment he'd learned of Harve's involvement in Fred and Stella's death. Standing on the edge of the clearing and seeing the destruction of their dream, Stirling realized that every moment sitting in the bottom of the Zodiac had added to that knot until it filled up his stomach and sat on his lungs, a vast, immoveable weight.

If he opened his mouth to scream, he expected swords and shrapnel to vomit forth and take out every soul in his path.

He was so angry.

He and Molly hadn't taken their family for granted. They had *known* what it was like to live without. They had *known* what a windfall they'd had in Fred and Stella—and it wasn't about money. The money was nice, of course it was, but the *time*. The *affection*. The goddamned kindness and fucking whimsy. That had been the true gift, and their birth son had given the order to stop all of that dead and bleeding in its tracks.

Stirling couldn't fathom as to why.

But all of that was on the inside. He turned to the lead guard, who was pale and shaking now, spooked by the illness that had suddenly beset his fellows and probably feeling some effects himself. "Lead the way," he said, absolutely impassive.

From the corner of his eye, he saw Molly lurking back in the masking foliage of the jungle, her bright hair tucked up under a black scarf. She'd been wearing a scarlet silk skirt and white peasant blouse when she'd left with Talia, and they'd both been beautiful, but somehow—perhaps she'd brought her own change of clothes—she'd gotten hold of dark green pants and a long-sleeved black-and-green shirt, and while she was just as beautiful, the only reason Stirling had spotted her was because he'd known she'd be there.

Molly had a plan. He had no doubt she and the others had a plan.

He was glad the guard wasn't looking at him as they continued down the litter-strewn path. Stirling was afraid his expression was no longer impassive.

He might, in fact, have been looking highly satisfied.

A few minutes later, though, he was back to rage.

The remaining lackey who had eaten the poison fruit deserted them the moment they entered the house through a stately open foyer and two great front doors. As he ran off for what Stirling assumed was the bathroom, Stirling had a chance to glance around and mourn for what this dream could have been. The place had been furnished—Stirling recognized Stella's love of colors in the tapestried couches and the Persian rugs—and it had been lovely.

Once.

Trash was now piled high in the kitchen, and the stench was overwhelming. He could smell the bathrooms from the foyer, and the smell of cigarettes and stale alcohol permeated the floorboards.

He wondered if Molly felt the same rage he did, and somewhere outside, he heard sounds of a scuffle and figured she might be working that out even as he was herded past the living room and into a first-floor study that had probably been designed as a den or a library.

Now it held an ugly military-style desk, with bent corners and uncovered feet that had torn up the exquisite hardwood floors.

Stirling didn't have to know what kind of wood it was or what kind of furniture to know it had been abused and destroyed from sheer carelessness and disdain.

A new guard—or a new threat—intercepted them as the leader shouldered his way toward the desk.

Thank God he spoke English, although Stirling thought that maybe he'd work with Josh when he studied Russian, because it certainly would have come in handy over the past few days.

"Who the fuck is this?"

"Harvey Christopher's foster brother" came the thick reply. "He's got a… a *time bomb* on his computer. Says he can bring the authorities down on us if he doesn't log back in and type in the password."

There was a stunned silence. "The actual fuck? What does he want?"

"To talk to Harve! He managed to poison all my men—they're all shitting themselves and dying on the path to the dock." A moan issued from the back of the house, followed by gastric sounds that almost shook the floorboards. "And I don't think he's here alone. I… it's very strange out there," he finished forlornly, and Stirling barely contained his smile.

"Where the fuck is the *mudak*?" spat the first guard, and Stirling shuddered, because even *he* knew that was a terrible insult in Russian. "He should have been back with you. He said he was going to take a look to see if more people landed with that other guy. Fucking asshole. Had us lock up that guy he found on the beach in one of the back bathrooms, and the guy fucking disappeared. We keep hearing him *in the goddamned walls* like a ghost or something, and the plumbing is backing up!"

Ah, Michael. Stirling *really* approved of Carl's boyfriend. It was like he'd been born to be a Salinger—much like himself and Molly, really.

"So there's a random *guy* running around the house in the walls?" The guy Stirling was starting to think of as *his* guard—they'd seen guys shit themselves together, after all—was sounding more and more freaked out. "And half my men are rolling around in their own feces. And"—Stirling could tell this had just occurred to him—"*two of them are missing*! I sent them to check out where this one landed, and they never came back. Look at him! He's not even that big, and he looks about twelve! How can he cause this much trouble?"

"You think that's bad," the other guard muttered. "The guy in the walls is—" He muttered a word in Russian that Stirling didn't understand, but it sounded *foul*.

"How do you know?"

"He kept saying his 'boyfriend's' family was going to fuck us all up." The guard shuddered. "If he's the one making the plumbing back up, I think he's bad enough."

Stirling couldn't help it. He chuckled.

"You!" said the guard afraid of Michael and bad plumbing. "What are you laughing at?"

"Oh, buddy," Stirling murmured. "You guys are *so* not ready for us. You both should probably jump in the ocean right now and try to swim for Barbados. That at least is even odds."

The two guards looked at each other, and overhead the lights crackled and went out. Before either of them could react, Stirling called, "We're gonna need Wi-Fi, Michael. Don't kill the whole electrical grid!"

There was a gentle flicker, the fan started whirring again, and Stirling was relieved on behalf of the Wi-Fi router.

The guard who had accompanied him from the beach raised the stock of his semiautomatic weapon as if to strike Stirling in the face, only to be stopped by a blow from the other man, a quick slap across the back of his head.

"Stop it! I thought you said there's a time bomb on his computer. We need to make him take that down."

"I'm telling you, this is bad," Stirling's guard said. "I say we cut and run!"

"But Harve Christopher is *here*," the other man retorted. "He had to be. Kadjic's guys are going to be picking the guns up in *hours*. One more shipment and we are home free."

Stirling kept his face impassive, which was hard with the unexpected knowledge that Harve Christopher was *physically* there on the island, but he filed the rest of the information away for later. Kadjic—the man who had killed Tienne's father and who had left Danny Mitchell for dead. It seemed that Andres Kadjic was a specter from the past who would eventually need to be vanquished.

But not today. Today, Stirling was going to get his and Molly's island back. He hadn't even known he wanted it until he'd seen what Fred and Stella had planned. It wasn't even that he wanted to live in the Caribbean. He wanted that final reminder that Fred and Stella had loved them and planned to be a family for many years to come.

"If Harve's here, where the fuck is he?" Stirling's guard demanded. "Wouldn't he be in the house?"

"He's out checking on the shipments!" the house guard told him. "Do you want to go fetch him? He's got the right idea, counting the fucking guns. Man, you do not want to be here if Kadjic finds his shipment missing. That man has green blood and ice water in his veins."

Stirling slow-blinked at that. For one thing, the metaphor was very apt, and for another, the idea that the guards were as wary of Kadjic as the Salingers was important and potentially useful.

"Then where's Cawthorne? Levka Dubov, that fucking *mudak*, is supposed to get here too. He went the back way from the path to see if there were any more strangers that way."

Oh God. The knowledge that Lawrence Cawthorne, Fred's caretaker, was in on this disaster was secondary to that other piece of information. Dubov was out there? Dubov was out there with Stirling's gentle artist? *Run, Tienne, run!* Stirling's heart started thundering, and he had to concentrate on the conversation in front of him.

"Cawthorne is upstairs," the house guard said. Then he held his finger to one nostril and snorted through the other, and Stirling wanted to groan. It was the universal signal for snorting drugs, and that's *all* they needed. "I'd be careful how you woke him up," the guard finished, and Stirling's guard grimaced.

"Yes, but to not wake him up could get us shot anyway. I'll go get him. You let this one set up his computer so he can stop that damned clock from ticking!"

"After I talk to my brother," Stirling clarified. The knowledge that Harve was *actually on the island* had not changed this requirement one damned bit.

"Yes, yes, whatever!" his guard said, waving his hand. "He'll be inside eventually to bitch at us for not taking care of the house, and then he'll threaten to shoot us when the man hasn't done a lick of work in his life. You talk to your brother, and then we'll drop your body into the ocean, like we did everybody else's." He stalked out of the office, presumably upstairs to risk getting his head blown off by his own boss for waking the guy up in the middle of a drug binge.

Stirling was starting to see why the others enjoyed dealing with these assclowns in person. It really *was* satisfying when you knew they were going to get what was coming to them.

The house guard watched the other guy go. "You must have really spooked Vlade," he said, his thick accent making "spooked" sound even more frightening. "He *really* hates Cawthorne. Tell me what you need me to do?"

"Give me the Wi-Fi password and I'll do the rest," he said amiably, not bothering to tell this man that it was too late, the packet of information had already been sent out. Stirling had no doubts—none whatsoever—that his crew had done their jobs. But to be on the safe side, since he knew Harve was here, he had some other ideas.

The house guard narrowed his eyes. "But will you kill the time bomb he was talking about? What sort of bomb is it?"

"It's a mass-send email to every agency who gives a shit that Harve and his buddies set up a shell corporation to launder money from illegal gun sales from this island."

The house guard took a step back, and his eyes shot open. "Can you kill this bomb?"

Stirling looked at him, trying to discern what kind of man he was, whether he should tell the guy no, he couldn't, and that the guy should probably run now, or whether Stirling should bluff it out. In the end, he couldn't make the decision and simply held his tongue. If he was wrong, the guy might shoot him where he stood.

"The only way to find out is by letting me talk to Harve," he said after a moment.

It must have been the right thing to say, because the house guard began to activate the laptop.

In a moment, Stirling had a text box open to Josh. It had not escaped his notice that this was exactly what they'd planned—to get somebody on the island to access the Wi-Fi and pull all the pertinent info out for an airtight case. Only it had happened a day early, the timeline precipitated by the very chaotic Grace.

Holy shit, are you guys okay?

We're sort of split up at the moment, he texted back. *I'm on the internal Wi-Fi—on their computer. Consider this your bug and start pulling and transferring files to add to what you already sent. While you're sorting information, can you piggyback off the signal and tape what shows up here? I think I have a way to keep us all off the official radar and still incriminate the hell out of Harve.*

The fuck?

Harve's here, Stirling typed. *Kadjic's goons are coming. It's about to get VERY interesting.*

In the meantime, Harve's thick, snarling voice echoed through the house. "Victor? The fuck? Where's Cawthorne or Dubov? Kadjic's guys are going to be here tonight, and I can't find a goddamned lackey!"

Victor, who was considerably younger than Vlade, the lead guard from the beach, called out into the hallway, "In here! There has been a wrinkle." He cast a green look to Stirling. "That's the word, yes?"

Stirling nodded. It was indeed. His fingers continued to fly on the computer, and on top of the standard laptop, he saw the red light of the laptop camera activate.

In the textbox, Josh typed, *I've got you. Package is sent. What I'm getting from Harve's laptop nearby will be the icing on top.*

Wait until the video.

"What sort of a fuckin'—" Harve's voice signaled he was about to enter the room, and Victor, apparently aware all this was over his pay grade, simply stood back and indicated Stirling as he entered. Stirling angled himself to the side of the laptop; the camera would get Harve Christopher and anybody who came in behind him, but not the people to the side.

With a few clunky steps, Harve entered, looking hot and uncomfortable in a boxy tan American suit. He had all of Fred and Stella's average-folk homeliness—big ears, receding hairline, slightly bulbous nose—but none of the kindness or laughter that made them beautiful to Stirling and Molly. Stirling had once thought that Fred and Stella were what God had in mind when he'd made middle-aged parents. Harvey Christopher was younger than Fred had been when Stirling and Molly had been adopted, but hatred and greed had made him look pig-eyed, old, and mean.

And when he saw Stirling, he looked very surprised. "Oh. You. The actual hell?"

"I'm just curious," Stirling said, his voice sounding far away, "whether or not you had the balls to talk to your father and mother before ordering them killed."

Stirling watched him swallow, and from five feet away, he could smell Harve's fear stink. "You have no way of knowing—" He stopped abruptly and grimaced. "They died in a boat wreck." Harve's shoulders heaved up and down as though he were squaring up to an opponent. He had sweat stains seeping through his suit jacket, and Stirling couldn't help contrasting him with Felix or Carl, who would have removed the jacket, rolled up their shirtsleeves, and found a pair of flip-flops if they'd ever had to fly to Barbados in their work clothes.

And they'd still look more commanding and more organized than Harvey Christopher did in his full kit.

But Harve was too busy lying to fix his wardrobe malfunction. He obviously hadn't realized he'd already lost.

"We have the reports that prove otherwise," Stirling said, thinking about Danny's wounds, and Josh and Felix's panic. "They were shot. They were shot within hours after radioing to the port at Barbados that they'd been blown off course and were coming to their own property. And minutes after they made a giant withdrawal from their vacation funds to buy life insurance for people they barely knew. An hour after that radio call, you got a ten-minute call from this island. Specifically. There was nowhere else it could've come from. An hour after that, their chartered yacht was pushed out to sea toward another storm, but my parents and everybody aboard the yacht were already dead."

"*They weren't your parents!*" Harve shouted, spittle flying from his mouth, but Stirling wasn't frightened. Not of *this* man. His crew had his back. They always did. Felix had told him that he was the mastermind in this one, but it wouldn't matter if he was still in the van. Like Carl had told him, *this* was what they did. They fixed wrongs. And what had been done to Fred and Stella was very, very wrong.

In the ensuing silence, several noises crackled about them. From the stairs there were rapid footsteps and swearing in Serbian, the hollow, shambling steps of somebody trying to negotiate floors and railings.

From outside in the front came a boom loud enough to shake the windows, along with shouts and calls, and from the back door—Stirling would wager it was near the kitchen—came sounds of a scuffle, grunts, thuds, and one "Ouch, you *fucker*!" that sounded *very* familiar.

Stirling started to smile.

"What?" Harve demanded, as though trying to regain control after his outburst. "What is that expression? Victor, go see what the fuck that was! Cawthorne, what in the hell is going on here?"

"It's all under control." Stirling glanced behind Harve as a thin man with lank mousy hair stumbled into the room. His eyes were red, as was his nose, and he looked very much like a man pulled out of a drug bender. "No worries. We have it in hand—" The man Stirling assumed was Cawthorne paused and blinked from Harve to Stirling. "Who the fuck are you?"

Stirling got a glimpse of Victor the house-guard's face as he started to edge toward whatever the hell was going on outside and saw a man who was very much regretting his life choices at this point. Ignoring Cawthorne and even Harve, Stirling nodded at him and mouthed, "Run," before turning back to his brother.

"They were too my parents," he said calmly, ignoring the chaos around them. "They took me into their home. They gave me and my sister—"

"She doesn't even look like you!" Harve retorted spitefully, and Stirling cocked his head the other way, as though he was examining a particularly obnoxious bug.

"Why do you hate us so much?" he asked. "You were out of the house. You had all the money and all the privilege in the world. Why did it bother you so much that Fred and Stella loved us?"

"They didn't *love* you," Harve snarled, lost in bitterness. "They *admired* you. They wouldn't fucking shut up about how talented you both were. That foulmouthed bitch was 'strong' and 'brave' and 'brilliant,' and you? You were 'a creative genius' and 'quirky.' God, if I had to hear Fred tell me one more time what 'great kids' you both were, I was gonna puke!"

"He didn't say the same things about you?" Stirling asked analytically. He wanted to understand—he really did—where Harve's irrational hatred came from.

"Well, yes! But I was his *son*! And he had more money than God—enough money to buy this entire fuckin' island—but he wouldn't help me out when I needed it!"

"Because of your gambling," Stirling said evenly, because that was the conclusion he and Josh had come to, and Harve's face turned a bright, unhealthy shade of red.

"He told you about the *gambling*?" It was a combination of fury and embarrassment, and Stirling shook his head.

"Of course not. We analyzed your financials. You had steady output that correlated with certain events, and you kept getting deeper and deeper into debt with no other obvious source of expenditures. That usually points to addiction, and since the cash withdrawals were so large and you showed no physical symptoms of addiction, well, that indicated gambling. It was a logical deduction. Killing your parents was not."

The noises outside had changed from explosions to shouts, along with that ongoing scuffle coming from the back. Stirling continued to occupy Harve, wondering when things would come to a head.

"You said it," Harve said, and his face was crumpling, although he kept his voice hard. "They blew off course and got to the island too early. Dad wouldn't fork over the money, and I was in too goddamned deep to a Serbian gangster, which would have been okay— guy was an easy mark—but he turned my marker over to Andres Kadjic." Harve shuddered. "You don't fuck with Kadjic. He told me I had resources to help pay him back, and by the time Mom and Dad got to the island, it was…." He wiped his sweating face with his palm. "It was too late. I… the others who were in on it with me kicked it up to Kadjic. He would have killed me, you understand, if I had let them live. But it was all Dad's fault, you see, because he wouldn't *give me the fuckin' money*. And he had it! That's the thing that burns me the most—he *had it*. I don't know where he was getting it, but he kept building more and more and more. He bought this fuckin' island, for God's sake, and put it in your name. He had the fuckin' money, and he wouldn't tell me where it came from, and he *wouldn't give it to me*."

As if to punctuate Harve's words, there was a crash through the back door and footsteps in the hallway. Harve jumped and whirled around, searching the hallway for whatever fresh hell had entered.

A very dear, *very* familiar female voice echoed through the halls. "Oh dear God, what is that smell!" and another familiar, equally dear male voice—this one accented in French—replied, "It's a good thing this place is going to blow up very soon, because I don't think you can clean that out of carpeting."

"Wait, what?" Harve muttered, staring at Stirling. "What did he say? What did he mean, blow up very soon?"

Stirling smiled. "He means we need to finish this conversation in about five minutes. Did you think I came alone?"

"There was another man," Victor said. "He arrived right after you did, Mr. Christopher. We locked him in the bathroom, and he escaped into the walls. We think he blew up the plumbing."

"So what? Two, three people?" Harve said, glancing around the sizable den as though he could suddenly see through the walls. "One of them's his fuckin' sister. You got one idiot-savant, one guy in the walls, and his fuckin' sister? How bad can it be?"

"Oh, Harve," Molly said, striding in with one of the guard's semiautomatic weapons in her hand. "It can be very, very bad." She looked at Stirling. "How's it going?" Her face was dirty, and her hair was escaping the black scarf she'd wrapped around it. She had bruises on her cheek and blood coming from the corner of her mouth, and her knuckles looked very, very bruised. Stirling wanted to get her some ice and some ibuprofen and a big coffee drink, but only because he loved her and she'd had a rough day. Other people saw Molly the socialite or Molly the actress. Molly the squealing, excited girl who loved to dance and to shop and swooned over pretty clothes.

This Molly was the Molly who had grabbed Stirling's hand at eight and had never, ever let him go.

He loved this Molly the best of them all.

"It's good," Stirling said. "I got him to confess to ordering the killing of our parents, but he hasn't explained the life insurance for the employees on the yacht yet."

"I bet it was a payoff," Tienne said, drawing to Stirling's side, and even as Stirling pulled Tienne out of the camera's range and gestured with his chin that Molly should do the same, Stirling tried not to moon too much over him. Tienne, too, looked as though he'd hauled ass through the jungle and beat the shit out of some bad guys. His long hair was out of its queue, and it hung in his face like a dirty blond mane, but his blue eyes were alight with confidence and a pride Stirling hadn't seen before, and Stirling wanted to hold him forever and ever and exchange the stories of their day.

He also, he thought darkly, would make whoever had left fingerprints around Tienne's throat wish he'd never been born.

"A payoff," he said instead, reaching for Tienne's hand, relieved when their fingers twined together. "That's interesting." He glanced at Harve, thinking that this was so much more delicious in person—particularly since it hadn't yet dawned on Harve that he had never been so fucked.

Harve swallowed. "The people on the yacht were local," he said, looking away. "We've got a local on our payroll. He told us that if we ever had to… to take care of somebody, if we took care of their families, the islanders would help protect us."

"So life insurance?" Molly said. "Oh my God. Like somebody wouldn't look at that and think it's fishy?"

"Nobody looked at it until now!" Harve snapped. "Jesus, you fucking nosy little assholes! Wasn't it enough that you got the house and your fucking trust funds? Why aren't you out there spending that money on cars and blow? I've been waiting for you to fucking crash a Maserati into the goddamned lake and get the fuck out of my life!"

Molly and Stirling met eyes. "You've never been in our lives," she said. "You're… you're sort of deluded, aren't you?"

"He's mad because Fred didn't pay off his gambling debts," Stirling repeated, and then frowned. "I admit, I don't know why Fred didn't. I mean, you know." He gave a surreptitious glance at the computer. "Fred had the money."

Molly gave Stirling a look laden with compassion before flitting her eyes toward the computer as well, acknowledging that things were being taped. "Wait, little brother," she said softly, "we need to get out of here now, but when this is over, I'll tell you."

"Tell me now!" Harve demanded, and Molly raised the gun in her hand with an absolutely dead-eyed glare.

"You are in no position to demand anything," she said, and Harve lost his mind.

"Cawthorne! Vlade! Victor! You've got guns! Don't let her threaten me!"

Stirling frowned, wondering if he'd missed something or if—

"What a ridiculous thing to say," Tienne murmured. "Besides, I don't see this Victor. Who is he talking about?"

"I told him to run," Stirling told him. "I think he took my advice."

"Oh!" Tienne raised his voice so Harve could hear him. "Victor slid out the back as we entered." He frowned. "And Grace disappeared."

"You found Grace?" Stirling was impressed. If Grace wanted to disappear, he usually did.

"I threw a gun at him," Tienne said, and Stirling nodded as though this made perfect sense.

"Who *is* this kid?" Harve demanded. "And what's happening to all my men!"

"Which kid?" Cawthorne asked. Belatedly, he reached into the back of his pants where, Stirling assumed, a gun would be, but he came up empty. Tienne, who had brushed by Cawthorne as they entered, reached behind his back with his free hand and showed Stirling, who grinned and nodded. He'd finally gotten to make a lift! "And where did Victor go?" Cawthorne continued before he glanced around. "Vlade, make her drop that gun."

All Molly had to do was arch an eyebrow and Vlade dropped his own gun, and Stirling turned back to Harve.

"Look, you little assholes," Harve began, but Stirling was done. He could still feel the wind on his face and in his ears from that long ride in the boat, and his head hurt from the march through the jungle in the sun. Tienne was there, safe and sound, and Molly apparently could take on a much larger army. He'd wanted to know what had happened with their parents, and now he knew.

His disappointment in Harvey Christopher, who could have been his brother, and with humanity in general, was so deep right now, he knew the only thing that could heal the wound was time with his family. He might spend half of it curled up behind the couch, leaning against Tienne, but hearing their voices wash over him in the babble of brilliant nonsense they usually spewed would be enough.

It would fill up the empty places until eventually they would heal. It would remind him of all the time he and Fred Christopher had spent in the den, making sports bets, watching six games at once and cheering when their team won, whether or not they made money. It would remind him that when Molly had dragged him into that meeting, that all-important second meeting when she should have been looking out for herself, Stella Christopher had looked almost sideways, as though realizing he wasn't great at eye contact, and she'd said, "So this is your sister?"

"Yes," he'd said.

"Well, we can't split you two apart. Would you mind being our son?"

"Harvey," Stirling said now, tired to his bones. He wanted to know if Danny and Carl were okay, and he wanted to see Josh and Grace and tell them thank you for everything, from middle school on.

He wanted to sit on the couch with his sister by his feet and his lover by his side and watch a stupid movie and laugh.

"What?" Harve stared at him, still glancing around the den in Fred and Stella's dead dream as though possessed. "What could you possibly say right now that would make me listen to—"

Another explosion went off somewhere in the front, and those remaining in the house flinched.

"It's over," Stirling said. "What I told Victor and Vlade about the time bomb was a lie. The bomb went off as soon as we landed. Hooking up the laptop here enabled us to copy your hard drive and stream it to the authorities. My partners and I have sent enough information to prosecute you and your cronies about six hundred ways to Sunday. You're finished. Your business is finished. Your gang activity and gun running is finished. Your gambling debts and lawyer fees will eat away at whatever you have left. My friends and I have a way off this island, and you're not welcome. You can stay here and wait for Interpol—" He frowned and looked at Molly. "—right?" Liam would have taken care of that.

"Oh yes. I figure we've got about an hour before they get here."

"So we don't need to blow up the house?" he asked, and Tienne shrugged.

"I got the feeling," he said, "that people were very excited about it, but it is up to you."

Stirling shrugged. Perhaps with some work and some money, it could be lovely again. Perhaps he would give it to Lucius as another place for battered women to hide and to heal, as well as their children. If one didn't eat the manchineel fruit, it *could* be paradise.

"So we're not blowing up the house. This means you can wait for Interpol, or you can wait for Andres Kadjic to come get you." His eyes burned. "I figure it's a better choice than you gave our parents."

Harvey's face went white, and he glanced around the ruined house helplessly, as though finally seeing what he'd let slip through his fingers.

"They weren't your parents," he mumbled.

"They were," Molly said. "But they're not yours now. Not anymore. We have all the good memories now, Harve. You've got prison time and your own self-hatred." She paused and handed the gun to Tienne, who let go of Stirling's hand and took it awkwardly. "And a broken jaw."

Harve stared at her with incomprehension even as she strode up to him and swung.

Very Small, Very Large

Fifteen minutes earlier…

AS THEY hauled ass across the jungle, heading for the big house and Stirling, Tienne remembered watching Grace dance in the studio. He thought he'd seen something that day, but watching the man dance from shadow to shadow as they crossed the jungle was like watching smoke move, or water.

Tienne tried to follow along without making too much noise, and for the first time, he noticed the chatter of the monkeys in the trees overhead. He thought wistfully of sometime sitting under the trees and looking up—maybe even sketching the monkeys, that would be fun—but realized that he needed to keep his attention to the ground. They'd estimated between eight and sixteen more guards, and all of them had guns.

In his earbuds, though, he heard heavy breathing and the thud of flesh. As he and Grace neared the mouth of the other trail, Hunter said, "Three for me, two for Liam."

So that made eleven—or three. Still, better odds than they'd walked on the island with. Something that had not gone unremarked upon.

"Hey, Molly," Grace murmured. "Did you hear?"

"Bwah!"

That last was from Tienne, who had not seen the young woman crouched in the shadow of another lignum vitae tree, her bright hair covered, her clothing and face dark and stained with mud. She was practically her own shadow, but she winked at Tienne, and he saw her bright green eyes peering at him and could smile back.

"Gotcha, didn't I?" she said with an impertinent grin.

"You should have maybe left me back on the yacht," he muttered, his victory over Levka diminished by every step the people around him took.

"Are you kidding?" She chuckled wickedly and gestured toward her ear. "I've heard everything, you know. You and my brother took out eight guys? I mean, that's pretty impressive."

Tienne snorted. "Seven. And they took themselves out, most of them. Who eats other people's food?"

Her fierce smile made him answer in kind. "Bad guys," she said, eyes dancing. "Ready to come help me get my brother back?"

Tienne swallowed hard at the thought of Stirling— practical, solid, no-bullshit Stirling, who could touch him so tenderly it made him cry—in the hands of the people they'd seen operating on the island. It filled him with so much terror, he was surprised he could still breathe.

"We have to get out of here before Kadjic arrives," he rasped, hoping everybody understood that was the deadline he was *really* worried about.

"Interpol's going to get here first," Liam murmured over the coms. "I think you all should be absent before that. Hunter, *duck*!"

Tienne blinked, and Molly laughed. "Oh, they're having a good time. Let's take some more out for Team Christopher."

They started toward the house at a jog, and Grace asked, "Am I in Team Christopher? Is that disloyal to Team Hunter and Grace? Which team is Josh on?"

"You're on Team Christopher until you drive us too crazy to keep," Molly said, her patience obviously at an end. They were approaching the side of what had once been a dignified two-story plantation home, but even from up the litter-strewn driveway, they could see signs of wear. Black marks on the side of the porch from items being dragged, piles of trash that they could see—and smell—from where they were.

"You know," Molly muttered, "it's not the money—it's the dream. This place was nice. They were going to make this a family house for us. You can tell. Stirling made him and Fred piles of money, and I know they gave a buttload to charity because Stirling did their taxes, but this was just... it was a gift. And these fuckers killed my parents and shit on their gift, and now I'm pissed all over again."

She paused—they all did—and took in the figure in the top story of the house, waving madly at them through a large window.

"Molly?" Felix's voice came in through the coms. "Molly girl, are you all right?"

"Carl," Grace said, "your boyfriend's okay."

Carl's voice was strained and breathless. "You're sure?"

"I think he's escaped," Tienne said as they all waved bemusedly back. "Molly, aren't we supposed to come in from the other side?"

Molly nodded and pointed toward the rear of the great house, making the gesture pronounced. Her effort was rewarded when Michael pointed in the same direction and nodded, then made a thumbs-up, grinning.

They all sucked air in through their teeth when he smiled; even from that distance, they could see the split on his lip and his cheek.

"He's okay, right?" Carl said.

"He was roughed up a little," Molly said, her voice even. "I'm looking forward to getting some payback for that, and hey, oh look! Guards!"

"Can you wait a moment?" Felix asked. "When we give the signal—"

"Oh, Felix," Molly murmured, sounding almost unhinged. "How about we get in the old-fashioned way."

"But Molly, there's five other guards coming in from the gun sheds to—"

Molly took off running, and Grace followed her. Tienne had barely enough wind to breathe, "Hurry, Felix, I don't think she can wait," before following them both.

He was fast. He'd known that in a peripheral way, but until he found himself keeping up easily with Molly and Grace after all they'd done that day, he hadn't realized how much his lonely time running in the city had given him.

Right now, it gave him the ability to keep up with his friends and not get left behind, and given that their whole purpose was to get to Stirling, he was good with that.

They swung around to the back of the house and ran into a contingent of guards, all of them carrying weapons and none of them ready for Molly to charge the guy in front, leaping at his chest and taking him down while his friends stared at him stupidly.

Tienne remembered how he'd taken down Levka, and while the two guards were staring at Molly as she gave the guy in the middle a solid beating, he ran at one of them from the side, using the guy's kneecap to push off and up, and then his shoulder, and then his head.

The guard fell to the ground, moaning, his gun lying forgotten by his side.

Tienne took it away anyway and turned to see if Grace needed any help.

Grace had his guard's gun and was in the process of smacking him on the back of the head with it. When they were both done, they turned to Molly.

Tienne and Grace met eyes over her head.

The guy was KO'd, eyes rolled back, head lolling, face turning purple and pulpy as she continued to beat him, and Tienne realized she was about to do something she'd regret.

"Come on," he said, approaching her from behind, Grace on her other side. "Time is wasting, Molly. We need to go!"

But Molly was lost, the stress of the night, the fear for her brother, and probably the rage of her parents' deaths pulling her further and further away.

She swore, she gibbered, and she cursed, and Tienne knew he was taking his life in both hands, but he couldn't—couldn't—let Stirling's sister, whom he was beginning to love as much as Stirling did, become a thing she would hate.

"Stop it!" he yelled, grabbing her upper arm and holding on for dear life. Grace did the same on her other side, and together they pulled hard at her while he tried to get through. "Molly! Molly! They've got him inside. We're almost there. Don't get distracted—we need you!"

Grace helped as well. "Molly, goddammit, your brother needs you! Stop fucking around and lead the charge!"

Molly's fist came up and caught Tienne on his jaw, but Tienne wasn't afraid of pain, not right now. "*Molly*!" he snapped. "We *need you back*! Stirling needs his sister, not an animal. Please, Molly. For all of us! We need you!"

He punctuated that with a hard shove backward, hard enough to unbalance her so she went tumbling back over her downed opponent's legs and had to roll quickly or she'd be left vulnerable in the dust.

She came up flailing, and Tienne and Grace both stepped back, hands up, captured guns held awkwardly. For a moment, Tienne thought she was going to take them both out, and all he could do was stare at her mutely, pleading.

In the sudden silence, Chuck's voice, shouting at Molly over coms to quit fucking around so he could blow shit up, penetrated the brain fog brought on by violence.

Tienne and Molly both put their palms to their ears, because he was screaming loudly enough to send feedback through their coms, the shriek of it sobering, if his obvious panic hadn't been.

"I'm okay," she muttered, eyes darting wildly as she tried to remember what they were doing. "I'm fine. Don't come back here, Chuck. You guys stay and—"

Boom!

A wall of flame appeared about fifty feet from the front of the house, and while Tienne had no idea what Chuck had blown up, he knew that was their cue to go in and get their boy back.

With a grim look and a nod, Molly wiped the blood from the corner of her mouth, her bloodied hands leaving another smear on her chin. Without another word—or even a glance back—they left the three incapacitated guards moaning where they lay. Tienne did check to make sure the one Molly had beaten so badly was still alive and was reassured to see him struggling to stand up.

He fell back down in the dust, much to Tienne's relief. The guy had earned his rest.

As they drew near the back porch, the door burst open, and one guard sprinted past him, no gun in sight. He was heading toward the path in the jungle that led to the cove and the dock, and Tienne wished him Godspeed. Next came two more guards from the side, running as though they were actually going to do something, and Tienne and Grace stepped back.

"It's probably better," Grace said, watching Molly completely wipe the floor with the two men. "She needs to get it out of her system before she has to talk to people inside. Ouch! Oh God. He's not coming back from that."

"Kickboxing move," Tienne said, watching the first opponent crumple to the ground. "Nice."

She was engaging with the second opponent when they heard a clatter from above them and saw a pair of legs slide over the edge of the porch overhang.

Michael's unmistakable Texas twang could be heard from the awning over their heads, as he flailed and kicked his way to the porch below.

"Goddammit sonuvafuckin' bastard fuckin' *balls*!"

Tienne and Grace moved to help him down, reaching up to steady him until he could swing from the gutter around the awning and allow himself to drop.

"That was some prime-A swearing," Grace told him with a pat on the shoulder. "You didn't even swear that much when the boat took off."

Michael scowled. "That was a real nice house those assholes trashed. I wanted to thump some heads." His expression shifted. "You okay? I was worried about you after they took me. There's bad shit in that jungle."

Grace snorted. "There *was* bad shit in that jungle, but Tienne clocked it on the head with a gun, and then everybody else killed it."

The words were punctuated by the thud of flesh hitting flesh and a groan, and they looked up to see Molly finishing off the second guard.

"Come *on*," she ordered, and Tienne followed her in without a second thought.

Oh God, he was so happy to see Stirling, he didn't even notice that Michael and Grace had disappeared. For a few moments he was distracted, making sure Stirling wasn't hurt too badly, cataloguing his bruised face, his angry glare, the devastating sadness behind his eyes. It wasn't until Molly handed him her gun and strode forward to break Harve Christopher's jaw that he remembered he had duties.

He waited until her first blow landed—the silence was so profound in the moment that everybody left in the den recoiled from the crunch of bone—before grabbing Stirling's hand. "Come *on*," he urged. Then, remembering that terrible moment when he wasn't sure if Molly would be able to rein in her temper, he called to her. "Molly, we've got to go!"

She looked to where Harve lay at her feet and then turned to Stirling. "Are we good here, little brother?"

Stirling thought for a moment, then turned to the laptop that had been open on the desk. He bent quickly and typed before shutting the lid and grabbing it.

"Let's go," he said.

She nodded and aimed a savage kick at Harvey Christopher's side, and he moaned some more. Then she stalked away, heading toward the back door, not even bothering to look behind her.

Tienne followed her—at this point he would have followed Stirling's sister into hell—but Stirling paused and crouched down by Harvey as he lay groaning.

"Your wife," Stirling said carefully. "Did she know about the guns? About Kadjic? About my parents?"

"Mmmooooo," Harve moaned miserably, not even trying to sit up from his huddle on the floor. "Dimm no. Lllv er lone…."

"If Kadjic comes here and kills you, will he go to her for your debt?" Stirling asked, and Harve's tautly indrawn breath told Tienne everything he needed to know. Carolyn might not have known about what her husband had been doing, but that didn't mean she wasn't going to be put into protective custody for possibly the rest of her life.

"I hope you're very, very afraid," Stirling said, before standing up and taking Tienne's hand. Together they followed Molly out the back door and into the smoke-filled sunlight, where Felix, Hunter, and Chuck stood waiting.

"Are we done, Molly girl?" Chuck asked. He looked to his left, where the guards she'd taken on were still breathing but not moving anytime soon.

Molly nodded, and Tienne watched her lower lip quiver before she got it under control. "Where's Grace and Michael?" she asked. "They're not micced—"

Felix held up the phone Danny had shoved into his hands. "They're headed back to the Zodiacs," he said. He looked at Tienne. "You told Grace that Carl had been hurt. I'm going to assume that's something Michael would want to know."

Tienne nodded. "Grace has a very big heart and a *very* unusual brain," he said, shaking his head. Then he looked at Stirling. "What do we do now?"

Stirling looked to Felix, and Tienne read his genuine bewilderment, and Molly's too. They were both shell-shocked, he realized. Confronting their adoptive brother, realizing all over again what had been taken from them—neither of them were okay.

"Is it enough?" Felix asked, as another explosion rocked the area where the gun crates were kept. Beyond the house, they could see a spectacular orange halo from something truly horrific. They all gave Chuck an exasperated look.

"That wasn't me," Chuck said, trying—and failing—to look innocent. "There were only two golf carts and not that much kerosene!"

"My bad," Liam's voice said over their coms. "There was an entire case of hand grenades and RPGs. To be honest, I didn't want them aimed at us as we took off."

"Good thinking," Felix muttered. "Are your people on their way?"

"Yes. In about an hour, I think. I don't need to be here, though. I'm undercover as far as they're concerned. I'll head out with you lot. Go toward the boats."

And Felix took stock of Stirling and Molly again. "Will it be enough?" he repeated. "We know what happened to them, and it was terrible. There's nothing we can do to bring Fred and Stella back, but I'm pretty sure the killers will all be punished. Can you live with this as it is, or…?" He swallowed hard, and Tienne realized the enormity of what he was doing, asking them to make a choice between vengeance and justice. They were both so young, Tienne thought wretchedly. Could he make a choice like that and do it wisely? What would he give to have Andres Kadjic's throat under his palette knife?

"Harve can either go to prison or be executed by the mob," Stirling said, looking at his sister. "His cronies are about to be arrested in their homes in Chicago. They have no idea it's coming. I'm… I'm satisfied. I mean…." Tienne squeezed his hand, watching emotions play on Stirling's face that Stirling so rarely showed. "It's going to hurt again, but at least I know. Molly?"

She gave a troubled look to the man she'd almost beaten to death.

"I broke Harve's jaw," she said. "And his ribs. I think that's going to have to be enough. He let his bitterness kill all the good inside him, and eventually it killed Fred and Stella too. I think I need to keep that monster locked in my heart and only let it out on a leash, or it could destroy—" She gave them all a watery glance. "—everything."

Far off, they heard the *whop, whop, whop* of chopper blades, and the acrid black smoke from Chuck's handiwork was making it hard to breathe.

"I think we've done quite enough," Felix said. "Let's get back to the yacht and see if Julia is going to let us live."

To Live and Let Live

LIAM STAYED with one watercraft and helped to get Carl *and* Danny onto the medevac chopper. He used his Interpol credentials and spun a story about agent assets and, on Tienne's whispered advice, used the name Carlson Sternburg for Carl and Denny Julius for Danny. Tienne had made both of the fake IDs, and they'd all exchanged "alternate information" before they packed. You knew someone had your back when they had your alias too.

It would all be okay when they got back to the yacht.

Stirling repeated that to himself over and over. He had to get back to the yacht. What he really wanted was his cozy little room next to the Salingers' den. He wanted to sit there and patrol the web and work on his next set design and go upstairs for dinner to be with all his family and then lie down next to Tienne somewhere that didn't move or vibrate or blow wind in his face.

His rational mind knew that wasn't possible, not for quite some time, so he told himself that the yacht would do. Once he got back on board, it would all be okay.

His brain sort of fuzzed out on the trip there, though, and he missed the complete and thorough ass-chewing Julia gave everybody else except Molly when they arrived back.

Instead, he staggered to the shower and washed the smell of that awful house off his skin and then fell into bed and slept for hours.

He woke up, groggy and disoriented and vaguely disappointed that Tienne wasn't by his side.

"He's up in the lounge," Julia said, surprising him. "Getting you both dinner. He didn't want to leave you alone, so I told him I'd sit here and listen to your stomach grumble."

"Is it fish?" he asked, feeling sad and spoiled to even worry about that.

Julia's delicately manicured fingertips skated across his temples. "Hamburgers, darling. Josh insisted."

Stirling's eyes burned. God bless him. Bless them all. "How's Josh?" He'd been so pale, so barely recovering.

"He woke up right before I came to check on you," she said, and her smile let him know how exhausted she was too. "And before you ask—or forget, because it's a lot—we'll dock in Barbados tomorrow, and Danny and Carl will board there. They're fine but will be expected to rest and actually vacation for the rest of the trip. Liam reported that what was left of the guns were confiscated." She grimaced. "Apparently Charles had rather too much fun with the kerosene and batteries. I understand there wasn't much left of Andres Kadjic's gun shipment when his thugs arrived to claim it." She shrugged. "What a pity."

Stirling smiled. "So sad," he agreed, and then, much more soberly, "And Harve?"

"Was arrested," she said with a little shrug. "And not by the US—by the combined forces of the French and English governments, who don't like their territories used badly. By the way, Molly has fielded a number of apologetic calls letting her know that your property was being used in a most inappropriate way. I have the feeling Barbados is going to clean that right up in order to apologize to you for the oversight."

Stirling smiled grimly, remembering how Danny had needed to break into their government building to get the papers. Harve's sources had been right—giving the locals some sort of recompense for their loss had bought a lot more than insurance. Stirling couldn't really blame them, though. People working for a living would need that money to make up for a productive family member. It was a lot harder to grieve when you were trying to survive.

"Sorry Leon didn't get to help," he murmured, remembering Leon's eagerness to contribute.

She shrugged, looking happy. "He helped in other ways. That medevac helicopter was all his doing, and Carl and Danny would have been much worse off if that hadn't happened. Although Lucius was a little put out." Her expression grew grimmer. "As were all of us left behind. That wasn't fair of you all. You realize that."

Stirling grimaced. "So many people," he said.

She sighed and nodded. "Yes, I know. But Torrance Grayson *did* get the scoop of the century. He even had some of his employees staked out in Chicago, got some great handcuff footage of Harve Christopher's cohorts being arrested. And he got to interview the agent from Interpol, who talked exclusively about what Harve had done to his parents. It's great stuff," she said, and her voice lowered tenderly. "Even if it's not going to make up for what you and Molly lost."

Stirling closed his eyes tightly. "How's Molly?" They had huddled together on the ride back, and while he'd had Tienne on one side and Molly on the other, Molly'd had nobody else but him.

"She cried herself to sleep on Chuck," Julia said softly. "And you know Charles—he's got a soft spot for women in distress. He'll be her favorite uncle as long as she needs him."

Stirling sighed. "You'd think, with all we *can* do, that we could find her a straight man to date."

Julia's chuckle warmed him. "One thing at a time," she murmured. There was a sweet silence; then she spoke again. "I saw the footage, you know. Not the doctored stuff that Torrance used, but the raw footage of your confrontation with Harve. Josh and I sat, hands clenched, and watched it together as it happened, since we could do nothing else."

Stirling let out a soft groan. "I wasn't on camera, was I?"

"None of you were," she said, then held out a hand. "Until Molly broke Harve's jaw, of course. But I heard you ask Molly why Fred didn't simply give Harve the money. Have you figured out the answer?"

Stirling frowned, trying to get past the muzziness in his head. "No," he said at last. "I thought it was because of the house and the island, but Fred and Stella were practical. I mean, they had all the money, but they'd put their kids first. That's why Molly and I loved them so much."

She *hmm*ed. "Now, don't you see?" she said softly. "That's what they did."

Stirling stared at her, nonplussed. "I don't understand."

"How did Fred get all that money?" she asked, and he frowned because she knew this.

"Fred and I made it gambling. You know that." Felix and Julia had been the only people in Fred and Stella's acquaintance who *had* known that. Something about them had made Fred and Stella take them into their confidence.

"You did," Julia said softly. "You, more than Fred. If it had been Fred who was gambling, he would have won or lost, and it would have been a game. But you made it highly profitable. And then he invested the money, and with a little help from Felix and some more from you, the two of you really did have a magic refillable purse. What would have happened if Fred had given Harve that money?"

Stirling sighed. "He would have wanted more. He never would have stopped." He'd seen Harve's bank records—that was an addiction as serious as the caretaker, Cawthorne's, had been.

"And eventually he would have figured out where Fred was getting his money from," Julia prompted.

"But I didn't mind making it!" Stirling cried, his eyes stinging. "I would have made Harvey all the stupid money he wanted if only Fred and Stella had been there."

"Stirling," Julia said, "that's no way to live."

Stirling caught his breath. "Me," he squeaked. "*I'm* the reason he didn't give Harvey the money."

"You are," she agreed. "He loved you too much to put you under a contract with Harvey. He knew his son. I saw his will. That's why he and Stella locked down yours and Molly's trust so tightly. That's why they locked down the house for you. They knew Harve could come after it—could come after *you*—if he realized that you were the golden goose. Your parents loved you, Stirling. Both you and Molly. They couldn't have loved you more if you'd been their own flesh and blood. And now you know *exactly* what that means."

Stirling heard the first moan coming out of his throat and thought, *Oh no. Not this again.* And then he was sobbing against the pillow while Julia Dormer-Salinger rubbed his back and told him in no uncertain terms that he and Molly were never going to have to do this alone.

WHEN HE woke up, it was to the tantalizing smell of hamburger coming out from under the hot plate. Suddenly he was *starving*. He pushed himself up to a sitting position and saw Tienne sitting next to the bed, midway through his own meal.

Tienne's blue eyes—red-rimmed but bright and oddly merry—took him in as he swallowed the bite he'd been working on. Like Molly and Chuck, he was very, very pink, and odds were good none of them were leaving the yacht any time soon.

"Are you okay?" Tienne asked. "You… you cried again and I wasn't here. I'm sorry. I'm falling down in my job."

Stirling found a smile stretching his mouth.

"Did you bring me food?" he asked urgently. "If you brought me food, you've officially won the boyfriend prize of the day."

Tienne grinned and handed him his plate. Stirling folded his legs underneath him and began to eat, every bite a salty, ketchupy, blissful salute to charred beef and fried potatoes. They ate in silence until their plates were clean, and then Tienne took his plate from him and stacked it on the tray.

"Julia told me to set this out in the hallway," he said. "Like a hotel. Apparently the staff was complaining that we were all too self-sufficient. I think that might be a lie, but I'm not sure, so I think this once we can be very rich and not care."

Stirling laughed, his heart warming with affection as he watched Tienne—wearing sleep shorts and a T-shirt and looking very much like a bohemian artist—clean up after their meal. When the plates were stacked on the tray in the hallway, Tienne came back and sat next to him on the bed.

It was the most natural thing in the world for Stirling to simply lean back into his arms. The physical contact, real and electric and solid, warmed so many places in Stirling's soul that he refused to count them.

"Can you live now?" Tienne asked gently. "Now that it's finished?"

Stirling thought about it and realized that after his conversation with Julia, some of the numbness that had followed him ever since he'd been told of Fred and Stella's death had dissipated.

"Yes," he said. "I sort of miss home, but I want to see the end of this vacation without the job hanging over us. And I want to go back to the snow in Chicago and think, 'Ah, yes, I miss the sun,' even when I'm grateful for the snow. I want...." He swallowed. "I want you in my room, in my bed, in my house if I should ever move out of the basement. I want you there. For as long as we can stand each other."

"Mm...," Tienne hummed, kissing the top of his head. "I think that shall be a very long time."

"Good." Stirling closed his eyes. "Are *you* okay? Kadjic—or at least his flunkies—came really close today. Are you ever going to want revenge there?"

Tienne hummed again. "I think," he said, "if I was painting a picture of all of us, all the people with their lovers, all the parts in our past and the pieces of the puzzle that is all of the many people on this boat, that Andres Kadjic would be a big missing piece. But it's one that we must all eventually fill in. Not now, though. Now I think we will sleep tonight, and eventually we'll dock in Venezuela and spend some time in the hotel, being very civilized and visiting beaches and eventually going home, like you said, to Chicago, where you will all be busy and brilliant and happy."

"And...?"

"And the rest of the picture will fill in someday," Tienne said thoughtfully. He shifted so he could look Stirling seriously in the eyes. "But not now. Now we will make love and be young and happy, and we will be what we have always been—the quiet bubble in the middle of the people tornado."

Stirling nodded. "But we'll be together in that bubble. And we'll be okay."

"Yes." Tienne lowered his mouth and tasted Stirling, and Stirling tasted back.

They made love, a gentle, touching sort of sex that was more about feasting their skin on each other's in lieu of passion. Stirling knew his heart was a little raw for passion this night, but by the time they reached Venezuela, they'd probably find it again.

And when they were done, they wandered up to the lounge, where they found Josh, Grace, Liam, Torrance Grayson, Talia, and Molly all watching a stupid action movie, while Chuck gave Lucius commentary about which parts they'd actually done while they'd been on the island.

Somebody had made popcorn, and the staff had configured the couch cushions so they could all cuddle together amid cushions and blankets.

Stirling rested his head on Tienne's chest while Molly rested her weight on his hip, and around them the babble, the chatter, the teasing and banter, eddied and swirled and rang.

This, Stirling thought, his eyes closing as he felt himself about to fall asleep in the middle of all of it, this was a family. A real family. And they all knew the value of what they were doing in that moment. They were in luxury in that moment, but they could have been in a cheap apartment, or somebody's parents' basement.

And tomorrow, these people would still be his family of the heart, and Tienne would still be his lover, and there would be more fun to be had, more games to play, and another job to do.

Sometime toward the end of the movie, Danny came out and took a moment to lean down and check to make sure Stirling and Molly were okay.

Stirling nodded, smiling, and Tienne kissed his temple.

They were okay into a world of tomorrows, and the painting of their picture of life could take a lifetime of their days to complete.

And he was more okay with that than he had been in his entire life. It was going to be a glorious picture. After all, true love was the best con of all.

Ladies' Tea with Julia

By Amy Lane

JULIA DORMER-SALINGER took a deep breath of cold air in late October and let it out.

This could be the last day she could meditate in the backyard, and she was saying goodbye to the pleasant little spot Felix had made up for her birthday a few years back. He'd planted a willow tree, installed a small pond, and made sure the grass grown in that little patch of heaven was a soft, sweet Kentucky blue. There was a cherry tree nearby for blossoms in the spring, a maple tree on the other side for gold leaves in the fall, and generally, it was the perfect place for contemplation and tranquility.

But Julia was too restless for contemplation and tranquility.

She should have been fresh as a daisy, and it irritated her to no end.

After some very precarious weeks, it appeared the two bone marrow transplants Josh had undergone would be enough to get him through his next rounds of chemo, and his prognosis was good—so much better than it had been in early September. Just thinking about the difference in hope made her want to cry.

And she'd just spent a very... stimulating two weeks with a handsome man who challenged her and made her laugh and could play chess like a champion and did not mind in the least that she and two gay men, one of them her ex-husband, had been laying schemes and doing crime in order to keep their family together. The fact that he, too, had a rough past, and could empathize with doing the illegal thing to right a wrong made him extra amazing, and Lord, was that man handsome.

He could kiss like a dream.

But that's where Julia had drawn the line. They'd had a suite—a living room space and a bedroom space, and she'd taken the bedroom.

After a torrid kiss good-night, that is.

But the point was, she, a supposedly mature woman of newly forty, was as balky as a high school virgin.

In fact, she distinctly remembered giving her virginity up much more quickly to this same man's brother over twenty years ago.

Perhaps, she thought sadly, she knew what it was like to be hurt now, and knew what it was like to hurt others, whether you meant to or not. It made her a little more selective—and a lot more cautious—about giving her heart and her body.

Particularly to *this* man, who, she could sense, could mean so very, very much to her.

There was just not enough meditation in the *world*.

She needed to *do* something.

After her yoga and meditation, she stalked restlessly through the mansion and found Hunter, Molly, Stirling, Chuck, Carl, and Michael, all praising Phyllis for a batch of snickerdoodles hot from the oven.

"What are you all doing here?" she asked, pleased down to her toes that her home had become this bustling hive of activity. Josh had chemo this week—he was resting in his room, and probably would be sleeping for most of the day—but in the meantime, she had his friends to play with. "And where is Grace?"

Hunter gave a tired look toward the upstairs. "Grace is with Josh, although Josh keeps telling him to get out of the house." He sighed. "Grace *really* needs to get out of the house."

That morning, Julia had found her closet rearranged by skirt length and her earrings rearranged by gem cut and clarity. She had to agree.

"Hm… I do have an idea. Sort of a project for you gentleman that might give Grace the outlet he needs, but I need someone on coms here at the house with Josh."

"I can do that," Michael said, eager to help, and she gave him a sweet smile.

"You'd be perfect, darling, but I have plans for you, if you wouldn't mind going in costume. Stirling, Carl, I think you'd be best. Chuck, I do believe I'll need you in one of your snazziest suits. You too, Hunter."

"What about Grace?" Hunter asked, eyes bright. He was definitely looking forward to, well, *anything*.

"Grace will need a waiter's tuxedo, and Michael, I hope you don't mind valet red. Molly, if you can help him find the outfit—it's in the panic room."

"Absolutely," Molly said, eyes dancing with curiosity. "What should I wear?"

"Your society afternoon best, my child. We're going out to ladies' tea."

Molly squealed, jumping up from her stool and brushing snickerdoodle crumbs off her chest. "Oh, you guys," she said, looking at everybody at the table. "You have no idea what you're in for. And all of us? Oh, this is going to be... it's going to be *fabulous*. Come *on*!"

"I'll meet you all back here in an hour," Julia said. "Costumes and props, my children. Chuck, Michael is going to need your handy little master key. Stirling, everybody needs a bug in their ear. Carl needs the hookup by Josh's bed, but you're welcome to come with us into the restaurant if you like."

Stirling gave her a sideways look. "I could either go to the Society Tea Room in a suit and run an op from my phone there, or hang out here with Josh and Carl and run the op from here? These are my choices?"

Julia suppressed a smile. "Those are, indeed, your choices."

"Carl," Stirling said, "I'm going to get my laptop and the long-distance coms. Don't forget to bring snickerdoodles up to Josh's room when you come."

"Deal," Carl said. "But I'll be getting my laptop as well." He turned to Julia. "Is there anything you'll need specifically?"

Julia wrinkled her nose. "Dirt, darling. I'm going to need all the dirt you can find."

AN HOUR and a half later, everybody had left the house, leaving Josh, Stirling, and Carl up in Josh's bedroom. Josh had a hospital bed and an IV installed, and while he was wearing some warm fleece sweats, he also had a sublimely fluffy throw blanket over his knees and another one over his shoulders as he balanced his keyboard on his lap.

"You guys," he warned softly, "you know I'm mostly here as a witness. I...." He yawned. "I can't promise I'll stay awake throughout the hijinks."

"We know," Stirling said, looking at him worriedly. "But since Carl and I couldn't be at the site, we sort of wanted you to have a chance to participate."

Josh gave him a faint smile. "I do miss the game," he murmured.

Just then, Grace's voice crackled over their earbuds. "Shh. You guys, we're in position. Julia, Molly, Chuck, and Hunter are at the table. Michael is out with the cars, and I'm bussing tables. By the way, my boyfriend looks totally hot in his sport coat and ponytail thing, and I bet you're all jealous I get to hit that."

"Yeah, Grace," Josh replied, suppressing a grin. "So jealous. Now hush."

Stirling and Carl exchanged glances of relief. Grace, it seemed, understood why the coms van was all the way back in Glencoe when they were in Chicago.

What they didn't exactly understand was the game.

Then Julia spoke quietly for coms only.

"Heads up, boys and girl, here comes our first mark." Then her voice pitched for somebody else. Judging by her tone, somebody she didn't like very much. Looking through the closed-circuit camera installed in the brooch she'd chosen, they could all view her intended victim on Josh's laptop screen.

"Tessa Ventura!" Julia purred. "So nice of you to visit our table. How are you doing these days?"

The woman approaching the table—and peering *down* to where Julia sat—was of middle height, with a flat bob of brown-blond hair at her shoulders and blue eyes in an elfin face. Possibly in her midforties, she gave off an air of someone much younger. Right until she spoke.

"Julia. I see you've recovered from Felix's little… setback, in the spring."

Everybody sucked in a breath. Felix had been accused of some heinous things that March, but he'd been very publicly exonerated, and the person who'd accused him had her credibility shot to shit and was now in prison for doing way worse than she'd falsely accused Felix of doing.

But apparently some people still had friends.

"What setback?" Julia asked blandly. "I do believe stock in the network is at a higher premium than ever. What about your husband's company? I do recall him having to ask for a loan recently. I trust that was… approved?"

"It was not," Carl said; he was the first to pull up the business records with Tessa's name. "But Julia, you knew that."

Stirling's laptop had the camera picture from Molly's brooch, and through it they could see that Julia's expression didn't give a thing away.

"She totally did," Josh murmured.

"Now?" Grace asked.

"Hold on," Stirling murmured. Then: "Michael?"

"Yeah?"

"I need you to find a wasp-yellow Humvee in the parking lot." He rattled off the license number. "Grace," he added, "wait until Michael finds the vehicle or you'll be wandering around the parking lot with a plate full of fish."

"Sole meunière," Grace murmured. "Precooked. Ah, the best."

They turned their attention back to Julia and Tessa.

"My husband doesn't need a loan," Tessa sniffed. "He's in the middle of a business deal right now with a magnate from Springfield who's going to invest in his company and make all our troubles go away."

Everybody perked up at the mention of a "magnate from Springfield" because that sounded suspiciously like Chuck's boyfriend, Lucius. Uh-oh.

"Is he," Julia purred. "But isn't your husband still under investigation for labor violations and discrimination? I could have sworn I read something like that. Firing women for getting pregnant, denying birth control in the health insurance—that sort of thing?"

Tessa's expression darkened. "Those people," she muttered. "As if women who can't keep their legs closed are the company's problem!"

"Mm…," Chuck murmured. "So compassionate. I'll be sure to tell Lucius."

Molly turned toward him, and they got a glimpse of Chuck texting wildly.

"Lucius?" Tessa said quickly. "Lucius who?"

Chuck's voice was nothing but velvet. "Lucius Broadstone. My boyfriend. I assume that's who your husband was having a meeting with today?"

Julia and Molly both turned quickly enough to give them a dual view of Tessa's face losing all color and her hand reaching out to the back of Hunter's chair.

"If you'll excuse me," she said faintly, and they got a glimpse of her retreating back as she headed to the ladies' room, pulling out her phone.

"Car is located," Michael said happily. "Grace, you're on."

"One fish surprise, on its way," Grace murmured. "I bet a Humvee has all *sorts* of great hiding places."

"Well done," Julia murmured. "Next target?"

"Wait a minute, Mom," Josh said. "Stirling's doing a facial recognition sweep of everyone captured by your cameras, and Carl and I are running names."

"You do you, dear," Julia said indulgently. "Look alive, boys, incoming."

"Uh-oh," Stirling murmured. "Molly, get me a face."

The face that appeared on their cameras was wide and sweet, with highlighted blond hair in a chignon and pink lips. The woman attached to the face was wearing a mauve suit with a pink flowered scarf, and Stirling would have given much to capture his sister's wide-eyed horror at such a getup.

"Julia," the woman said effusively, coming in for the air kisses on either side of Julia's cheeks. Once again, Stirling noted, Julia did not get up to greet this woman. She stayed seated and, according to Molly's camera, peered upward with a mild, open expression on her face.

"Marion!" she said, just as Carl caught the name.

"Marion Kavanaugh," he said. "Her husband owns and profits off all the prisons recently built in Illinois. Slave labor, if you will."

"She drives a Maserati," Stirling said. "Firebird red, with baby seal upholstery."

Josh and Carl both snorted.

"Well, calfskin," Stirling amended, scowling, "but seriously—"

"It's insured for over a hundred thousand dollars," Carl said.

"One more fish surprise," Grace said happily. "Michael?"

"Looking for it," Michael hummed.

Then they tuned into what Julia was saying.

"So," Marion said nervously. "Did you get my email about the fundraiser?"

"For pro-forced-birth?" Julia asked, and Stirling wondered if there was any oxygen left in the room.

"Now, Julia, I know you don't believe that—"

"Oh, but I do," Julia said. "I chose to have my son, but I had options. Look at us, sitting here surrounded by options. I won't take those options away from other women. That's cruel and demeaning."

"But Julia, the church says—"

"Oh, Marion, I get that your church says slavery is okay, which is why your husband profits from human labor, but I really haven't read that passage in the Bible that says you get to make decisions for other people based on your beliefs. I rather doubt it's there."

"Then why did you come here for lunch?" Marion asked bitterly.

"So, so many reasons," Julia murmured, and Marion paled.

"Serpentus just canceled her insurance," Carl said quietly.

"Torrance Grayson is on the way to the restaurant with a film crew to put her on the spot," Josh said, sounding more animated than he had in a month.

"I added broccoli to the fish," Grace said, happy as a clam.

"And I put sugar in her gas tank," Michael added, sounding very pleased with himself.

"And I'm going to disable the cameras," Hunter muttered. Then, out loud, he said, "If you ladies will excuse me...."

Julia smiled at Marion, all teeth. "Thank you so much for stopping by," she said, "but if you'll excuse me, the waiter is about to serve wine."

Her face blotching an odd shade of mauve, Marion stepped aside and made her way woodenly to her table.

"When's Torrance getting here?" Julia asked.

"Before your meal is served and after you finish your wine," Carl told her. "Why, are you done already?"

"Oh no." Julia gave an ecstatic little shiver. "Molly, do you have any prey?"

"Mm...," Molly murmured. "That's a tough one. See that young man there, having lunch with his mother?"

"Yes, dear?"

"Petitioned the college to cancel the LGBTQ booth for rush week and attends Proud Boy events. Is, in fact, currently screwing his African American pool boy because blackmail. The boy's father works for his parents, and Cambridge there threatened to have him fired."

So. Many. Deep. Breaths.

"Josh?" Julia said. "We need a new, better job for Cambridge Barret's pool boy, and another one for his father. What does the boy's father do?"

"Engineer—"

"On it," Chuck murmured. "Carl, get me stats and—oh. There's his LinkedIn profile. Excellent."

"Well," Carl added, "once she mentioned Cambridge Barrett, I was able to access all sorts of things. Did you know Cambridge has wrecked three different

Mercedes in the span of three years? Poor boy also seems to have a substance abuse problem."

They all heard Michael blow out a breath. "Fuck."

"Just because he's got a substance abuse problem doesn't mean he's not a douchebag," Carl said gently.

"Yeah, but we need his douchebaggery to stand on its own."

"He's right," Julia said softly. "Let's get his victim to safety and see if we can't nail him on hypocrisy without—"

"His Grindr profile is filthy," Stirling said.

"Outing him," Julia muttered. "Good God. This is a tough one. How do we expose this man for a scumbag without punishing his victims or—"

Stirling started to laugh, low and dirty, then Josh, and then Carl.

"What am I missing?" she asked.

"Nothing," Josh said soothingly. "Stirling just… well, put a little truth on his Grindr profile."

"What sort of truth?"

Chuck held up his hands. "Don't look at me. I've never used the app."

"Bibles full of truth," Carl said dryly. "No pictures of his victims and definitely no names—just a confessional of the things he's done, how much he loves oxy, how many cars he's wrecked, his affiliation with the Proud Boys. That sort of thing. Didn't out his pseudonym, didn't mention his parents. Just a list of his misdeeds. He may never get laid again."

"And if he does, they're duly warned," Josh added. "Some people love that bad guy—not even the bad *boy* but the bad *guy*. But now they know."

"Excellent," Julia said. "Good enough, Molly?"

"Absolutely," Molly said.

"But what kind of car does he drive?" Michael asked. "I've got more sugar for his gas tank!"

"Oh!" Stirling said. "My bad. Small black Mercedes. License plate…," he rattled off the numbers.

"Hunter's going to help me put fish in the seat lining, aren't you, Hunter?" Grace sounded absolutely besotted.

"Sure." So did Hunter. "Why the seat lining?"

"Harder to spot," Grace said. "Isn't he cute?"

"So cute," Molly muttered. "An absolute doll."

"Hush, children," Julia murmured. "Here's the wine service."

At that moment the sommelier approached and filled the four glasses—even Hunter's—with chardonnay.

"Can I take your order?" said the waiter when the sommelier was done. "But first, I need to tell you, we're running low on sole meunière."

"Not a problem," Julia said. "I'm feeling very predatory today. What are your red-meat specials for lunch?"

There were more marks after that—three more, in fact—before the kitchen ran completely out of fish and Michael's sugar supply for the gas tanks ran low.

Josh had fallen asleep two marks ago, and it was time to leave.

As Julia led her family out of the restaurant—after leaving a *very* generous tip for everyone inconvenienced, of course—she neatly bypassed Torrance Grayson's meal of Marion Kavanaugh and continued to where Michael stood by the SUV, ready to drive them all home. Chuck took over the driving—Michael looked a little tuckered, because apparently he'd also been parking cars as a valet, as he'd felt bad about leaving the other guys panting, with all the tow trucks they'd needed to call and everything—and the SUV made its way home.

That evening, Danny and Felix arrived at the mansion, and Lucius followed them a few moments later. As everybody was enjoying drinks and chatter in the living room before dinner, Felix came alongside the woman he'd been married to for nearly twelve years and wrapped his arm around her waist in a very platonic gesture of affection.

"You look happy, darling. What did you do with your day?"

"Not much," she said. "Took the children to lunch, put my thumb on a few scales, bought the restaurant out of fish."

The look of admiration on Felix's face was worth a thousand yoga/meditation sessions. "Oh, you are such a devoted mother, Julia. You shall have to tell Danny and I what games you played."

She gave him a kiss on the cheek. "I'd rather let the children do it. Even Josh had a hand."

Felix sobered. "Now that's the best news I've had all day."

They had hope now, but worry was still their shadow.

But for the length of dinner that evening, as all of Julia's playmates recounted the story of ladies' tea, it was the hope that fed their souls.

Keep Reading for an Excerpt from
The Rising Tide
by Amy Lane

Prologue

HELEN HAD waited a long time to do this—maybe too long.

As she buzzed along the suburban streets of Folsom, California, on her beloved Ducati, she had to admit that the neighborhood had changed in the last thirty years since she bought her cottage. She'd seen it happening in increments, but it hadn't really hit her until some damned fool had put up three prefab houses on her once empty cul-de-sac and those damned college kids had moved in.

She felt her shoulders hunch, which she couldn't let happen because once you hit a certain age, hunching over a motorcycle could be considered an actual injury.

Okay, okay, breathe out. Remember, resentment trapped the bad feelings in. The bad feelings created the shackles that held you down.

Sounded like new age crap, but after a long talk with her mentor, she'd come to realize that it was something more. It was the reason her life had *gone* to crap over the last ten years. Held grudges, a refusal to move, to motivate herself to break the chains that had bound her. She was a powerful witch. Age made those powers stronger, not weaker, and her metaphorical chains had become magical, physical manifestations very quickly.

She'd needed to break them before they consumed her, but in her panic, she'd done the unthinkable.

She'd shoved the keys to her *very* magical witch's cottage into the hands of the most responsible of the young people who'd moved into her cul-de-sac and had run.

That poor kid. God knows what had happened to him once he'd taken her keys and her hurried admonition not to touch any of the distilled oils. The kid had been smart as a whip. Friendly, kind. Offered to help her with her groceries once a week, was gentle to the nine feral cats she fed. She'd been desperate, but holy Hecate and blessed Brigid, what had she done?

As she rounded the corner of the perfectly normal little suburb, the chill wind of February settled more firmly into her bones. This wasn't snow country, but the wind still had a bite on top of a motorcycle, and for a moment she was concentrating on a small spell to warm herself.

And then she realized where she was and almost laid out the damned bike.

"The actual hell…," she murmured.

The cul-de-sac was deserted.

The three prefab houses had signs on the front proclaiming new developments to come from Asa Bryne, but judging by the dust on the windows, they'd been vacant for months. Helen's eyes sharpened—she'd been out in the world. She knew that vacant houses often attracted squatters, drug addicts, indigents. But in spite of the likelihood of that happening, all she saw were a couple of turkeys wandering desultorily across the cul-de-sac and some owls perching on the gutters of the house in the middle. The house on the end appeared to have more than its fair share of squirrels, and there were starlings everywhere.

What in the everloving hell?

And then she saw her own cottage—or what had once been her own cottage—and for a moment, she had to fight hard to breathe.

It was… it had been….

It had… *imploded*.

That was the only word for it. The little shake roof, the neat wooden walls, the rickety front porch—all of it had been demolished in a way that implied a giant vacuum from the inside had sucked all the walls inward and the house had collapsed, the roof falling mostly intact on top of it.

Her feral cats, all of them more or less enchanted, had left.

She felt a pull toward the middle of the cul-de-sac and turned to see three stars, marked in faded tape and with the power of what had once been much use.

The first star was three-pointed and close to the center of the four houses. The next star had five points, and it was set a little farther back from the three-pointed one. Enough space stretched between them for a circle of people to form around each star, with nobody bumping elbows. The next star—seven-pointed—was set farther back from that, and Helen stared at the lot of them, stunned.

She could sense their power from the sidewalk. Those college kids had done this. Or rather those *post*-college kids had done it. Every iota of energy emanating from those circles had gone into keeping this neighborhood safe from the forces Helen herself had unleashed.

Her eyes burned.

Oh, those brave damned kids.

They'd taken her cottage, her library, her years of accumulated knowledge and run with it. And when the presence of ennui, of abnegation, had gotten too large, started taking over the neighborhood, they'd used those powers to fight it.

They weren't here slaving away, growing old and hopeless, locked in the dance that the presence had locked Helen in for so many years. In fact, she felt… nothing. Nothing but the faint buzz of their protection and the residue of one holy hell of a spell. And the lingering scent of patchouli and rosewater and the myriad other oils she'd accumulated during the years, which had probably been released when her house had been destroyed.

They'd done it. What she'd failed to do for years. They'd broken those chains, and now she was well and truly free.

And so in debt to the universe she could hardly breathe.

She reached into her saddlebag and pulled out her satellite phone to call the one number she had.

"Marcus?"

"Helen," he said warmly. "Have you visited your neighborhood? Have you made it right?"

She swallowed. "I found it, and the presence has been vanquished. But Marcus, those kids did it themselves. They… they took all my knowledge and, you know, fixed it. Fixed the world. I…." Her voice broke. "I owe such a debt. I should find them and—"

"No," Marcus said softly. "They've started on their own path and apparently taught themselves. Do they have your library? Your familiars?"

She smiled sadly, thinking of her nine furry companions. "Yes. The nine are gone, and the library…." She looked toward the destroyed house and could spot nary a page. "I think they took the library with them." She let out a sad laugh. It had taken thirty years to build that library, rare book by rare book, estate sale by lucky find. "They earned it if they could free this area from the presence that took it over."

"Yes," Marcus agreed. "They did. But we need you back here, honey. You'll make amends. Maybe not with those people specifically, but I think there will be ways you can pay the universe back." His voice took on a sad, thready quality she could never remember it having, not after thirty years of friendship, some of those years more than friendly. "Spinner's Drift needs you, Helen. We need you back here. I feel it. All your karma… you can pay it back here."

"Of course," she said softly. Marcus had taken her in two years ago, listened to her barely coherent tale of the witch's cottage that had begun to dominate her life. Of the presence that had sucked all her animation away, all her personality, all the energy she'd once offered the world.

He'd listened, and he'd kissed her, and he'd healed her. She'd left to see if she was needed and to sell the property outright and clear up some of her finances so she could start again.

"Are you sure I shouldn't…?" Those kids. All of them right out of college, starting their lives. They'd been so fresh-faced and optimistic. So ready to find their places in the world. What a terrible burden she'd placed on their shoulders.

"Your paths will cross again," he said softly. "I feel it, Helen. It's written in the starlight. But Spinner's Drift needs you." His voice lowered humbly, as it wouldn't have done thirty years ago when she'd left the first time. "I need you."

And that decided her. It was true that hedge witches and wizards tended to live astoundingly long lives, but sixty was sixty, and she was too old to take another minute for granted.

"Let me clear up my finances," she promised. "I should be back in two weeks or so."

"What are you going to do?" he asked.

She thought about it, about her personal library, now out in the world to do what she sensed had been so much good. "I'm going to buy a bookstore," she said, "that also sells coffee and pastries. And has cats." The thought of it gave her a pleasant magical buzz. Oh yes. The karma gods liked this idea.

"What will you call it?" he asked.

"I don't know yet." She smiled, that buzz pulsing along her skin, making her graying ponytail lift from the back of her neck with static. "But it's going to be extraordinary."

The Wide World

ALISTAIR QUINTERO'S voice thundered in Scout's ears. There was a terrific whooshing wind, a clap of thunder and white light, and shazam!

Scout was exiled from the only home he'd ever known and alone in the woods that surrounded the wizard compound, the family home he'd grown up in and had never managed to escape, even to see the surrounding area.

Until now, when he wasn't allowed back in.

Holy Goddess, Alistair was a dick.

He suppressed a whine—he was twenty-four, godsdammit, and whining was *not* attractive—and looked around, trying to discern east from west to figure out in which direction the road was. They'd been allowed to look at maps; he wasn't *completely* in the dark about modern geography. But the compound was really several buildings surrounding the family mansion, with acres of land, developed and wilderness, inside the perimeter. He didn't know any of the landmarks outside the compound, and his head ached fiercely from the portal his father had banished him out of as well.

Scout tried not to fume. He understood that most of the time, portals made a person tired anyway, but that *Alistair's* portals tended to be a lot louder and more violent than the usual.

Again. Holy Goddess, what a dick.

He took a deep breath and fought off another childish impulse—this one to cry. As he did so, he felt a thump against his ribs, coming from a pocket in his ceremonial robes, and he stiffened.

His brother, Josue, had dropped the robes off by his quarters and helped him dress, giving him emergency instructions as he did so. Scout had been too nervous to pay attention—Josue was a mother hen most days, telling the younger boys (men now!) to remember fennel in their spells to deceive deceivers or oak for strength. Telling them to remember their blue shirts to show fealty to Alistair or their red socks to show care for their mothers. But this time he'd been practically whispering, muttering things that, Scout now realized, had been instructions and warnings.

"He's going to banish you no matter what, Scout. Be ready for it. I've put things in your robes that will help. Don't forget to check the pockets. Remember—I love you, your brother Macklin loves you, and you're not the only one to get out of this hellhole and thrive."

Scout reached into the robes, which he realized were Josue's. He must have given Scout his so he'd have time to put things in the pockets. In one pocket Scout found a wallet with a forged driver's license with Scout's picture on it and his official name: Scotland Damaris Quintero. Oh heavens, Josue had known. He'd said it. *He's going to banish you no matter what.* He must have had this ready for months. There were two cards, both of them with bank account numbers and passwords taped to them, and Scout had to swallow against tears, moved by love and gratitude as he hadn't been by fear and anger.

Five thousand dollars each. Josue, who held a job out of the compound to manage the compound's investments, had squirreled away ten thousand dollars for Scout because he'd known. He'd known Scout wasn't going to make it. He'd known Alistair would banish him. He'd known, and he'd silently prepared for it, and....

Scout wiped under his eyes with his palm and felt the thing in his other robe pocket buzz. He reached inside and found a cell phone, a thing he knew from books that most children knew how to use at ten but that the kids in the compound were not given. Computers they could use for their studies, but the use was closely monitored. Phones? Not necessary. Books were to be read in paper format so any adult could read it. Allowance could only be spent on approved books or magic supplies.

But Josue had bought him a phone and had written the passcode on another Post-it swacked to the back.

Scout tapped the passcode in and smiled through the burning behind his eyes.

His brother had sent him a text.

Sorry, brother. He found your stash of forbidden books. It didn't matter if you made a portal or not, he was going to send you away.

Scout grimaced. "Forbidden" in this case meant "romance." The kind with two male romantic leads. He'd been refusing to choose a wife for years now, making vague excuses, but obviously Alistair had not been fooled.

Our brother Macklin has been waiting for your call. Here's his number. Call immediately, and he'll be there.

Scout stared at this. Macklin? Macklin had left when Scout was a kid—off to sow his wild oats,

Alistair had sneered often enough. Not quite a year ago, though, something had changed. Alistair had shown up for breakfast one morning looking as though he'd been pecked to death by ducks, and after that the first person to ask about Macklin's long-anticipated return had been blown through a wall.

Scout's younger sister, Kayleigh, had woken up after a week, unable to remember what had happened, and nobody had dared to mention Macklin Quintero again.

Apparently, whatever had happened, Macklin had come out on top, and Alistair was not happy about it.

That decided Scout. Anything that pissed Alistair off was enough to make him a fan.

He looked around the woods again, thinking he may have heard cars to the southeast, and cursed the fact that wearing his ceremonial robes when he'd been banished meant he was barefoot.

Seriously. Alistair Quintero. Fuck that guy.

With a bit of fiddling—these little devices were really very self-explanatory—he thought he had it.

Macklin? This is Scout. Josue told me you could help me?

He stared at the screen, thinking, Wait? Don't these things need internet or something? But whatever Josue had done to charge and power this thing—and Scout felt a small soft-sided box in his pocket that he assumed held power cords—it apparently was ready to work.

Scout? Where are you?

I, uhm, don't know. Out in the woods by the compound, maybe? I was just banished.

There was a pause, and Scout noticed little bubbles by where Macklin's reply would appear. Very comforting, those bubbles, he thought.

And he just left you there? What. A. Dick!

And that, right there, was when Scout realized Macklin might be the family member he loved the most.

Right?

He sent it almost without thinking. He was going to ask questions then, but Macklin beat him to it.

Do you need anything? Money? Transportation? A map?

Shoes? Scout typed in, angry all over again.

We'll be there in ten minutes.

Scout frowned. Be there? They'd be there? Who would be there? But... but Macklin was presumably banished too. Granted, he was supposedly the pride of the Quintero wizard family before he'd been banished, but didn't that mean he wasn't allowed to do magic anymore?

Could *Scout* still do magic?

Ooh... interesting question.

The *stated* reason for Scout being banished had been that he didn't have enough magical power to be more than a (disdainful sniff) hedge witch. That was how Alistair said it too, like being a hedge witch was too small to even worry about. Certainly not talented enough to ever be real family.

But Scout *had* possessed power. Sometimes it was wonky, and sometimes it listened to his heart instead of his head, but it was there. Once, he'd been asked to conjure a crossbow. Why, he had no idea. They didn't hunt their own food. They had it shipped in, in giant quantities. Were they hunters now? Because that didn't really work for Scout, who was much happier with some toast and jam than raw bleeding deer meat on the hoof. But a crossbow he'd been asked to conjure.

He'd gotten toast and jam instead. *He'd* been delighted, but Alistair had thrown it away dismissively and told him to do some *real* conjuring.

This time, Scout got an entire loaf of bread, a brick of butter, and a *jar* of jam. His favorite.

He hadn't let Alistair throw *that* away, insisting that it must have come from the kitchen and he'd return it. The fact that he'd taken it to the kitchen, toasted himself a snack, and disappeared for the rest of the day had never been mentioned again.

And he'd never learned to conjure weapons either.

So Scout wasn't really a brilliant wizard, but he *did* have power, and he rather enjoyed the feeling it gave him. Not that he could lord it over people or conjure a crossbow to lay waste to his enemies or anything. That never occurred to him. It was the feeling of oneness it gave him with the rest of the world. The wizard compound was stifling, and all the boys were housed in the same quarters, and Scout wondered if it was possible to have a thought not permeated with stinky gym socks and the midnight sounds of the teenaged and twenty-something boys masturbating in the dark.

Meals were family affairs, everybody seated at the table looking suitably grateful and chastened that the women—who were never given a word of thanks from Alistair or the elders—had slaved away for the meals before them.

All of this togetherness, and the only time Scout *didn't* feel alone was when he snuck some toast and jam and wandered off into the wooded part of the compound. He'd bring his sketch book and write poems or sketch badly, or bring Kayleigh, his favorite sister, and they'd find pictures in the clouds or talk about the things they'd snuck into their reading or away from their studies that Alistair hadn't seen.

If they missed lunchtime, they conjured food. If they needed a book from their study, they conjured that.

If they wanted to try their hand at levitation or talking to the animals, they did so, and failed and tried again and failed and sometimes succeeded.

Those moments of peace, of playing with Kayleigh, throwing words or ideas or potions back and forth, those had made him feel more connected than anything. And not to Kayleigh, but to, well, the world. Even without Kayleigh, those moments in the woods, alone with his thoughts, had made him less lonely.

But still, Kayleigh had helped, and he thought about her now, mourning one of the two people in the compound who had given a damn where he was. Would he be able to see her again? She was pretty powerful, but she was also twenty-one, and Alistair was trying to marry her off to "strengthen the bloodline." Scout had managed to evade Alistair's machinations for three years, but Kayleigh was supposedly betrothed to someone from the south already. Oh Goddess. Kayleigh, with her sparkling brown eyes and apple cheeks. The thought of her married to a hovering despot like Alistair made him physically ill.

He started to pace, looking at his phone, wondering if he could ask Macklin to help him get her out. Could they mount a rescue? Alistair had *thrown her through a wall* for simply asking about Macklin. What would he do to her for protesting Scout's banishment?

His worry for her grew, and that power, that oneness he'd always felt when alone in the woods, grew too. He found himself reaching out for her, wanting to grab her hand and just *yank* her out of the now-invisible compound. He closed his eyes and conjured her image behind them—brown eyes, sleek brown hair in a ponytail, apple cheeks, and all, and thought, *Kayleigh!*

"What?"

Her voice was so real and so honest that his eyes popped open, and then he screamed and she did too, because she was right there. Or rather he was right there in their spot in the compound, and she was sitting under a tree crying.

"*Scout*?"

"*Kayleigh*?"

"Did you just rescue me?"

He stared. "We're still in the compound, so I'm going to say no!"

She stared back. "But the portal is right behind you."

"I can't conjure porta—"

She didn't give him time to finish. She launched herself at him and hugged him so tight his eyes almost popped out of his head, sobbing, "I'm free! I'm free! I'm free!" and he stumbled back, through the gateway of space and time he'd apparently opened up. In a heartbeat, they were back in the spot Scout had recently left, the portal had closed, and he was freezing his ass off in his ceremonial robes in the New England woods in the brisk early days of September.

And that's where they were when a guy in his late thirties—not too tall but not short, with the Quintero black hair, square jaw, and Scout's cobalt eyes—appeared in the forest through another portal about twenty feet from them.

"Scout?"

"Macklin?" His eyes strayed to the objects dangling from Macklin's fingers. "Oh my Goddess, are those *shoes*?"

Those eyes—so much like their father's that Scout quailed a little when he first saw them—had crinkles at the corners that one only associated with kindness.

Macklin smiled and his eyes crinkled, and the family reunion was complete.

Award winning author AMY LANE lives in a crumbling crapmansion with a couple of teenagers, a passel of furbabies, and a bemused spouse. She has too damned much yarn, a penchant for action-adventure movies, and a need to know that somewhere in all the pain is a story of Wuv, Twu Wuv, which she continues to believe in to this day! She writes contemporary romance, paranormal romance, urban fantasy, and romantic suspense, teaches the occasional writing class, and likes to pretend her very simple life is as exciting as the lives of the people who live in her head. She'll also tell you that sacrifices, large and small, are worth the urge to write.

Website: www.greenshill.com
Blog: www.writerslane.blogspot.com
Email: amylane@greenshill.com
Facebook: www.facebook.com/amy.lane.167
Twitter: @amymaclane

A LONG CON ADVENTURE

The Mastermind
AMY LANE

"Delicious fun." — *Booklist*

A Long Con Adventure

Once upon a time in Rome, Felix Salinger got caught picking his first pocket and Danny Mitchell saved his bacon. The two of them were inseparable… until they weren't.

Twenty years after that first meeting, Danny returns to Chicago, the city he shared with Felix and their perfect, secret family, to save him again. Felix's news network—the business that broke them apart—is under fire from an unscrupulous employee pointing the finger at Felix. An official investigation could topple their house of cards. The only way to prove Felix is innocent is to pull off their biggest con yet.

But though Felix still has the gift of grift, his reunion with Danny is bittersweet. Their ten-year separation left holes in their hearts that no amount of stolen property can fill. A green crew of young thieves looks to them for guidance as they negotiate old jewels and new threats to pull off the perfect heist—but the hardest job is proving that love is the only thing of value they've ever had.

www.dreamspinnerpress.com

A LONG CON ADVENTURE

The Muscle

AMY LANE

A Long Con Adventure

A true protector will guard your heart before his own.

Hunter Rutledge saw one too many people die in his life as mercenary muscle to go back to the job, so he was conveniently at loose ends when Josh Salinger offered him a place in his altruistic den of thieves.

Hunter is almost content having found a home with a group of people who want justice badly enough to steal it. If only one of them didn't keep stealing his attention from the task at hand....

Superlative dancer and transcendent thief Dylan "Grace" Li lives in the moment. But when mobsters blackmail the people who gave him dance—and the means to save his own soul—Grace turns to Josh for help.

Unfortunately, working with Josh's crew means working with Hunter Rutledge, and for Grace, that's more dangerous than any heist.

Grace's childhood left him thinking he was too difficult to love—so he's better off not risking his love on anyone else. Avoiding commitment keeps him safe. But somehow Hunter's solid, grounding presence makes him feel safer. Can Grace trust that letting down his guard to a former mercenary doesn't mean he'll get shot in the heart?

www.dreamspinnerpress.com

A LONG CON ADVENTURE

The Driver

AMY LANE

A Long Con Adventure

Hell-raiser, getaway driver, and occasional knight in tarnished armor Chuck Calder has never had any illusions about being a serious boyfriend. He may not be a good guy, but at least as part of Josh Salinger's crew of upscale thieves and cons, he can feel good about his job.

Right now, his job is Lucius Broadstone.

Lucius is a blueblood with a brutal past. He uses his fortune and contacts to help people trying to escape abuse, but someone is doing everything they can to stop him. He needs the kind of help only the Salingers can provide. Besides, he hasn't forgotten the last time he and Chuck Calder collided. The team's good ol' boy and good luck charm is a blue-collar handful, but he is genuinely kind. He takes Lucius's mission seriously, and Lucius has never had that before. In spite of Chuck's reluctance to admit he's a nice guy, Lucius wants to know him better.

Chuck's a guaranteed good time, and Lucius is a forever guy. Can Chuck come to terms with his past and embrace the future Lucius is offering? Or is Good Luck Chuck destined to be driving off into the sunset alone forever?

www.dreamspinnerpress.com

A LONG CON ADVENTURE

The Suit

AMY LANE

A Long Con Adventure

Two and a half years ago, Michael Carmody made the biggest mistake of his life. Thanks to the Salinger crew, he has a second chance. Now he's working as their mechanic and nursing a starry-eyed crush on the crew's stoic suit, insurance investigator and spin doctor Carl Cox.

Carl has always been an almost-ran, so Michael's crush baffles him. When it comes to the Salingers, he's the designated wet blanket. But watching Michael forge the life he wants instead of the one he fell into inspires him. In Michael's eyes, he isn't an almost-ran—he just hasn't found the right person to run with. And while the mechanic and the suit shouldn't have much to talk about, suddenly they're seeking out each other's company.

Then the Salingers take a case from their past, and it's all hands on deck. For once, behind-the-scenes guys Michael and Carl find themselves front and center. Between monster trucks, missing women, and murder birds, the case is a jigsaw puzzle with a lot of missing pieces—but confronting the unknown is a hell of a lot easier when they're side by side.

www.dreamspinnerpress.com